UNTIL THY WRATH BE PAST

UNTIL THY WRATH BE PAST

Åsa Larsson

Translated
by Laurie Thompson

MacLehose Press

MacLehose Press
An imprint of Quercus
New York • London

© 2008 by Åsa Larsson
Translation © 2011 by Laurie Thompson
Originally published in Sweden as *Till dess din vrede upphör* in 2008 by Bonnier
First published in the United States by Sterling in 2011

Any member of educational institutions wishing to photocopy part or all of the work for classroom use or anthology should send inquiries to Permissions c/o Quercus Publishing Inc., 31 West 57th Street, 6th Floor, New York, NY 10019, or to permissions@quercus.com.

ISBN 978-1-62365-169-5

Library of Congress Control Number: 2013913483

Distributed in the United States and Canada by
Random House Publisher Services
c/o Random House, 1745 Broadway
New York, NY 10019

This book is a work of fiction. Names, characters, institutions, places, and events are either the product of the author's imagination or are used fictitiously. Any resemblance to actual persons—living or dead—events, or locales is entirely coincidental.

Manufactured in the United States

2 4 6 8 10 9 7 5 3 1

www.quercus.com

O that thou wouldest hide me in the grave,
that thou wouldest keep me secret, until thy wrath be past,
that thou wouldest appoint me a set time, and remember me!
If a man die, shall he live again?
All the days of my appointed time will I wait,
till my change come.

Thou shalt call,
and I will answer thee:
thou wilt have a desire to the work of thy hands.
For now thou numberest my steps:
dost thou not watch over my sin?
My transgression is sealed up in a bag,
and thou sewest up mine iniquity.

And surely the mountain falling cometh to nought,
and the rock is moved out of his place.
The waters wear the stones:
thou washest away the things which grow out of the dust
    of the earth;
and thou destroyest the hope of man.

Thou prevailest for ever against him, and he passeth:
thou changest his countenance and sendest him away.
His sons come to honour, and he knoweth it not;
and they are brought low, but he perceiveth it not of them.
But his flesh upon him shall have pain,
and his soul within him shall mourn.

Job 14:13–22

UNTIL THY WRATH BE PAST

I remember how we died. I remember, and I know. That's the way it is now. I know about certain things even though I wasn't actually present when they happened. But I don't know everything. Far from it. There are no rules. Take people, for instance. Sometimes they are open rooms that I can walk into. Sometimes they are closed. Time doesn't exist. It's as if it's been whisked into nothingness.

Winter came without snow. The rivers and lakes were frozen as early as September, but still the snow didn't come.

It was October 9. The air was cold. The sky very blue. One of those days you'd like to pour into a glass and drink.

I was seventeen. If I were still alive, I'd be eighteen now. Simon was nearly nineteen. He let me drive even though I didn't have a license. The forest trail was full of potholes. I liked driving. Laughed at every bump. Sand and gravel clattered against the chassis.

"Sorry, Bettan," Simon said to the car, stroking the cover of the glove box.

We had no idea that we were going to die. That I would be screaming, my mouth full of water. That we only had five hours left.

The trail petered out at Sevujärvi. We unpacked the car. I kept stopping to look around. Everything was divinely beautiful. I lifted my arms toward the sky, screwed up my eyes to look at the sun, a burning white sphere, watched a wisp of cloud scudding along high above us. The mountains embodied permanence and times immemorial.

"What are you doing?" Simon said.

I was still gazing at the sky, arms raised, when I said, "Nearly all religions have something like this. Looking up, reaching up with your hands. I understand why. It makes you feel good. Try it."

I took a deep breath, then let the air out to form a big white cloud.

Simon smiled and shook his head. Heaved his weighty rucksack up onto a rock and wriggled into the harness. He looked at me.

Oh, I remember how he looked at me. As if he couldn't believe his luck. And it's true. I wasn't just your average girl.

He liked to explore me. Count all my birthmarks. Or tap his fingernail on my teeth as I smiled, ticking off all the peaks of the Kebnekaise massif: "South Peak, North Peak, Dragon's Back, Kebnepakte, Kaskasapakte, Kaskasatjåkko, Tuolpagorni."

"Upper right lateral incisor—signs of decay; upper right central—sound; upper left central—distal filling," I'd reply.

The rucksacks containing our diving equipment weighed a ton.

We walked up to Lake Vittangijärvi. It took us three and a half hours. We urged each other on, noticing how the frozen ground made walking easier. We sweated a lot, stopped occasionally to have some water, and once to drink coffee from our thermos and eat a couple of sandwiches.

Frozen puddles and frostbitten moss crackled beneath our feet.

Alanen Vittangivaara loomed on our left.

"There's an old Sami sacrificial site up there," Simon said, pointing. "Uhrilaki."

That was a side of him I loved. He knew about that sort of thing.

We finally got there. Placing our rucksacks carefully on the slope, we stood in silence for a while, gazing out over the lake. The ice resembled a thick black pane of glass over the water. Trapped bubbles traced patterns like broken pearl necklaces. The cracks resembled crumpled tissue paper.

Frost had nipped at every blade of grass, every twig, making them brittle and crispy white. Sprays of lingonberry and stunted juniper bushes were a dull shade of wintry green. Dwarf birches and blueberry sprigs had been squeezed into shades of blood and violet. And everything was coated with rime. An aura of ice.

It was uncannily quiet.

Simon became withdrawn and thoughtful, as he usually did. He's the type who can tell time to stand still. Or was. He was that kind of person.

But I've never been able to keep quiet for long. I just had to start shouting. All that beauty—it was enough to make you burst.

I ran out onto the ice. As fast as I could without slipping. Then I stood with my legs wide apart and slid a long, long way.

"You try it!" I shouted to Simon.

He smiled and shook his head.

That was something he'd learned to do in the village where he'd grown up. How to shake his head. They're good at that in Piilijärvi.

"I better not," he shouted back. "Someone has to be here to repair your legs when you've broken them."

"Chicken!" I yelled as I ran and slid again.

Then I lay down and gazed up at the sky for a while. Stroked the ice affectionately.

Somewhere down below there was an airplane. And nobody knew anything about it, apart from us. Or so we thought.

Standing up, I caught Simon's gaze.

You and me, his eyes said.

You and me, my eyes said.

Simon collected some dry juniper twigs and birch bark so that we could start a fire and have something to eat before we made our dive. To give us the strength to keep going.

We grilled some smoked sausages on skewers. I didn't have the patience to do it properly—mine were burned black on the outside and raw inside. Hungry jays gathered in the trees around us.

"People used to eat them," I said, nodding at the birds. "Anni told me about it. She and her cousins used to hang a length of string between the trees and thread pieces of bread onto it. The birds would land on the string, but it was so thin that they couldn't stay upright and found themselves hanging upside down. Then all you had to do was pick them off. Like picking apples. We ought to try it—have we got any string?"

"Wouldn't you rather have a piece of sausage?"

One of Simon's typically marvelous sardonic comments. And no hint of a smile to show that he was joking.

I gave him a thump on the chest.

"Idiot! I didn't mean that we should eat them. I just wanted to see if it worked."

"No. We ought to get going. Before it gets dark."

Instantly I became serious.

Simon gathered some more dry twigs and bark. And he found a hollow birch log—they burn well. He raked some ash over the glowing embers. As he said, with a bit of luck we would be able to blow the fire back to life after the dive. It would be good to be able to warm ourselves quickly when we emerged from the freezing water.

We carried our tanks, regulators, masks, snorkels, fins, and black army-surplus diving suits out onto the ice.

Simon led the way with the GPS.

In August we had brought the kayak, towing it through water whenever possible, along the River Vittangi as far as Lake Tahko. Then we'd paddled to Vittangijärvi. We'd plumbed the depths of various parts of the lake, and, once we finally found the right place, Simon had keyed it into the GPS under the heading Wilma. He named it after me.

But during the summer there were vacationers staying in the old farmhouse on the lake's western shore.

"You can bet your life they're all lined up with their binoculars," I'd said, squinting across. "Wondering what the hell we're up to. If we dive now, everyone for kilometers around will know about it in no time."

So once we'd finished, we'd paddled over to the western shore, beached the kayak, and strolled up to the old farmhouse, where we'd been invited in for coffee. I went on about how we were getting paid a pittance by the Swedish Meteorological and Hydrological Institute for charting the depth of the lake. Something to do with climate change, I guessed.

"As soon as they close down the summer cottages for the winter," I'd said to Simon as we struggled home with the kayak, "we'll be able to use their boat as well."

But then the ice came, and we had to wait until it was thick enough to bear our weight. We could hardly believe our luck when it didn't snow—we'd be able to see through the ice. A meter or so at least. But of course we'd be diving down much deeper than that.

Simon sawed through the ice. He started by hacking a hole with an axe—the ice was still thin enough to do that—and then he used a hand saw. A chainsaw would have been too heavy to carry, and besides, it would have created a hell of a noise; the last thing we wanted was to attract attention. What we were doing suggested a book title to me: Wilma, Simon, and the Secret of the Airplane.

While Simon was sawing through the ice, I nailed some lengths of wood together to form a cross we would place over the hole after attaching a safety line to it.

Stripping down to our thermal underwear, we pulled on our diving suits. Then we sat down at the edge of the hole.

"Go right down to four meters," Simon said. "The worst that can happen is that we lose our air supply if the regulators freeze up. The start is the riskiest bit, just beneath the surface."

"Okay."

"We might also run into trouble lower down. You can't trust mountain lakes. There could be an inlet somewhere, causing currents. The temperature could be below zero. But, the riskiest place is just beneath the surface, remember that. So, down you go. No hanging around."

"Okay."

I didn't want to listen. I wanted to get down there. Right away.

Simon wasn't an expert on the technical side of diving, but he'd read up on it. In magazines and on the Internet. He continued his unhurried preparations.

"Two tugs on the line means 'come up.'"

"Right."

"Maybe we'll find the wreck right away, but probably not. Let's get down there and take it as it comes."

"Okay, okay."

And so we dive.

Simon goes in after me. The cold water is like a horse kicking us in the face. He places the wooden cross with the safety line attached to it over the hole in the ice.

He checks the dive computer during our descent. Two meters. As bright as day. The ice above us acts as a window, letting the sunlight in. When we were standing up there the ice looked black. From underneath it is light blue. Twelve meters. Murky. Colors disappear. Fifteen meters. Darkness. Simon is probably wondering how I'm feeling. But he knows I'm a tough customer. Seventeen meters.

We head straight for the wreck. Land on top of it.

I don't know what I'd been expecting, but not this. Not that it would be so easy. I can feel laughter bubbling up inside me, but it can't come out just now. I'm looking forward to hearing Simon's comments when we're back by the fire getting warm. He's always so calm, but the words will come tumbling out after this.

It feels as if the plane has been lying down there waiting for us. But we'd sounded the depth; we'd already done the searching. We knew where it ought to be.

Even so, when I see it at the bottom in the greeny-black darkness, it seems so unreal. It's much bigger than I'd imagined it would be. Simon shines his flashlight on me. I realize that he wants to see my reaction. The happy expression on my face. But of course, he can't read my face behind the oxygen mask.

He moves his outstretched hand up and down. Remain calm, he means. I notice how heavily I'm breathing. I need to collect myself if the air is going to last.

There might be enough for twenty minutes. We'll be very cold by then as well. We shine our flashlights on the plane, the beams of light working their way over the mud-covered fuselage. I try to make out what model it is. A Dornier, perhaps? We swim over the hull, wiping away mud and slime with our hands. No, the metal is corrugated. It's a Junkers.

Following the wing, we come to the engine. Something isn't right, something seems . . . We swim back. I'm close behind Simon, holding on to the safety line. He finds the landing gear. On top of the wing.

Facing me, he sticks his hand out, palm facing down, then turns his outstretched hand over. I understand: The plane is upside down. That's why it looks so odd. It must have flipped over when it hit the water. Turned a somersault, then headed down into the depths, its heavy nose first. But settling on its back.

If that's how it happened, I expect they all died instantly.

So how can we get in?

After searching for a while, we find the side door just behind the wing. But it's impossible to open it. And the side windows are too small to wriggle through.

We swim to the nose. There used to be an engine there, but it's gone. It probably happened just as I suspected. The nose hit the water first. The engine broke off. Then the fuselage sank to the bottom of the lake. The cockpit windows are shattered. It'll be a bit difficult to get through them because the plane is upside down. But we'll manage somehow.

Simon shines his flashlight inside. Somewhere in there the remains of the crew are floating around. I steel myself for the sight of what is left of the pilot. But we can't see anything.

No doubt Simon is regretting not having bought a reel line, like I said he should. But we'll be okay. There's nowhere to fasten the safety line, but I hold onto it, and we both check that it's attached securely to his weight belt.

He shines his flashlight on his hand. Points at me. Then points straight down. That means I should stay where I am. Then he holds up the fingers of one hand twice. Ten minutes.

I shine my flashlight at my own hand and give him the thumbs up. Then I blow him a kiss from the regulator.

He slides his arms in through what was the window, grabs hold of the back of one of the seats and pulls himself gently into the plane.

He must move carefully now.

So as to stir up as little mud as possible.

I watch Simon disappear into the plane. Then I check my watch. Ten minutes, he'd signaled.

Thoughts drift into my mind, but I push them away when they try to take shape and distract my attention. For instance, what happens in an old wreck that has been lying at the bottom of a lake for more than sixty years when someone swims inside it and suddenly starts moving the water around? Just breathing out could be enough to break something loose. Something might fall on top of Simon. He might become trapped. Under something heavy. What if that were to happen, and I couldn't pull him free? If I run out of air, should I save myself and swim away? Or die with him in the darkness?

No, no. I mustn't think like that. This will be easy. A piece of cake. And then it will be my turn—I can't wait!

I shine my flashlight around a bit, but the beam doesn't penetrate very far. Besides, we've stirred up a lot of mud, and visibility has become poor. It's hard to imagine that just up there, not far away at all, a mere few meters, the sun is shining on a sheet of sparkling ice.

Then I realize that the ascent line running between me and the wooden cross lying over the hole in the ice is floating slack in my hand.

I pull at it, to make it tighter. But it doesn't tighten. I haul it in. One meter, two meters.

Three.

Has it come loose? But we tied it so securely.

I haul away at it more and more quickly. Suddenly I have the other end in my hand. I look at it. Stare at it.

My God, I must get up there and refasten it. When Simon emerges from the plane, we won't have time to swim around under the ice, looking for the hole.

I let a little air into my drysuit so that I move slowly upward. Up out of the darkness, through the gloom; it's getting lighter. I'm holding the line in my hand.

I'm looking for the hole, a source of light through the ice, but I can't see it.

Instead I see a shadow. A black rectangle.

There's something covering the hole. I swim over to it. The wooden cross is no longer there. Instead there's a door lying over the hole. It's green. Made of simple planks with a slat running diagonally across them. A door from a shed or a barn.

For a moment I think it's been lying around and the wind has blown it across the hole. I barely have time to register the thought before I realize how wrong it is. It's a sunny day up there, not a breath of wind. If there's a door lying across the hole in the ice it's because someone's put it there. What kind of joker would do that?

I try to push the door to one side, using both hands. I've dropped the line and the flashlight; they've both sunk slowly to the bottom of the lake. I can't move the door. My heavy breathing echoes like thunder in my ears as I tug at the door in vain. It dawns on me that the joker is standing on top of it. Someone is standing on the door.

Swimming away from the door, I take out my diving knife. Start hacking a hole in the ice. It's hard. The water makes it difficult to move my hand quickly enough. There's no strength in my thrusts. Twisting the knife, I stab at the ice. At last I break through. It's easier now. I rotate the knife around the hole, scraping away at the sides. It's getting bigger.

Simon swims through the wreck as carefully as he can. He has passed the radio operator's seat behind the cockpit and continued into the cabin. He thinks he feels a slight tug on the line. He wonders if it is Wilma signaling to him. But he had said two tugs to come up. What if her airline is blocked? Worried now, he decides to swim out of the wreck. It is impossible to see anything in any case. The air and his own movements have stirred up so much mud that if he holds out his arm and shines his flashlight on it, he cannot even see his hand. It is like swimming through pea soup. They might as well go back up.

He pulls at the line tied to his weight belt so it will tighten and allow him to follow it out. But it does not tighten. He hauls in more and more of the line, meter after meter. Eventually he is holding the end of the line in his hand. Wilma is supposed to be holding on to it. And the end is supposed to be fastened to the wooden cross over the hole in the ice.

Fear hits his solar plexus like a snakebite. No line to follow. How is he going to find his way back to the cockpit window? He cannot see a damn thing. How is he going to get out?

He swims until he bumps into a wall. Groping around, he starts swimming in the opposite direction, no longer knowing which is backward, forward, sideways.

He bumps into something that is not fastened down. Something that floats off to one side. He shines his flashlight. Sees nothing. Gets it into his head that it is a body. Flounders around. Swims away. Quickly, quickly. Soon he will be swimming through masses of limbs floating around. Arms and legs that have come away from bodies. He must try to calm down, but where is he? How long has he been down here? How much longer will his air last?

He has no concept of up or down, but does not realize this. Fumbles for one of the seats—if he can grab onto one, he will be able to work his way forward through the passenger cabin, but he is groping around on the ceiling, so he does not find a seat.

He swims back and forth in an aimless panic. Up and down. He cannot see a thing. Nothing at all. The line attached to his belt keeps catching, on cargo hooks on the floor, on a seat that has been wrenched from its moorings, on a loose safety belt. Everywhere. Then he begins swimming into the line. Gets tangled up in it. It is all over the inside of the plane like a spider's web. He cannot find his way out. He dies in there.

I've managed to hack a hole in the ice with my diving knife. I'm battling to make it bigger. Stabbing away. Working the knife around the edge. When it's as big as my hand, I check the pressure meter. Twenty bars left.

I mustn't breathe so rapidly. I must calm down. But I can't get out. I'm trapped under the ice.

I stick my hand up through the hole. I do it without thinking. My hand reaches out for help of its own accord.

Someone up there grips my hand firmly. At first I'm relieved to know that someone is helping me. That someone is going to pull me out of the water. Save me.

Then whoever it is really does start pulling on my hand. Bending it backward and forward. And then it dawns on me that I'm a prisoner. I'm not going anywhere. I try to jerk my hand free but only succeed in banging my face against the ice. A pink veil spreads across the light blue.

Eventually I realize what's happening: I'm bleeding.

The person up there changes his grip. Clasps hold of me as if we were shaking hands.

I press my knees against the ice. My trapped hand between my legs. And then I push away. I'm free. My hand slides out of my diving glove. Cold water. Cold hand. Pain.

I swim away under the ice. Away. Away from whoever it was.

Now I'm beneath the green door again. I thump it hard. Hammer on it. Scratch at it.

There must be another way up. A place where the ice is thinner. Where I can break through it. I swim off again.

But he runs after me. Is it a he? I can see the person through the ice. Blurred. From underneath. Above me the whole time. Between breaths, when the air I'm exhaling isn't thundering in my ears, I can hear footsteps on the ice.

I can only see whoever it is for a brief moment. The air I'm breathing out has nowhere to go. It forms a big, flat bubble like a mirror beneath the ice. I can see myself in it. Distorted. Like in the hall of

mirrors at a fairground. Changing all the time. When I breathe in,
I can see the person on the ice above me; when I breathe out, I can
see myself.

Then the regulator freezes. Air comes spurting out of my mouthpiece. I stop swimming. I have to devote all my strength to trying to
breathe. A few minutes later the tank is empty.

My lungs heave and heave. I fight to the bitter end. Mustn't
inhale water. I'm about to burst.

My arms are flailing. Banging in vain against the ice. The last
thing I do in this life is tear off my regulator and my mask. Then I
die. There's no air now between me and the ice. No reflection of me.
My eyes are open in the water. Now I can see the person up there.

A face pressing against the ice, looking at me. But what I see
doesn't register. My consciousness ebbs away like a retreating wave.

Thursday, April 16

At three fifteen in the morning Östen Marjavaara opened his eyes in his cottage in Pirttilahti. The light woke him. In the middle of April it was never dark at night for more than an hour or so. The fact that the blinds were closed did not make much difference. The light forced its way in between the slats, trickled in via the cord holes, poured through the gap between the blind and the window frame. Even if he had boarded up the windows, even if he had slept in a window-less room, he would still have woken up. The light was out there. Prodding and tugging at him. Gently but persistently, like a lonely woman. He might as well get up and make a pot of coffee.

Once out of bed, he opened the blinds. The floor was freezing cold against his bare feet. The thermometer outside the window said minus two. It had snowed during the night. The hard crust that had formed the previous week after some milder weather and a few days of sleet had become even firmer now—strong enough for him to ski along the bank of the River Torne toward Tervaskoski. There were bound to be grayling lurking behind stones in the rapids there.

When the fire had taken hold in the kitchen stove, Marja-vaara took the red plastic bucket standing in the hall and went down to the river to fetch some water. It was only a few meters to the riverbank, but he made his way carefully: There were plenty of potentially treacherous ice patches beneath the fresh snow and you could easily injure yourself.

The sun was lying in wait just below the horizon, painting the cold, wintry sky with golden-red strokes. Soon it would peer over the spruce forest, setting the red wooden panels of the cottage aglow.

The snow lay over the river like a whisper of nature. Hush, it said, be quiet. There is only you and me now.

He did as he was told, stood still with the bucket in his hand, gazing out over the river. It was true. You never come closer to owning the whole world than when you wake up before everyone else. There were a few cottages dotted along both banks of the river, but his was the only chimney with smoke rising from it. Most likely the people were not even there. They were probably fast asleep in their town houses, poor fools.

At the far end of the jetty was the water hole Marjavaara had cut in the ice. He had covered it with a polystyrene lid to prevent it from freezing over. Brushing the snow off the lid, he lifted it up. When Barbro was with him at the cottage, they always brought tap water from the town—she refused to drink water from the river.

"Yuck!" she always said with a shudder, raising her shoulders almost to her ears. "All the shit from all the villages upstream!"

She used to go on about the hospital at Vittangi, how it was a good thing they lived upstream from there. How there were no sewage-treatment plants or anything. No doubt someone's appendix would be floating down the river, and God only knew what else.

"Don't talk such rubbish!" he would say, as he had done a hundred times before. "You're talking nonsense, woman!"

He had been drinking that water since he was a child, and his health was better than hers.

He squatted down to dip the bucket into the water. There was a length of rope attached to the handle so that he could let it sink and fill before hauling it back up again.

But he could not get the bucket to sink. There was something in the way, just beneath the surface. Something big. Black.

Maybe a waterlogged tree trunk, he thought.

You did not often find tree trunks in the water nowadays. It had been more common when he was a child, when logs were still floated down to the sawmills at the mouth of the river.

Marjavaara dipped his hand in the freezing water in order to push the log out of the way. It seemed to have gotten wedged in the jetty. And it was not a log. It seemed to be made of rubber or something similar.

"What the hell . . ." he said, sliding the bucket to one side.

He took hold of it with both hands, tried to get a firm grip, but his hands would not function properly in the cold water. Then he managed to get hold of an arm. Pulled at it.

An arm, he thought impassively.

His mind was unwilling to understand.

An arm.

Then a battered face floated into view in the water hole.

Marjavaara cried out and leapt to his feet.

A raven answered from the forest. Its call sliced through the silence. Several crows joined in the chorus.

Marjavaara ran back to the cottage, slipping but regaining his balance.

He dialed the emergency number. Then it occurred to him that he had drunk three glasses of water with his dinner yesterday. And coffee after the meal. He had fetched the water from the river. From the hole in the ice. And the dead body had been lying there. Right next to it, no doubt. That white, battered face. A gash where the nose had been. Teeth in a mouth with no lips.

Someone answered the phone, but he cut them off and vomited on the spot. His body spat out everything in it, kept on spitting long after there was nothing left.

Then he dialed the emergency number again.

Never again would he drink water from the river. And it would be years before he would even go for a swim after his sauna.

I'm looking at the man who found me. He's throwing up. He calls the emergency number and vows never to drink water from the river again.

I'm thinking about the day I died.

We were dead, Simon and I. I was standing on the ice. It was evening. The sun was lower now. The door was smashed, floating in the hole in the ice. I could see that it was green on one side and black on the other.

On the riverbank, a man was rummaging in our rucksacks.

A raven flew past. It was calling in its characteristic way, sounding like a stick being hit against an empty oil drum. It landed on the ice, right next to me. Turned its head away and looked at me in the way birds do. From the side.

I must go home to Anni, I thought.

And even before I'd finished thinking, I was back at Anni's house.

The transition made me dizzy. Like when you step off a carousel.

I've gotten used to it now.

Anni was whisking pancake batter. Sitting on a chair by the kitchen table, whisking.

I like pancakes.

She didn't know I was dead. She was whisking away, thinking about me. She was looking forward to seeing me sitting at the table and tucking into the pancakes while she stood at the stove, cooking them. She placed a plate over the bowl containing the pancake batter and put in to one side. But I never came. The bowl of batter went into the fridge. She couldn't let it go to waste,

so in the end she cooked the pancakes and froze them. They're
still in the freezer.

Now they've found me. Now she can cry.

Snow, thought district prosecutor Rebecka Martinsson, shivering with pleasure as she got out of her car at the house in
Kurravaara.

It was seven in the evening. Snow clouds enveloped the village in a pleasant, dusky haze. Martinsson could barely make
out the lights from the neighboring houses. And the snow
was not just falling. Oh no, it was hurtling down. Cold, dry,
fluffy flakes cascaded from the sky, as if someone up there were
sweeping them down, doing the housework.

My *farmor*, my father's mother, of course, Martinsson
thought with a trace of a smile. She must always be on the go,
scrubbing the good Lord's floor, dusting, hard at work. I expect
she's sent Him out to stand on the porch.

Her *farmor*'s house, faced with gray, cement-fiber Eternit
siding seemed to be hiding itself in the gloom. It appeared to
have taken the opportunity to have a nap. Only the outside light
above the green-painted steps whispered quietly: Welcome
home, my girl.

Her cell phone pinged. She took it out of her pocket. A text
from Måns Wenngren.

"Pouring rain in Stockholm," it said. "Bed empty and lonely.
Come back. Want to lick your breasts & hold you. Kiss all your
lovely places."

She felt a tingling sensation.

"Infernal man," she keyed in. "I have to work tonight. Not
think about you."

She smiled. She missed him, missed his company. A few
years ago she had been working for him at the corporate law

firm Meijer & Ditzinger in Stockholm. He thought she should move back there and start working as an attorney again.

"You'd earn three times as much as you're getting now," he would say.

She looked over toward the river. Last summer he had knelt with her on the jetty, giving all of her *farmor*'s rag rugs a good scrubbing. They had sweated in the sunshine. Salty rivulets had trickled down their backs and from their brows into their eyes. When they had finished scrubbing they had dipped the rugs into the water to rinse them. Then they had stripped off and swum naked like excited dogs.

She tried to explain to him that this was how she wanted to live.

"I want to stand out here re-puttying the windows, glancing out over the river from time to time. I want to drink coffee on my porch before going to work on summer mornings. I want to dig my car out of the snow in winter. I want frost patterns on my kitchen windows."

"But you can have all that," he tried to persuade her. "We can come up to Kiruna as often as you want."

But it would not be the same. She knew that. The house would never stand for such half-measures from her. Nor would the river.

I need all this, she thought. I am so many difficult people. The little three-year-old, starved of love; the ice-cold lawyer; the lone wolf; and the person who longs to do crazy things again, who longs to escape into the craziness. It is good to feel small beneath the sparkling northern lights, small beside the mighty river. Nature is so close to us up here. My troubles and difficulties just shrivel up. I like being insignificant.

I like living up here with lining paper on the shelves and spiders in the corners, and a broom to sweep the floor with, she thought. I do not want to be a guest and a stranger. Never again.

A German pointer came galloping along at full speed through the snow. Her ears were flapping at right angles to her head, and her mouth was open wide as if she were smiling. She slid along on the ice beneath the snow as she tried to stop and say hello.

"Hello, Bella!" Martinsson said, her arms full of dog. "Where's the boss?"

Now she could hear furious shouting.

"Heel, I said! Heel! Are you deaf?"

"She's here," Martinsson shouted back.

Sivving Fjällborg gradually materialized through the falling snow. He was jogging along tentatively, afraid of falling. His weaker side was lagging slightly, his arm hanging down. His curly white hair was hidden under a green and white knitted hat. The hat was wearing its own little cap of snow. Martinsson did her best to suppress a smile. He looked magnificent. He was big anyway, but he was wearing a red padded jacket that made him look enormous. And everything was crowned by that little cap of snow.

"Where?" he puffed.

But Bella had vanished into the snow.

"Huh. I expect she'll turn up when she's hungry," he said with a smile. "What about you? I'm going to make some dumplings. There'll be plenty for both of us."

Bella appeared just as they were about to go in, scampering down into the cellar ahead of them. Fjällborg had moved into his boiler room several years before.

"You can always find what you're looking for, and it's easy to keep tidy," he would say.

The house above was neat and tidy, but was used only when the children and grandchildren came to visit.

The boiler room was sparsely furnished.

Nice and cozy, Martinsson thought as she kicked off her shoes and sat down on the padded wooden bench next to the Formica table.

A table, a chair, a stool, a bench—what more could you want? There was a made-up bed in one corner. Rag rugs on the floor to prevent the chill seeping up.

Fjällborg was standing by the hot plate, wearing an apron that had once belonged to his wife tucked into the waistband of his trousers. His stomach was too big for him to knot it at his back.

Bella had lain down next to the boiler, in order to get dry. There was a smell of wet dog, wet wool, wet concrete.

"Why not have a little rest?" Fjällborg said.

Martinsson lay down on the padded bench. It was short, but if you piled two cushions under your head and tucked up your knees it was comfortable enough.

Fjällborg cut a dumpling into thick slices. He swirled a large pat of butter around the hot frying pan.

Martinsson's cell phone pinged again. Another text from Wenngren. "You can work some other time. I want to put my arms around your waist and kiss you, lift you up onto the kitchen table and hoist up your skirt."

"Is it from work?" Fjällborg said.

"No, it's from Måns," Martinsson said archly. "He's wondering when you're going to go down to Stockholm and build him a sauna."

"Bah, the idle fool. Tell him to come up here and do some shoveling. All this snow—a bit of mild weather is all we need, and it'll be sheer hell. Tell him that."

"I will," Martinsson said, and wrote: "Mmm . . . More."

Fjällborg tipped the sliced dumpling into the pan. The fat hissed and spat. Bella raised her head and sniffed happily.

"And me with my messed-up arm," Fjällborg said. "Build a damn sauna? You must be joking. No, we should all do what Arvid Backlund has done."

"What has he done?" Martinsson said, not looking up.

"If you can tear your eyes away from that thing for one second, I'll tell you."

Martinsson switched off her phone. She spent far too little time with her neighbor. Now that she was here, the least she could do was give him her full attention.

"He lives on the other side of the creek. He turned eighty-two last week. He worked out how much firewood he was going to need for the rest of his life . . ."

"How can he do that when he doesn't know how much longer he's going to live?"

"Maybe you'd like me to give you a doggy bag so you can eat at home on your own? I'm trying to tell you a story."

"Sorry! Go on!"

"Anyway, he ordered a load of wood and got them to tip it in through his living-room window. So it's nice and handy. Enough to keep him warm for the winters he has left to him."

"In the living room?"

"A damn big pile in the middle of the floor."

"I bet he hasn't got a wife," Martinsson said.

They both burst out laughing. The moment went some way toward salving Martinsson's guilty conscience over calling on Fjällborg so seldom and his resulting disappointment. Fjällborg's stomach wobbled beneath his apron. Martinsson had a coughing fit.

Then Fjällborg changed tack completely, becoming fretful.

"Not that there's anything wrong in that," he said in Arvid Backlund's defense.

Martinsson stopped laughing.

"At least he can manage at home on his own now," Fjällborg said vehemently. "Of course he could have his firewood in the woodshed like everyone else. Then go out there one morning, slip, and break his leg. At his age. You never come home from the hospital when you're that old. You just get shoved off into a nursing home. It's easy to laugh when you're young and healthy."

He slammed the cast-iron pan with the fried dumpling onto the table.

"Time to eat!"

They put lumps of butter and heaps of lingonberry preserve and fried pork on their plates. Piled the butter and preserve and meat onto the slices of dumpling. Ate without talking.

He's scared, Martinsson thought.

She would have liked to tell him. Explain that she was never going to move back to Stockholm. Promise to clear the snow from around his house and do his shopping for him when the time came.

I will look after you, she thought, watching him as he drank from his glass of milk, taking big gulps.

Just like he looked after my *farmor*, she thought as she cut into her dumpling and the knife made squeaking noises against the plate. When I had moved away and left her. He shoveled snow for her and kept her company. Even though she grew anxious toward the end and nagged at him all the time. Even though she kept complaining about the way he cleared the snow. I want to be the kind of person who looks after someone else. That is who I want to be.

"I had a hell of a case last Friday," she said.

Fjällborg didn't react. He ate his dumpling and drank his milk as if he had not heard, still in a bad mood.

"It was sexual assault," she said, disregarding the lack of response. "The accused had called two officials at the Employment Office and masturbated during the conversations. One of the ladies was fifty and the other over sixty, and they were terrified they might actually meet him. They thought that if he found out what they looked like, he would jump them and rape them if they happened to encounter him at the supermarket. So I asked for the ladies to be questioned without the accused being present."

"What does that mean?" Fjällborg said, annoyed that he needed to ask but too curious not to.

"He was put in a neighboring room so that he could listen to what they said without being able to see them. My God, but those poor ladies found it incredibly difficult to describe what had happened. I had to push them quite hard in order to clarify the sexual nature of the complaint. Among other things I asked them what made them think that he was masturbating."

Martinsson paused to put a large piece of dumpling into her mouth. She chewed away at it, seemingly in no hurry. Fjällborg had stopped eating altogether and was waiting for her to go on.

"And?" he said impatiently.

"They said they had heard rhythmic slapping noises, and at the same time he was panting heavily. One of them said he had ejaculated, so then of course I had to ask her what had made her think so. She replied that he had started breathing even more heavily and that the rhythmic slapping noises had grown more and more intense, then he had groaned loudly and said, 'Yeesss, that's it!' Poor things. And all the while Hasse Sternlund from the local paper was sitting there taking notes—his pen was practically on fire. That didn't make matters any easier."

Fjällborg stopped being irritable and started chuckling.

"The accused was a shifty, greasy individual in his thirties," Martinsson said. "He already had several convictions for sexual assault. But he always denied everything and claimed that he suffered from asthma—what the ladies at the Employment Office had heard was him having an asthma attack, not masturbating. At that point the defense counsel asked the accused to demonstrate what it sounded like when he had an asthma attack. You should have seen the judge and the jury. Their faces were twitching, and the judge pretended to have a coughing fit. They were all desperately trying not to burst out laughing; the situation was utterly absurd. The man refused, thank goodness. The defense counsel told me afterward that the only reason he asked his client to demonstrate an asthma attack was to see if he could knock me off balance. I had been so cold and clinical while interrogating both the plaintiffs and the accused. Whenever he calls me now about anything to do with work, he always starts breathing heavily and asks, 'Is this the Employment Office?'"

"Was he convicted, then, the pervert?" Fjällborg said, deliberately dropping some pieces of meat on the floor. Bella slurped them up in an instant.

Martinsson laughed.

"Of course. I mean, who'd want a job like mine? Those poor women—you try imitating the sound of someone beating off!"

"Never! I'd rather be sent to prison."

Fjällborg laughed. Martinsson felt happier. At the same time she was thinking about the older of the two plaintiffs. She had screwed up her eyes and stared at Martinsson. They had been sitting in the prosecutor's office before the trial. The woman's voice was rough and shrill, tainted by smoking and alcohol. Her lipstick had bled into the wrinkles above her upper lip. A thick layer of powder covered her open pores, the color quite lifeless.

"This is all I need," she had said, pursing her lips. And she had told Martinsson how she was bullied at work. That one of her colleagues had invited everyone to a party—everyone except her, that is. "They're whispering behind my back all the time, just because at last year's party I might have had a bit too much to drink and fell asleep on the terrace. They're still going on about that. And they lie about me to the boss. I hate the whole damned lot of them. I ought to take them to court."

Martinsson had felt completely exhausted after her meeting with the woman. Drained and depressed. Found herself thinking about her mother. If only she had not died so young. Would her voice have become like that woman's at the end?

Fjällborg interrupted her thoughts.

"You seem to have a pretty exciting job, at least."

"Oh, I don't know. There's nothing happening at the moment. Drunk driving and domestic violence all day every day."

It is still snowing when she walks home. But it is calmer now. The flakes are not hurtling down like they were, but drifting, dancing attractively. The kind of snowfall that makes you feel happy. Big flakes melting on her cheeks.

Although it is quite late, it is not dark. The nights are getting lighter. The sky is gray, covered in snow clouds. Buildings and trees are blurred at the edges. As if they had been painted on wet watercolor paper.

She has reached the porch. She pauses, raises her hands, palms facing downward. Snow flakes land on her gloves and lie there, sparkling.

Without warning Martinsson is overcome by a feeling of pure white happiness. It flows through her body like wind blowing down a mountain valley. Power surges up from the ground. Through her body and into her hands. She stands absolutely still. Dares not move for fear of frightening the moment away.

She is at one with it all. With the snow, with the sky. With the river as it flows along, hidden beneath the ice. With Fjäll-borg, with the villagers. With everything. Everyone.

I belong here, she thinks. Perhaps I do belong, irrespective of what I want or feel.

She unlocks the door and goes up the stairs.

The feeling of reverence remains with her. Brushing her teeth and washing her face are a sacred ritual. Her thoughts remain still; nothing is bustling inside her head, just the sound of the toothbrush scrubbing and water running from the tap. She puts on her pajamas like a christening suit. Takes the time to put clean sheets on the bed. The television and radio remain blind and silent. Wenngren calls her cell phone, but she does not answer.

She lies down between the sheets, which have that unused, slightly crisp feel; they smell clean.

Thank you, she thinks.

Her hands are tingling; they are as hot as the stones in a sauna. But it is not an unpleasant feeling.

She falls asleep.

She wakes up at about four in the morning. It is light outside; the snow must have moved on. A young girl is sitting on her bed. She is naked. She has two rings in one eyebrow. Freckles. Her red hair is wet. Water is running from her hair down her spine, like a little stream. When she speaks, water dribbles constantly from her mouth and nose.

"It wasn't an accident," she tells Martinsson.

"No," Martinsson says, sitting up in bed. "I know."

"He moved me. I didn't die in the river. Look at my hand."

She holds up a hand to show Martinsson. The skin has been torn away. The knuckles are sticking out through the gray flesh. The little finger and thumb are missing.

The girl looks sorrowfully at her hand.

"I broke my nails on the ice when I was trying to scratch my way out," she says.

Martinsson gets the feeling that she is about to disappear.

"Wait," she says.

She goes after the girl, who is running among the pine trees in a forest. Martinsson tries to follow her, but in the forest the snow is deep and wet, and she sinks up to her knees.

Then Martinsson is standing at the side of her bed. She hears her mother's voice in her head: That's enough now, Rebecka. Relax.

It was just a dream, Martinsson tells herself. She gets back into bed and drifts off into different dreams. Open sky above her head. Black birds flying up from the tops of the pine trees.

I go to visit the prosecutor. She's the first person to see me since I died. She is wide awake. Sees me clearly when I sit down on her bed. Her farmor is standing in the bedroom as well. She is the first dead person I've seen since I died myself. The first dead person I've ever seen, in fact. The grandmother eyes me up and down.

You can't just come and go as you like here, stirring up trouble.

The prosecutor has a stern protector. I ask permission to speak to her granddaughter.

I've no desire to frighten or upset anybody. All I want is for them to find Simon. I don't know where to turn.

I can't bear to see them: Anni is at home in her house with the pink siding, gazing out the window in the direction of the road. She sometimes goes for days without speaking. Occasionally she takes her kicksled and wanders through the village. Now and then she struggles up the stairs to my room and looks at my bed.

Simon's mother stares at his father with hatred in her eyes as he wolfs down his food and then rushes out of the house. Their relationship is sterile; they have nothing to say to each other. He can't stand the sight of her. She tried to talk when it first happened. Wept and woke him in the night. But she's stopped now. He'd simply take his pillow and go to sleep on the sofa in the living room. When she begged him to say something, he merely said he had to get up and go to work the next day. She has run out of accusations and pleas. She needs to be able to bury her son.

She tells another woman that her husband doesn't seem to be bothered. But I can see him when he's driving, passing other cars in the most dangerous circumstances imaginable. Long-distance truck drivers keep sounding their horns at him as he overtakes them, even when it is impossible to see anything through the swirling snow. He'll soon kill himself, driving like that.

I pass over the village. It's nighttime, but as light as day. Fresh snow has covered the thick blanket of old snow that had become dirty, as it does at this time of year, stained brown by soil and grit.

Hjalmar Krekula is awake. He's standing outside his house like a bear, fat after a summer spent feeding. Wearing only a T-shirt and long johns. Two ravens have landed on his roof, making their grating calls. Hjalmar tries to chase them away. He fetches some firewood from the shed and throws it at them. He doesn't dare to shout and bawl at them; the village is asleep after all. He can't sleep, but in his mind he blames the black birds and the sunlit night, and perhaps something he's eaten.

The ravens fly off and perch in a tall pine tree instead.

He's not going to get rid of them.

My body was discovered last night. Maybe people will start talking in the village. At last.

Friday, April 17

"Fuck me sideways!"

Inspector Krister Eriksson, dog handler, slammed the car door and cursed into the cold, dry winter air.

His black German Shepherd bitch Tintin was sniffing around in the fresh snow in the police station parking lot.

"Are you all right?" someone said behind him.

It was Martinsson, the prosecutor. Her long brown hair hung down beneath her wool hat. She wore jeans, no makeup. Not in court today, then.

"It's the car," Eriksson said with a smile, embarrassed by his swearing. "It won't start. They've found Wilma Persson, the girl who disappeared last autumn."

Martinsson shook her head, not recognizing the name.

"She and her boyfriend disappeared at the beginning of October," Eriksson said. "They were both young. People thought they had gone off to do a winter dive, but nobody knew where."

"Ah yes, I remember now," Martinsson said. "So they've found them, have they?"

"Not them, just the girl. In the River Torne, upstream from Vittangi. It was a diving accident, just as people thought. Anna-Maria phoned and asked me to go up there with Tintin and see if there's any trace of the boy."

Inspector Anna-Maria Mella was Eriksson's boss.

"How is Anna-Maria?" Martinsson said. "It's been ages since I spoke to her, even though we work in the same building."

"She's okay, I think, but you know what it's like with a house full of kids. She's always on the go, like most people, I suppose."

Martinsson was sure he was not telling the truth. All was not well with Mella, in fact.

"The atmosphere between her and her colleagues isn't as good as it used to be," he said. "Anyway, I told her that Tintin isn't really working at the moment. Her puppies are due soon, but I can let her have a quick look around. I was thinking of taking the new dog as well. Let him have a sniff. It won't do any harm. If we don't find anything, they can send for another dog, but the nearest one is in Sundsvall, so that would take ages."

He nodded toward the back of his car. There were two dog cages in the luggage space. In one of them was a chocolate-brown German Shepherd.

"He's lovely," Martinsson said. "What's his name?"

"Roy. Yes, he's certainly handsome. It remains to be seen if he's going to be any good as a police dog. I can't let him out at the same time as Tintin. He chases after her and winds her up. And Tintin needs to take things easy until she whelps."

Martinsson looked over at Tintin.

"She's good, from what I've heard," she said. "She found the vicar in Vuolusjärvi, and tracked down Inna Wattrang. Amazing."

"Oh yes, she certainly is good," Eriksson said, turning away to hide his proud smile. "I always compare them with my previous dog, Zack. It was a privilege to work with him. He taught me all I know. I just followed him. I was so young in those days, didn't have a clue. But I've trained Tintin."

The dog looked up when she heard her name and came trotting over to them. Sat down next to the trunk of Eriksson's car as if to say, "Shall we get moving?"

"She knows we're going out on a job," Eriksson said. "She thinks it's great fun."

He turned to Tintin.

"It's no good," he said. "The car won't start."

The dog tilted her head to one side and seemed to think this over. Then she lay down in the snow with a resigned sigh.

"Why don't you take my car?" Martinsson said.

It dawned on her that she was talking to Tintin, so she turned to face Eriksson.

"Sorry," she said. "I expect you'll be the one doing the driving. I don't need my car today."

"Oh no, I couldn't possibly . . ."

As she pressed the keys of her Audi A4 Avant into his hand, he kept asking whether she was sure she would not need the car that day. In any case, there was sure to be another solution. They could come and fetch him, for instance.

"Why can't you just say thank you?" she said. "I'm going inside. Unless you need some help moving the dog cages. Just go! They'll be waiting for you."

He said he could manage the cages himself. So she left him to it, pausing in the doorway to give him a wave.

She had not even taken her jacket off when he knocked on the door of her office.

"Sorry," he said. "It's a stick shift. I can't cope with them."

She smiled.

That doesn't happen very often, he thought.

Other women went around smiling all day long. Whether they were happy or not. But not this one. And she did not just smile with her mouth, oh no, you had to look deep into her eyes. A merry tune was playing at the very back of her eyes when she looked at him.

"What about Tintin?" she said.

"No, she's used to an automatic as well."

"It's dead easy, you just—"

"I know!" he said, interrupting her. "That's what everyone says, but . . . It's no good, I just can't do it."

Martinsson looked at him. He met her gaze without a trace of embarrassment or shyness. Held her gaze.

She knew he was a lone wolf.

And it's not just because of how he looks, she thought.

Eriksson's face was badly scarred by severe burns. A house fire when he was a teenager, she had heard. His skin was shiny with patches of pink, his ears two newly opened, crinkled birch leaves, no hair, no eyebrows or lashes, his nose just two holes in the middle of his face.

"I'll drive you," she said finally.

She expected him to protest. To start going on about how she was supposed to be at work. That she no doubt had all kinds of other things to do.

"Thank you," he said, smiling mischievously to show that he had learned his lesson.

It suddenly turned warm as they were driving. The sun's hot breath. Melting snow dripped from spindly pine trees and from the branches of birches already taking on a violet tone. Patches of open water had begun to appear around the stones in the river. The ice was beginning to recede from the riverbanks. But the cold would return when night fell. It had not surrendered yet.

Martinsson and Eriksson followed the forest trails north of the Torne. The police had marked the route with strips of red plastic tape. If they had not done so, it would have been virtually impossible to find the right place out here in the wild. There were trails running off in all directions.

The barrier across the trail leading to the summer cottages on the promontory at Pirttilahti was standing open. The site was covered with wooden cottages, huts, and several outhouses made out of spare bits of timber. People seemed to have built haphazardly, wherever they could find room. There was also an old red-painted wooden hut on wheels with dark green window frames. It was propped up on railroad ties, and there were flounced flowery curtains at the windows. It made Martinsson think of a small, tired traveling circus troupe. Here and there lengths of wood had been nailed up between pine trees. Hanging from them were swings with graying ropes, or ratty fishing nets weighed down by fragments of ice that had not yet melted in the spring sunshine. Along the walls of the cottages were stacks of rotting wood, unlikely to be much good for burning. Lying all over the place were things that might come in handy one of these days: part of an old porch, a pretty but broken wooden gate leaning against a tree, stacks of timber only just adequately covered by tarpaulins, piles of old bricks and paving stones, grindstones, a street lamp, an old tractor, rolls of fiberglass insulation, an iron bed.

And lots of rowboats in among the trees. Upside down and covered in snow. Made of wood and plastic, in varying states of repair.

By the side of a permanent landing pier was a floating jetty that had been dragged up onto the riverbank. The police and forensic teams were gathered there.

"What a place!" Martinsson said with delight, switching off the engine.

Tintin and Roy immediately started howling and barking with excitement.

"Some of us can't wait to start work," Eriksson said, laughing.

They got out of the car quickly.

Inspector Mella came over to them.

"What a commotion!" she said with a chuckle.

"They just go mad, they're so desperate to get to work," Eriksson said. "I don't want to shush them up as I want this to be a positive experience. But I'm not at all sure that it's good for Tintin. She shouldn't get this excited in her condition. She needs to get to work, then she'll calm down. Where do you want us to search?"

Mella looked over toward the river.

"The forensic team has just arrived. They're working down by the jetty, but I thought you and Tintin could check along the riverbank. The girl was out diving with her boyfriend, so he must be here somewhere. Maybe his body has floated ashore nearby, who knows? It would be helpful if you could search a little way upstream and downstream from here, and then we can go up to the rapids. Some people dive in the rapids to retrieve lost fishing tackle—a decent Rapala can set you back a hundred and fifty kronor after all. So they go looking for a few of those . . . As I said, I've no idea. But young people are always short on money. Such a tragic accident. A damned shame if ever there was one. They had the whole of their lives to look forward to. It would be nice for the relatives if we could find both of them."

Eriksson nodded.

"Tintin can make a start," he said. "But she's not going to walk three kilometers. I'll take Roy out later."

"Okay. Maybe we can let her search the promontory here, and then up by the rapids. It's open water there, and we can cross over to the far side later. I've got some officers out looking for the car, but they're keeping away from the riverbank. A hundred meters, I told them."

Eriksson nodded his approval. Letting Tintin out of the car, he strapped her into her work coat.

She stopped barking and scuttled excitedly around his legs; he had to disentangle himself from the lead.

When he had disappeared, being dragged down toward the promontory by an excited, whimpering German Shepherd, Mella turned to Martinsson.

"What brought you out here?"

"I'm just the chauffeur," Martinsson said. "Krister's car wouldn't start."

They eyed each other for a long moment. Then both said at the same time, "How are things?"

Mella answered first. "Fine, just fine." Martinsson looked her over. Inspector Mella was short, barely five feet tall. But it had never registered with Martinsson that Mella was small. Until now. The inspector was almost swallowed up by her black leather jacket. Her long, light blond hair hung down her back in a thick braid as usual. It struck Martinsson that she had seen very little of Mella recently—for the last year or so, in fact. Time really did fly. It was obvious from Mella's eyes that things were not fine at all. Just over a year ago, she and her colleague Sven-Erik Stålnacke had been involved in a gunfight; both of them had been forced to shoot to kill. Mella had been responsible for getting them into that situation. She hadn't wanted to wait for backup.

Of course Stålnacke's angry, Martinsson thought. No doubt he feels bad, thinks it was all her fault.

And he's right, really, she reasoned. Mella had put both her own life and his at risk. There had been a wild horse in this mother of four. But now that horse's spirit had been crushed.

"I'm fine," Martinsson replied to Mella's question.

Mella looked hard at Martinsson. She did seem to be in good shape. A hell of a lot better than she had been. Still thin, but not nearly so pale and wretched. She was doing a good job as district prosecutor. Had some kind of relationship with her old boss from Stockholm. Not that he was much to write home about. One of those well-heeled types who sail through life, getting by on charm and good looks. He drank too much, anybody could see that. But if he made Martinsson feel good, so be it.

One of the forensic officers shouted to Mella. They were going to take the body away. Did Mella want to see it before they did? Shouting "I'm coming," she turned back to Martinsson.

"I want to have a look at her," she said. "It will feel better, somehow, if I've seen her when I talk to her next of kin. They usually want to view the deceased, to reassure themselves that it really is their relative we've found. So it's good to know what state the body is in. I can well imagine. She's been in the water since last autumn."

Mella suddenly bit her tongue. For Christ's sake, she should not be babbling on about dead bodies to Martinsson. Martinsson had killed in self-defense. Three men. Smashed the skull of one and shot the other two. She had been on sick leave for a long time. Nearly two years later, when Lars-Gunnar Vinsa killed his son and took his own life, it had all been too much for her. Martinsson had ended up in a psychiatric ward.

"I'm okay," Martinsson said, as if she had read Mella's mind. "May I have a look as well?"

The skin on the girl's face was white and bloated from the water. One hand was without its diving glove, and there was next to nothing left of it. The flesh had come away and exposed the bones. The little finger and thumb were missing. So was her nose. Most of her lips, too.

"That's what happens," one of the forensic officers said. "When they've been in the water for a long time. The skin tears easily and peels away, and then they drift around and bump into things. That causes noses and ears and such to fall off. Pike might have been nibbling at her as well. We'll have to see how she holds together when the pathologist cuts away her diving suit. Will Pohjanen be doing the autopsy?"

Mella nodded, keeping an eye on Martinsson, who was staring at the girl's battered hand as if transfixed.

A little way off, Inspector Sven-Erik Stålnacke pulled up in his Volvo, got out, and shouted to Mella.

"We've found the kids' car. Over by the rapids."

He walked toward them. Gingerly, legs wide apart so as not to slip, just as they all were doing.

"It was parked in the felling area," he said. "A hundred and fifty meters from the rapids. They must have driven as far as they could over the rough ground so they wouldn't have to carry their heavy diving gear."

He rubbed the back of his neck thoughtfully.

"Then of course it was covered in snow during the winter. They're digging it out now. That's what we thought was so odd when they disappeared last autumn—the fact that nobody had seen their car. But it's obvious now. If it was in the forest, completely covered in snow . . . Not even people riding snowmobiles along the riverbank would have noticed it. The young man did well to drive it that far, though. The trees have all been felled down toward the rapids, but the area's full of big stones and stumps."

Martinsson seemed to snap out of her trance, standing there in front of the girl.

"She might have been the one driving," she said, nodding toward the body. "According to the statistics, women are better drivers than men."

She gave Stålnacke a knowing smile.

Normally, he would have responded with a snort, making his graying scrubbing brush of a mustache stick straight out. He would have said that stastistics were lies, damned lies, and then asked where Martinsson got her ideas from. He would have had a self-satisfied giggle while Martinsson and Mella rolled their eyes.

But all he said was: "You may be right."

He asked Mella what she wanted them to do with the car.

Oh dear, Martinsson thought. Things really are frosty between the pair of them.

"There's no reason to suspect a crime," Mella said. "If we can get hold of a spare key, someone can drive it back to town."

"Well, we can try, I suppose," Stålnacke said doubtfully. "If we can get it onto the road, that is."

"I'm only asking you to try," Mella said, a splinter of ice in her voice.

Stålnacke turned on his heel and walked away just as Eriksson was returning.

"Oh," Mella said, disappointed. "I'd hoped to hear her barking."

"No, she didn't find anything. I'll take a walk with Roy, but I don't think the boy is here."

"What do you mean?" Mella said.

Eriksson shrugged.

"I don't know," he said. "But I'll take a walk with Roy, and we'll see."

Patting Tintin, he told her what a good job she had done. Opening the trunk of Martinsson's car, he allowed the dogs to change places. Roy could not believe his luck. He danced the dance of the happy tracker dog, in the end not knowing what to do with all the joy in his body. So he sat down and gave a huge yawn.

Tintin was not happy with the changeover. She barked away in desperation. Was that little nothing going to go out with the boss and have fun while she, the alpha bitch, was shut up in the car? Unacceptable. Totally unacceptable.

Her barking penetrated the bodywork of the car as she spun around and around in her cage.

"Not good," Eriksson said, as he watched her through the rear window. "She's not supposed to get stressed in her condition. I'm sorry, Anna-Maria, but this is no good."

"Should I put her on her lead and take her for a walk?" Mella said. "Maybe if she's outside . . ."

"That would only make things worse."

"I could take her back to town with me," Martinsson said. "Do you think that would calm her down?"

Eriksson looked at her. Now that the sun was out, she had taken off her wool hat. Her hair was slightly tousled. Those sand-colored eyes. That mouth. He wanted to kiss that mouth. She had a scar running from her upper lip to her nose, from the time Lars-Gunnar Vinsa had thrown her down the cellar steps. A lot of people thought it was ugly, felt sorry for her, went on about how pretty she had been before. But he liked the scar. It made her look vulnerable.

Desire coursed through his body like a jet of hot water. Her beneath him on all fours. One hand sifting through her hair. The other gripping her hip. Or she's sitting astride him. His hands cupping her breasts. He whispers her name. A strand of her hair is sticking to her face, wet with perspiration. Or she's on her back beneath him. Her knees drawn up. He thrusts into her. Slowly now.

"What do you say?" she said again. "She can wait in my office. Nobody will mind. You can come get her when you've finished."

"Yes, why not?" he said, averting his eyes in case she saw through him. "That would be fine."

Mella and Stålnacke were standing by the car that had been discovered near the river, a Peugeot 305.

"I found the key," Stålnacke said. "It occurred to me that they'd probably done the same as people who go berrypicking. They don't want to take the car key with them, because if you drop it and lose it in the forest you have a hell of a time getting home, way out here in the wild. I usually hide mine inside the back bumper. They'd hidden theirs on top of one of the tires, under the wheel arch."

"Really?" Mella said patiently.

"Anyway, I thought I'd try to drive it out onto the road before the snow melts too much in the heat—there are a hell of a lot of stones and rocks, and . . ."

Mella glanced involuntarily at the clock on her cell phone. Stålnacke hurried to get to the point.

"When I turned the key, the car started right away, no problem."

"Really?"

"But . . ."

He raised a finger to emphasize that they had reached the point he wanted to talk to her about.

". . . but it ran out of gas after only a few seconds. So there was only a drop in the tank. I thought you'd want to know that."

"Really?"

"So they'd have been stuck. They'd never have made it back to Piilijärvi. The nearest gas station is in Vittangi."

Mella made a sort of humming noise to indicate surprise.

"It's strange, don't you think?" Stålnacke said. "I mean, they weren't stupid, were they? How did they think they were going to get home?"

"I've no idea," Mella said with a shrug.

"Oh well," Stålnacke said, obviously irritated by the fact that she did not share his puzzlement over the empty gas tank. "I just thought you might be interested."

"Of course." Mella made an effort. "Maybe someone siphoned off the gas while the car was standing here during the winter. Someone on a snowmobile, perhaps?"

"There aren't any scratches on the cap to the gas tank. Mind you, if I could find the key, no doubt anybody else could have as well. I still think it's odd, though."

"Everything okay?"

Eriksson knocked on the open door of Martinsson's office. He remained standing in the doorway. This time he took a good look around the place. The desk was piled high with legal documents. A cardboard box full of material having to do with some environmental investigation occupied the visitor's chair. It was obvious that she was working her ass off. But he had known that already. Everyone in the police station knew it. When she had taken up her post in Kiruna, she had set lawsuits in motion at such a rate that the local lawyers complained. And God help any police officer who submitted inadequate preliminary investigation documents—she would chase them down, thrust instructions detailing what needed to be done into their hands, then phone and nag them until they did what she wanted them to do.

Martinsson looked up from the file on a drunk-driving case.

"No problems at all. How did it go out there? Did you find him?"

"No. What have you done with Tintin?"

"She's here," Martinsson said, rolling back her desk chair. "Under my desk."

"What?" Eriksson said. His face was one big smile as he bent over to investigate. "Now look here, old girl; did it take just one afternoon for you to forget your boss? You're supposed to jump up and dance out to greet me the moment you hear my footsteps in the corridor."

When Eriksson bent down and started talking to her, Tintin got up and walked over to him, her tail wagging.

"Just look at her," he said. "Now she's ashamed because she didn't show me the respect I deserve."

Martinsson smiled at Tintin, who was arching her back submissively, wagging her tail excitedly and trying to lick her master on the mouth. Then she suddenly seemed to remember Martinsson. She hurried back, sat down beside Martinsson's chair and placed her paw on the woman's knee. Then she scurried back to Eriksson again.

"Well, I'll be damned!" Eriksson said. "Amazing! She stayed under your desk even as I was approaching. And now this. She's giving you the highest possible marks. She's normally very loyal to her master. This is most unusual."

"I like dogs," Martinsson said.

She looked him in the eye. Did not avert her gaze. He returned the look.

"Lots of people like dogs," he said. "But dogs obviously like you. Are you thinking of getting one?"

"Perhaps," she said. "But the dogs I have in mind are those I played with as a child. It's difficult to find intelligent hunting dogs now. Mind you, I don't hunt myself. I want a dog that runs loose around the village during the winter, but that's not allowed any more. That's how it was when I was a girl. They knew everything that was going on. And hunted mice in the stubblefields."

"One like her, in other words?" he said, nodding toward Tintin. "Wouldn't that be the right dog for you?"

"Of course. She's lovely."

Several long seconds passed. Tintin sat between them, looking first at one, then the other.

"Anyway," Martinsson said eventually, "you didn't find him."

"No, but I knew we wouldn't from the start."

"How could you know that? What do you mean?"

Eriksson looked out of the window. Sunshine and a light blue sky. Softening up the icy crust on the snow. Icicles hung in pretty rows dripping from gutters. The trees were suffering the pains of spring.

"I don't know," he said. "It's just that I sometimes get a feeling. Sometimes I know the dog is about to find something even before it starts barking. Or that we aren't going to find anything, as on this occasion. It's when I feel . . . how shall I put it? . . . maybe *open* is the right word. A human being is something special. There's more to us than we realize. And Mother Earth is more than just a lump of dead rock. She's also alive. If there's a dead body lying somewhere in the countryside, you can feel it when you reach the place. The trees know, and vibrate with the knowledge. The stones know. The grass. They create an atmosphere. And we can perceive it if we just . . ."

He shrugged as a way of finishing the sentence.

"Like people do when they are dowsing for water," Martinsson said, feeling that this sounded awkward. "They don't really need a divining rod. They simply know that the water is there."

"Yes," he said softly. "Something like that, perhaps."

He gave her a searching look, suspected that there was something she wanted to tell him.

"What's on your mind?" he said.

"The girl they found," Martinsson said. "I had a dream about her."

"Really?"

"It was nothing much. Anyway, I have to go home now. Need a lift?"

"No, but thanks all the same. A friend of mine's coming to help me with the car. So you saw Wilma, did you?"

"I dreamed about her."

"What did she want, do you think?"

"It was a dream," Martinsson said again. "Don't they say that all the people in your dreams are really yourself?"

Eriksson smiled.

"'Bye," was all he said.

And off he went, with the dog.

Mella drove down to Piilijärvi, some sixty-five kilometers southeast of Kiruna. The snow had melted from the road. All that was left was an icy ridge in the middle. Mella needed to inform Anni Autio, Wilma Persson's great-grandmother, that Persson had been found, and that she was dead. It would have been helpful to have Stålnacke with her, but that was out of the question. He could not forgive her for what had happened during the shooting in Regla.

"And what the hell am I supposed to do about that?" Mella said aloud to herself. "He'll be retiring soon, so he won't have to put up with me much longer. He can stay at home with Airi and her cats."

But it nagged at her. She was used to laughing and joking with her colleagues. It had always been fun, going to work. But now . . .

"Not much damn fun at all!" she said to herself as she turned off onto the narrow, winding road leading from the E10 to the village.

And things were not getting any better. She rarely asked the others if they wanted to grab lunch somewhere as a group. Often she just drove home and forced down some yogurt and muesli on her own. She had started calling her husband from work. In the middle of the day. To talk about nothing at all. Or she would invent errands: "Did you remember Gustav's extra pair of gloves when you took him to day care?" "Can you pick up some shopping on the way home?"

≋

Anni Autio lived in a pink paneled house in the middle of the village, by the lake. The wooden steps up to the front door were stained brown, carefully looked after, and generously sanded to prevent falls. The handrail was black-painted iron. A handwritten note inside a plastic pocket, attached to the front door with a thumbtack, read:

RING and WAIT.

It takes ages for me to get to the door.

I AM at home.

Mella rang the bell. And waited. A few ravens were frolicking in the thermals above the lake. Black and majestic against the blue sky. Their cries filled the air. One of them was wheeling around and around in concentric circles. Without a care in the world.

Mella waited. Could feel every nerve in her body itching to hurry back to her car and drive away. Anything to avoid coming face-to-face with another person's sorrow.

A cat came strolling across the parking area, caught sight of Mella, and quickened its pace. Stålnacke was a cat person. Mella's thoughts turned back to him. He was good at this kind of thing. Telling people what they least wanted to hear. Hugging and consoling them.

Damn him, she thought.

"Damn," she said out loud, in an attempt to banish her depressing thoughts.

At that same moment the door opened. A thin, stooped woman in her eighties was clinging onto the handle with both hands. Her white hair hung down her back in a string-like plait. She was wearing a simple blue dress buttoned up to her neck and a man's cardigan. Her legs were encased in thick nylon stockings, and her pointed shoes were made of reindeer skin.

"Sorry," Mella said. "I was lost in my thoughts."

"Never mind," the woman said in a friendly tone. "I'm pleased that you're still here. You wouldn't believe how many people don't have the patience to wait, despite the note I pinned to the door. I struggle this far only to see them driving away. I'm always tempted to shoot them. I look forward to a nice little chat, then find myself cheated. Mind you, the Jehovah's Witnesses always wait."

She laughed.

"I'm not so particular nowadays. They're welcome to stay for a chat. But you're not religious, are you? Are you selling raffle tickets?"

"Anna-Maria Mella, Kiruna police," Mella said, showing her ID. "Are you Anni Autio?"

The smile disappeared from the woman's face.

"You've found Wilma," she said.

Anni Autio supported herself against the walls and held onto strategically placed chairs as she shuffled to the kitchen. Mella took off her winter boots and left them in the vestibule, which was almost completely filled by a large, humming freezer. She accepted Autio's offer of coffee. The kitchen gave the impression of having been untouched since the 1950s. The tap shook and the pipes shuddered as Autio filled the coffee pot. The conifer-green cupboards reached all the way to the ceiling. The walls were crammed with photographs, poems by Edith Södergran and Nils Ferlin, children's watercolors now so faded that it was impossible to see what they were meant to represent, miniature prints of birds, framed pages torn out of old flower books.

"We haven't managed to find her mother," Mella said. "According to the electoral register, Wilma lived with you, and the police report on her disappearance names you as next of kin. She was your granddaughter—"

"My great-granddaughter, in fact."

Autio hunched over the stove as she waited for the water to boil. Listening to Mella's account of how Persson had been found, she occasionally lifted the saucepan lid with an embroidered potholder.

"Tell me if there's anything I can do," Mella said. Autio made a dismissive gesture.

"Do you mind if I smoke?" she asked when she had finished pouring out the coffee. "I know it's flirting with death, but I was eighty last January, and I've always smoked. Some people look after their health . . . But life isn't fair."

Tapping her cigarette against the glass jar she used as an ashtray, she said again, "Life isn't fair."

She wiped her nose and cheeks with the back of her hand.

"I'm sorry," she said.

"Cry as much as you like," Mella said, just as Stålnacke used to do.

"She was only seventeen," Autio said with a sob. "She was too young. And I'm too old to have to live through all this."

She looked angrily at Mella.

"I'm totally fed up," she said. "It's bad enough outliving nearly everyone my own age. But when you start outliving the youngsters, well . . ."

"How come she lived with you?" Mella asked, mainly to have something to say.

"She used to live in Huddinge with her mother, my granddaughter. Went to school, but was having trouble getting through all the work. She insisted on taking a break and coming up here to live with me. She moved in last Christmas. She worked for Marta Andersson at the campsite. And then she met Simon. He's a relative of Kyrö, who lives in the red wooden cottage over there."

She gestured toward the building.

"Simon thought the world of Wilma."

She stared hard at Mella.

"I've never been as close to anyone as I was to Wilma. Not to my daughters. Certainly not to my sister. Mind you, here in the village nobody has much time for anybody else. But Wilma gave me a feeling of freedom. I don't know how to explain it. My sister Kerttu, for instance—she's always been better off than me. She married Isak Krekula. He runs the hauling firm."

"I recognize the name," Mella said.

"Anyway, none of them have exactly been pals with the police. It's his sons who run the firm nowadays, of course. That Kerttu is always annoying me. All she wants to talk about is money and business and what big shots her boys keep meeting. But Wilma used to say, 'Take no notice. If money and that sort of stuff make her feel good, then fine. You don't need to be any less happy on her account.' I know it sounds simple and straightforward— but last summer . . . I'd never felt so liberated and so young. You can think whatever you like, Ann-Britt, but—"

"Anna-Maria."

"But she was my best friend. An eighty-year-old and a teenager. She didn't treat me like a useless pensioner."

It is the middle of August. Blueberry time. Simon Kyrö is driving along a forest trail. Wilma Persson is in the passenger seat. Anni

Autio is in the back, her walker beside her. This is the place they were looking for. Blueberries and lingonberries growing right by the trail. Autio wriggles out of the car unaided. Kyrö lifts out her walker and her basket. It is a lovely day. The sun is shining, and the heat is squeezing threads of attractive scents from the forest.

"I haven't been here for years," Autio says.

Kyrö gives her a worried look. Of course not. How on earth could she have negotiated any kind of rough terrain with her walker?

"Would you like us to come with you?" he says. "I can carry your basket."

"Just leave her," Persson says, and Autio emits a loud expletive in Tornedalen Finnish, shooing him away as if his interpolation were a fly buzzing around her. Persson knows. Autio needs to be alone in the silence. If she finds it impossible to move around and does not manage to pick a single blueberry, that will not matter. She can sit down on a rock and just be herself.

"We'll come back and collect you in three hours," Persson says.

Then she turns to Kyrö with a cheeky smile.

"I know how you and I can figure out how to spend the time."

Kyrö's face turns as red as a beetroot.

"Stop it," he says, glancing over at Autio.

Persson laughs.

"Anni's nearly eighty. She's given birth to five children. Do you think she's forgotten what people can get up to when they're on their own?"

"I haven't forgotten," Autio says. "But stop embarrassing him."

"Make sure you don't die while we're away," Persson says chirpily before she and Kyrö get back into the car and drive off.

They do not go far. The car stops. Persson sticks her head out of the window and shouts so loudly that her voice echoes through the forest, "Mind you, if you do die, it's a fantastic day and place for it."

It was five thirty in the afternoon when Mella entered the autopsy unit of Kiruna's hospital.

"You again?" was her sardonic greeting from the pathologist Lars Pohjanen.

His thin body always looked frozen inside his crumpled green autopsy coat.

Mella's mood improved immediately—here was someone who still pulled her leg just as in the old days.

"I assumed that you just couldn't wait to see me again," she said, giving him a one-hundred-watt smile.

He chuckled, though it sounded as if he was simply clearing his throat.

Wilma Persson was lying naked on the stainless steel autopsy table. Pohjanen had cut away her diving suit and underclothes. Her skin was grayish-white and looked bleached. Next to her was an ashtray full of Pohjanen's cigarette butts. Mella did not comment—she was neither his boss nor his mother.

"I've just been talking to her great-grandmother," she said. "I thought perhaps you'd be able to tell me what happened."

Pohjanen shook his head.

"I haven't opened her up yet," he said. "She's a bit of a mess, as you can see, but all this damage happened after she died." He pointed to Persson's face, her missing nose and lips.

"Why is her hair all over the floor?" Mella said.

"Water rots the roots, so the hair becomes very loose."

Holding up Persson's hands, he contemplated them through narrowed eyes. The little finger and thumb of her right hand were missing.

"I noticed something odd about her hands," he said, clearing his throat. "She's lost a lot of nails, but not all of them. Take a look at her right hand—oops! I have to be careful, the skin detaches itself from her fingers before you know where you are. As you can see, the little finger and thumb are missing from the right hand, but the middle and ring fingers are still there. Compare that with the other hand . . ."

He held up both hands, and Mella leaned forward somewhat reluctantly to take a close look.

"The nails on her left hand, the ones she has left, are polished black and neatly filed—they're in quite good shape, don't you think? But the nails on the middle and ring fingers on her right hand are broken, and the polish is almost scraped away."

"What does that imply?" Mella said.

Pohjanen shrugged.

"Difficult to say. But I scraped the underside of the nails. Come and see what I found."

He laid Persson's hands down with care, then led Mella to his workbench. On it were five sealed test tubes labeled "right middle," "right ring," "left thumb," "left middle," "left index." In each of the tubes was a flat wooden toothpick.

"Under both the nails on her right hand there were flakes of green paint. That doesn't necessarily mean it had anything to do with the accident—she might have been scraping window frames, or painting, or something of the sort. Most people are right-handed."

Mella nodded and glanced at her watch. Dinner at six, Robert had said. Time to go home.

≈≈≈≈

A quarter of an hour later, Pohjanen was standing once more with Persson's hand in his. He was taking her fingerprints. This was something he always did when identification was difficult due to intense facial damage, as in this case. The skin of Persson's left thumb had come away just as he was about to press it onto the paper. Such things happen, and he did what he usually did, sliding his own finger inside the pocket of Persson's skin and pressing it down on the paper. As he did so he heard someone in the doorway. Assuming it was Inspector Mella, he did not turn around but said, "Right, Anna-Maria. All done here. You'll be able to read the autopsy report as soon as it's written. Assuming it ever gets written."

"Sorry to interrupt," said a voice that was not Mella's.

When Pohjanen finally turned around, he saw that his visitor was district prosecutor Rebecka Martinsson. He had met Martinsson once before, when he had been called in to advise on one of her cases having to do with domestic violence. The husband and wife had given different explanations for the woman's injuries. But Pohjanen and Martinsson had never spoken outside the courtroom. He could see that she was staring at the thimble of dead skin he was wearing on his index finger.

Introducing herself, she reminded him that they had already met. He said he recalled the circumstances clearly, and asked what she wanted.

"Is that Wilma Persson?" she said.

"Yes, I was just taking her fingerprints. You have to get everything done as quickly as possible—things change very rapidly when you take a body out of the water."

"I was just wondering if there was any way of establishing whether she actually died at the place where she was found."

"What makes you think she might not have?"

Martinsson appeared to steady herself. He noticed how she pursed her lips, shook her head as if to clear it of unwanted thoughts, and then looked at him as if begging his indulgence.

"I had a dream about her," she said, after a moment's hesitation. "In the dream she said that she had been moved. That she had died somewhere else."

Pohjanen looked long and hard at Martinsson without speaking. There was not a sound, apart from his own wheezing and the hum from the air-conditioning.

"As far as I'm aware, the cause of death was accidental drowning. Is it your intention to turn the case into something more elaborate?"

"No, er, well . . ."

"Is there something I ought to know? How the hell am I supposed to do my job if nobody tells me anything? If you say there's no suspicion of a crime having been committed, that's the basis on which I will conduct my examination. I don't want to be told later on that I've missed something. Is that clear?"

"I'm not here to—"

"But you're here, just the same."

She held up her hands.

"Forget it," she said. "Pay no attention. I should never have come. I was being silly."

"Yes, I've heard that you often are," Pohjanen said unkindly.

Turning on her heel, she left the room. His comment hung in the air. Rang through the autopsy lab like a church bell.

The silly bitch should stop poking her nose in, Pojhanen said to himself defensively.

But his guilty conscience gnawed away at him. The dead spirits surrounding him were unusually silent.

They can go to hell, the whole lot of 'em, he said to himself.

A week passes. Snow crashes down from the trees. Sighs deeply as it collapses into the sunny warmth. Bare patches appear. The southern sides of anthills heat up in the sun. The snow buntings return. Martinsson's neighbor Fjällborg finds bear tracks in the forest. The big sleep of winter is over.

"Have they found the boy yet?" Fjällborg asks her.

Martinsson has invited Fjällborg and Bella over for supper. She has served sushi, which Fjällborg is forcing down with a skeptical expression on his face. He pronounces it *sishu*, making it sound like a sneeze. Having settled on the sofabed, Bella is lying on her back, hind legs apart, fast asleep. Her front paws keep twitching.

Martinsson says they have not.

"Piilijärvi," Fjällborg says. "That's the last place on earth I'd like to live in. That's where the Krekula brothers live."

"Krekula Haulers," he says when he sees that Martinsson has not understood. "Tore and Hjalmar Krekula. They're about the same age as my kid brother. A seasoned pair of crooks if ever there was one. It was their father who set up the hauling business, and he was just as bad when he was in his prime. He must be almost ninety now. The elder brother, Hjalmar, is the worst. He's been charged with assault loads of times—I don't know how many other people there are who are too scared to report him. It was the same when they were kids. That was quite a scandal. Surely you've heard about it? About the Krekula brothers? No? No, come to think of it, it was long before your time. Hjalmar could hardly have been nine, and his little brother must have been about six, maybe seven. They were out in the forest. They were taking the cows to their summer pasture. Not all that far away, in fact. Hjalmar left his kid brother behind. Came back home without him. That started a major fuss—soldiers, mountain rescue, the police. But they didn't find him. They gave up after a week. Everyone thought he was dead. Then out of the blue the little kid turned up at the front door. It was headline news all over Sweden. Tore was interviewed on the radio, and all the papers wrote about it. The boy survived. A damn miracle, there's no other word for it. That Hjalmar, well, he's as cold as a dead fish. Always has been. Even in primary school the pair of 'em used to go around collecting debts—real ones and made-up ones, it was all the same to them. One of my cousins, Einar— you've never met him, he moved away ages ago, been dead for years. Had a heart attack. Anyway, he was at school with the Krekula brothers. And he and his friends had to pay up. If they didn't, they'd have Hjalmar on their backs.

"Ah well," Fjällborg says, scraping the wasabi off the rice, "not everything was better in the old days, I guess."

Friday, April 24

Pathologist Lars Pohjanen telephoned Inspector Anna-Maria Mella at eleven fifteen on the night of Friday, April 24.

"Have you got a moment?" he said.

"Of course," Mella said. "Marcus rented a movie; it's supposed to be deep, profound even. But Robert fell asleep after a few minutes. He woke up just now and said, 'Are they still sitting around blabbering? Haven't they solved the world's problems yet?' Then he fell asleep again."

"Who is it?" Robert shouted, sounding distinctly drowsy. "I'm awake."

"It's Pohjanen."

"This damn film is just a gang of people lounging around on a park bench talking, going on and on nonstop," Robert yelled, loud enough for Pohjanen to hear. "It's Friday night, for Christ's sake! What we need is a car chase or two, a few murders, and a dollop of sex."

Pohjanen chuckled.

"I apologize," Mella. "I was drunk one night and he got me pregnant."

"They are not sitting on a park bench. Can you just shut up, please?" Mella's eldest son, Marcus, said.

"What's the film?" Pohjanen said.

"*The Lives of Others*. It's in German."

"I've seen that," Pohjanen said. "It was good. It made me cry."

"Pohjanen says he cried when he saw it," Mella advised Robert.

"Tell him I'm crying my eyes out as well," Robert yelled.

"There you are, you see," Mella said to Pohjanen. "The last time he cried was when Wassberg beat Juha Mieto in the 1980

Olympics. Can you be quiet now so I can hear what Pohjanen wants?"

"One hundredth of a second," Robert said, touched by the memory of that famous skiing victory. "Fifteen kilometers, and he won by five centimeters."

"Can't you all shut up so I can watch this film?" Marcus said.

"Wilma Persson," Pohjanen said. "I tested some water from her lungs."

"And?"

"And I compared it with water from the river."

Her son was looking daggers at Mella, who stood up and went into the kitchen.

"Are you still there?" Pohjanen said grumpily. Then he cleared his throat.

"Yes, I'm still here," Mella said, sitting down on a kitchen chair and trying to ignore Pohjanen's phlegmy wheezing.

"I . . . *khrush, khrush*. . . I sent the samples to the Rudbeck Laboratory in Uppsala. Told Marie Allen to push them through *rapido*. They . . . *khrush*. . . did a sequential analysis of the samples. Very interesting."

"Why?"

"Well, this is cutting-edge technology. You can identify the genetic material in anything living in water. Bacteria, algae, that sort of thing. As you probably know, everything is made up of four building blocks. Even us humans. A person's DNA has three million of these building blocks in a particular sequence."

Mella looked at the clock. First a profound film in German, then a DNA seminar with Lars Pohjanen.

"Anyway, I don't suppose you're all that interested in such things," Pohjanen said with a rattling squeak. "But I can confirm that the water in Wilma Persson's lungs had entirely different algae and microorganic flora from the water in the river where she was found."

Mella stood up.

"So she didn't die in the river," she said.

"No, she didn't die in the river," Pohjanen said.

saturday, April 25

Sven-Erik Stålnacke was woken up by his cell phone.

Feeling the familiar wave of early-morning fatigue flow through his body, he answered the phone.

"It's me," Anna-Maria Mella said, sounding chirpy.

Holding the phone at arm's length, he squinted at the display. Twenty past seven.

Mella was an early bird. He was a night owl. They had always had an unspoken agreement that it was okay for either of them to call and wake the other one up. Stålnacke might think of something at one in the morning and phone Mella. She might phone him bright and early, already in her car and on the way to pick him up. But that had been then.

Then, before Regla, Stålnacke would have said, "Are you up already?" and Mella would have said something about having to drag Gustav out of bed and take him to day care during the week, while on the weekend he would be jumping up and down on her head at dawn, begging her to turn on the kid's shows on TV.

"Sorry to disturb you so early," Mella said.

She regretted having phoned him; she had done it without thinking. But things were not as they had been.

Stålnacke could hear the change in her voice and felt a mixture of regret and bad conscience.

Then he became angry. It was not his fault that things had turned out as they had.

"Pohjanen called me late last night," Mella said, as if to stress that she was not the only one who phoned colleagues at odd times.

In bed next to Stålnacke, Airi Bylund opened her eyes. "Coffee?" she mimed. He nodded. Bylund got up and pulled on her red terrycloth robe. Boxar the cat, who had been fast asleep on Stålnacke's legs, jumped eagerly down from the bed and tried to grab the belt of Bylund's robe as she tied it around her waist, making it jiggle up and down irresistibly.

"He's taken samples of water from Wilma Persson's lungs and from the river, and that's not where she died," Mella said.

"You don't say."

"You thought that business of the car with no gas in the tank was odd. Why venture into the middle of nowhere without enough juice to get them home again? Now we hear that she didn't die in the river. So how did she get there?"

"You tell me."

Neither spoke for a while. Finally she said, "I'm going to drive out to Piilijärvi today and ask if anybody there knows where the kids intended to go diving."

Now was his chance, his opportunity to say he would accompany her.

"Didn't they ask questions like that when she disappeared?" he said instead.

"Yes, no doubt they asked the people closest to her. But the situation has changed. Now I'm going to ask everyone."

"Fair enough. Do that. Good luck."

The silence between them was heavy with disappointment and accusation.

"Thank you," she said, and hung up.

Bylund came in with coffee and open sandwiches on a tray. "What was all that about?" she said.

"Anna-Maria," Stålnacke said. "She rings and wakes you up on a Saturday morning and expects you to drop everything and be at her beck and call. She can forget it."

Bylund said nothing. Handed him his mug of coffee.

"She's so damn inconsiderate," he said.

"You know," Bylund said, sitting down on the edge of the bed, "I've heard you say that so often this year. But I think that being inconsiderate means thinking maybe you shouldn't do something and then doing it anyway. That business at Regla— she just . . . Well, it just happened."

"She doesn't think!"

"That may be. But it's how she is. She's impulsive, quick to act. I love you, darling, but it would be pretty boring if people were all the same. All I'm trying to say is that I don't think she just stood there and said to herself, 'All right, I'm going to make myself and Sven-Erik risk our lives.'"

Stålnacke got up. Pulled on his trousers. Shoved Boxar exasperatedly to one side just as she went on the attack.

"Anyway," he said, "it's going to be pretty mild today. I'd better go home and check that there isn't any snow still lying on the roof. It'll be wet and heavy if it is."

"I know," Bylund said to Boxar with a sigh when Stålnacke had left. "It's a waste of time trying to reason with him."

Morning sun and pink clouds above the treetops. But all Mella saw was black forest on all sides, and dirty snowdrifts. Her eyes searched automatically for reindeer wandering along the edge of the road, but otherwise concentrated on the frost-damaged tarmac.

Her mood improved significantly when she got out of her car outside Anni Autio's house.

"There's a lovely smell of baking in the air," she said when Autio opened the door.

Once in the kitchen, Autio packed buns and cookies into plastic bags for Mella to take home with her.

"What else is there for me to do with them?" she said when Mella tried to protest. "All the old folk in the village have freezers chock-full with their own buns and cookies. Surely you can let me offload the odd goodie on you, especially as they're newly baked? You're not on a low-carb diet, are you?"

"Good Lord, no."

"Well, then, dunk away!"

Mella broke a corner off a cinnamon cookie and dipped it in her coffee.

"Did Wilma and Simon tell you where they were going diving?" she said.

"I didn't even know they were going diving. I told the police that when they went missing. Nobody knew anything at all. Simon's mother said that his diving gear had disappeared from the garage, so we assumed they had gone diving. But as you know, they didn't find the car. No sign of it."

"I see. Do you think they might have told someone? Their friends in the village, perhaps?"

"There are hardly any young people left in the village. Just us old-timers. The children live in Kiruna or somewhere in the south. They argue among themselves about who's going to look after the houses they've inherited from their parents. They make no attempt to sell them, and they never come to the village, not even in the summer. The houses are falling to pieces. I usually refer to my nephews, Tore and Hjalmar Krekula, as 'the boys'—but they're over sixty, for God's sake. And Tore has two sons of his own; they do a bit of driving for their dad, but they also live in Kiruna. So Wilma and Simon used to stay at home most of the time. They drove into Kiruna now and then. He had an apartment there. More coffee?"

"No thanks, I've had three cups already! Can I take a look at her room?"

"Of course. I won't come with you; it's upstairs."

Autio suddenly looked worried.

"It's very cold up there. I turned off the heat when she . . . I mean, she wasn't . . . I suppose I was just thinking of the expense."

She fell silent, standing by the countertop. Anxiously brushed traces of flour from her apron.

"It's okay," Mella said. "It costs a lot of money to keep a house warm. I know. I live in one myself."

"It's not okay. The heat should have been on. The house and I ought to have been ready for her."

"Do you know what?" Mella said. "You can be practical at the same time as you're worrying or grieving. I reckon you were doing both."

"I don't want to start crying again," Autio said, looking entreatingly at Mella as if hoping that she would be able to stop her going on about it. "You should have felt what the house was like when she was living here. So full of life. I still keep waking up and thinking it's time to make her breakfast. I don't suppose you believe me, knowing that I turned the heat off."

"Listen, Anni, I couldn't care less about the heat being off."

Autio smiled wanly.

"I was so happy back then. I enjoyed every day, every morning when she was here with me. I didn't take it for granted, though. I knew she could move back to Stockholm at any moment."

This isn't a typical teenager's room, Mella thought as she entered Persson's room.

An old office desk stood in front of the window. A blue-painted Windsor-style chair served as a desk chair. The bed was narrow—two and a half feet, perhaps. On it was a white embroidered bedspread. There were no posters on the walls, no ancient teddy bears or other plush toys to remind Persson of her childhood. A photograph of her with Kyrö was pinned to the wall beside the bed. It looked as if Persson had taken it herself. She was roaring with laughter; he was smiling in mild embarrassment. Mella's heart bled as she looked at it.

She searched the desk drawers. No maps. No diary.

She could hear Autio struggling up the stairs, and hastened to open the wardrobe and look through the clothes piled at the bottom. When Autio entered the room, Mella was standing on a chair, examining the top of the wardrobe. Autio sat down on the bed.

"What are you looking for?" she said—not aggressively, she was just interested.

Mella shook her head.

"I don't really know. Something that might indicate where they went. Where they were going to go diving."

"But you found her in the river at Tervaskoski. Isn't that where they were diving?"

"I don't know."

"Maybe you should talk to Johannes Svarvare," Autio said. "He lives in that little red house with the glassed-in porch on the right just after the curve as you enter the village. He used to lend maps to Wilma and Simon when they were going exploring in the forest. I'm going to lie down here for a while. Perhaps you could come back and help me down the stairs before you drive back to town?"

Mella felt the urge to give Autio a big hug. To console her. And hopefully find a bit of consolation for herself.

But all she said was, "Thanks for the coffee. I'll stop back on my way home."

≈≈≈≈

Johannes Svarvare also offered Mella coffee. She accepted even though she was feeling a bit queasy from having drunk so much already. He fetched the best china from the glass-fronted cupboard in the living room. The cups clinked against the saucers as he put the tray down on the kitchen table. They were delicate, with handles you could not fit your finger through, ivory-colored with pink roses.

"Please excuse the mess," Svarvare said, gesturing toward himself. "It never occurred to me that the forces of law and order would come visiting on a Saturday afternoon."

His hair was unkempt, and he looked as if he had slept in his clothes. His brown woolen trousers were almost falling down. His crumpled shirt had several stains down the front.

"How nice to have a wood-burning stove in the kitchen," Mella said, in an attempt to lessen his embarrassment.

Christmas curtains were still hanging in the windows. Rag rugs lay chaotically on the floor, one on top of the other, to keep the heat in. The floor itself was covered in crumbs.

His eyesight can't be all that good, Mella thought. He doesn't see that the place could do with a good vacuuming.

What a fascinating village, she thought. It's just as Anni said: In a few years' time there'll be nobody left. At best, the houses will have become summer cottages for surviving family members. The place will be completely deserted in winter.

"This is a big loss for poor old Anni," Svarvare said, moving his jaw from side to side. "A tragic accident."

It looked as if his false teeth were a bad fit. There was a glass of water on the draining board—no doubt that was where he normally kept them. Mella suspected that he only put his teeth in when he was about to eat or expecting visitors.

"I'm trying to find out what happened," she said, cutting to the chase. "Various details are unclear. Did she tell you where they were going to dive?"

"Didn't you find her downstream from Tervaskoski?"

"Yes . . . even so."

"'Even so?' What do you mean, are there details that are unclear?"

Mella hesitated. She preferred not to put her cards on the table. But sometimes you had to take a gamble to get results.

"There are indications that she didn't drown in the river," she said.

Svarvare slammed his cup down on the saucer.

"What do you mean?"

"I don't mean anything at all! Really! It's just that I need to investigate this death in a bit more detail. And then, of course, we want to find Simon Kyrö as well."

"She came here," Svarvare said. "She came here . . ."

As he spoke, he made sweeping gestures with both hands on the kitchen table.

"We chatted. The way one does. People need to talk. I mean, the only people left in the village are us old wrecks. As a result, perhaps we talk too much."

"What do you mean?" Mella said.

"What do I mean? What do I mean?" Svarvare said, lost in thought. "Do you know that just over a week before they disappeared, Isak Krekula had a heart attack? He's back home now, but I haven't even seen him going to his mailbox to collect the newspaper."

"I'm sorry to hear that," Mella said. "But I don't understand what you're getting at."

Svarvare poked at a scratch on the kitchen table with a dirty fingernail. He looked at the wall clock. It had stopped at seven. In fact it was 12:05.

"Oh dear," he said, sounding as if he had made up his mind. "I need to lie down. I'm an old man, you know."

He stood up, removed his dentures, and put them in the glass of water on the draining board. Then he lay down on the bench, his arms crossed over his chest, and closed his eyes.

"Of course," Mella said, feeling like an idiot. "But can't you explain what you meant?"

There was no response from the bench. The conversation was over. Svarvare's chest rose and fell rapidly.

"For fuck's sake!" Mella said as she got into her car.

She knew she ought to have let him talk. He had been on the way to telling her something. Stålnacke would have sat there quietly, waiting. Let Svarvare speak in his own good time. Damn that Stålnacke! And what was all that about Isak Krekula having a heart attack? How was it relevant?

"We'd better have a word with Isak Krekula," Mella said to herself as she turned the ignition key.

The Krekulas' houses formed a group of three at the far end of the village. Mella parked, got out of the car, and stood beside it. So this was where Tore and Hjalmar lived, and their parents as well. She tried to guess which house belonged to whom. All were clad in red-painted wooden panels. One of the houses was older than the other two and had a barn attached, with a roof of irregular corrugated-iron sheets. Embroidered curtains in the windows. This had to be where the parents lived.

Mella hesitated. A feeling of unease swept over her. In a pen at the side of the older house, a hunting dog was hurling itself over and over again at the wire netting, barking for all it was

worth. Baring its fangs. Gnawing at the wooden frame. Snarling and snapping at the air. Barking and barking. Tireless and
aggressive.

Spruce trees grew close together along the boundary of the
plot. The house stood in deep shade. Nobody ever seemed to
have bothered to thin the trees. They were very tall, seemingly
bent forward. Black, straggly, and threatening. The branches
looked wispy and weak, drooping down onto the slope. The
image they evoked was of a father in a bedroom doorway, belt
in hand, ready to attack. Of a mother, her feeble arms dangling
at her sides.

Don't go in there, a voice said deep inside Mella.

The hair stood up on the back of her neck.

Afterward, she would recall the feeling. But now she was
paying no attention to it.

The dog was scratching away at the netting. The air was a
thick soup of hostility. One of the curtains twitched slightly.
Someone was at home.

A notice on the door proclaimed: NO BEGGARS. NO HAWK-
ERS. When Mella rang the bell, the door opened a fraction. The
face of an old woman wondered what she wanted. Mella introduced herself.

Anni's sister, she thought. What had Anni said her name
was? Kerttu. Mella tried to see if there was a family resemblance.
Perhaps, but then Mella realized that what she had noticed most
about Autio were the signs of old age. Her bearing, her many
wrinkles, her scraggy hands. Mella tried to imagine what the
sisters had looked like when they had been her age. Autio had
little hair left. Her face was long and narrow, just like Mella's
own. Kerttu Krekula still had thick hair. Her cheekbones were
high. No doubt she had been the pretty sister. She was younger,
as well.

But Autio had been happy. Except when she was grieving over Persson, of course.

The sides of Kerttu Krekula's mouth were drawn downward, as if she had a devil on each shoulder pulling at them with a boat hook.

"I don't usually allow strangers in my house," she said. "You never know."

"You are Anni Autio's sister, is that right?"

"Yes."

"I've just come from Anni's. She's been baking."

"I never bake. What's the point? When you can buy stuff. Besides, my hands are so bad."

At least she's talking, Mella thought.

"Do you have a bathroom?" she said.

"Yes, of course."

"Do you think I might use it? I badly need a pee. It's a long way back to town."

"Come in, then, before you let the winter in with you," Kerttu Krekula said, opening the door just wide enough for Mella to squeeze through.

"No, I didn't think much of Wilma. She filled my sister's head with no end of nonsense, if you ask me."

They were sitting at the kitchen table. Mella had hung her jacket over a green-painted chair.

"In what ways did she fill your sister's head with nonsense?"

"In all kinds of ways. Last summer they went swimming in the lake, stark naked. Not after a sauna or anything like that. In broad daylight. For no reason at all. Anni's tits were hanging down to her belly. Disgusting, it was. Made you feel ashamed. But Wilma didn't seem to have anything against displaying herself to all the men for miles around. Flashed her pussy and her tattooed bottom."

The dog started barking again in its pen. A man's voice shouted, "Shut up!" to no effect whatsoever. There was a sound of feet stamping off snow outside the front door. Shortly afterward two men appeared in the kitchen doorway.

Tore and Hjalmar, Mella thought.

She had heard about them. A long time ago, just after she had moved back to Kiruna after completing her course at police college, an accusation of assault had been withdrawn by the injured party. Mella recalled the fear in the plaintiff's eyes as he begged the prosecutor to drop the case. It was Hjalmar Krekula who got off on that occasion. Hjalmar Krekula already had a record for several assaults. Two or three, she seemed to remember. And there were several other cases that had never progressed past suspicion. She had heard that Hjalmar Krekula was big. And he certainly was. Head and shoulders taller than his brother. Well built and decidedly overweight. He leaned listlessly against the doorjamb. Washed-out-looking skin hung from his cheekbones, which were badly in need of a shave.

Not much in the way of fruit and vegetables in his diet, Mella thought. Both men, in their sixties, were wearing work trousers. Tore Krekula's hair was close-cropped. He seemed unable to keep still. There was something restless about him.

"So you have visitors, eh?" he said to his mother, without introducing himself to Mella.

"From the police," Kerttu Krekula said curtly. "Asking about Wilma and Simon."

"The police?" Tore Krekula said, staring at Mella as if she were from another world. "Well, I'll be damned. We don't see the likes of you very often. What do you think, Hjallie?"

Hjalmar Krekula stayed leaning against the doorjamb and said nothing. His face was expressionless, his eyes blank, his mouth open. It was impossible to say if he had heard what his brother had said. A shiver ran down Mella's spine.

"When Stig Rautio's summer cottage was burgled, could we get you out here to investigate?" Tore said. "Like hell. We told you what you needed to do—check cars with Polish registration. If you'd done that, you'd have found his stuff in a flash. They've caught on to the fact that it's a waste of time picking berries up here. They can break into people's property and earn themselves a bundle, no risk at all, 'cuz the police . . . fuck only knows what you get up to, you seem to have more important things to do than catch thieves. Bikes, outboard motors, no matter what gets stolen, everyone knows it's no point going to the police. Our drivers have stuff stolen all the time. The crooks cut open the tarps and take whatever they like. There hasn't been a single thief brought to justice all the years I've worked for the firm."

He leaned over the table. Thrust his face close to Mella's.

"You don't give a fuck about us," he said. "Snotty-nosed kids vandalize cars and smash windshields, and the worst that can happen is that they end up with some old crone at Social Services who tells them what deprived childhoods they've had. Half-witted, feather-brained old crones. That's what the whole damn lot of you are, if you ask me. So what are you nosing around here for?"

"If you back off, I'll be pleased to inform you," Mella said, slipping into the measured, professional tone of voice she used when dealing with people who were aggressive or drunk and looking for trouble.

"You think I should back off, do you?" Tore Krekula said, without shifting a millimeter.

He jabbed his index finger hard on the table in front of Mella.

"I pay your wages. Just bear that in mind, constabitch. Me, my brother, my father. People like us with real jobs who actually do something useful and pay taxes. You could say you're my employee. And I think you do a damn awful job. Am I allowed to think that?"

"You can if you like," Mella said. "I'm leaving."

Tore Krekula's face was still pressed up against hers. Now he backed off slightly and waved his hand about in front of her face.

"There's no charge for fresh air, I suppose you know that?" he said.

"Didn't you want to use the bathroom?" Kerttu Krekula said. "You came in because you wanted to go to the bathroom. It's to the right in the hall."

Mella nodded. Hjalmar Krekula moved unhurriedly to one side, so that she could get past him.

Once safely in the bathroom, she took a deep breath. What ghastly people.

She stood there for a while, trying to pull herself together. Then she flushed the toilet and turned on the tap.

There was no sign of Hjalmar Krekula when she came out. Tore Krekula was sitting at the kitchen table. Mella took her jacket from the chair and put it on.

"You can't go yet," Tore Krekula said. "Hjalmar has let Reijo out. He'll gobble you up."

"Could you ask him to shut the dog in again, please?" Mella said. "I want to go now."

"He's just letting him do a quick lap around the house. Are you in a hurry? Lots to do?"

Don't let them see you're afraid, Mella told herself.

"Do you know where Wilma and Simon were planning to go diving?" she said, her voice steady as a rock.

She heard a faint groan coming from the little room next to the kitchen. It was the sound of a restless sleeper. An old man.

"How is he?" Tore Krekula asked his mother.

She replied with a shrug and an expression on her face that seemed to signify same as usual.

Mella wondered if the sleeping man was Isak Krekula. She supposed it must be. She ought to ask about what Johannes Svarvare had told her, about Isak Krekula having a heart attack a week or so before the kids disappeared, but she couldn't bring herself to do it. Nor could she manage to ask again whether any of them knew where Kyrö and Persson were planning to go diving. She was sweating, and all she wanted to do was get away. The kitchen really was ugly. Painted various peculiar shades of green, as if they had mixed green paint with a bit of white here and there. There were hardly any countertops, and what little space there was had cheap, ugly ornaments crammed into it.

The door opened and Hjalmar Krekula came in.

"Can she go now?" Tore Krekula asked his brother in an odd tone of voice.

Hjalmar Krekula did not reply, did not look at Mella.

"Goodbye, then," she said. "I may be back."

She left the house. The dog was barking nonstop. Both brothers followed her out. They stood in the porch, watching her.

"What the hell?" she said when she got to her car.

All the tires were flat.

"My tires!" she said, aghast.

"Well, fuck me!" Tore Krekula said. "No doubt some kids did it."

He smiled so there could be no doubt that he was lying.

Someone has to come and get me, Mella thought, fumbling for her cell phone in the inside pocket of her jacket. Her first thought was Stålnacke—but no, that was out of the question. She would have to call Robert. He would have to bring Gustav with him.

The phone was not in the pocket where she usually kept it. She felt in her other pockets. No phone. Had she left it in the car? She checked. No.

She looked at the brothers standing in the porch. They had taken it. While she had been in the bathroom.

"My cell phone," she said. "It's missing."

"I hope you're not suggesting that we took it," Tore Krekula said. "That would really piss me off. Come out here and start casting aspersions. Do you need a lift into town?"

"No. I need to borrow a phone."

She looked at the dog. It was running around, barking gruffly. Typical behavior for a dog that would run off if it got the chance. Hjalmar Krekula had not let it out at all. If he had, it would be several kilometers away by now. Besides, the snow around the pen was unmarked.

"Mother's telephone is out of order," Tore Krekula said. "Hop into the red Volvo. Me and Hjallie are going to town anyway. You can come with us."

They must be out of their minds, she thought.

A series of images flashed through her mind. Tore Krekula has driven onto a forest trail. Hjalmar Krekula wrenches open the back door and drags her out of the car. Hjalmar Krekula grabs hold of her hair and bashes her head against a tree trunk. He pins her arms down while Tore Krekula rapes her.

I'm not getting into a car with them, she thought. I'd rather walk all the way back to town.

"I'll manage," she said. "I'll come back with some colleagues and collect the car."

Turning on her heel, she strode off. Followed the village street in the direction of Anni Autio's house. Halfway there she was overtaken by Tore and Hjalmar Krekula in their car, on the way to Kiruna. She half-expected them to stop and for

Tore Krekula to offer her a lift again, but they just sailed past without even slowing down. She forced herself to walk at normal speed.

I'll borrow Anni's telephone, she thought.

Then she remembered that she'd promised to go back and help Autio down the stairs.

Good Lord, she thought. I'd forgotten all about that.

Autio was fast asleep upstairs in Persson's room. She had pulled the bedspread over her. When Mella sat down on the edge of the bed, she opened her eyes.

"Back already?" she said. "How about a cup of coffee?"

"If I drink another cup of coffee, I'll drop down and die," Mella said with a wry smile. "Can I borrow your phone?"

Autio did not sit up, but her eyes were suddenly wide open and searching.

"What's happened?" she said.

"Nothing," Mella said. "I just can't start my car."

Robert did not answer the phone. He was probably out playing in the snow with the kids. Ringing Stålnacke was a not an option. She could not call any of her other colleagues either.

It's Saturday, she thought. They're off duty. I got myself into this situation. The last thing I need is another story about how inconsiderate I am.

In the end she dialed Rebecka Martinsson's number. Martinsson picked up after two rings.

"I'll fill you in later," Mella said, glancing at Autio, who was in the kitchen getting some yogurt and bread. "Can you come and get me, please? I hate having to ask you."

"I'll be there right away," Martinsson said, without asking any questions.

~~~~~

Forty minutes later, Rebecka Martinsson pulled up at Anni Autio's house.

Mella was standing outside, waiting for her. Slammed the passenger door as she got into the car.

"Let's go," was all she said.

Once they had left the village, the story came tumbling out.

"The bastards," she said, bursting into tears. "What a bunch of fucking cunts."

Martinsson said nothing, concentrated on her driving.

"And they knew the score exactly," Mella snuffled. "I can't prove a damn thing. Not that Hjalmar slashed my tires, not that they stole my phone, nothing."

Shame raged inside her. She had allowed herself to be terrified. Tore Krekula must have felt like a bloated rat on top of a garbage can when he offered to drive her into Kiruna and she said no.

"He enjoyed every minute of it," she said to Martinsson.

I ought to have made a scene, she thought. I ought to have raised hell and screamed and accused them. I should have insisted that they drove me into town. Instead I let them see that I was scared shitless.

"I'll give them hell!" she roared, slamming her fist down on the glove box. "I'll reopen every suspended investigation, check out every retracted accusation involving those damned brothers. You can charge them. They'll regret the day they started fucking with me."

"You'll do nothing of the sort," Martinsson said calmly. "You'll keep a cool head and act in a professional manner."

"You saunter in all serene and innocent," Mella said, "and they launch an all-out attack!"

"Some people . . ." Martinsson said, without finishing her sentence. "Do you think this has anything to do with Simon and Wilma?"

"Simon and Wilma. I'm going to find Simon. And I'm going to discover exactly how they died."

"Yes, you do that," Martinsson said. "That's your job."

"I'll call in the media and appeal to the public for information. And I'll call the Krekula brothers and suggest that they turn on their televisions."

She slapped her forehead.

"Oh, shit!" she said. "I was supposed to pick up Jenny from the stables. What time is it?"

"Quarter past two."

"I can just make it . . . that is, if you . . . Is it okay if we pick her up?"

There was no sign of Jenny at the stables. Mella ran into the coffee room, checked all the seats around the riding track, every box, every stall. She asked all the stable girls she could find, becoming desperate when they shrugged and said they had no idea where Jenny might be. Martinsson was hard on her heels. They finally discovered one of Jenny's friends behind the main building. She was busy splitting bales of hay open for the horses in the paddock.

"Hi, Ebba," Mella said in an uncharacteristically cheerful voice, trying to subdue the suspicions that were beginning to creep up on her. "Where's Jenny?"

Ebba looked at Mella in confusion.

"But you sent her a text," she said. "Jenny was so upset. She texted you back, then called you, but you didn't pick up."

Mella went ice-cold with horror.

"But I haven't sent any texts," she said, her voice no more than a whisper. "I haven't . . . My phone . . ."

Martinsson's phone rang. It was Måns Wenngren. She ignored the call.

"What did the text say?"

"Surely you must know what you wrote?" Ebba said.

Mella groaned, covering her mouth with her hand to prevent herself from screaming.

"Oh my God!" Ebba said, looking scared. "You texted Jenny that she should meet you. Immediately. She was pretty annoyed about it, having to go back to town."

"Where to?" Mella screeched. "Where was she supposed to go?"

"To that old open-air stage in the park by the railway station. We thought it seemed odd. A peculiar place to meet. She tried to call and text you, but you didn't answer. Neither did Robert. Your text said to come immediately—Jenny was afraid something might have happened to you."

The stage in Järnvägsparken, Martinsson thought. There won't be a soul anywhere in the vicinity.

"Are you saying it wasn't you who sent that text?" Ebba said, sounding worried.

But Mella was already racing for the car. Martinsson ran after her.

Mella's heart was thumping. She could envisage Tore and Hjalmar Krekula telling Jenny that her mother had had an accident. She could see them driving off with Jenny in their car.

How many times had Mella found herself observing her only daughter surreptitiously? Since she had become a teenager? Mella had contemplated Jenny's budding breasts, her perfect pink skin. Prayed for divine protection. Please God, don't let anything awful happen to her. And now . . . Please, please God . . .

Martinsson set off with Mella on her phone, trying to ring Jenny. No answer. Please, please God . . . Don't let anything happen to her. Please don't let anything happen to her. We'll be there very soon.

Martinsson drove through the park along the pedestrian walkway to the stage. There was Jenny. She looked frozen to death in her stable girl's light jacket. Mella leapt out of the car, yelling out her daughter's name. "Jenny! Jenny!"

"I'm here, can't you see?" Jenny said, breaking free from her mother's embrace.

She was furious. Scared as well, Mella could see that in her eyes.

Mella flew into a rage.

"Why didn't you answer your calls?" she thundered.

"I tried to call you. My battery ran out. God knows how long I've been standing here waiting. Nobody answered the phone! You didn't. Dad didn't. What's going on? Why are you crying?"

The late news on North Swedish Television carried pictures of Wilma Persson and Simon Kyrö. The newscaster said that although the young people had disappeared in October, Persson's body had only just been found. Mella stood in front of the camera asking the public for any leads. Anything and everything was of interest, she said. Did anyone know where the kids were planning to go diving? Had anybody spoken to them before they disappeared?

"Don't be afraid to call us," she said. "Rather a call too many than one too few."

Mella was sitting on the living room sofa, watching the late news. Robert was beside her. Each of them had a pizza in a box on their knees. Jenny and Petter had already finished eating. There were empty boxes and soda cans on the table. Marcus was staying over at his girlfriend's place. Gustav had been asleep for ages.

All around Mella and Robert, behind them and on the floor in front of the sofa, was clean, crumpled laundry waiting to be sorted and folded. Robert had been out with Gustav all day. They had had lunch at his sister's.

It would never occur to him to volunteer to fold newly washed laundry, Mella thought disapprovingly. Everything was such a mess. She would need to devote an entire vacation to catching up with the housework. And she would have much preferred a real dinner instead of this nasty, greasy pizza. She made a point of dropping the slice in her hand into the box and pushing it away.

Out of the corner of her eye she could see Robert folding pieces of pizza and stuffing them into his mouth while caressing her back absent-mindedly.

She was irritated by this monotonous, aimless stroking. As if she were a cat. What she needed were some real, sensuous caresses. Fingertips alternating with the whole of his hand. A trace of desire. A kiss on the back of her neck. A consoling hand stroking her hair.

She had told him what had happened, and he had listened without saying much. "Well, everything turned out all right in the end," he had said at last. She had felt like screaming, "But what if it hadn't turned out all right? It could have been very nasty indeed!"

Do I always need to cry in order to be consoled? she said to herself. Do I always have to fly into a rage before he does anything to help in the house?

She had the feeling that Robert thought he was being very generous in not complaining. She was the police officer after all. If she had a different job, none of this would have happened. The unspoken accusation made her angry. That he seemed to think he had the right to be furious, but that he was sufficiently kind and generous to forgive her. She did not want to be forgiven.

She wriggled her shoulders, a leave-me-alone gesture.

Robert took his hand away. Washing down the last piece of pizza with the dregs from a Coca-Cola can, he stood up, collected all the boxes and empty cans, and went out to the kitchen.

Mella stayed where she was. She felt abandoned and unloved. Part of her wanted to go after Robert and ask him for a hug. But she did not. Turned her attention listlessly back to the television, feeling that, deep inside, she had become hardened.

I'm paying a visit to Hjalmar Krekula. His place is a real bachelor pad. His mother, Kerttu, still changes the curtains for him. Every spring and autumn. He told her to stop a few years ago, so she no longer puts up Christmas curtains. She's filled the window ledges with plastic geraniums. He hasn't bought a single item of furniture for his house. He got most of his things from Tore. When his younger brother changed his woman, the new woman replaced all the old furniture. Whatever was left from Tore's previous marriage was either too dark, too light, too worn, or just plain wrong. Tore let her do whatever she wanted, as they do in the beginning. All the old furniture ended up in Hjalmar's house.

But he bought the television himself. A big, expensive one. He's just turned off the late-night news bulletin from North Swedish Television. They showed pictures of me and Simon. He senses that I'm there when I sit down next to him on the living room sofa. I notice him glancing quickly to the side. Then he moves away, tries to stop feeling my presence, closes all the doors to the house that is his self.

He hurries to turn on the television again.

He's surprised by that little policewoman.

He remembers how Tore leaned over, in a way that showed he was used to doing it, and searched her pockets while she was in the bathroom.

Kerttu didn't say a word. Isak was in bed in the little room off the kitchen, gasping for breath.

Tore took out her cell phone, put it in his pocket, and told Hjalmar to go out and fix her car.

"That'll stop the bitch rooting around in my business," Tore said as they drove off to town, passing the policewoman on her way to Anni's.

Then they sent the text message to the policewoman's daughter. It was dead easy to figure out the girl's name from the saved texts.

They've found my body. Things should start happening now. Tore's on a high, although he's trying to disguise it. He wants to convince Hjalmar that all this was just a job that had to be done, merely another aspect of the firm's business.

I can sense how Hjalmar's mind is working. Knowing that Tore thrives in such situations. Not so much on the violence itself as on the threat of violence. Tore feeds off other people's fear and impotence. It fills him with strength and a lust for work. Spurs him on to tidy up the cabs of the trucks, polishing everything with Cockpit Shine or changing the paper in the tachographs. Hjalmar is pretty much the opposite. Or used to be. He's never understood the point of making threats; it's always been Tore who's looked after that side of things. But Hjalmar knows all about violence. Always assuming his opponent is someone to be reckoned with, preferably superior to himself.

That feeling of getting involved in a fight, perhaps against three opponents. The initial fear. Before the first punch has been delivered. Then the blood-red rage of fury. Unrestrained by thoughts or feelings other than the determination to survive, the desire to win. I was also a fighter until I moved to Piilijärvi and met Simon. I know the pleasure there is to be derived from fighting.

But Hjalmar only fought like that when he was young. It's been a different matter since he became an adult.

Now he's sighing deeply, as he only does when he's alone. He's standing up.

These days he indulges in violence with a sort of mechanical listlessness. Beating up some poor soul who owes money or has to be made to close down his business to reduce the competition, or making sure someone grants the necessary permission to set up a greasing pit, that sort of stuff.

Generally speaking, violence isn't necessary. The brothers are known far and wide. People usually do as they're told. But Inspector Anna-Maria Mella hasn't allowed herself to be intimidated.

Now Hjalmar goes out onto his porch. It's a Saturday evening. Still light outside. He checks Tore's house: Tore and his wife are watching television. Hjalmar wonders if Tore has seen the news bulletin. No doubt Kerttu has helped Isak to sit up, pulled the tea cart over, and is feeding him spoonfuls of rose-hip soup and bread that has been dipped into it.

Hjalmar would love to go off into the forest. I can tell by looking at him. He's gazing at the spruce trees along the edge of their plot like a chained-up dog. He has a little cottage at Saarisuanto on the banks of the River Kalix. I know about it. I bet that's what he's thinking about.

He likes the remoteness there. He loves to get away from people. I wonder if he's always been like that. Or if it began after the incident.

There was an incident in the village. A story that's told behind the brothers' backs.

It is early in the morning of June 17, 1956. Hjalmar Krekula is preparing to drive the cows out to their summer pasture. That is one of the tasks he has to perform during the summer holidays. The farms within the village are fenced in, and the cows are sent into the forest during the day to graze. In the evening they nearly always come home of their own accord, udders bulging, to be milked. But sometimes Hjalmar Krekula has to go to get them. They are especially difficult to bring home toward the end of summer. When they have been eating mushrooms among the trees. It can take hours to find them. Mushrooms tend to make them behave oddly.

The boys' mother is in the kitchen, making packed lunches to put in their rucksacks.

"Does Tore have to come as well?" Hjalmar Krekula says, fastening the only three buttons left on his flannel shirt. "Can't he stay at home with you?"

Hjalmar Krekula is eight years old, will be nine in July. Tore Krekula is six. Hjalmar Krekula would prefer to be in the forest on his own. Tore Krekula is a nuisance, following him around all the time.

"Don't argue," his mother says in a voice that will not tolerate contradiction.

She is spreading butter on bread for her boys. Hjalmar Krekula notices that she is spreading the butter more thickly on one of the slices. She wraps the sandwiches in newspaper, and the one with the most butter goes into Tore Krekula's rucksack. Hjalmar Krekula makes no comment. Tore Krekula is sitting on the kitchen stool, sliding his new knife up and down in its sheath.

"Don't play with knives," Hjalmar Krekula says, just as he has been told not to do many times.

Tore Krekula does not seem to hear him. Their mother says nothing. She pours a little yogurt into a small wooden flask and puts a piece of salted fish into an old flour bag. These Hjalmar Krekula will carry in his rucksack.

~~~~~

The family keeps only three cows, to supply their own needs. Isak Krekula, their father, runs the hauling firm, while Kerttu Krekula looks after the house and the cattle.

The boys have their rucksacks. They are wearing caps, and shorts that just cover their knees. Hjalmar Krekula's boots are too big for him and flop around. Tore Krekula's boots are a bit too small.

Before they have even crossed the main road, Tore Krekula cuts off a birch switch with which he pokes the cows.

"You don't need to hit them," Hjalmar Krekula says with annoyance. "Star is bright. She follows you if you lead the way."

Star, the lead cow, follows Hjalmar Krekula. She has a bell attached to a leather strap around her neck. Her ears are black, and she has a black star on her forehead. Rosa and Mustikka traipse along behind. Their tails are twitching, aiming at flies. They occasionally run a few paces in order to get away from Tore Krekula and his confounded birch switch.

Hjalmar Krekula presses on. He is leading the cows to the edge of a bog a kilometer or so away. It is a good grazing spot. The sun is warm. The forest is fragrant with wild rosemary, which has just come into bloom. Star trots happily after Hjalmar Krekula. She has learned that he takes her to good grazing grounds.

Tore Krekula keeps on holding them up. He stops to poke a big branch through an anthill, back and forth, back and forth. And he feels the need to cut notches in tree trunks with his new knife. Hjalmar Krekula looks the other way. His own knife is nowhere near as sharp. One of his father's employees had used it to scrape rust off one of the truck. There is a big hack in the cutting edge, too big to be ground away. Tore Krekula's knife is brand new.

Tore Krekula prattles away behind his brother and Star. Hjalmar Krekula wishes the younger boy would keep quiet. You have to keep silent in the forest. When they reach the edge of the bog, they unpack their lunches. The cows immediately start grazing. They drift farther and farther from the boys.

The bog is white with cloudberry flowers.

When the boys have finished eating, it is time to head for home.

They have been walking for ten minutes when they catch sight of a reindeer. It is standing absolutely still, watching them with big black eyes. The Lapps have already taken their herds up into the mountains; this is one they missed.

The boys try to sneak up on it, but it stretches its neck and sets off at a brisk trot. They hear the clippety-clop of its hooves, and then it is gone.

They try to follow it for a while, but give up after ten minutes. The reindeer is no doubt a long way away by now.

They set off for home again, but after a while Hjalmar Krekula realizes that he does not know where he is. Even so, he continues in the same direction—no doubt he will soon see the familiar rocks and clearings. But before long they come to a swamp that he has never seen before. Spindly, stunted pine trees are growing in the middle of it. Beard lichen hangs from the branches, looking burned. Where on earth are they?

"We're lost," Hjalmar Krekula says to his brother. "We must retrace our steps."

They retrace their steps. But after an hour or so, they find themselves on the edge of the same swamp.

"Let's cross over it," Tore Krekula says.

"Don't be silly," Hjalmar Krekula says.

He is worried now. Which way should they go?

They hear a cow lowing in the distance, very faintly.

"Hush," he says to Tore Krekula, who is prattling on about something or other. "It's Star. It's coming from over there."

If they can find the cows, they will be able to get home. Star will find the way as milking time approaches.

But after only a few steps, they realize that they can no longer hear any lowing. They cannot follow the sound. Neither of them is sure where it came from.

They lie down in a clearing to rest. The moss is dry and the sun is warm. They feel sleepy. Hjalmar Krekula is no longer on the verge of tears; he is just tired. He drops off to sleep. Tore Krekula's legs twitch, and he says something in his dream.

Hjalmar Krekula is woken up by his brother shaking his arm.

"I want to go home now," Tore Krekula whimpers. "I'm hungry."

Hjalmar Krekula is also hungry. His stomach is rumbling. The sun is low in the sky. The forest is filled with different sounds. The heat drains away from the trees, making them crackle. The noise is almost like footsteps. An eerie sound must be a barking fox. It is chillier now, and the boys are cold.

They set off aimlessly.

After a while they come to a creek. Kneeling down, they fill the mugs they have with them. Drink until they are no longer thirsty.

Hjalmar Krekula thinks.

What if this is the same creek that flows past Iso-Junti's farmhouse on the edge of the village?

Hjalmar Krekula had once thrown pieces of wood into the creek. They had floated off in the direction of the Kalix. So, if they follow the creek upstream, they should find themselves in the village.

Always assuming it is the same creek, of course. They could well be following one that goes somewhere else.

"Let's go this way," Hjalmar Krekula says to his brother.

But Tore Krekula does not like being told what to do. Nobody is going to tell him which way to go. Except his father, perhaps.

"No," he says. "Let's go that way."

He points in the opposite direction.

They start arguing. Tore Krekula's opposition makes his older brother certain that following the creek upstream is the best thing to do.

Tore Krekula refuses absolutely. Hjalmar Krekula calls him a stupid brat, tells him he is being idiotic, that he must do as he is told.

"You don't tell me what to do," Tore Krekula howls.

He starts blubbering and shouts for his mother. Hjalmar Krekula slaps him. Tore Krekula punches Hjalmar Krekula in the stomach. Soon they are both on the ground. The fight does not last long. Tore Krekula does not have a chance. Age wins the day. And Hjalmar Krekula is big.

"I'm going now," he bellows.

He is sitting on top of his brother. Lets go of his arms, but grabs them again when Tore Krekula tries to hit him in the face. The younger boy gives up in the end. He has lost the fight. But not the battle. When he eventually stands up, he marches off resolutely in the direction he had chosen to begin with.

Hjalmar Krekula shouts after him.

"Don't be an idiot. Come with me! Now!"

Tore Krekula pretends not to hear. After a while Hjalmar Krekula can no longer see him.

At eleven fifteen that night Hjalmar Krekula comes to the main road to Vittangi. He starts walking along it, and just over an hour later a truck stops and picks him up. It is one of his father's trucks, but his father is not driving it. The driver is Johannes Svarvare. In the passenger seat is another villager, Hugo Fors. They pull up fifty meters in front of Hjalmar Krekula, and both men open their doors and shout to him. Their soft caps are askew over their sunburned faces. Shirt sleeves rolled up. Hjalmar Krekula feels his chest opening up as joy and relief flood in. He will soon be home.

They laugh as they help him to clamber up into the truck. He is allowed to sit between them. By Jove, my boy, they say, your mother and father have been worried sick. Since the evening milking, practically everyone in the village has been out shouting and looking for them. Hjalmar Krekula wants to reply, but the words stick in his throat.

"Where's Tore?" they ask.

He cannot produce a single word. The men exchange worried looks.

"What's happened?" Svarvare says. "Out with it, my boy. Where's your brother?"

Hjalmar Krekula turns his head toward the forest.

The men do not know how to interpret that movement. Has his younger brother got stuck in one of the bogs?

"Let's get you home," Fors says, placing his hand on Hjalmar Krekula's head. "We can talk about it later."

His voice is as calm as a lake in the evening, but beneath the surface a shoal of worry glints like a sheet of steel.

They are gathered outside the Krekulas' house. It is like a Laestadian prayer meeting. Ten grown-ups in a circle around Hjalmar Krekula. The women are whimpering and shouting with emotion—but not too loudly; they do not want to miss a word of what is said. Kerttu Krekula does not whimper. She is white and as frozen as an icicle. Isak Krekula is red and sweaty; he has run all the way home from the forest.

"Right, let's hear what's happened to Tore," he says.

Hjalmar Krekula forces the words out.

"He's still in the forest," he says.

The grown-ups stand around him. Like black pine trees on a summer night. He is alone in this particular clearing.

"You mean you left him in the forest?"

"I didn't want to. I told him to come with me. We were lost. He didn't want to come."

He bursts into tears. One of the women shouts, "Oh, Lord!" in Tornedalen Finnish, and presses her hand over her mouth.

Kerttu Krekula stares at Hjalmar Krekula.

"This is the punishment," she says to her husband, without taking her eyes off her son. "We'll never find him."

Then she turns slowly, just as slowly as an icicle would turn if it were alive, and goes into the house.

"Take him away," Isak Krekula bellows to the crowd. "Someone had better take him home before I hurt him. You left him in the forest. You left your little brother in the forest."

Elmina Salmi takes Hjalmar Krekula home with her. He turns several times and looks back at his house. His father ought to have given him a good hiding with his belt. That would have been better.

"When will I be able to go home?" he says.

"God knows," Elima says. She is very religious. "We must pray that they find poor little Tore."

My name is Wilma Persson. I'm dead. I don't really know what that involves yet.

Hjalmar is on his knees outside his house, pressing snow onto his face. He doesn't want to think about it any more. He doesn't want to think at all.

Enough now, enough, he says to himself.

~~~~~

I'm looking at Anni. She's lying in bed asleep, on her side. Her clothes are folded neatly over the back of a chair in the bedroom. She's sleeping with one hand under her cheek. It's like a dish for her head to rest in. Her other hand is open, on her chest. She makes me think of a fox. How it snuggles down for the night. Curls up into itself. Uses its tail to keep its body warm.

The policewoman Anna-Maria Mella is lying awake in her bedroom. Her husband has turned away from her and is snoring. She feels lonely and can't keep herself warm like a fox. She wishes he'd given her that hug now. So that she didn't need to feel angry and abandoned. Her life has been torn apart today.

I sit down on her side of the bed. Place my hand against her heart.

If you want to go to sleep in his arms, then do it, I tell her.

After a while she wriggles closer to Robert. Lies behind him. Wraps her arms around him. He wakes up sufficiently to turn over and embrace her.

"How do you feel?" he says sleepily.

"Not good," she says. He caresses her, squeezes her, kisses her forehead. At first she thinks it's a damn scandal, having to beg him to do this, having to make all the moves. But she no longer has the strength to be bothered. She relaxes and falls asleep.

sunday, April 26

On Sunday someone phoned the police station in Kiruna to say that he had information about the two kids who had featured in the late-night news bulletin the day before. He said his name was Göran Sillfors.

"I don't know if what I have to tell you is all that significant," he said, "but you said yourselves, 'Rather a call too many than one too few,' so I thought . . ."

The receptionist put him through to Anna-Maria Mella.

"Absolutely right," Mella replied when Sillfors repeated what he had already said.

"Anyway, those two kids. They were out in a canoe on the lake at Vittangijärvi last summer. We have a summer cottage up there. I always say that not all young people sit glued to their computers from morning to night. This pair carried and dragged their canoe along the river, paddled over Tahkojärvi, and up as far as the lake. That's a hell of a long way. I don't know how much they were being paid by the Swedish Meteorological and Hydrological Institute, but it can't have been all that much."

"What do you mean, paid by the MHI?"

"They were taking soundings in the lake for the MHI—that's what they told us when they came by for a chat and a coffee. First-class young people, they were. I didn't know they'd gone missing—we were abroad when it happened. Our daughter and her partner had bought a hotel in Thailand, so we went out there for a three-week vacation. Obviously we had to pitch in—you know how it is: When anything needs doing, Father's the only one who knows how."

"They came by for a chat and a coffee . . . What was it they said?"

"Not much."

No, Mella thought. No doubt you did most of the talking.

Sillfors continued.

"They were taking some kind of measurements for the MHI. What did you say?"

"I beg your pardon?"

"No, not you, I was responding to my wife. She says they were taking depth soundings in the lake. I recognized them the moment I saw them on the television. The girl looked a bit dangerous with those little daggers stuck through her eyebrows. Huh! I asked her if she was into that what-do-you-call-it—you know, when you hang yourself from a rope with hooks you stick into your skin. Christ Almighty, I saw a program on the TV about these characters with piercings all over their bodies, hanging themselves up on a washing line. But no, she said she only had them things in her eyebrows and ears."

"Can you remember what they said about the lake? Were they thinking of going diving there, for instance?"

"No. They asked if I fished there."

"And you said?"

"That I did."

"Anything else?"

"No, nothing else."

"Think hard, now. If you were drinking coffee, you must have had time to chat about all kinds of things."

"I suppose so. We spoke a bit about fishing. I said there was a particular place where the fish always seem to bite. I thought maybe they were interested in fishing themselves. We usually joke about that spot in the middle of the lake and reckon there must be a meteorite or an especially big rock there. Somewhere the fish can hide, because that's always where they bite the most. But the kids weren't going fishing. Hang on a minute, my wife is trying to say something."

He doesn't hear what I'm saying, Mella thought. That's because I'm not saying anything. He's doing all the talking.

"You what?" Sillfors shouted to his wife. "Why should she be interested in that? Talk to her yourself if you must."

"What's all that about?" Mella said.

"She's going on about the door to our shed. How someone stole it last winter."

Mella's heart skipped a beat. She recalled the flakes of green paint Pohjanen had found under Wilma Persson's fingernails.

"What color was the door?" she said.

"Black," Göran Sillfors said.

Mella's hopes collapsed. It had been too good to be true. She heard Sillfors's wife saying something in the background.

"Ah yes. You're right," he said. "It was black on the outside— that was the side I painted a couple of years ago. You know how weather and especially wind ruins paintwork. I had a bit of black paint left over from when I helped our neighbor to paint our fences. There wasn't much, but I thought I might as well give the outside a coat at least . . ."

"Go on," Mella urged, concealing her impatience with difficulty.

"The inside was green. Why do you want to know?"

Mella gasped. This was it. Damn it to hell, this was it!

"Stay where you are," she yelled into the telephone. "Where do you live? I'm on my way."

Göran Sillfors and his wife, Berit, took Mella to their cottage at Vittangijärvi. It was a brown-painted timber house with white window frames. The porch was unusually wide with a little roof supported by carved wooden columns. Göran Sillfors drove the snowmobile with Mella in the sled.

"Shall we go in?" Berit Sillfors said when they arrived.

Mella shook her head.

"Where's the shed door?" she said.

"There isn't a door," Göran Sillfors said. "That's the problem."

The snow on the shed roof had melted and then frozen again. An enormous cake of ice hung ominously from the edge.

Mella took off her wool hat and unzipped her snowmobile overalls. She was much too hot.

"You know what I mean," she said with a jolly smile. "Show me where the door was. At the back?"

The opening, at the gable end, had been boarded over.

"I'll sort out a new door in time for the spring," Göran Sillfors said. "We're not here in the winter, so this is a bit amateurish."

Mella examined the doorframe. No sign of green paint, or of black paint, come to that.

"Could you remove the boards, please?" she said. "Just so I can go inside and take a quick look around."

"Might one ask what you're looking for?"

"I'm hoping there's a bit of green paint left on the inside of the doorframe. So that we can take some samples."

"No, there won't be any. It must be, let's see, fifteen years ago that I painted it green. I unscrewed the hinges and laid it down on trestles. So there won't be any paint on the frame."

Göran Sillfors's expression changed from pride at having done the painting so carefully to worry when he saw how disappointed Mella was.

"But do you know what?" he said. "One of the doors inside the cottage was painted with the same stuff. From the same can. I painted it the same day, if I remember rightly. Will that do?"

Mella's face lit up, and she threw her arms around a some-what surprised Göran Sillfors.

"Will it do?" she shouted in delight. "You bet your life it will!"

"Shall we go inside after all, then?" Berit Sillfors said. "It would be good if I could check the mousetraps while we're here."

Scraping a bit of paint from the green door between the cottage's vestibule and large hall, Mella put the flakes carefully in an envelope.

"Scrape as much as you like," Göran Sillfors said generously. "It needs repainting anyway."

Berit Sillfors emptied the mousetraps in the upstairs wardrobes and beneath the sink. When she had finished she showed the result to Mella and her husband: five frozen mice in a red plastic bucket.

"I'll just go and dispose of them," she said.

"I'm finished," Mella said.

She looked out through the hall window. The whole lake still seemed to be covered with ice. With a lot of snow on top of it.

What if they made a hole in the ice and went diving through it? Mella asked herself. And then someone laid the door over the hole so that they would drown? That might be what had happened. But why move her body? And where is his? Is the door still out there on the ice, hidden beneath the snow?

"Can I go out on the ice and have a look?" she said.

"I wouldn't recommend it," Göran Sillfors said. "It's slushy and unreliable."

"Is there anybody who spends time out here in winter?" Mella said. "Who owns the other house? I'm just wondering if there might be someone who could have seen something or met Wilma and Simon."

"No, there's never anyone in the house next to ours," Berit Sillfors said sadly. "The man who owns it is too ill and too old, and his nephews and nieces have shown no interest in it at all. But there's Hjörleifur—"

"That's enough!" Göran Sillfors said. "You can't send her to Hjörleifur."

"But she was asking."

"Leave Hjörleifur out of this! He can't cope with the authorities."

"Anyway," Berit Sillfors said, shaking the bucket with the dead mice as if to attract attention, "Hjörleifur Arnarson lives in a remote farmhouse about a kilometer from here. Do you know who he is?"

Mella shook her head.

"He bathes in the lake. Walks here through the forest, summer and winter alike. He usually cuts a hole in the ice by our jetty. He's become very grumpy. You have to agree, Göran."

"Hjörleifur has nothing to do with this," Göran Sillfors said firmly. "He's as crazy as a loon, but there's no evil in him."

"I'm not suggesting that there's any evil in him," Berit Sillfors said defensively. "But he's become very grumpy."

"What do you mean, grumpy?" Mella said.

"Well, for example, he doesn't like intruders up here. He borrowed your shotgun without permission, didn't he, Göran? And scared off some fishermen. Was that two years ago?"

Göran Sillfors gave his wife a dirty look that said, Hold your tongue!

Mella said nothing. She was not going to go on about Göran Sillfors evidently not keeping his shotgun locked up in a gun safe.

Unconcerned, Berit Sillfors went on talking. "I sometimes call in on him to buy some of the anti-mosquito oil he concocts, and we have a little chat. Last summer when I went to see him, I found his billy goat hanging in a tree."

"Eh? How do you mean, hanging in a tree?"

"I asked him: 'What on earth's happened here, Hjörleifur?' He told me the goat had butted him, and he was so angry that he killed it and threw its body into the air with all his strength. The poor thing ended up in the birch tree outside Hjörleifur's house, got stuck there with its horns. I helped him get it down. If I hadn't, the crows would have started pecking at it. Hjörleifur was so sorry. The billy goat had merely been rutting—that makes them obnoxiously affectionate."

Berit Sillfors turned to look at Mella.

"But Hjörleifur would never do anything to people. I agree with Göran. He's a bit crazy, but there's no evil in him. Just be careful how you handle him. Would you like us to go with you?"

Mella checked her watch.

"I have to go home now," she said with a smile. "If I don't, my husband will throw me up into the birch tree."

It's Sunday evening at the hauling firm's garage. I'm sitting on top of the cabin, watching Hjalmar. He's opened up the hydraulic lift on the back of one of the trucks and is oiling the pistons. He attaches the greasing gun to the nipples and fills them. He doesn't hear Tore come in. Suddenly Tore is standing by the truck, yelling at him.

"What the hell do you think you're doing?"

Hjalmar glances at Tore but continues working. Tore races to fetch some supports and jams them under the hydraulic platform.

"You fucking idiot!' he says. "You can't work under the hydraulic platform without making it secure, surely you realize that?"

Hjalmar says nothing. What is there to say?

"I can't run this firm on my own," Tore says. "It's bad enough having Father in bed and unable to help with the bookkeeping. You're no use to me as a cripple or a corpse. Is that clear?"

Tore is upset. He spits as he talks.

"Don't you dare let me down!" he says, pointing a finger at Hjalmar.

When Hjalmar doesn't respond, Tore says, "You're an idiot! A damn idiot!"

Turning on his heel, he leaves.

No, Hjalmar thinks. I won't let you down. Not again.

They spend five days and nights looking for Tore. Volunteers from the old Emergency Service and the Mountain Rescue Service are out searching. Police officers and a company of soldiers from the I 19 regiment in Boden are also taking part. An airplane makes two reconnaissance flights over the wooded areas north of Piilijärvi. No sign of Tore. The men from the village spend most of their time outside the Krekulas' house. Drinking coffee. They are either on their way into the forest or on their way back from it. They want to talk to Hjalmar Krekula, ask him where he and his brother went, what the route looked like. What the swamp looked like. Hjalmar Krekula does not want to talk, tries to keep out of the way, but he is forced to answer questions. He is back at home now, having spent the first couple of nights with Elmina Salmi. On the morning of the second day, she took Hjalmar Krekula home and said to Kerttu Krekula, "You have a son here who is alive. Be grateful for that."

Kerttu Krekula gave him some porridge, but did not say anything. She still has not said anything to Hjalmar Krekula.

When the men ask him questions, he turns himself inside out trying to answer them. But he does not know. Cannot remember. In the end he starts making things up and telling lies, just to have something to tell them. Did they see Hanhivaara Mountain? Yes, maybe. Was the sun on their backs as they walked?

Yes, he thought it was. Had the trees been thinned? No, they had not been.

They search the forest to the north of the village. That is where he came from when he emerged onto the main road. And everything he says suggests that it is where the boys got lost.

He has to get used to days like this. To people falling silent when he approaches. To comments such as, "May God forgive you," or "What the hell were you thinking of, boy?" To head-shakings and piercing looks. To his mother's silence. Not that she ever had much to say for herself. But now she does not even look at him.

Once he overhears his father say to one of the men from the village, "What I'd really like to do is kill the little shit, but that wouldn't bring Tore back."

"*Jumala on antanu anteeksi,*" the man says, who is a believer. God has forgiven that sin.

But Isak Krekula does not believe in God. He has nothing to console him. Nor can he do as Job did, wave his fist in the air and cry out to the Lord. He mutters something evasive and embarrassed in reply. But he clenches his fists whenever he looks at his son.

On the sixth day, the search for Tore Krekula is called off. A six-year-old boy is incapable of surviving for five days and nights in the forest. He has probably been sucked into one of the bogs. Or perhaps he has drowned in the creek the brothers were standing by when they parted. Or he has been savaged by a bear. The house feels empty. Some of the villagers consider it their duty to spend an hour there in the evening on the sixth day. But all of them have their own lives to lead. What is the point of looking for someone who is already dead?

That night Hjalmar Krekula lies awake in the little bedroom. He can hear his mother sobbing through the wall.

"It's our punishment," she wails.

He can hear the bed creaking and complaining as his father gets up.

"That's enough of that—shut up!" he says.

Hjalmar Krekula listens to his mother crying, then suddenly the bedroom door is wrenched open. It is his father.

"Get up," he bellows. "Get up, and down with your shorts."

He lashes his son with his belt. As hard as he can. Hjalmar Krekula can hear his father grunting with the strain. At first the boy is determined that he is not going to cry. No, no. But in the end the pain is too much for him. Tears and screams just flow out of him, whether he wants them to or not.

Not a sound from the big bedroom.

Now she is the one lying silent, listening to him.

The miracle occurs on the morning of June 23, 1956. At about five, before his mother has gone to the cowshed, before his father has even gotten up, Tore Krekula trudges up to the front door. Going into the kitchen, he shouts, "*Paivää!*" Hi there!

His mother has been in the bathroom, putting her hair up. She emerges and stares at Tore Krekula. Then she bursts into tears. Shouts, screams. Hugs him so tightly that he howls in pain and she has to let him go.

He has been so badly bitten by mosquitoes, gnats, and horseflies that his shirt collar is soaked in blood and appears to be stuck to his neck. His mother has to cut it loose with scissors. His feet are tender and swollen. For the last few days he has been carrying his boots—something people laughed about later, the fact that he did not want to lose his boots no matter what.

All day, villagers keep popping in to watch Tore Krekula eating. Or to watch Tore Krekula lying asleep on the kitchen sofa. Or to watch Tore Krekula eating again.

The story gets into the newspapers, and is repeated on the radio. The Krekulas receive letters from all over the country. People send presents—clothes, shoes, skis. People turn up from Kiruna and Gällivare to see Tore Krekula with their own eyes. Sweden's most popular singer, Ulla Billquist, sends a telegram.

Kerttu and Tore Krekula take the train down to Stockholm, and the boy is interviewed by the legendary Lennart Hyland on the children's television program *Roundabout*.

Hjalmar Krekula sits listening to it all. Thank God Tore Krekula did not say anything on the radio about his brother hitting him. But word has spread around the village. Hjalmar Krekula hit his little brother, three years younger than he is. And then abandoned him in the forest.

monday, April 27

Morning meeting in the conference room at Kiruna police station. Inspectors Sven-Erik Stålnacke, Fred Olsson, and Tommy Rantakyrö were waiting for Anna-Maria Mella.

Stålnacke's mustache dipped into his coffee mug as he drank. It had hung down beneath his nose like a dead gray squirrel until his steady relationship with Airi Bylund had begun; since then he had kept it tidily trimmed.

More like an angry hedgehog nowadays, was Rantakyrö's comment. Stålnacke also trimmed his nasal hair and had lost weight, despite being an enthusiastic consumer of Bylund's cooking.

Olsson was playing with his Blackberry. Rantakyrö had already asked his usual "But can you make telephone calls with it?" and was listening with half an ear while Olsson went on about push functions and gigabytes.

Mella strode into the room, ruddy-faced, still in her street clothes. She pulled off her wool hat. Her hair was neither braided nor brushed. She looked totally untamed.

"Lousy morning, eh?" Olsson said.

"Sorry I'm late," Mella said, trying to sound calm. "You don't want to know. I've spent so much energy on my four-year-old today . . . First I had to force him into his snowsuit while he fought and screamed the house down. Then I had to wrestle with him to get it off again. With the day care staff watching patiently the entire time. I expect Social Services will take him away from me before the day's out."

She took off her jacket and sat down.

"I just wanted to fill you in regarding the investigation into Wilma Persson's death and Simon Kyrö's disappearance. Persson's body was found in the River Torne just downstream from Tervas-koski. But when Pohjanen sent samples of water from her lungs to Rudbeck Laboratory, the DNA pattern didn't fit. She didn't die in the river. Last summer the kids were canoeing in the lake at Vittangijärvi and stopped for a coffee with Berit and Göran Sillfors—they own one of the summer cottages there. Wilma and Simon told the Sillforses that they were taking depth soundings for the MHI. But I phoned the MHI and they hadn't ordered soundings in Vittangijärvi. Persson and Kyrö have never done any work for them. So what were the kids really doing there? And someone stole the Sillforses' shed door at some point during the winter. One side of it was painted green. Pohjanen found flakes of green paint under the fingernails of Persson's right hand—the few fingers that she had left, that is."

"So you think they were diving in the lake, and someone placed a door over the hole in the ice?" Rantakyrö said.

"I don't know, but I want to investigate further. There's too much that doesn't add up."

"But don't you wear gloves when you go diving in winter?" Rantakyrö said.

Mella shrugged.

"I've sent the paint samples from Persson's nails and from the door to the National Forensic Laboratory in Stockholm," she said. "Today we'll take some water samples from the lake and send them to Rudbeck Laboratory to see if they match the water in her lungs. I think they were diving in the lake."

"Maybe it was the boyfriend who put the door over the hole," Rantakyrö said.

"But why was her body moved?" Olsson said.

Mella said nothing. If Persson had been murdered, one reason for moving the body could have been that the murderer lived nearby, or that it was widely known that he often visited the lake. Hjörleifur Arnarson lived not far from there. And he often visited it. But there was no point in mentioning him to her colleagues.

It's not him, she thought. Those damn Krekula brothers have something to do with this, I'm sure of it.

But she also needed to talk to Hjörleifur Arnarson. Preferably not on her own.

"How's your daughter?" Olsson asked.

"She's okay," Mella said. "It was mostly me who was scared."

"What a pair of swine!" Rantakyrö said with feeling. "Have you had her number changed?"

"Of course."

"They must be involved in some way or other," Rantakyrö said vehemently. "We need to get them back for what they did to you, Mella."

"I don't know about that," Stålnacke said. "I don't think what they did necessarily has anything to do with the two kids. You went to see them. They took the opportunity to cause trouble. If you'd been from the Inland Revenue or the local council, or if you'd been a traffic warden or anybody else they have it in for, they'd have treated you just the same."

"But it's also possible that they tried to scare me off because they know something or are mixed up in this business."

Stålnacke's tone of voice went up a notch. "Or else your emotions are running ahead of your brain—and it wouldn't be the first time."

Mella stood up.

"You can go to hell," she said calmly to Stålnacke. "Go home to Airi or do whatever the hell you please. I'm going to investigate the death of Wilma Persson and the disappearance of Simon Kyrö. I think he's somewhere under the ice. If they were murdered, I'm going to find out who did it."

She strode out of the room.

"What are you staring at?" Stålnacke said after she had left.

His colleagues did not respond. They did not want an argument. Olsson shook his head almost imperceptibly and pretended to concentrate on his Blackberry. Rantakyrö picked his nose conscientiously.

Rebecka Martinsson was getting out of her car outside the police station as Mella came storming out of the door.

Then Mella had a brainwave. She could ask Martinsson to go with her to talk to Arnarson. Even if it was not a good idea to go out there on her own, she could keep her colleagues out of it for the time being.

"Hello," she said. "Do you feel like coming into the forest and having a chat with the most eccentric character in Kiruna? I have—"

"Hang on a minute," Martinsson said, fumbling for her phone, which was ringing away inside her briefcase.

Wenngren. Rejecting the call, she switched off her phone. I'll call him later, she thought.

"Sorry," she said to Mella. "What were you saying?"

"I'm going to talk to Hjörleifur Arnarson," Mella said. "Do you know who he is? He lives near Vittangijärvi, and I think that's where Wilma and Simon were diving when they disappeared. I'd prefer not to go out there on my own. My colleagues are, er, busy with other things this morning. Would you like to come with me? Or do you have something important that needs doing?"

"No, I've nothing special going on," Martinsson said, thinking of the work piled up on her desk.

If all went well, she should be able to deal with most of the backlog that evening.

≈≈≈≈

"So you've never heard of Hjörleifur Arnarson," Mella said as they drove out to Kurravaara.

They had the police snowmobile in the trailer so they would be able to get to Vittangijärvi.

"Tell me about him."

"I hardly know where to begin. When he first moved to Kiruna, he lived out at Fjällnäs. His mission was to raise a new breed of pig. The idea was that these pigs would be able to survive in the forest up here and tolerate the winter temperatures. So Arnarson crossed wild boar and Linderöd pigs. My God, those pigs! They had no intention of staying in the forest when they could root around in his neighbors' potato fields. The whole village was in an uproar! The neighbors were furious, called us up, wanted us to drive out there and capture the pigs. Arnarson tried to fence them in, but they kept escaping. The pigs, that is, not the neighbors. In the end someone in the village shot them all. My goodness, that was such an ordeal!"

Mella chuckled at the memory.

"And then a few years ago there was a big NATO exercise in the forests north of Jukkasjärvi, Operation North Storm. Arnarson made a contribution to world peace by running around naked in the woods while they were on maneuvers. They had to interrupt the exercise and go looking for him."

"Naked?" Martinsson said.

"Yes."

"But that North Storm exercise was in February, wasn't it?"

"Yes."

"February. Twenty, thirty degrees below zero?"

"It was an unusually warm winter," Mella said with a laugh. "Not much more than minus ten. He had a pair of boots and a blanket under his arm when they caught him. He's a nudist. Only in the summer normally; his contribution to world peace was a special effort. He never wears clothes in summer. He believes that his skin absorbs solar energy, so he also hardly eats anything then."

"How do you know all this?"

"When that neighbor shot his pigs . . ."

"Yes?"

"It led to a court case. Taking the law into his own hands or malicious damage, I can't remember which, but the case went to court in the summer. You should have seen the judge and jury when Arnarson turned up as the plaintiff."

"I can imagine!" Martinsson said, roaring with laughter. "The spring sunshine is pretty strong today. Think we'll get a peek?"

"You never know," Mella said with a smile.

There were no roads leading to Hjörleifur Arnarson's house, which was a two-story building, timber-clad and painted red. In what passed for a garden were an old bathtub and masses of other junk: rabbit cages, traps of various types and sizes, bales of hay, a plow, and sundry bits of wood nailed together and looking like the early stages of some building project.

Several hens were wandering and scratching away in the soft spring snow. A friendly dog, short-haired but with the sharp snout of a collie, came trotting over to greet them, wagging its tail.

"Hello!" Mella shouted. "Is anybody home?"

She looked over at Martinsson. Perhaps it had been a mistake, bringing her along. Martinsson's appearance seemed too elegant somehow. It would be easy to peg her for a slick Stockholm lawyer. But then again, if you allowed an excited dog to lick off all your makeup, as Martinsson was doing, you might pass muster. Mella tried not to think about Stålnacke. He always had a calming effect on people.

I miss him, she surprised herself by thinking. I'm as angry as hell with him, but I hate not having him around.

"Hi there!" a man said, appearing from behind the house.

Hjörleifur Arnarson was wearing incredibly filthy blue overalls that hung loosely around his skinny body. His hair was long and curly, although the crown of his head was bald. His face was deeply tanned and weatherbeaten. He looked much the same as he had done the last time Mella had seen him. That must have been about fifteen years ago, she thought. He was carrying a basket of eggs. The hens assembled devotedly around his feet.

"Women!" he said with a broad smile.

"Er, yes," Mella said. "We're from the police."

She introduced herself and Martinsson.

"You're welcome, even so," Arnarson said. "Maybe you'd like some eggs? Environmentally friendly. They'll make you more fertile. Do you have any kids?"

"Yes," Mella said with a laugh, a bit taken aback. "Four."

"Four!"

Arnarson paused and stared at her in admiration.

"All with the same man?"

"Yes."

"That's not so good. It's best to have children with as many different men as possible. That ensures a richer gene pool. Increases your chances of a biological bull's eye."

He turned to Martinsson.

"Do you have any children?"

"No," she said.

"That's not good. Is it intentional or accidental? Forgive my frankness, but infertile women are useless for the future of humankind."

"Perhaps it leaves us free to get some work done instead," Martinsson said. "While the rest of you are busy making children."

"We can do all the work ourselves," Arnarson said. "As well as make children. But I expect you are fertile in fact. Probably just one of them career women. With the right man you ought to be able to produce loads of children."

"With the right men, surely, you mean," Mella could not resist saying, and was delighted to note the cut-it-out look she received from Martinsson.

"But only one at a time," Arnarson said, eyeing Martinsson appraisingly. "Come in."

Martinsson gave Mella a look that said, Come in and be impregnated, is that what he means?

"We just wanted . . ." Mella said, but Arnarson had disappeared inside the house.

All they could do was follow him.

Arnarson was putting the fertility-boosting eggs into an egg box on the kitchen counter. He wrote the date on each of them with a pencil. Mella looked around with a mixture of horror and elation. She was impressed to see a kitchen as messy and dirty as this one—it made her own kitchen look like an ad in a home-improvement magazine.

In front of the wood-burning stove was a big pile of shavings and bark from timber Arnarson had sawed. There was a cork mat on the floor, but it was impossible to see what color it was under all the layers of dirt. A rag rug under the table was the same grayish-brown shade. The cloth on the kitchen table was stiff with congealed grime. The window panes had been half-heartedly wiped in the middle so that it was just about possible to see out. There were no curtains. Instead Arnarson had installed shelves in front of the windows, on which were rows of tins and potted plants. An old-fashioned zinc bathtub stood in the middle of the floor, and washing was hanging in front of the stove. There were piles of dirty dishes everywhere. Mella suspected that Arnarson never washed up, simply using the plate and mug nearest to him as needed. A yellowish-green sleeping bag lay on the bench. The ceiling was black with soot, and the paraffin lamp hanging from it was covered in dust and spiders' webs.

Both women declined the offer of ecological herbal tea.

"Are you sure?" Arnarson said. "I make it myself. It's high time you started eating in an environmentally friendly way, if you don't already. Only ten percent of us will give birth to children sufficiently capable of coping with life to ensure that our genetic heritage will survive for the next three generations."

"You usually bathe at Vittangijärvi, is that right?" Mella said, thinking that it was time to change the subject.

"Yes."

"Have you ever seen these two down by the lake?"

She showed Arnarson a photograph of Persson and Kyrö.

He looked at the picture and shook his head no.

"I think they were diving in the lake on October 9. That must have been shortly after the ice formed. Did you ever see or meet them? Have you noticed anything happening down by the lake? Do you know about Göran and Berit Sillfors's shed door? Seems it was stolen last winter."

Arnarson's expression changed. He looked grumpy.

"Questions, questions," he said.

Waiting, Mella said nothing.

"They may have been murdered," she said eventually. "It really is important that you tell me anything you know."

Arnarson remained silent the way little children do, his mouth tightly closed.

"Come back tomorrow," he said finally. "Maybe I might have seen something."

"Tell me now," Mella said. "I . . ."

"Maybe I haven't seen anything at all," Arnarson said.

He eyed Mella defiantly. It was clear that she was not going to get anything out of him today.

She gritted her teeth.

The stubborn old goat, she thought.

She opened her mouth to urge him to tell her what he knew, but Martinsson got there first.

"Thank you so much for being willing to help us," she said. "We'll be happy to come back tomorrow."

She smiled at him, revealing her perfect teeth. Her eyes gleamed.

"What's the name of your lovely dog?" she said.

Aranrson melted.

"Vera," he said with a smile. "So there we are then. Come back tomorrow. I'll boil a few eggs for you."

Arnarson stood outside his front door watching Mella and Martinsson drive away. Martinsson had put him in a good mood, but now he was anxious about their next visit.

When they came back tomorrow, what if they brought handcuffs with them? What if they took him to the police station and locked him up? What if he was no longer free? Unable to get out? Locked up in a gray concrete cage?

Going back into the house, he fished his cell phone out of a cupboard. He hardly ever used it. But this was an emergency. Holding a piece of aluminium foil between his head and the phone, he dialed the number of Göran and Berit Sillfors.

"What have you told the police?" he said in an agitated voice when Göran Sillfors answered.

Göran Sillfors sat down on a stool in the kitchen and took his time to convince Arnarson that he and his wife had not said anything at all, and that nobody believed that Arnarson had anything to do with the disappearance of the young couple.

Once Arnarson had calmed down, Göran Sillfors couldn't resist inquiring, "And what about you? What did you tell them?"

Arnarson could feel the vibrations coming from the telephone. They heated up his ear and gave him a headache.

"Nothing. They'll be back again tomorrow," he said curtly.

And hung up.

It is not easy to be Göran Sillfors. He is a talker, a blabbermouth. He likes the sound of his own voice. He will hold forth about anything under the sun, especially himself. He is the type about whom people say, "He gossips like an old woman" and use phrases like "verbal diarrhea" to describe him. He is the type of person other people want to shut up.

Of course he senses that this is how he is regarded. But instead of being quiet, he just talks some more. He has learned to talk without pausing so that it is impossible for people to end conversations with him.

Now Göran Sillfors really has got something to talk about. Something that other people really will be interested in, especially people living in Piilijärvi. The police suspect that Persson and Kyrö were murdered. The police have been talking to Arnarson, who might know more than he has admitted. Sillfors is sitting on a piece of red-hot news, and now he calls his cousin's former workmate, who lives in Piilijärvi.

He cannot know what a terrible mistake that is. What consequences that telephone call will have.

After taking the call, his cousin's former workmate puts on his jacket and goes into the village.

The word spreads like water beneath late-winter snow.

≈≈≈≈

Mella and Martinsson arrived back at the police station at twelve thirty.

"I'd love to go looking for that shed door," Mella said as they were getting out of the car. But it would have to wait. The ice was too unreliable to walk on. Almost half a meter thick, but there was still a danger of falling through it. "I wonder if Krister Eriksson would be able to put Tintin on the trail of a wooden door . . . I'm sure he could," she went on. "I think that dog makes him porridge every morning."

"What happened to his face?" Martinsson said.

"I'm not sure," Mella said, "but according to what I've heard, admittedly not from him directly . . ."

She came to a sudden stop.

"What's the matter?" Martinsson said.

Following Mella's gaze, she saw Hjalmar and Tore Krekula sitting in their car in the police station parking lot. When they noticed Mella, they got out and came toward her. Mella could feel her stomach churning with fear and anger. She thought about Jenny, her daughter.

"I just thought I'd inform you," Tore Krekula said, "that we've been to see your boss to complain about police harassing people in Piilijärvi."

"What?" Mella said.

"It's your attitude," Tore Krekula said. "You march around the village acting so damned superior, and people feel they are being accused and harassed. Lots of us feel that way. And lots of us are going to complain to your boss."

"Do that," Mella said, looking him straight in the eye. "Done much texting lately?"

"Sure," Tore Krekula said casually, returning her gaze.

Neither of them looked away.

In the end Martinsson took Mella by the arm.

"Come on," she said.

She looked hard at Hjalmar Krekula.

Hjalmar Krekula put his hand on his brother's shoulder.

Martinsson and Hjalmar Krekula stood there like two dog owners, each with their pit bull terrier on a lead.

In the end Mella allowed herself to be led away. Tore Krekula shrugged off his brother's hand.

"Shall we go?" Hjalmar Krekula said.

Tore Krekula spat in the snow.

"Bitch," he called after Mella as she entered the police station.

His phone rang and he answered it. Listened for a while without speaking. As he hung up he said, "Let's get going. Time to pay Hjörleifur Arnarson a visit."

I'm with Anni. She's gone down to the lake on her kicksled. The sun is hiding behind the treetops. There's been a midday thaw, and there's a strange, magical haze above the lake.

She hears a hare scream on the far shore. It sounds like the cry of a little baby. Ghostly through the haze. The hare was probably taken by a fox. Hares get careless in the mating season.

There are some who sacrifice their lives for love, she thinks.

As that thought comes to her, she becomes aware of her sister standing behind her.

Kerttu. Also on a kicksled, she parks next to Anni and gazes out over the lake.

"You shouldn't talk to the police," she says. "You shouldn't let them in."

Anni says nothing. I try to glide in between them, but there are so many threads connecting the two sisters.

Anni doesn't turn her head. Instead she sees Kerttu in her mind's eye. The Kerttu she is looking at is young and smooth-skinned. It doesn't seem that long ago, but in fact more than sixty years have passed.

It is May 1943. Kerttu is on her way home, her hair in curlers, expecting Isak Krekula to pick her up in his truck. She is sixteen years old. Many years will pass before she weeps over the loss of her son in the forest. Isak Krekula is twenty-two, but already owns eight trucks, has his own hauling firm and eight employees. For many years now he has been the hero of his village. He has transported supplies across the border into Finland, to both German and Finnish troops during the Winter War and the Continuation War against Russia.

He has returned home to the village full of adventure stories. Sat in people's kitchens and recited the Swedish mantra, "Finland's cause is ours," and perhaps sounded self-important, but his listeners have encouraged that. They have brewed real coffee, produced cookies to dunk, and laughed when Krekula has told them about how he jokes with both the Finnish and the Swedish soldiers to keep their spirits up—after all, he speaks both languages fluently, just like the rest of the villagers. "I came to Kousamo. My God, but the men were freezing. And hungry. I told them, 'Those damn Russkies will all have frostbitten asses, and *perkele*, they'll starve to death.' They couldn't stop themselves laughing. Then we'd unload food and tobacco and weapons. There were tears in plenty of eyes, believe you me."

The villagers would have been sitting by their radios listening to reports from the front line; the women would have been knitting mittens and sweaters and socks for the Swedish volunteers. They would have handed the clothes over to Krekula for delivery to the troops, and would have felt extra pleased when he came back and told them how the boys nearly ended up fighting over the sweaters the women had made, and how they sent greetings and thanked them all from the bottom of their hearts. "And they wondered if I couldn't bring a few pretty unmarried girls with me next time."

The volunteers had been welcomed back to Sweden with parades and receptions in town halls and cathedrals.

Krekula's pockets are full of cash. He earns a lot of money from these transports. His hauling firm grows bigger and bigger. But nobody begrudged him that before the winter of 1943.

Then comes Stalingrad, and the tide turns against the Germans. Foreign minister Christian Günther, who had urged Sweden to follow the example of Finland and support the Germans against the Soviet Union, had backed the wrong horse. Sweden supports the Allies. Finland's cause is not ours, dammit. Finland is a German lackey.

Now the returning volunteers are greeted with silence and averted eyes. Krekula still transports goods across the border, but he no longer circulates around the kitchens of the village. He takes Kerttu with him in his truck. They have been going steady since she was fourteen, and she is as pretty as a picture. Spends ages posing in front of her mirror and avoiding doing any chores, and Anni is tempted to give her a good smacking. Krekula seldom comes in to say hello, hangs around in the road instead. Matti, the girls' dad, looks away and growls grumpily when Kerttu bids them a hasty goodbye and runs outside. He keeps the family going on the little he earns from farming and fishing. But he feels the shame of the poverty-stricken when his daughter comes home with a new dress that Krekula has bought her, or a fancy headscarf or some perfumed soap. Anni and her mother are a stark contrast to all that finery. If the family were better off, perhaps Kerttu would not be so head-over-heels in love—but what can Matti do?

Kerttu continues to strut through the village and could not care less what people say. Not that they dare say very much, as several of the local men drive trucks for Krekula and others are involved in building him a new garage. The bottom line being that they all need to earn a living.

But Anni knows about the gossip. One day when she is visiting one of the families in the village, the youngest daughter catches sight of Kerttu through the window. She starts singing, "If you want to see a bright star, look at me." One of her sisters immediately shuts her up and gives Anni a look combining shame and scorn. She does not apologize. Anni knows that the song is often sung behind Kerttu's back.

The singer who made it popular, Zarah Leander, is out in the cold now, hated by everyone for fraternizing with the Nazis. On the other hand, the anti-fascist composer and revue artist Karl Gerhard's songs are being played on the radio again. The wind changes direction rapidly. Kerttu is the village's little Zarah Leander.

All those threads between the sisters. Anni is over eighty, the age Kerttu soon will be. But they're unable to say a word to each other about what they think and know. Eventually, Anni says she's going back indoors. Whereupon Kerttu heaves her kicksled around and heads off home.

Anni stays put for a while, watching the mist. Then, suddenly, she senses my presence.

"Wilma," she says.

I wish I were able to touch her. Instead, I remind her of when we went swimming in the lake. She even swam underwater. Came up snorting.

"I didn't know I was still capable of that!" she had gasped in jubilation. "Why do we stop doing things simply because we grow old?"

I had shouted back to her, "I'm not going to stop. I'll carry on swimming until I'm ninety!"

Later, in the kitchen, when we were both sitting in front of the stove with fluffy towels wrapped around us, Anni had grinned and said, "So you'll stop swimming when you're ninety, will you? Why?"

Now she starts crying as she turns around and trudges back to her house.

I move on.

I'm sitting on the edge of the autopsy bench, observing myself.

The pathologist is in a bad mood. Angry because he's been forced to do his autopsy examination again. A week ago my body looked quite decent. But now, after being exposed to the air, I'm bluish and swollen. My flesh is distintegrating.

Now he's cutting up my right hand, and suddenly his bad mood seems to have blown away. He starts humming. Is it a song? What a voice he has! It sounds like two stones being rubbed together.

He takes off his gloves and makes a phone call. Asks to speak to Anna-Maria Mella. He starts by complaining about what a hell of a nuisance it is, having to repeat the autopsy, and how he'd be grateful if in the future he'd be informed when there's suspicion that a death has been anything other than accidental so he knows what to look for. I can hear that the woman at the other end of the line is being very patient with him. He grumbles and groans, but in the end can't contain himself any longer. He simply has to tell her about the hand.

"I thought you might be interested in something," he says, and when he hears her tense, expectant silence, he pauses dramatically, coughing and clearing his throat, and almost succeeds in driving her mad.

"Khrush . . . khrush . . . " *he croaks before continuing.* "She has a fracture in her fifth metacarpal . . . that is, you know, the bone in the hand behind the little finger, on the way to the wrist. A common injury caused when defending oneself. It could very well have been caused by her . . . by her hitting her hand against a door, for instance."

I must get away from here. I can't bear to look at this body any more. Not long ago the skin was tight and alive. I had fantastic breasts. I think about how Simon used to hug me. I remember how he would stand behind me, kiss my ears and my neck, and put his hands inside my clothes. The soft, sweet noises he would make that meant he wanted to make love to me. Saying "Mmm" to each other, we knew exactly what we meant.

Now I have no body. That blue, swollen, disintegrating lump of flesh on the steel bench beneath the fluorescent lamps isn't really my body.

I am so terribly lonely.

Hjörleifur Arnarson is also lonely. I'm standing outside his house. His dog can sense my presence. She's staring in my direction. The fur on her back bristles, and she whimpers restlessly.

Several weeks can pass between occasions when Hjörleifur talks to other human beings. Not that he misses the contact. He thinks a lot about women, of course, but it's been more than thirty years since he had a relationship with one. He dreams about a woman's soft skin and rounded body. He leads his own eccentric, wild existence out here in the forest. In summer he wanders around naked and sleeps outdoors. Every day, summer and winter, he bathes in Lake Vittangijärvi.

He didn't see us when we were there, diving. When he arrived at the lake we had already been dead for two hours. I wasn't even in the lake any more. He wondered about that hole in the ice, too big to be used just for fishing. He thought perhaps there was someone enjoying a wintry bath in the lake, just like him. But why in the middle of the lake? And the remains of the door were floating around in the hole, lots of bits of wood; he couldn't fit them together.

Then he saw our rucksacks at the edge of the lake. Assumed they belonged to people who would be returning shortly. He hung around for a while. Investigated the contents of the rucksacks, but didn't take anything. He was curious, hoping for an opportunity to chat. But nobody turned up, of course.

When he came back for his dip the next day, the rucksacks were still there. And the following day. It started snowing the day after that. The rucksacks were covered in snow. So he took them home.

Now he goes upstairs and takes the rucksacks out of a cupboard. He has shut them away very carefully, so that mice and rats couldn't get at them and poke around and crap all over them.

No doubt the rucksacks belonged to the kids that policewoman was asking about, he thinks. He'll hand them over when she comes back tomorrow, tell her exactly where he found them and about the bits of wood floating around in the hole—which doubtless came from the door she was also asking about.

But before he does that, there are one or two things he wants to remove. There's a first-rate, brand-new Trangia stove in one of the rucksacks, and a big merino wool pullover with a windproof lining in the other one. Hjörleifur has never owned such a splendid pullover. And the kids no longer need the stuff, so there's no reason why he shouldn't keep it.

He carries the rucksacks downstairs. It's so cold upstairs. Much nicer in the kitchen, where the wood-burning stove is crackling and spitting away, warming the place up with its living heat.

He is so busy unpacking the rucksacks and sifting through the contents, picking out what he wants to keep and what he'll put back, that he doesn't hear the snowmobile pull up not far from his house.

It doesn't worry him that the dog starts barking—she does that sometimes. For all sorts of reasons. A squirrel, perhaps. Or a fox. Or snow tumbling down from the trees. She's such an old softie.

It's only when he hears the front door closing and footsteps approaching down the hall that he realizes he has visitors. Two men appear in his kitchen.

"Now then, Hjörleifur," one of them says. "We hear you've had a visit from the police."

He looks at them. His instinct tells him to run. But there's nowhere to run to.

Only one of them does the talking. The other one, who's big and fat, stands leaning against the doorframe.

"What have you told the police, Hjörleifur? What did they ask you about? Come on, let's hear it!"

Hjörleifur clears his throat.

"They were asking about a couple of kids who disappeared. If they'd been to the lake. If I'd seen them."

"Well, did you? What did you tell them?"

Hjörleifur doesn't answer. Remains kneeling by the rucksacks.

It's only now that Tore notices them. Two top-class rucksacks made from high-tech nylon material. Not the kind of thing Hjörleifur would normally have. He uses army surplus and homemade stuff he nails together or sews by hand from animal skins he's tanned himself.

"So you found the rucksacks by the lake," Tore says, feasting his eyes on them. "That's right, isn't it, you thieving bastard?"

"I didn't think about it," Hjörleifur says. "There was nobody who—"

That's as far as he gets. Tore takes a piece of wood from the pile beside the stove, holds it with both hands like a baseball bat, and uses all his strength to bash it against the back of Hjörleifur's head.

I hear the sound of Hjörleifur's skull cracking. I hear the thud as his body slumps to the floor. I hear the forest catch its breath in horror. The earth shudders, appalled by the blood being spilled.

Outside the house, the dog stiffens and bristles, then lies down in the snow. She doesn't go indoors, despite the fact that the brothers have carelessly left the door open.

The whole area smells of death. The birch trees are writhing. Birds are calling. Only the field mice carry on scampering beneath the snow. This means nothing to them.

I also feel strangely cold and unaffected. But perhaps I was like that even when I was alive.

Hjalmar moves away from the doorframe.

"That was unnecessary, for Christ's sake," he says.

Hjörleifur Arnarson's legs twitch and kick as life drains out of him.

"Don't be such an old woman," Tore says. "Put your gloves on. We need to rearrange the furniture here."

tuesday, April 28

"Why the devil don't you pick up when I call you?"

Måns Wenngren sounded annoyed.

Rebecka Martinsson rolled her desk chair over to the door and kicked it shut.

"But I do," she said.

"You know what I mean. I've been trying to get you on your cell phone, and I don't like my calls being rejected."

"I'm working, remember," Martinsson said patiently. "So are you, Måns. Sometimes when I call you."

"But then I call you back as soon as I can."

Martinsson said nothing. She had intended to call him back, but had forgotten. Or perhaps could not summon up the strength. She had worked late following the trip to Hjörleifur Arnarson's with Anna-Maria Mella. Then Sivving Fjällborg had invited her to dinner, and she had fallen asleep the moment she had gotten home. She ought to have phoned Wenngren and told him about Arnarson. How he ran around naked in the forest and wanted to give her some ecological eggs that would boost her fertility. That would have made Wenngren laugh.

"I don't get it," he said. "Are you playing games with me? Now you see me, now you don't? Just say the word and I'll join right in."

"I don't do that sort of thing," Martinsson said. "You know that."

"I know nothing. I think you're playing a little power game. Make no mistake, Rebecka, you're wasting your time. It'll just cool me off, that's what it'll do."

"Sorry, that's simply not the case. I'm really no good at . . . I think you're great," she ended lamely.

Silence.

"Move back here, then," he said eventually. "If you think I'm so great."

"I can't," she said. "You know that."

"Why not? You're partnership material, Rebecka. And you're wasted messing around as a prosecutor up there. I can't possibly move north."

"I know," Martinsson said.

"I want to be with you," he said.

"And I want to be with you," Martinsson said. "Can't we just carry on as we are? We get together fairly often, in fact."

"It will never work in the long run."

"Why not? It works for lots of people."

"Not for me. I want to be with you all the time. I want to wake up with you every morning."

"If I worked for Meijer & Ditzinger we'd never see each other."

"Give me a break!"

"It's true. Name one woman working for the firm who's in a successful relationship."

"Work as a prosecutor here in Stockholm, then. No, you don't want to do that either. It seems to suit you just fine to keep me at a distance, to answer the phone only when you feel like it. When you've nothing better to do. I have no idea what you were doing yesterday evening."

"Oh stop it. I was having dinner with Sivving."

"So you say."

Wenngren continued talking. The door to Martinsson's office opened, and Mella popped her head around it. Martinsson shook her head and pointed at the telephone, indicating that she was busy. But Mella took a piece of paper from her desk and scribbled on it in large letters HJÖRLEIFUR ARNARSON is DEAD!!!

"I've got to go," Martinsson said to Wenngren. "Something's happened. I'll call you."

Wenngren broke off his musing.

"Don't bother," he said. "I'm not the type to hang around where I'm not wanted."

He waited for Martinsson to respond.

She said nothing.

He hung up.

"Man trouble?" Mella said.

Martinsson made a face, but before she could reply Mella said, "I tell you what—let's forget about men for the moment. I heard a couple of minutes ago from Sonja on the switchboard that Göran Sillfors found Hjörleifur dead. Sven-Erik and Tommy are already there. You might ask why they didn't call me, but never mind that."

Sven-Erik will be furious, she thought. Pissed off because I didn't tell him I was going to visit Hjörleifur Arnarson yesterday.

Wilma Persson was buried on April 28 at ten in the morning. The mourners stood in the churchyard, clustered around the grave. Hjalmar Krekula looked around. He had not bothered to take his dark suit out of the wardrobe that morning. It was God knows how many years since he had grown out of it.

Standing in front of the bathroom mirror, he had shaved and thought, I can't cope with this. I can't take any more.

Then he had sliced up a whole loaf of rye bread for breakfast. Spread each slice thickly with butter. Eaten it while standing by the drainboard. Eventally he had calmed down. His heart had stopped pounding against his rib cage.

Now he was standing beside the grave containing the coffin, feeling uncomfortable in his camouflage trousers and jacket—although at least he had had the sense not to wear his duffel coat. Lots of young people had turned up, each carrying a red rose to drop onto the coffin. All of them were dressed in black with jewelry in their eyebrows and noses and lips; all had black makeup around their eyes. But none of that could conceal their smooth skin, their rounded cheeks.

They're so young, he thought. All of them are so young. Wilma as well.

Ashes to ashes, dust to dust.

Wilma's mother had traveled up from Stockholm. She was sobbing loudly. Shouting "Oh my God!" over and over again. A sister was holding one arm, a cousin the other.

Anni Autio stood there like a shriveled autumn leaf, teeth clenched. There seemed to be no room for her sorrow. Persson's mother took up all the available space with her shrill shrieks and loud sobbing. Hjalmar Krekula was angry on Autio's behalf. Wished he could get rid of those shrieks, so that Autio had room to cry.

There Persson lay in her coffin.

There was a lot for him to think about now. He needed to get away from there soon. Before he also started shouting and shrieking.

Not long ago her cheeks had been just as rounded as those of the girls standing nearby, holding one another's hands. He did not dare to look at them. He knew what their faces would express if they caught his eye: disgust with the fat pervert.

It was not long ago that Persson had been sitting at his kitchen table. Her hair, the same red color as that of all the women in her family—her mother, grandmother, great-grandmother, Autio, and his own mother, Kerttu. Persson's red hair, tumbling down on both sides of her face as she struggled with her math homework. She spoke to him like, well, just like she spoke to everyone else.

But then.

Her hands hammering away at the ice beneath his feet.

Now she was hammering away at her coffin lid. On the inside of his skull.

It'll soon be over, he thought. Nothing shows.

Afterward, at the funeral reception, he forced down several slices of cake. He was aware that people were looking at him. Thinking that he ought to resist the temptation, that it was no wonder he was so fat.

Let them look, he thought, stuffing a few sugar lumps into his mouth, chewing and then letting them dissolve. It eased the pain, made it easier to take. Eating helped him to calm down.

Inspector Tommy Rantakyrö was squatting down outside Hjör- leifur Arnarson's house, stroking Arnarson's dog, when Mella and Martinsson parked their snowmobile not far away.

He stood up and went over to meet them.

"She's refusing to move," he said, nodding toward the dog.

Mella was annoyed to see that the other inspectors had parked their snowmobile immediately in front of the porch.

"Can you move the snowmobile?" she said curtly to Rantakyrö. "We need to tape this area off so the forensic team can search for clues. How many people have touched the front door handle?"

Rantakyrö shrugged.

Mella stamped off to the house.

Martinsson went over to the dog.

"Now then, my girl," she said softly, scratching the dog's chest gently. "You can't stay here, I'm afraid."

"We'll have to have her put down," Rantakyrö said.

Yes, I suppose so, Martinsson thought.

She stroked the dog's triangular ears: They were very soft, one of them sticking straight up and the top of the other one folded down. The animal was black with white markings, with a white patch around one eye.

"What sort of a mutt are you, then?" she said.

The dog made licking movements in the air. A signal that she was well-disposed toward Martinsson, who stuck out her own tongue and licked her lips in response. She was friend, not foe.

"Do you recognize me?" she said. "Yes, of course you do."

Then she heard herself saying to Rantakyrö: "She has intelligent eyes, like a border collie—see how she looks right at you? She doesn't feel threatened when you look back at her. Isn't that so, my love? And you're friendly like a Labrador, aren't you? Don't take her away. I'll look after her. If he has a relative who's prepared to take her on, okay—but if he hasn't, well then . . ."

Wenngren will have a fit, she thought.

"Okay," Rantakyrö said, looking pleased and relieved. "I wonder what her name is."

"Vera," Martinsson said. "He said it yesterday."

"I see," Rantakyrö said. "Was it you who was here with Mella yesterday, then? Sven-Erik is pretty pissed off about that. I can see his point."

Stålnacke was in the kitchen, talking to Göran Sillfors.

Arnarson was lying on his back on the kitchen floor in front of the pantry. Next to him was a collapsed stepladder. The door to the cupboard above the pantry was open. There were two rucksacks on the floor.

"What the hell's going on?" Mella said when she entered the kitchen. "You can't just go wandering around in here. The forensic boys will have a fit. We must tape the whole place off."

"Who are you bursting in here and telling me what to do?" Stålnacke said.

"No doubt you'd have preferred me not to come at all," Mella said. "When I got to work, Sonja told me about Hjörleifur."

"And I heard from Göran Sillfors that you'd already been here and questioned Hjörleifur. Great. It didn't occur to you to mention that to your colleagues at yesterday's meeting, did it?"

Sillfors looked first at one and then at the other of them.

"Hjörleifur called me yesterday, after you'd been here," he said. "I'd given him a cell phone with a prepaid card. He thinks that using them will make you die young . . ."

Cutting himself short, he looked down at Arnarson lying dead on the floor.

"Sorry," Sillfors said. "Sometimes words just come tumbling out. Anyway, he was reluctant to use the phone. But I told him that one of these days he might break a leg and need help, and that it didn't matter if he kept it in a drawer somewhere, switched off. The card was on special offer, so it didn't cost much. Sometimes you get a new bike or goodness knows what else when you buy a new phone, although then you need to agree to a contract, of course. Anyway, I reckoned it was worth spending a bit on a fellow human being. And we used to get honey and mosquito repellant off him—not that I think much of his mosquito repellant, but still . . . Anyway, he used it yesterday—the phone, I mean. Called me to say that you'd been here. He wondered what the hell we'd told the police, and I had to calm him down. What did you say to him? This morning I thought I'd better drive out and see how he was. And of course make sure he didn't think we'd been telling tales about him, or anything like that. The dog was outside, and the door was wide open. I realized right away that something had happened."

"There's nothing for the forensic team to investigate," Stålnacke said. "It's obvious what's happened here."

Lifting up one of the rucksacks, he showed Mella an address label sewn inside it: WILMA PERSSON.

"One was standing on the floor here, the other was up there."
He pointed to the open door of the cupboard above the pantry.

"He killed them and took their rucksacks," he said. "You frightened him yesterday with your questions. He clambers up the stepladder to fetch the rucksacks from the cupboard, intending to get rid of them, falls, hits his head, and dies."

"That's an odd place to keep them," Mella said, looking up at the cupboard. "Cramped, and awkward to get at. He didn't do it. This doesn't add up."

Stålnacke stared at her as if he felt tempted to pick her up and shake her. His mustache was standing on end.

Mella pulled herself up to her full height.

"Get out!" she said. "I'm in charge here. This is a suspected crime scene. The forensic team will have a look, and then Pohjanen can take over."

That afternoon Mella appeared in the doorway of the autopsy room. She noted the look of annoyance on the face of the technician, Anna Granlund. Granlund didn't take kindly to anybody who came nagging her boss.

The way Granlund looked after her pathologist boss, Lars Pohjanen, always made Mella think of the way trainers looked after sumo wrestlers—not that Pohjanen bore the least resemblance to a sumo wrestler, skinny as he was, and the color of putty, but nevertheless . . . Granlund made sure he always had a sensible lunch, telephoned his wife when Pohjanen was summoned to some crime scene or other, and put a blanket over him when he fell asleep on the sofa in the coffee room, having first removed the glowing cigarette from his hand. She took on as much of his work as she could. And did her best to make sure that nobody quarreled with or pressured him.

"He should be left alone to do what he's best at and be free of any other responsibilities," Granlund would say.

She never commented on Pohjanen's smoking habit. Listened patiently to his wheezing and his lengthy coughing fits, and always had a handkerchief handy when he needed to spit out the phlegm he had coughed up.

But Mella didn't care about any of that. If you wanted results, you needed to keep at them. Nudge them, nag them, stir up trouble. If a corpse turned up on the weekend in suspicious circumstances, Anna Granlund always wanted to wait until Monday before carrying out the autopsy. And she never wanted Pohjanen to have to work in the evenings. All of these things sometimes led to arguments.

"We have to make them understand that passing the buck to the police in Luleå has its price," Mella would say to her colleagues. "If they do that, then they deserve to be put under pressure."

"What do you want?" Lars Pohjanen said in his usual complaining tone.

He was leaning over Hjörleifur Arnarson's sinewy body. He had sawn open the skull and removed the brain, which was lying on a metal tray on a cart next to the table.

"I just want to know how things are going," Mella said.

Taking off her wool hat and mittens, she entered the room. Granlund folded her arms and swallowed thousands of words. It was cold in there, as always. A smell of damp concrete, steel, and dead bodies.

"I don't think it was an accident," Mella said, nodding in the direction of Arnarson's body.

"I'm told he fell off a stepladder in his kitchen," Pohjanen said, without looking up.

"Who told you that?" Mella said, annoyed. "Sven-Erik?"

Pohjanen looked at her.

"I don't think it was an accident either," he said. "The injuries to the brain suggest a powerful trauma to the head, not a fall."

Mella pricked up her ears.

"A blow?" she said.

"Very likely. With a fall there is always a contrecoup injury."

"Do you mind if I phone for an interpreter? It's several years since I studied Latin, and—"

"If you just let me finish, Mella, you might learn something. Imagine the brain hanging inside a box. If you fall on your face, the brain swings forward and you get a contusion in the frontal lobe of the cerebral cortex. And a corresponding injury on the occipital lobe when the brain bounces off the inside of your forehead and swings back, crashing into the back of your skull. This is not what we have here. In addition, there were tiny fragments of bark in the wound."

"A blow from a piece of wood?"

"Most likely. What do forensics say?"

"They say that the doorframe in the kitchen has been wiped. You can see it quite clearly; it was pretty filthy, but at one point it is very clean, at a height where you would place a hand if you were leaning on it . . ."

Mella drifted into silence. The image of Hjalmar Krekula standing in the doorway of Kerttu Krekula's kitchen came into her mind's eye.

"Anything else?" Pohjanen said.

"The body seems to have been moved. He was wearing blue overalls, and they were crumpled up at the back of his neck in a way suggesting that he'd been dragged along by the feet. But that kind of thing can be misleading. You know that yourself.

You might not die immediately. You might try to stand up, and there are death throes to take into account."

"Any blood on the floor?"

"One place that had been wiped."

Mella looked at Arnarson's body. It was sad that he was dead, but now this was a murder case, no question about it. Now it was justified to drop all other lines of inquiry and concentrate on this one. Stålnacke would not like it. She had been right. He had been tramping around the crime scene. The forensic team was annoyed.

But that's not my problem, she thought. He can go off and work on something else if he likes.

She zipped up her jacket.

"I have to go," she said.

"Okay," Pohjanen said. "Where?"

"Rebecka Martinsson. I need to get permission to search a house."

"By the way, this Rebecka Martinsson," Pohjanen said, sounding curious. "What's she all about?"

But Mella had already left.

At the Kiruna police station Mella gave a brief summary of the pre-liminary autopsy report on Hjörleifur Arnarson to District Prosecutor Martinsson. Mella's colleagues Stålnacke, Olsson, and Rantakyrö were also present.

Vera was lying at Martinsson's feet. Rantakyrö had taken the dog from Arnarson's house, left her in Martinsson's office, and then galloped off to the supermarket to buy some dog food. Rejecting the food, Vera had drunk a little water and lain down.

Speaking of dogs, Martinsson thought, contemplating the police officers crowded into her office.

Mella was a different person from when Martinsson had seen her last. She was the leader of the pack once more, enthusiasm for the hunt obvious in her every movement. She had not even taken her hat off, nor had she sat down. Olsson and Rantakyrö were wagging their tails eagerly; their tongues were hanging out expectantly, and they were straining at their leads. Only Stålnacke sat listlessly on Martinsson's extra chair, staring out of the window at nothing.

"We've had a response from the National Forensic Laboratory regarding the flakes of paint under Wilma Persson's fingernails. They match the paint on the door at the Sillforses' summer cottage. And Göran Sillfors used the same paint on the shed door that was stolen. So we can now be sure that someone placed that door over the hole in the ice when Wilma Persson and Simon Kyrö were diving. They were murdered."

"Kyrö hasn't been found yet," Martinsson said.

"That's correct. And now Hjörleifur Arnarson. I'd like permission to conduct searches at Hjalmar and Tore Krekula's places."

Martinsson sighed.

"There needs to be reasonable suspicion," she said.

"So what?" Mella said. "That's the least thing required by law. Come on, Martinsson. It's not as if I want to go and arrest them—but 'reasonable suspicion' . . . Let's face it, that could apply to someone who, say, shopped at the same supermarket as the victim. Seriously. This would never have been a problem for Alf Björnfot."

Chief prosecutor Alf Björnfot was Martinsson's boss. These days he worked mostly in Luleå and let Martinsson take care of Kiruna District.

"That may be, but you're dealing with me now, not him," Martinsson said slowly.

Olsson's and Rantakyrö's tails stopped wagging. The hunt had been called off.

"They've threatened me and tried to scare me off the case," Mella said.

"There's no proof of that," Martinsson said.

"I called Göran Sillfors. He told me that he'd mentioned to someone who lives in Piilijärvi that we'd paid a visit to Hjörleifur. Piilijärvi's a village! If one person knows something, everyone knows it! Tore and Hjalmar Krekula must have heard that we had been talking to Hjörleifur Arnarson. They no doubt went straight to his place after they'd spoken to us in the parking lot."

"But we don't know that for sure," Martinsson said. "If you can prove it—if someone has seen them near or even in Kurravaara, you'll get your permission."

"Oh, for Christ's sake . . ." Mella groaned.

The whole pack, apart from Stålnacke, looked imploringly at Martinsson.

"We'd be reported to the parliamentary ombudsman," she said. "The Krekula brothers would just love that."

"We'll never catch them," Mella said dejectedly. "It will be another Peter Snell case."

Fifteen years earlier, a thirteen-year-old girl, Ronja Larsson, had gone missing one Saturday evening after visiting some friends. Peter Snell was an acquaintance of the family. One of the girl's friends had said that he had made advances, and that Larsson had thought he was "creepy." The morning after her disappearance, Snell had poured gas into the trunk of his car and set fire to it in the forest. When interrogated, he had denied committing a crime, but could not give a satisfactory explanation for burning his car.

"He doesn't need to," chief prosecutor Alf Björnfot had said to Mella. "There's no law to stop you burning your own car if that's what you want to do. It proves nothing."

There had been vain attempts to find DNA traces in the burned-out wreck. The girl's body was never found. The case was written off, closed as far as the police were concerned. They knew who the murderer was, but couldn't produce enough evidence to charge him. Snell owned a towing firm. Before the Ronja Larsson case, the police had frequently used his tow trucks in connection with traffic accidents and similar situations. Following the case, they cut him off. He threatened to sue.

Martinsson said nothing for a few seconds. Then she smiled mischievously at the Kiruna police officers.

"It'll be okay," she said. "We'll establish a link between them and the crime scene. Then we'll be able to turn their houses inside out."

"And how will we do that?" Mella said doubtfully.

"They'll tell me of their own accord," Martinsson said. "Sven-Erik?"

Stålnacke looked up in surprise.

"Have you got my direct line on your cell phone?"

Stålnacke and Martinsson pulled up outside Tore Krekula's house at five fifteen on April 28. His wife answered the door.

"Tore's not at home," she said. "I think he's at the garage. I can phone him."

"No, we'll go over there," Stålnacke said with a good-natured smile. "You can come with us and show us the way."

"You can't miss it. You just need to drive back through the village and—"

"You can come with us," Stålnacke said in a friendly voice that clearly expected to be obeyed.

"I'll just go and get my jacket."

"No need for that," Stålnacke said, ushering her gently along. "It's nice and warm in the car."

They drove in silence.

"I apologize for the smell," Martinsson said. "It's the dog. I'll give her a good wash this evening."

Laura Krekula glanced casually at Vera, who was lying in the back compartment.

Martinsson keyed a text message into her cell phone. It was to Mella. It said: "Laura Krekula out of the house."

The garage was built out of cinderblocks. Standing outside it were several buses, snowplows, and a brand-new Mercedes E270 station wagon.

"In there—the office is on your right as you go in," Laura Krekula said, pointing to a door remarkably high up in the wall. "Can I walk back? It's not all that cold."

Martinsson checked her phone. A text from Mella. "We're outside now," it said. Martinsson nodded almost imperceptibly.

"Yes, that'll be okay," Stålnacke said.

Laura Krekula set off. Stålnacke and Martinsson stepped over the high threshold of the staff entrance. There was a faint smell of diesel, rubber, and oil.

The office was on the right. The door was open. It was barely more than a cupboard. Just enough room for a desk and chair. Tore Krekula was sitting at the computer. When Martinsson and Stålnacke came in, he swung around to face them.

"Tore Krekula?" Martinsson said.

He nodded. Stålnacke seemed to be embarrassed and was staring at the floor. He had his hands in his jacket pockets. Martinsson was doing the talking.

"I'm district prosecutor Rebecka Martinsson, and this is inspector Sven-Erik Stålnacke."

Stålnacke nodded a greeting, his hands still in his pockets.

"We met yesterday," Tore Krekula said to Martinsson. "You're a bit of a celeb here in Kiruna, not someone we'd forget easily."

"I'm investigating the death of Hjörleifur Arnarson," Martinsson said. "We have reason to believe that it wasn't accidental. I'd like to ask you if —"

She was interrupted by her phone ringing, and looked at it.

"Excuse me," she said to Tore Krekula. "I have to take this call."

He shrugged to indicate that it did not matter to him.

"Hello," Martinsson said into the phone as she walked out through the door. "Yes, I sent you the material yesterday . . ."

The door closed with a click, and they could no longer hear her.

Stålnacke smiled apologetically at Tore Krekula. Neither spoke for a moment.

"So Hjörleifur Arnarson is dead, is he?" Tore Krekula said. "What did she mean, it wasn't an accident?"

"It was a nasty business," Stålnacke said. "It seems that someone killed him. I don't really know what we're doing here, but my boss is in league with the prosecutor."

He nodded in the direction of the door through which Martinsson had disappeared.

"And you seem to have annoyed my boss," Stålnacke continued. "I don't know how much of what she's told me is true, but she has a talent for rubbing people the wrong way."

Krekula said nothing.

"Anyway," Stålnacke said with a sigh, "I assume you know about that insane shoot-out at Regla."

"Of course," Tore Krekula said. "There was a lot about it in the papers."

"It was all her fault," Stålnacke said vehemently. "She exposes her staff to danger without a moment's thought. I had to take sick leave afterward—"

He broke off and seemed to be lost in thought.

"And now she can't wait for the forensic boys to complete their job. If in fact someone has been out at Hjörleifur's place, we'll soon know all about it. My God, it's amazing what the tech wizards can do nowadays. If someone has left a strand of hair behind, you can bet your life they'll find it. They're going through Hjörleifur's house with a fine-tooth comb."

Tore Krekula ran his hand over his head. His hair had not thinned with age.

"Not that it proves anything even if someone has been there," Stålnacke said, looking up at the ceiling and speaking as if he had forgotten that Tore Krekula was there. "I mean, you can have paid someone a visit, but that doesn't mean you killed them."

At that moment the door opened and Martinsson came back into the office.

"Sorry about that," she said. "As I was saying, Hjörleifur Arnarson has been found dead in his home. Have you been out there? You and your brother?"

Tore Krekula looked at her slyly.

"I won't deny that we were there," he said after a while. "But we didn't kill him. We simply wanted to know what he'd seen. I mean, the police don't tell any of us in the village a damned thing. But that was where they lived, after all. My Auntie Anni was Wilma's great-grandmother. You'd have thought they would have given her a bit of information."

"So you were there," Martinsson said. "What did he say?"

"Nothing. He probably thought you'd be furious with him if he said anything to us. We left none the wiser."

Martinsson checked the time on her phone.

"It's 5:56. I confirm herewith that the police will search the houses of Tore and Hjalmar Krekula, both of whom we have good reason to suspect of the murder of Hjörleifur Arnarson."

She turned to Tore Krekula.

"Take your clothes off. We'll be taking them with us. You can keep your underpants on. We have some things in the car that we can lend you."

The police are searching the houses of Tore and Hjalmar Krekula. I'm sitting on the roof of Tore's porch. There's a raven perched next to me. It knows I'm there, I'm convinced of it. It leans its head to one side and studies me, even though there's nothing for it to see. It moves a step closer, then steps away again. Tore's wife, Laura, is standing outside the front door, shivering. When she arrived home from the garage the police were already here—the blond police-woman with the long braid, and three uniformed colleagues. They wouldn't allow Laura into the house. Then the policewoman's cell phone rang. It was a short call. She simply said "Okay," and they went inside.

Now they're taking Tore's clothes away. I assume they're hoping to find bloodstains from Hjörleifur.

Tore arrives and stands watching them. He says nothing at first, tries to catch the policewoman's eye, but fails. He smiles scornfully at her colleagues instead and asks if they'd like to search his dust-bin. Which they do. Tore's wife says nothing. She doesn't dare ask what they're looking for. She has learned not to wind Tore up.

The raven caws and clicks and clucks—it seems to be trying out different sounds to see if I'll react to any of them. I can't respond. Giving up, it flies off to Hjalmar's house one hundred and fifty meters away. Perches in the big birch tree and calls to me. In a flash I'm sitting beside it on a branch.

Hjalmar opens the door when the police ring the bell. He seems half asleep. His mop of hair resembles a spiky tuft of winter grass. His stubble is like a sooty shadow on his cheeks and neck. His belly sticks out like an overfed pig under his tentlike T-shirt. When the police officers ask him politely to wait outside until they've finished, he doesn't put any pants on, just steps outside in his underwear. The older officer, the one with the shaggy mustache, takes pity on him, and allows him to sit and wait in the police car.

I land in the prosecutor's hair. I'm like a raven on the top of her head. I dig my claws into her dark locks. I turn her head to look at Hjalmar. She sees him sitting there in the police car, blinking. She opens the door and talks to him. I peck at her head. She must wake up now.

Olsson, Rantakyrö, and Stålnacke carried clothing out of Hjalmar Krekula's house and searched through the garage looking for a murder weapon. An hour and a half later they announced that they had finished.

Martinsson contemplated Hjalmar Krekula. She saw how he was leaning against the car window. It looked almost as if he were about to fall asleep. His eyelids were half-closed.

Suddenly he felt her watching him. He turned his head slowly and looked at her through the car window.

She felt as if she were being stabbed inside. His gaze dug into her just like a pike clamping its jaws around the bait. And her gaze dug into him. Like when the hook pierces the pike's cheek.

Fleeting images flitting through her consciousness.

Nobody has been kind to him since he was a very little boy. Torture and pain are tangled in all that fat. This loneliness is something he can't eat himself out of. He is at the end of the line.

But I've touched him, she thought—although it wasn't so much a thought as an insight. He was young. I was not that old either. Fifteen, perhaps. I held him under his arms and lifted him up toward the heavens. The sun at its zenith. Dry soil under my bare feet. He slept in my arms. Was he my little brother? My child? My little sister?

Her heart felt as if it might burst with compassion. She wanted to place her hand on the car window. So he would place his hand against hers on the other side of the glass.

"Hello," Olsson said beside her. "I said we're finished."

Following her gaze, he saw Hjalmar Krekula.

"That asshole!" he said between gritted teeth. "Let him suffer. Did they think they could fuck with Mella and get away with it? Let him sit there and stew in his filthy underwear."

Martinsson nodded absentmindedly. Then she went over to Stålnacke's car and opened the back door.

"We've finished," she said to Hjalmar Krekula.

He was sitting there like a lump of lard, looking at her. Stålnacke had draped a red-and-black synthetic blanket over his bare legs.

They had slashed Mella's tires, Martinsson reminded herself. Stole her cell phone and lured Jenny to Järnvägsparken to scare the shit out of her. I must get a grip.

"We're taking you to the station for questioning," she said. "You're not under arrest, so I'll give you a lift home when we've finished."

She controlled any feelings of sympathy. Made sure they were not noticeable. She caught sight of a raven perched on the porch roof.

"We'll get you a pair of pants."

Transcript of the Interrogation of Tore Krekula.
Place: Kiruna police station.
Date and time: April 28, 7:35 p.m.
Present: Inspectors Anna-Maria Mella and Sven-Erik Stålnacke, and District Prosecutor Rebecka Martinsson.

A-MM: Interrogation begun at 7:35 p.m. Can you tell us your name, please?

TK: Tore Krekula.

A-MM: You have told the police that you and your brother, Hjalmar Krekula, paid a visit to Hjörleifur Arnarson yesterday. Why did you do that?

TK: We heard that the police had been there and asked questions about Wilma Persson and Simon Kyrö. We were relatives of Wilma's. She lived with her great-grandmother Anni Autio. And Anni and our mother are sisters. But the police never tell us a damn thing. So we wanted to know what the hell was going on.

A-MM: Can you tell us about your visit to Hjörleifur Arnarson?

TK: What do you want to know?

A-MM: Just tell us what happened.

TK: We asked what he'd spoken to the police about. He said, "nothing in particular." He said you'd asked about Wilma and Simon, but he knew nothing.

A-MM: Who did the asking? You or your brother?

TK: Me. I asked the questions. Hjalmar isn't much for talking.

A-MM: And what happened then?

TK: What do you mean, what happened then? Nothing happened then. We went home. He didn't know anything.

A-MM: Did you touch anything while you were in his house?

TK: It's possible. I don't remember.

A-MM: Think hard.

TK: As I said, I don't remember. Is that all? Some of us need to earn enough money to pay your wages, you know.

A-MM: Interrogation concluded at 7:42 p.m.

Transcript of the Interrogation of Hjalmar Krekula.
Place: Kiruna police station.
Date and time: April 28, 7:45 p.m.
Present: Inspectors Anna-Maria Mella and Sven-Erik Stålnacke,
and District Prosecutor Rebecka Martinsson.

A-MM: Interrogation begun at 7:45 p.m. Can you tell us your name, please?

HK: —

A-MM: Your name, please.

HK: Hjalmar Krekula.

A-MM: You and your brother visited Hjörleifur Arnarson yesterday. Can you tell us about the visit?

HK: —

A-MM: Can you tell us about that visit?

HK: —

A-MM: Should I interpret your silence as meaning that you . . .

HK: He didn't say anything. Can I go now?

A-MM: No, you can't go now, we have only just—Sit down!

HK: Can I have a word, please?

A-MM: It's 7:47 p.m. We are taking a short break.

"We have to let him go," Martinsson said to Mella and Stålnacke. "We've got their clothes. We have to hope that the forensic examination gives us some results."

They were standing in the corridor outside the interrogation room.

"But they haven't said anything!" Mella said. "We can't just let them go!"

"They are not under arrest. They've said what they're going to say."

"Nevertheless we have the right to keep them here and interrogate them for six hours. Those bastards can sit in there for six hours."

"Do you want to be charged with professional misconduct?" Martinsson asked calmly. "We have no justification for holding them."

Olsson and Rantakyrö came out into the corridor, attracted by the sound of raised voices.

"Rebecka says we have to let them go," Mella said.

"We'll nail them regardless," Olsson said by way of consolation. Mella nodded.

We simply have to, she thought. I won't be able to cope otherwise. Please God, let them find something on their clothes.

"We managed to search the houses after all," Rantakyrö said.

"Well done, Svempa."

Stålnacke looked at the floor. Cleared his throat to show that he had noted the compliment.

"By God, we did!" Rantakyrö said, making a clumsy effort to transform the gloomy atmosphere. "I'd have given anything to have been there."

"Yes, it was perfect timing with the telephone," Martinsson said, giving Stålnacke a congratulatory look. "Anyway, let's say goodbye to the Krekula brothers for now. Anna-Maria, do you have the documentation for Wilma, Simon, and Hjörleifur?"

"Of course," Mella said.

"Okay. Since I'm taking over the investigation, I'll need to read all the material. I thought I'd do that this evening."

No one spoke. Everyone was looking at Martinsson.

"Having made the decision to search the Krekulas' houses, I'll be taking over the preliminary investigation," Martinsson said.

The three male officers turned to look at Mella.

"Of course," she said in an unnaturally offhand tone of voice. "But we're not used to being so formal. With Alf Björnfot it was business as usual. We simply kept reporting to him as work progressed."

"As I mentioned earlier today," Martinsson said, and now the words came flowing smoothly out of her mouth, "you're no longer working with Alf Björnfot, but with me. I want to read all the material. And I naturally expect you to report to me as soon as anything happens."

"'Expect,'" said Mella before she could stop herself. Then she darted into her office and fetched the documents lying on her desk to hand them over to Martinsson.

Having followed on her heels, Martinsson collected them in Mella's doorway, the other officers trailing after her like a tail.

"They're probably not in the right order," Mella said.

"That doesn't matter," Martinsson said.

She glanced at the bulletin board in Mella's office. Pinned up were photographs of Persson, Kyrö, and Arnarson, with the dates when the first two had disappeared and when Arnarson had been murdered. There were maps of the area where Persson had been found dead, and of Vittangijärvi. The names of the Krekula brothers were also posted.

"All that stuff," Martinsson said, pointing, "we'll move into the conference room tomorrow. So we have everything in one place. When shall we meet tomorrow? Eight o'clock?"

I don't care what they think, Martinsson said to herself as she walked off with the documentation under her arm. I'm responsible now, and everything will be done by the book. It's not my style to watch from the sidelines. If I'm in charge of the investigation, I'm the one who makes the decisions.

"Wow," Mella said when Martinsson had left. "Do you think we'll have to line up before the meeting tomorrow? In alphabetical order? Like at school?"

"But she did a damn brilliant job today with Tore Krekula," Stålnacke said. "Without her . . ."

"Yes, yes," Mella said impatiently. "I just think a little humility wouldn't go amiss."

The silence between them seemed to last for eternity. Stålnacke looked hard at Mella. Mella stared back at him, ready to fight her corner.

"Looks like it's time to go home," Olsson said, and was seconded by Rantakyrö, who explained that his girlfriend was getting annoyed—she'd called him about supper an hour ago now, and he had promised to check in and rent a movie on the way home.

Word soon gets around in a little town like Kiruna. Pathologist Lars Pohjanen tells his technical assistant Anna Granlund that Rebecka Martinsson saw Wilma Persson in a dream after the girl died and told him that Persson did not die in the river. That was why he took samples of the water in her lungs.

Granlund says she believes in that kind of thing—her grandfather's cousin was able to stanch blood by the laying on of hands.

Granlund's work is covered by hospital confidentiality rules, but she cannot resist telling her sister about this paranormal development over a pizza lunch at Laguna.

Her sister promises not to say anything about it, but close family does not count, of course, so she tells her husband that evening.

The husband does not believe in that kind of thing, however. That is precisely why he tells one of his friends about it while they are sitting in the sauna after a body-building session. Perhaps he feels the need to test the credibility of Martinsson's claim. Could it really be possible? He wants to see how his friend reacts.

His friend does not say much at all. Just pours more water onto the hot stones.

His friend often goes hunting with an old Piilijärvi resident, Stig Rautio. They bump into each other outside the co-op. He repeats the story to Rautio. Asks if he knew Wilma Persson. She was murdered, it seems. It was that district prosecutor Rebecka

Martinsson—the one who killed those pastors a few years ago—she was the one who . . .

Stig Rautio. He hunts on land owned by Tore and Hjalmar Krekula. He calls on Isak and Kerttu Krekula with the rent he owes Tore Krekula—Tore's wife has told him her husband is visiting his parents. There is no urgency regarding the rent payment, but Rautio is curious. Everyone in the village, indeed in the whole of Kiruna, knows that the police have searched the Krekula brothers' houses in connection with the murders of Wilma Persson and Hjörleifur Arnarson. Isak Krekula is in bed in the little room off the kitchen, as he always is nowadays. Kerttu Krekula is frying sausages and has made some mashed turnips for her boys. Hjalmar Krekula is eating, but Tore Krekula is only drinking coffee; he's already eaten at home—after all, he has a wife who cooks for him.

Kerttu Krekula does not ask if Rautio would like a mug of coffee. They realize that he is only nosing around, but they cannot tell him anything. He hands over the envelope with the rent. He had used the first envelope he could lay hands on, and it happened to be one of his wife's special ones, bought at Kiruna market. It looked as if dried flowers had been pressed into the handmade paper. Taking the envelope, Tore Krekula gives it a quizzical look. Aha, says the look, someone is trying to give the impression of being high-class, superior.

Rautio regrets not having looked for a different envelope; a used one with a window would have been better, but so what! He says he has heard that the police have been around—what a gang of idiots, halfwits! What the hell do they think they're doing? Next thing we know they will be knocking on his door as well. Then he tells them about that business concerning District Prosecutor Martinsson and the pathologist Pohjanen. That she had dreamed about Persson, and gone to the pathologist as a result.

"Before long they'll be buying crystal balls instead of chasing after thieves," he jokes.

Nobody reacts, of course. The joke hangs in the air, awkward and heavy-handed. The Krekulas carry on as if nothing had happened. Hjalmar Krekula eats his mashed turnip and pork sausages. Tore Krekula taps on his coffee cup with his fingernail and gets a refill from his mother.

It is as if nothing unusual has happened. They do not comment on what Rautio says about the police. The kitchen is as silent as the grave for what seems like an eternity. Then Tore Krekula checks the bills in the envelope and asks if there is anything else Rautio wants to discuss. No, there is nothing else. He leaves without any gossip to pass on.

When Rautio is gone, Tore Krekula says, "What a load of bullshit! Claiming that the prosecutor dreamed about her."

Kerttu Krekula says, "This will be the last straw for your father. It'll be the death of him."

"People talk," Tore Krekula says. "They always have. Let 'em."

Kerttu Krekula slams her palm down on the table. Shouts, "That's easy for you to say!"

She starts clearing the table. Despite the fact that Hjalmar Krekula has not finished eating yet. A clear signal that there is nothing more to be said.

There never is anything more to be said, Hjalmar thinks. It was the same then. Last autumn, when Father had his heart attack. When Johannes Svarvare got drunk and started blabbing. There was nothing more to be said almost before they started speaking.

It is late September. The sun is setting on the other side of the lake. Hjalmar Krekula has carried the outboard motor indoors for his father. It is lying on the kitchen table, on a layer of newspapers.

Johannes Svarvare usually dismantles it and gives it a service for Isak Krekula. The carburetor is blocked as usual.

Svarvare messes about with the motor. Isak Krekula serves him some vodka, by way of thanks. Tore Krekula's wife is at a Tupperware party, so he is having dinner with his parents. Hjalmar Krekula is there as well. There is no room to swing a cat in the kitchen. The table is piled high with plates of hamburgers and macaroni in white sauce alongside engine casing, screwdrivers, keys, a sheath knife, a plastic bottle with a long tube containing oil for the gearbox, new spark plugs, and a can of gas in which the filter will be soaked.

Svarvare is gabbling away a mile a minute. He is going on about old marine engines and various boats they have had or helped to build, and he even babbles on about the time he and his cousin loaded five sheep into his uncle's rowboat to take them to their summer grazing on one of the islands in the River Rautas, and how they hit a rock in Kutukoski and sunk, all the sheep drowned, and he and his cousin only just escaped with their lives.

They have heard the story about the drowned sheep in Kutukoski before, but Hjalmar and Tore Krekula continue eating and listen just like they used to do when they were children.

"Speaking of drowning," Svarvare says as he unscrews the carburetor, "do you remember that time in the autumn of 1943 when we were waiting and waiting for that transport plane that never arrived?"

"No," Isak Krekula says, sounding a warning note.

But Svarvare has been drinking, and does not hear any warning notes.

"It disappeared, didn't it? I've always wondered where it could have come down. It was coming from Narvik. It always seemed to me that the plane was bound to have followed the River Torne past Jiekajärvi and Alajärvi. But if you asked folk who lived up there, none of them had seen or heard such a plane. So I reckon it must have gone off course and turned south after Taalojärvi, then somehow turned off again and tried to make an emergency landing on the lakes at Övre Vuolusjärvi or Harrijärvi or Vittangijärvi. Don't you agree? The whole crew must have drowned like rats."

Tore and Hjalmar Krekula concentrate on their food. Kerttu Krekula is standing at the counter with her back to them and seems to be busy with something. Isak Krekula says nothing, merely hands Svarvare the key so that he can detach the float. Svarvare continues his outpouring.

"Anyway, I told Wilma—she and Simon go diving, you know—that this would be something for them to explore if they could find it. Try Vittangijärvi, was my advice. Because if it had gone down in Övre Vuolusjärvi we'd no doubt have heard about it by now. And Harrijärvi is so small. So Vittangijärvi would be as good a place to start looking as anywhere, don't you think?"

He unscrews the mouthpiece, puts it to his mouth, and blows out the flakes of metal. Then he holds it up in the light from the window. Squints through the little hole to see if it is clean. He turns to Tore and Hjalmar Krekula.

"I was only thirteen then, but your dad took me with him. We needed to work in those days."

"What did Wilma say?" Isak Krekula says casually, as if he was not really interested.

"Oh, she was as keen as anything. Asked me if she could borrow some maps."

Svarvare sounds satisfied now. It is evidently a pleasant memory. A keen young woman interested in something he had to tell her. Their fingers on the map.

He drops the filter into the can of gas. Dries his hands as best he can on his trousers, and knocks back the few drops left in the glass.

But instead of refilling it, Isak Krekula screws down the cork of the vodka bottle.

"Thanks for your help today; that's all for now," he says.

Svarvare looks a bit surprised. He had expected several more glasses of vodka while he fitted the engine back together. That was the usual pattern.

But he has spent his entire life in the village and had dealings with Isak Krekula since childhood. He knows it is prudent to pay attention when Isak Krekula says, "Time to go."

He says thank you, staggers unsteadily out of the house, and heads for home.

Kerttu Krekula remains standing absolutely still, her back to her family and her hands resting on the countertop. Nobody says a word.

"Is Father all right?" Tore Krekula says.

Isak Krekula has tried to stand up from his chair by the kitchen table. His face is white as a sheet. Then he falls. Makes no attempt to break his fall with his hands. Hits his head on the table as he collapses onto the floor.

Tore Krekula puts the fancy envelope with the rental payment into his pocket. As always, Hjalmar Krekula thinks that there is a lot of money around, of which he never sees a trace. He does not know what the firm's sales are. He does not know how much of the forest they own or what income it brings in. But then, Tore Krekula is the one with a family to look after.

There is a clattering of dishware as Kerttu Krekula nonchalantly drops plates, cutlery, and mugs into the sink.

"Two sons he's got," she says without looking at them. "And what good do they do him?"

Hjalmar Krekula notices how Tore Krekula reacts badly to what she says. The words stab him like knives. Hjalmar Krekula has been used to such rebukes ever since he was a little boy. All the abuse. Useless, thick as three planks, fat, idiot. Actually, most of it has come from Tore and Isak Krekula. Kerttu Krekula has not said much. But she never looks him in the eye.

Things are going downhill, Hjalmar thinks.

There is something almost comforting about that thought. He thinks about the prosecutor, Rebecka Martinsson. Who saw Persson after she had died.

Tore Krekula looks at Hjalmar Krekula. Thinks that he is keeping silent as usual. There is something the matter with him.

"Are you ill?" he says brusquely.

Oh yes, Hjalmar thinks. I'm ill.

He stands up, walks out of the kitchen, leaves the house, crosses the road. Trudges home to his sad little house full of furniture, curtains, clothes, you name it, none of which he has bought himself.

And then we spoke to Johannes Svarvare, he thinks. Father was in intensive care.

In his mind, Tore Krekula flings open Svarvare's front door. Marches into the kitchen.

"You bastard," Tore Krekula says, taking his knife from its sheath on his belt.

Hjalmar Krekula remains in the doorway. Svarvare is scared stiff, nearly shitting himself. He is lying on the bench in the kitchen, still suffering from yesterday's hangover, from when he sat in the Krekulas' house, taking their outboard motor to pieces. He sits up now.

Tore Krekula stabs his knife into Svarvare's kitchen table. He had better realize that this is serious.

"What the hell—?" Svarvare splutters.

"That airplane that disappeared," Tore Krekula says. "And all that was going on in those days. You've blabbed on about it like a silly old woman. Stuff that everyone's forgotten about, that ought to be forgotten. And now Father's in the hospital thanks to you. If he doesn't make it, or I hear that you've squeaked one more damn word . . ."

He wrenches the knife loose and points it at Svarvare's eye.

"Have you been gossiping to anybody else?" he says.

Svarvare shakes his head. Stares squint-eyed at the knife point.

Then they leave.

"At least he'll keep his trap shut now," Tore Krekula says.

"Wilma and Simon?" Hjalmar Krekula says.

Tore Krekula shakes his head.

"They'll never find anything anyway. Let them think of it as an old man's ravings. We'll keep our eye on 'em. Make sure they don't go diving there."

Hjalmar Krekula stands outside his house. Suppresses all thoughts of Svarvare, Persson, Kyrö, and all the rest of it. He has no desire at all to go into his own house. But what alternative does he have? Sleep in the woodshed?

Sven-Erik Stålnacke and Airi Bylund drive to Bylund's cottage in Puoltsa. They are only going to check on things—besides, it is such a lovely evening.

In the course of the journey, Stålnacke tells Bylund how he and Martinsson lured Tore Krekula into a trap.

Bylund listens, albeit absentmindedly, and says, "Good for you."

Stålnacke lapses into a bad mood. For no obvious reason. He says, "Every now and then I do something right, I suppose."

He tries not to think about how he trampled all over the evidence in Arnarson's house and pontificated about the cause of death without knowing what he was talking about.

He wants Bylund to say something along the lines of, "You always do the right thing, bless you," but she does not say a word.

Stålnacke is overcome by the feeling that he is not good enough for anybody. He becomes surly and silent.

Bylund does not say anything either.

And it certainly is not the sort of silence to make the most of. Usually it is uplifting for the two of them to share silence. Silence full of glances and smiles and sheer joy at having found one another. Silence occasionally broken by Bylund chatting to the cats or the flowers, to herself, or to Stålnacke.

But this particular silence is filled with the echo of Stålnacke's thought: She's going to leave me. There's no point anymore.

He can sense how fed up she has become with his dissatisfaction with his job. She thinks he goes on and on about Mella, about the shooting at Regla, about goodness only knows what else. But Bylund was not there. She cannot possibly understand.

They arrive at their destination. Getting out of the car, she says, "I'll make some coffee. Would you like some?"

All Stålnacke can manage to say is: "Yes, all right, if you're making some anyway."

She goes inside and he stands outside, at a loss, not knowing what to do next.

He trudges around the house. At the back Bylund has made a cat cemetery. All the cats she has ever owned are buried there, and also some that belonged to her friends. Hidden under the snow are small wooden crosses and beautiful stones. Last summer when he was off sick, he helped her to plant a Siberian rose. He wonders if it has survived the winter. He likes to sit on the veranda with Bylund and listen to her stories about all the cats lying there in her garden.

As he stands there thinking, Bylund turns up at his side. She hands him a mug of coffee.

He does not want her to go back inside, so he says, "Tell me about Tigge-Tiger again."

Like a little child, he wants to hear his favorite fairytale.

"What can I say?" Bylund begins. "He was my very first cat. I wasn't a cat person in those days. Mattias was fifteen, and he kept going on about how we ought to get ourselves a cat. Or at the very least a canary. Anything at all. But I said, 'Certainly not!' But then that gray-striped cat started visiting us. We lived in Bangatan at the time. I didn't let him in, obviously, but every day when I came home from work he was sitting on the gate-post. Meowing. Enough to break your heart. It was late autumn, and he was as thin as a rail."

"Some people are awful," Stålnacke growled. "They acquire a cat, then abandon it."

"I went around to the neighbors, knocking on doors, but nobody admitted to knowing anything about it. And it kept on following me wherever I went. If I was in the laundry room, it would sit on the window ledge outside, staring at me. If I was in the kitchen, it would sit on a decorative pedestal we had in the garden, glaring at me. It would jump up onto the front door, clinging onto the ledge over the window, meowing. It was driving me mad. The house was under siege. Every day when I came home from work I would think to myself, I hope to God it's not there again.

"Mattias came home late one evening. The cat was sitting out-side, meowing, really crying its eyes out. 'Can't we let him in,

Mother?' Mattias said. I gave in. 'Go on then,' I said. 'But he'll have to live downstairs with you. He'll be your cat.' Fat chance! That cat followed me wherever I went. He always sat on my knee. Only very rarely on Mattias's. But then Mattias moved out, and I sometimes went away on vacation. Then the cat would sit the whole evening, staring at Örjan. After three or four days he would eventually sit on Örjan's knee. But then when I came back home, like that time I'd been in Morocco—I'll never forget it— he slapped me with his paw, gave me a really solid smack, to show how angry he was."

"You had abandoned him, after all," Stålnacke says.

"Yes. Then all was forgiven. But before we got to that stage, he kept on smacking me. I remember when Örjan was depressed and in no state to do anything. Between us Tigge-Tiger and I built the May Day bonfire. He spent all day with me in the garden, working away. Then we sat together, gazing into the flames. And he was a terrific acrobat. When he wanted to come indoors in the evening he would cling onto the gutter with his front paws and swing toward the window, sort of knocking on it. So we'd open the window, and he would jump down onto the top of the frame and then into the house. I had lots of potted plants and cut flowers in vases on the window ledges, but he never knocked over a single one. Never ever."

They sit in silence for a while, looking at the birch tree under which Tigge-Tiger is buried.

"And then he grew old and died," Bylund says. "He turned me into a cat person."

"You grow attached to them," Stålnacke says.

Then Bylund takes hold of his hand. As if to demonstrate that she is attached to him.

"Life is too short for arguing and falling out," she says.

Stålnacke squeezes her hand. He knows she is right. But what is he going to do about that lump of anger lodged permanently in his chest?

8:32 p.m.: "You have reached Måns Wenngren at Meijer & Ditzinger. I can't take your call right now. Please leave a message after the beep."

Martinsson: "Hi, it's me. Just wanted to say I'm thinking about you and love you to bits. Call me when you can."

She looks at Vera, who is having a pee outside the front door. It is still light, a bright spring evening. She can hear the chuckling call of a curlew. She is not the only one pining for love.

"Why does life have to be so complicated?" she asks the dog.

9:05 p.m.: *Text from Rebecka Martinsson to Måns Wenngren:*
"Hi, sweetheart. Sitting here, reading up on murder investigation. Would rather be slipping into bed with you. Be nice to me, my love."

She puts her phone on the toilet lid and turns on the shower. Gives Vera a thorough rinse to follow up her shampoo.

"Stop all this rolling around in muck," she scolds her. "Is that clear?"

Vera licks her hands. It is clear enough.

11:16 p.m.: *"You have reached Måns Wenngren at Meijer & Ditzinger. I can't take your call right now. Please leave a message after the beep."*

Martinsson hangs up without leaving a message. She gives Vera some food.

"I don't deserve to be punished," she says.

Vera comes over to her and dries her mouth on Martinsson's pants.

4:36 a.m.: Martinsson wakes up and reaches for her phone. No message from Måns. No missed call. Documents concerning the murder investigation are scattered all around her on the bed. Vera is lying at the foot, snoring.

It's okay, she says to herself and makes a hushing noise into the darkness. You can go to sleep now.

wednesday, April 29

At 6:05 in the morning Rebecka Martinsson called Anna-Maria Mella. Mella answered in a low voice, so as not to wake Robert. Robert snuggled up behind her and fell asleep again, his warm breath fanning the back of her neck.

"I read the notes you made after talking to Johannes Svarvare," Martinsson said.

"Mmm."

"You recorded that he gave the impression of wanting to say something, but that he cut the interview short by lying down on the sofa and closing his eyes."

"Yes, although he first took out his false teeth and tossed them into a glass."

Martinsson laughed.

"Is it okay with you if I ask him to put his teeth back in and have a word with me?"

Mella vacillated between two reactions. Of course they would need to interview Svarvare again. She felt annoyed at not having reached that conclusion herself, and even more annoyed because Martinsson wanted to repeat the interrogation Mella had already done. But at the same time she realized that Martinsson was phoning her as a peacemaking gesture. That was decent of her. Martinsson was good. Mella decided not to sulk.

"That'll be fine," she said. "When I spoke to him we were still investigating what looked like an accidental death with a few details that needed clarifying."

"You wrote that he had been talking to Wilma, and had told her more than he ought to have."

"Yes."

Mella began to feel uneasy. She really had handled that interrogation badly.

"But he didn't say anything about what they actually discussed?"

"No. I suppose I ought to have pressed him, though I'm not sure how, but like I said, it wasn't a murder investigation then."

She fell silent.

Don't start making excuses, she told herself.

"Hey," Martinsson said, "you handled the situation extremely well. You made all these notes. Observed that there seemed to be something else he wanted to say. Okay, so we know what we need to concentrate on in round two, now that we've established what this case is really about."

"Thank you," Mella said.

"It's me who should be thanking you."

"For what?"

"For trusting me to go talk to him."

"I can always conduct round three, if necessary. When are you going to see him?"

"Now."

"Now? But it's only . . ."

"Yes, but you know what old people are like. When they finally get the chance to get the night's sleep they've always longed for, they wake up at four in the morning."

"I hope you're right."

"I am. I'm sitting in my car outside his house. He just looked out at me from behind his kitchen curtain for the third time."

"She's crazy," Mella said when she had hung up.

"Who?" Robert said as he caressed her breasts.

"Rebecka Martinsson. She's taken over the investigation. I like the woman, for Christ's sake—I mean, I saved her life back there in Jiekajärvi; that does things to you. And she's fun to talk to when she relaxes. Even if we are very different. She's a damn good prosecutor."

Robert kissed the back of her neck, and pressed his lower body against her backside.

Mella sighed.

"I suppose I'm annoyed because she seems to be taking everything over. I'd really prefer to run this case myself."

"She needs to realize that you're an alpha female," Robert said, squeezing her nipples.

"Yes," she said.

"Didn't you read a book recently? What was it called—*There's a Special Place in Hell for Women Who Don't Help Each Other?*"

"No, you're thinking of *There's a Special Place in Hell for Men Who Don't Have the Sense to Take Their Wives' Side in an Argument*. Hey, where do you think you're going with this?"

"I don't know," he said softly into her ear. "Where does the alpha bitch want me to go with it?"

Svarvare offered Martinsson a cup of coffee to start the day. Declining his best china, she asked for a mug instead. And accepted his offer of a sandwich. He smelled dirty the way old men do; hygiene was evidently not his strong point. He was wearing a vest under a knitted cardigan. A pair of black pants, very shiny at the rear, held up by suspenders. She could not suppress the feeling that she did not want to put anything in her mouth that he had touched. When had he last washed his hands? She shuddered at the thought that the fingers he had used to hold his false teeth had also been in contact with the bread and whatever he had put into the sandwich.

But then again I can allow a dog I have never seen before to lick my mouth, she thought.

She smiled and looked down at Vera, who was sniffing around under the kitchen table, gulping down scraps of food and crumbs, and licking the legs of the bench where something had trickled down and dried up.

Including you, you filthy little pig! she thought. I must be out of my mind.

"You knew Wilma, is that right?" she said.

"Yes, of course," Svarvare said, downing half his mug of coffee.

There are questions he is dreading that I might ask, Martinsson thought. I'll start with the easy ones.

"Can you tell me a bit about her?"

He seemed surprised. Relieved at the same time.

"She was so young," Svarvare said, shaking his head. "Much too young. But you know, it's a good thing if youngsters come to a village like this one. And when she moved in with Anni, Simon Kyrö also started to come and visit his uncle. The whole place seemed to come to life. Those of us who live here are all old-timers. But she and her friends—well, they looked like . . ."

He held up both hands and bent his fingers to look like claws, and made a face intended to be frightening.

"Black all around their eyes, and black clothes. But they were fun. And there was no harm in them. Once they borrowed kick-sleds from us old-timers and went racing around the village. There must have been ten of them. Careering around and shouting and laughing. Taking it in turns to give the others rides. Like a flock of crows. They say that young people nowadays just sit around indoors and gape at computers. Not her."

"Did she visit you sometimes?"

"Oh yes, often. She liked to hear me going on about the old days. It's not the old days for me, of course; everything seems to have happened quite recently. You'll understand what I mean

one of these days. It's only your body that grows old. Inside here
I feel . . ."

He tapped the side of his forehead and grinned.

". . . like a seventeen-year-old."

"Did you tell her anything you regret having told her?"

He fell silent. Stared at a deep scratch in the middle of the
kitchen table.

"You liked her, I think?"

He nodded.

"She was murdered, as you know. She and Simon went diving,
and someone made sure they never came back up again. At any
rate, *she* never came back up again. Strictly speaking the boy's
still missing, but presumably he's somewhere in Vittangijärvi."

"I thought they found her in the Torne, downstream from
Tervaskoski?"

"Yes, they did. But she'd been moved there. Don't you think
you owe it to her to tell me what's nagging at you?"

He stared at the scratch on the table.

"You should let sleeping dogs lie," he said.

Martinsson's hand shot out of its own accord and covered
the scratch in the table.

"But sometimes those sleeping dogs wake up," she said. "And
now Wilma's dead. I think you're an honorable man. Think of
Wilma. And Anni Autio."

Her last remark was a gamble. She had no idea what sort of a
relationship he had with Anni Autio.

He poured himself some more coffee. She noticed that he
placed his left hand over his right one in order to keep it steady.

"Well," he said. "But don't tell anybody I said anything, mind.
I told Wilma about an airplane that had been missing since
1943. It came down somewhere. I've spent ages thinking about
that airplane. Wondering where it might have crashed. I told

Wilma I thought it must have come down either in Vittangi-järvi, Harrijärvi, or Övre Vuolusjärvi."

"What kind of a plane was it?"

"I don't know, I never saw it. But it was German. The Germans had big storage depots in Luleå. One of them was right next to the cathedral. Oberleutnant Walther Zindel was in charge of them. The German troops in the north of Norway and Finnish Lapland needed weapons and food supplies, of course, and so the Germans used the port of Luleå in the north of Sweden. Their fleet was inferior to the British one, so they didn't dare rely on supplies reaching them via the Norwegian coast."

"I know, of course, that they were allowed to use our railway network," Martinsson said slowly. "For transporting troops going on leave and coming back again."

Sucking hard at his dentures, Svarvare eyed her up and down as if she were mentally deficient.

"Well, yes," he said. "Anyway, Isak Krekula was a hauler. I left school at the age of twelve and started working for him. I was strong, and I could carry things and load trucks. I also did a bit of driving now and then—they weren't so strict about it in those days. Anyway, that evening in the autumn of 1943, Isak drove one of his trucks to Kurravaara, and I went with him. Swedish Railways had stopped transporting German troops that summer, so we were never short on work—not that we had been before, come to think of it. The troops had to be provided for. So we sat there, waiting and waiting. There was me, Isak, and some of the guys from the village he'd hired to help with the unloading and reloading. But we gave up when morning came and nothing had happened. Isak paid one of the village men to stay and look out for the plane, and to call if it turned up. But it seemed to have been gobbled up somewhere. Isak heard eventually that nobody knew what had happened to it. But you know, people didn't talk about that sort of thing. Not then, and certainly not now. It was sensitive, you see."

How sensitive? Martinsson wondered. Sufficiently sensitive for two young people to be killed to prevent gossip starting up again? Surely that could not be possible?

"It's so long ago," Svarvare said. "It happened, and now it's in the past. Nobody wants to remember what went on. And before long all those who can will be dead and buried. The girls who used to stand by the railway lines and wave to the German soldiers in the trains on their way up to Narvik, all those who celebrated the arson attack on the *Norrskensflamman* in 1940—you know, the attack on the Communist, anti-German newspaper based in Luleå—and all those who fraternized with the Germans stationed in the north. And my God, you should have seen the fuss in support of the German consul Weiler—all the miners who were excused from military service because we were selling steel to Germany, they were all in favor of that. It was only afterward that they started going on about how we had to do it because we'd have had our throats slit if we didn't. Let's face it, even the king was a sympathizer."

Svarvare wiped away a drop of coffee that had trickled down the side of his mouth.

"I just thought it might be exciting for the kids to go looking for a wrecked airplane."

Martinsson thought for a moment.

"You asked me not to tell anybody that you'd been speaking to me," she said. "To whom shouldn't I say anything? Are you frightened of anybody in particular?"

Svarvare took his time, then sat up straight and looked her straight in the eye.

"The Krekulas," he said. "Isak has always been keen to jump in with both feet no matter what. He'd be quite capable of

setting fire to a house while the occupants were asleep. And
the boys follow in his footsteps. They were so put out when
I said I'd told Wilma about that plane. All that was done and
finished with, they reckoned. I've been working for them for
God only knows how many years, helped them with anything
that cropped up. I was always on call. Always. And then they
come here and . . ."

His hand dropped down on the table like a period at the end
of a sentence. Vera, who had been lying under the table, woke
up with a bark.

"Why? Was there something special about that plane?"

"I don't know. You've got to believe me. I've told you everything I know. Do you think that the Krekulas had something
to do with Wilma's death?"

"Do you think so?"

His eyes filled with tears.

"I should never have said anything to her. I just wanted to
make myself interesting. I wanted her to think it was fun to talk
to me. It's no fun, damn it all, being on my own all the time. It's
all my fault."

Once outside again, Martinsson took a deep breath.

As Strindberg said, she thought, you have to feel sorry for
people. I don't want to die alone.

She looked at Vera, who was standing expectantly by the car.

Dogs are not enough, she thought.

She switched on her phone. Ten past seven. No messages. No
missed calls.

Screw you then, was her unsent message to Måns Wenngren.
Screw some other woman if you want to.

*I'm sitting on Hjalmar's window ledge. Watching him as he wakes
up with a start. Worry is pounding away inside him. That worry is*

sinewy and has fists as hard as his father's. That worry has pulled his leather belt out of its loops.

He's sleeping a lot now. He's tired. Doesn't feel up to doing anything at all. But sleep is spasmodic and unreliable. Worry drags him to his feet. Usually at about three or four in the morning. It's light during the night now. Hjalmar curses the light, and tells himself that's why. But he knows the truth. His heart is racing. Sometimes he's afraid it will be the death of him. But he's started to get used to it. Knows his heart will calm down after a while.

Just think: I shall never, ever sleep again.

Hjalmar dreams about me sometimes. How I hacked a hole in the ice from underneath. He dreams about the water squirting out through the hole when I stuck my hand through it. In his dream more and more water comes spurting out, and he drowns in it. He wakes up, gasping for breath.

Sometimes he dreams that my hand clamps itself like a vise around his, and that I drag him down into the water.

He dreams about thin ice. Ice that gives way beneath him. Black water.

He doesn't have the strength to look after himself properly. He looked a right mess at my funeral. He hadn't had a shower for ages, and his hair was greasy.

Hjalmar Krekula checked the time on his cell phone: 7:10. He ought to have been at work ages ago. But Tore Krekula had not phoned to ask where the devil he was.

But maybe it was only fair to have a day off when you had helped to . . . No, he dismissed all thoughts and images involving Hjörleifur Arnarson. Pointless. The whole business was so damn pointless.

I'm used to doing whatever Tore wants me to do, Hjalmar thought. I was forced to do it at first. But then it became a habit.

No doubt it all goes back to when we got lost in the forest. I stopped thinking for myself. Making my own mind up. I just did as I was told.

It is October 1957. A Saturday. The older boys from the village are playing bandy on the ice covering the lake.

Tore Krekula asks his dad if he can go and watch. Yes, of course he can. He takes his bandy stick and sets off. Hjalmar Krekula is also going to watch, but first he has to carry firewood and water to the sauna down by the lake. Isak Krekula makes the sauna so hot that there is a danger of burning the whole place down. Tonight they are going to have a bath. He has sawn through the ice down by the jetty and made a hole so that Hjalmar Krekula can carry water up to the big tub that is heated by a wood fire.

Hjalmar Krekula does all the heavy stuff. Tore Krekula is excused, even though he has started school this autumn. On the first day of term Isak Krekula took Hjalmar by the ear and told him: "It's your job to look after your brother, is that clear?"

It is just over a year since the incident in the forest. Tore Krekula is still receiving letters and parcels—but less often, of course. His new bookbag is a present from the Friends of the Forest Club in Stockholm.

Hjalmar Krekula looks after Tore Krekula. That means that Tore Krekula rules the roost over his classmates, even the older pupils. Tore Krekula steals their money, threatens them, and decides which of his classmates is going to be beaten up after school every day. He concludes that it is going to be a skinny little boy with glasses by the name of Alvar. If anybody objects, or even hits back, Tore Krekula calls Hjalmar Krekula. Alvar has an older brother, but nobody wants to get involved in a fight with Hjalmar Krekula, so he doesn't intervene. Tore

Krekula and his mates have a lot of fun with Alvar. During the last lesson of the day, one of them might put up his hand and ask permission to go to the bathroom. When the bell rings, Alvar finds that his shoes are full of water. Or perhaps the sleeves of his jacket are crammed full of wet paper. After PE, they sometimes steal his pants so that he has to go home in his underwear. Alvar is frightened all the time. He runs home from school. He begs his teacher to let him go before the bell rings. Tells her he has stomachache. That is no doubt true. He comes home to his mother with his clothes and schoolbooks a mess, but he does not dare tell her who is responsible. His older brother says nothing either.

That is what Tore Krekula is really like, the little hero of the forest from Piilijärvi. But needless to say, the Friends of the Forest Club in Stockholm know nothing at all about it.

Hjalmar Krekula has carried all the necessary water and firewood to the sauna, ready for the evening's ablutions, so he can run to the other end of the village and watch the bandy match. They are using birch branches as goalposts. Not all of them have skates; some just have to run around in their ordinary shoes. Most of the bandy sticks are homemade.

Tore Krekula cheers up when he sees Hjalmar Krekula approaching, although he pretends he has not seen him. Hjalmar Krekula has the feeling that something stupid is about to happen. Something tells him he ought to go back home right away. But he does not.

Hans Aho shoots at the goal, but Yngve Talo makes a save. Someone tries to intercept the pass out, and there is a scrum inside the penalty area.

Tore Krekula takes the opportunity to jump down onto the ice with his stick and bandy ball. He hits the ball into the empty goal at the other end.

"What the hell do you think you're doing?" shouts the goalie, who has been upfield in support of his team's attack.

"Get off the ice, Tore," one of the girls in the crowd of spectators shouts.

But Tore Krekula does not listen. The goalie skates back and tells him again to get off.

Tore Krekula grins and leaves the ice, but he soon returns, dribbling the ball.

The game comes to a halt. The boys tell Tore Krekula to stop messing around and go home. Tore Krekula asks if they own the lake. Nobody has told him that they do.

"Hjalmar," he shouts. "Does this crowd own the lake? Have you heard anything about it?"

When the big boys are playing, the little boys keep out of the way. That is an unwritten law.

The bandy players look over at Hjalmar Krekula. A few are about the same age as he; most are older. They want to see if he is going to join in the sabotage. Everyone knows that the Krekula brothers stick together. Not that Hjalmar Krekula would stand a chance against the combined bandy teams, but the fact that he is outnumbered does not usually put him off. Everyone is wondering how serious the fight is going to be.

Hjalmar Krekula is furious. That damn Tore! Why does he always have to stir up trouble unnecessarily? But this time he can sort things out for himself. Hjalmar Krekula turns away and gazes out over the lake.

The bandy players register the signal. Hjalmar Krekula is not going to get involved.

One of them, Torgny Ylipää, who has been sick to death of Tore Krekula's antics for a long time, gives him a dig in the chest.

"Go home to Mommy," he says.

Tore Krekula hits him back. Hard. Ylipää falls over backward.

"Go home yourself," Tore Krekula says.

Ylipää is soon back on his feet. Tore Krekula raises his bandy stick, but one of the other boys grabs hold of it and prevents the blow. Ylipää seizes his chance and punches Tore Krekula in the nose.

"Go home, I said."

Tore Krekula starts crying. Maybe his nose is bleeding. Nobody is able to see. He runs away, clutching his face. He leaves his stick on the ice. One of the players picks it up and moves it to one side.

"Shall we keep going, then?"

They resume playing.

It only takes a quarter of an hour. Isak Krekula appears. He walks straight across the bandy pitch to Hjalmar Krekula. White with fury. The game stops again, and now all the players and spectators watch as Isak Krekula grabs hold of his elder son and drags him away without a word. He holds him firmly by the collar.

Isak Krekula utters not a word as he drags his son along the road through the village. But his heavy breathing reflects his fury as they reach the house. Hjalmar Krekula is scared stiff as his father frog-marches him down to the sauna. What on earth is he going to do?

"Father," he says. "Wait a minute. Father."

But Isak Krekula tells him to hold his tongue. He is not interested in explanations.

They are down at the jetty now. By the hole in the ice from which Hjalmar Krekula extracted a few buckets of water less than an hour ago.

Isak Krekula pulls off his son's wool hat and throws it onto the shore. Hjalmar Krekula struggles, but the grip on his coat collar has grown tighter. His father forces him down onto his knees at the edge of the hole, and the next thing he knows, his head is underwater.

He struggles with his arms. The cold threatens to explode his head. He is strong, and manages to raise himself up and gasp for air, but his father soon subdues him again.

I'm going to die now, he thinks.

And he does. Sunshine flows into his head. It is a warm summer's day. He is walking barefoot through the forest; pinecones and needles stick into his feet, but his soles are hardened. His task is to bring home the horses from their summer pasture. There they are, in among the pine trees, rubbing their necks against each other. Flicking away troublesome flies with their tails. There is a smell of wild rosemary and soil warmed by the sun. Bark, moss, resin. Ants are marching across the path in front of him. The horses whinny a greeting when they see him.

When he comes to his senses, he is lying on the floor of the dressing room in the sauna. The fire is burning in the grate. He raises himself on all fours and throws up lake water. Then he lies down on his back.

Isak Krekula is standing over him, smoking a cigarette.

"In our family we stick together," he says. "Remember that next time."

Rebecka Martinsson opened the heavy doors of the town hall. She enjoyed the feel of the attractive handles, carved in the shape of shamans' drums.

Once inside she admired the spacious hall with its high ceiling, its beautiful brick walls, and the *Sun Drum* tapestry, resplendent in the colors of summer and autumn.

She reported to the reception desk.

"I need to consult the town archives," she said to the young duty officer.

She was asked to wait a moment. After a while a man appeared, dressed in black jeans and a black jacket. His shoes were highly polished brown leather. His hair dark and combed back from his face.

"Jan Viinikainen. I'm in charge of the archives," he said, shaking Martinsson's hand. "What can I do to be of assistance to the police?"

Martinsson raised an eyebrow.

"Oh," Viinikainen said, "you're a celebrity here in Kiruna. There was a lot written about you when you killed those pastors. Self-defense, I know."

Martinsson overcame her instinct to turn on her heel and leave.

He doesn't understand, she thought. People don't understand; they think they can say whatever they like without hurting my feelings.

"I'm not sure what I'm looking for," she said hesitantly. "I want to know everything about an old firm in Piilijärvi, Krekula's Hauling Contractors."

Viinikainen shrugged, stretching out his hands in a gesture suggesting helplessness.

"How old?" he asked.

"They started in the forties or thereabouts. I need everything you've got."

Viinikainen stood there and thought for a while. Then he beckoned to Martinsson to follow him. Descending a spiral staircase to the basement, they passed what must have been Viinikainen's office just outside the white-painted wrought-iron gate into the archives. Unlocking the entrance to the holy of holies and making a sweeping gesture, he invited Martinsson to precede him through the gate.

They passed by row after row of archive shelves made of gray steel. Wherever Martinsson looked there were files of different

shapes and sizes with cloth, plastic, or metal binding. Paperback books, hardcover books, old manuscripts neatly and pret-
tily packaged using string and wax seals that hung down over
the edges of the shelves. On top of heavy oak document cupboards were old-fashioned manual typewriters. Card index files
were crammed alongside archival boxes made of brown cardboard. Here and there were paper scrolls in every imaginable
size. In one of the interior rooms there were sliding archive
shelves made of steel. Viinikainen switched on the mechanism
that controlled their movements.

"You can slide the shelves apart like this," he said, pulling at
a long black lever with a knob on the end and making the shelf
he was standing by slide slowly to one side. "If I were you I'd
start with the trade register, or possibly the *Swedish Commercial
Directory*. You'll find material from the Kiruna Technical Office
over there."

Martinsson took off her coat and hung it up. Viinikainen
withdrew to his desk.

Talk about looking for a needle in a haystack, she thought.
I've no idea what I'm after. She wandered around, examining
the shelves, glancing at the articles on phrenology from the thirties and forties, payment records from Jukkasjärvi's Poor Relief
Board, handicraft diaries from the Kiruna School archives.

Stop whining, she told herself. Roll up your sleeves.

Seventy minutes later she found Krekula's Hauling Contractors in a register of haulers in Kiruna municipality, listing how
many and what kind of vehicles they had, persons authorized to
sign on the firm's behalf, addresses, and so on.

She searched assiduously, untied bundles that hadn't
been opened for sixty years, opened archival boxes that had been
closed for just as long, turned up her nose when little clouds
of dust wafted up from the documents. In the end she had a

splitting headache from all the dust and cellulose she'd been breathing in.

Viinikainen appeared and asked how she was doing.

"Quite well," she said. "I've found a few things, at least."

Vera was waiting in the car. She stood up in her cage, wagging her tail affectionately when Martinsson got in.

"Thank you for being patient," Martinsson said. "Let's go for a spin."

She drove up Mount Luossavaara and let Vera out. The dog sat down immediately.

"I'm sorry, old girl," Martinsson said guiltily.

"Bad conscience, eh?" a voice said behind her.

It was Krister Eriksson. He was in his jogging clothes. An orange windbreaker clashed with the pink parchment-like texture of his face.

When he smiled at Martinsson, she noticed his teeth. They were white and even. The only aspect of his face that was not damaged by fire.

"Well, well, who's this then?" he said, looking at Vera. "Tintin's going to be jealous."

"It's Hjörleifur Arnarson's dog. I had to take her on, otherwise she'd have been given a one-way ticket to canine heaven."

Eriksson nodded solemnly.

"And you've taken over the investigation, I gather. Wilma Persson will be pleased."

"I don't believe in all that stuff," Martinsson said, embarrassed.

He shook his head and winked.

"Have you been out jogging?" she said, changing the subject.

"Yep. I generally exercise my back by running up the hill to the old mine entrance. I've just finished."

Martinsson looked up at the abandoned structure at the top of the mountain, gray and hollow-eyed.

If buildings can be ghosts, then that one certainly is, she thought. No doubt it says boo to whoever dares to walk past it at night.

"Pretty impressive, isn't it?" Eriksson said, as if he had read her thoughts. "Would you like to take a closer look? I could do with a bit more exercise to ease my muscles. Hang on a minute. I'll get my tracksuit from the car."

He came back wearing a cheap mint-green tracksuit that looked at least twenty years old and a veteran of goodness knows how many sessions in the washing machine.

My God, Martinsson thought. But perhaps he feels he looks so hideous anyway that he couldn't care less about the clothes he wears. It's a pity, she thought as he walked up the mountain a few paces in front of Vera, teasing her.

He was thin and in pretty good shape; he would look good in practically any clothes he chose to wear. Though not a tracksuit that looked like it had been discarded by an aerobics instructor circa 1989.

"What are you smiling at?" he said cheerfully.

"The view," she lied impulsively. "I love this mountain. What a magnificent panorama!"

They stopped and looked down at Kiruna, spread out below them. The iron mine with its gray terraces forming the background to the town. The Ädnamvaara massif to the northwest, with its typical pyramid-shaped peaks. The wind generators on the site of the abandoned Viscaria copper mine. The church faced with spruce cladding painted Falun red, designed to evoke a Lappish hut. The town hall with its iconic black clock tower—an iron shell with protruding decorations. It always reminded Martinsson of mountain birches in winter, or a flock of reindeer horns. The horseshoe-shaped railway depot with its little red-painted workers' cottages. The tower blocks in Gruv-vägen and Högalidsgatan.

"Look at that! You can see the Kebnekaise massif today." He pointed to the light blue mountain range in the northwest. "I can never work out which one is Kebne," he said. "I'm told it's not the one that looks the highest."

She pointed. He leaned toward her in order to see what she was pointing at.

"That's Tuolpagorni," she said. "The peak with the little crater. And the one next to it, to the right, is Kebne."

He moved away from her.

"Please forgive me," he said. "I'm leaning all over you, stinking of sweat."

"No problem," she said, and felt a wave of emotion surge through her body.

"The highest mountain in Sweden," he said enthusiastically, screwing up his eyes and gazing at the massif.

"The most beautiful building in Sweden, dating from 2001," Martinsson said, pointing at the church.

"The most beautiful building in Sweden, dating from 1964," Erkisson said, pointing at the town hall.

"The most beautiful town in Sweden," she said with a laugh. "The municipal architect really tried his best to make the town a work of art. In those days they still designed towns so that a network of streets all led to the square and the town hall. But the streets of Kiruna were allowed to wander along the hillside as they pleased."

"I can't get my head around the fact that they're talking about moving the whole town."

"Nor can I. Haukivaara was such a perfect mountainside to build a town on."

"But if the seam of iron ore turns out to run under the town . . ."

". . . then the town has to move."

"That's what the authorities say," Eriksson said. "I don't come from Kiruna myself. But I have the impression that the locals aren't too worried. When I ask them what they think about the town having to move, they just shrug their shoulders. My next-door neighbor is eighty, and she thinks that of course the town ought to move to the west because that way she'd be closer to the shops. I think it's all very odd. The only person who seems to have a view is someone who'll be dead and buried when the move actually takes place."

"I think people are concerned," Martinsson said hestitantly. "But the people of Kiruna have always been aware that the only reason we're here is that this is where the iron ore is. And if the mine isn't profitable any more, then we've no income to live off. So if the company needs to move the mine, well, there's nothing to argue about. So we accept the inevitable. But if we accept it, don't be misled into thinking that we don't care."

"But one thing doesn't exclude the other."

"No, I know. But I think we need time before we understand what it's really all about. Before we realize that although we have no choice, we can still regret that our town will never be the same again."

"There ought to be farewell concerts in the buildings that will be demolished," Eriksson said. "Weeping ceremonies. Music. Lectures. Storytelling."

"I'll be there," Martinsson said with a smile.

She remembered what it had been like when she'd walked up Mount Luossavaara with Måns Wenngren. He had felt cold and uncomfortable. She would have liked to point out the sites to him and talk about them. As she was doing now.

Martinsson was sitting on the bench in Sivving Fjällborg's boiler room. She was wearing thick woolen socks and a knitted sweater that had once belonged to her father.

Fjällborg was standing over the stove wearing one of Maj-Lis's aprons that Martinsson had not seen before. It had blue and white stripes with frills around the bottom and the armholes.

He was heating up some smoked pike in a cast-iron pan. One of Maj-Lis's embroidered potholders was hanging from the handle. Almond potatoes were boiling in an aluminium saucepan.

"I need to make a phone call," Martinsson said. "Is that okay?"

"Ten minutes," Fjällborg said. "Then we'll eat."

Martinsson dialed Anna-Maria Mella's number. Mella answered immediately. A child could be heard crying in the background.

"Sorry," Martinsson said. "Is this a bad time?"

"No, not at all," Mella said with a sigh. "It's Gustav. I locked myself into the bathroom, hoping to read the latest issue of *Luxury Living* in peace and quiet. Now he's rattling the door handle and yelling hysterically. Hang on a minute."

"Robert!" she bellowed. "Can you see to your son!"

Martinsson could hear a high-pitched male voice urging: "Gustav, Gustav, come to Daddy!"

"Come on, it's obvious he's not going to— Pick him up and get him away from the door!" Mella yelled. "Before I slit my wrists!"

After a while Martinsson could hear that the screaming kid was being carried away from the bathroom door.

"That's better," Mella said. "Now we can talk."

Martinsson summed up what she had heard from Johannes Svarvare about the airplane, and how he felt threatened by the Krekula brothers.

"I think you were right from the start," Martinsson said. "It's the brothers."

Mella hummed in agreement to show that she was listening.

"I was at the archives this afternoon," Martinsson said. "To dig out a bit of information about the hauling business."

"And?"

"I found a register of hauling contractors in Kiruna municipality. You know the kind of thing—how many vehicles were owned by the firm and how many drivers they employed. In 1940 Krekula's Hauling Contractors had two trucks, by 1942 they had four, by 1943 eight, and by 1944 eleven."

"Really? Wow!"

"Yes, their business expanded impressively during those years. By nearly five hundred percent. And they acquired five refrigerated vans during the same period. When I compared them with other hauling companies, none of them expanded anywhere near as much."

"Really?"

"Isak Krekula was on very good terms with the German army. There's nothing odd about that—lots of firms were. In Luleå, for instance, the Germans had enormous depots for weapons and provisions. Transport was needed to move all the stuff to the eastern front. I found a copy of a contract between the German army and Swedish Road Freight Center Limited. German soldiers were freezing to death in Finnish Lapland during the winter of 1941–42, and the German military attaché in Sweden ordered wooden huts from Swedish manufacturers. And so of course they also needed contracts with transport companies to carry those huts to the eastern front. That's what the SRFC contract was all about. So that winter there was nonstop shuttle traffic between the north of Sweden and the eastern front. Isak Krekula's hauling firm was one of the signatories to the contract between the SRFC and the German army. The contract was approved by the Foreign Ministry and the Swedish government."

"I see," Mella said, trying to resist the temptation to read an article about storage in her magazine.

"Once all the huts had been transported, deliveries continued to be made to the German front line. Including weapons, although there was nothing about that in the SRFC contract. And what's more," Martinsson continued, "I found a letter from Oberleutnant Walther Zindel, an army officer stationed in Luleå and in charge of the German depots in the region, to Martin Waldenström, the managing director of LKAB. In it Zindel asks for Isak Krekula to be released from his contract with the Kiruna mine concerning four trucks for transporting iron ore, so that they could be used by the German army in Finnish Lapland."

"Excuse me for being a bit slow on the uptake," Mella began.

"You're not slow on the uptake. All this doesn't necessarily mean a thing. But it's got me thinking. How come Isak Krekula's firm could grow so much more quickly than any of his competitors? A hauling firm was a lucrative business during the war. Obviously, everyone involved wanted to invest and expand. Where did Isak Krekula get all the money that enabled him to invest so much more than the others? It's just not possible for him to have earned so much from his hauling business alone— I mean, if that were the case, at least one or two of his competitors would have been able to expand at a similar rate. And my neighbor Sivving says that the Krekulas were farmers as far back as anybody can remember, so there's no money in the family."

"Are you suggesting he might have been doing something illegal?"

"Perhaps. He must have gotten the money from somewhere. And you have to ask where. And I wonder why Oberleutnant

Zindel asked the managing director of the mine to release Krekula from his three-year contract. Why Krekula? There were other haulers who had contracts with LKAB."

"So?"

"I don't know," Martinsson said. "I don't even know how to go about discovering what kind of a customer Isak Krekula was, or finding out about his dealings with Walther Zindel. In any case, it wouldn't be of any help to us. Even if we discovered that he was involved in dirty business with the Germans, that would have no bearing at all on whether Tore and Hjalmar Krekula had anything to do with the deaths of Wilma Persson and Simon Kyrö."

"Always assuming that Simon Kyrö is dead in fact," Mella said mechanically.

"Of course he's dead," Martinsson said impatiently. "We'll find him as soon as the ice on Vittangijärvi thaws."

"Hmm. I've been trying to keep an open mind. Might he have killed Wilma himself, for instance?"

"And then killed Hjörleifur Arnarson? Hardly, don't you think? Anyway, I reckon we should follow up on this line of investigation now—we don't have unlimited resources."

"We should probably just wait to see what develops," Mella said. "Hope that the forensic examination of Hjörleifur's body and his house, and the clothes Hjalmar and Tore Krekula were wearing, produce interesting results. And hope that we find the door and Simon Kyrö's body when the thaw comes, and that there are fingerprints on it, or something of the sort."

Clearing his throat, Fjällborg gave Martinsson a withering look.

"I've got to go," Martinsson said. "I'll see you at the meeting tomorrow."

"Johannes Svarvare told me that Isak Krekula had a heart attack just over a week before Wilma and Simon went missing,"

Mella said. "And when he said that, I had the impression that he wanted to say more, but was holding back for some reason."

"He's scared of them," Martinsson said.

"I can't help wondering if he had a heart attack because he'd heard that they were going to go diving to look for the plane. There's something about that damn plane. It's frustrating that the ice is melting, and that it's not possible to go diving there right now. We'll have to wait. I hate waiting."

"I hate waiting, too."

"So do I!" Fjällborg said, slamming the potato stew down on the table. "I hate waiting for food to get cold."

Mella laughed.

"What are you having to eat this evening?"

"Smoked pike."

"Smoked pike? I've never tried that."

"It's good! What are you having?"

"We've eaten already," Mella said. "Gustav was allowed to choose, so we had 'porky sausages.'"

"Hmm," Fjällborg said when Martinsson had hung up. "How's it going?"

"Not very well," Martinsson said. "I think the Krekula brothers are guilty, but . . ."

She shrugged.

"We'll have to hope the forensic examination turns up something good."

Fjällborg ate in silence. He had heard her talking about the Krekulas' hauling business and the Germans during the war. He knew exactly who Martinsson ought to talk to in order to get information about all that. But the question was, would that person be willing to talk?

≈≈≈

Måns Wenngren is sitting in his apartment in Floragatan. All the lights are out. The television is on, its flickering screen relieving the darkness. Some *Seinfeld* episode that he has seen before.

Martinsson has not called today. No text messages, nothing. The previous evening she had both texted and called him. He had not answered. She had left a message.

Now he regrets not having answered. But everything is arranged the way she wants it to be. She wants to live in Kiruna. She is busy with work and has no time to talk.

Yesterday. He had thought he would try to make it clear to her that he had no intention of playing the lovesick puppy, allowing her to trample all over him.

"Yes, I'm angry," he says to his empty apartment. "With good reason."

He puts down his phone. If there is no message from her tomorrow, he will call her.

"But I'm not going to say I'm sorry," he says out loud.

He longs to be with her. He imagines them back on good terms, imagines traveling up north to spend the weekend with her. He can take Friday off. He does not have any important meetings planned.

Thursday, April 30

A snowstorm was brewing. April in Kiruna. Martinsson woke up and all she could see through the window was the white, snow-laden wind howling around the house.

It was five thirty. She had just poured herself a cup of coffee when her cell phone rang. She could see from the display that it was Maria Taube, her former colleague at Meijer & Ditzinger. They had both worked for Måns Wenngren before Martinsson had moved back to Kiruna.

Pressing ANSWER, she gave a theatrical groan suggesting she was still half asleep.

"Oh dear!" Taube said. "I'm sorry! Did I wake you?"

Martinsson laughed.

"No, I was just teasing you. I've been up for some time."

"I knew you would be. You're a workaholic. It's okay to call you when everyone else is still asleep. But I thought that maybe the laid-back lifestyle of the northern Swedes we're always hearing about might have rubbed off on you."

"It has, but around here ladies of a certain age are up and about very early."

"Yes, I know how it is—first one up gets a medal. My aunts are like that; they sit at the dinner table competing to see who's been up longest. 'I woke up at five and thought I might as well get up and clean the windows.' 'I woke up at three thirty, but thought I'd force myself to stay in bed, so I didn't get up until four thirty.'"

"A bit like us, then," Martinsson said, taking a sip of coffee. "Are you at work already?"

"I'm on my way. And walking. Listen."

Martinsson could hear early birds singing.

"We've got a terrible snowstorm up here," she said.

"You're kidding! Down here all the cafés have set up their outdoor seating, and people are talking about how many tulips they've counted in their gardens in the country."

"Have you managed to go smell the tulips, my dear?"

"No, I haven't. I'm stuck in a rut, working myself to death and getting involved in destructive relationships."

"Better climb out of your rut," Martinsson said, sounding like a perky weather forecaster. "Your body can do other things; it's your mind that's getting in the way. Dare to do something different. Wear your watch on the other wrist. Have you tried walking backward today?"

"You really know how to torment a girl, you know," Taube said dejectedly. "I've actually read a book about mindfulness. It says that you've always got to practice compassion. I wonder if they've ever tried practicing compassion at Meijer & Ditzinger . . ."

"Is Måns being cruel and nasty?"

"Yes, he is in fact. Have you two had a fight or something? He's in such an awful mood. He flew into a rage yesterday because I'd forgotten to put Alea Finance on the list of firms allowed to make late payments."

"No, we haven't actually had a fight. But he's annoyed with me."

"Why? He's not allowed to be annoyed with you. It's your duty to keep him happy and well fed and satisfied so that he couldn't care less whether or not Alea Finance has to pay a late fee of five or six thousand. I mean, they have sales of two million. Not to mention the loss of prestige for M&D— I've heard the lecture before. Anyway, why is he annoyed with you?"

"He thinks I've been too reticent. And he doesn't like me set-tling in up here. What does he expect? Am I supposed to move in with him until he gets fed up with me and starts running off to the bar with the boys and screwing the trainee lawyers?"

Taube said nothing.

"You know I'm right," Martinsson said. "Some men and some dogs are just like that. It's only when you look the other way and signal that you're totally uninterested that they come running up to you wagging their tails."

"But he's in love with you," Taube said tamely.

She knew that Martinsson was right, though. It was good for Wenngren that Martinsson had moved up to Nowheresville. He was the sort of man who finds it hard to cope with an intimate relationship. Both she and Martinsson had seen him lose inter-est in attractive and gifted women who had simply become too attached to him.

"If he weren't like that," Taube said, "would you consider moving back here?"

"I think it would make me ill," Martinsson said, with no trace of humor in her voice.

"Stay there, then. You'll just have to have a hot long-distance relationship. There's nothing to beat a bit of longing for what you can't have."

"Exactly," Martinsson said.

Although I don't actually long to be with him any more, she told herself. I like him. I like it when he's here. It works well. I might sometimes miss the sex. I like sleeping in his arms. And now that he isn't getting in touch, I obviously feel scared of los-ing him. But I find it hard to cope with his restlessness after he's been up here for more than three days. When I start feeling that I need to think up some way of stopping him from getting into a bad mood. When he refuses to try to understand why I need to live here. And, now, when he's sulking. And refusing to answer his phone.

For a fleeting moment she wondered if she ought to ask Taube if she thought Wenngren had been with someone else. If there was a suitable candidate in the office.

But I'm damned if I will, she thought. In the old days I'd have been awake half the night, conjuring up all sorts of images in my mind's eye. But I don't have the strength now. I refuse to do that.

"I'm at the office now," Taube said, panting slightly. "Can you hear me walking up the stairs instead of taking the elevator?"

Martinsson was about to say, "You should keep asking yourself: What would Blossom Tainton have done?" But she could not keep the banter going any longer. They often spent ages on the phone joking like this. Presumably that was why both of them sometimes hesitated to call—things simply got out of control.

"Thank you for calling," she said instead, and meant it.

"I miss you," Taube panted. "Can we meet up the next time you come to Stockholm? That is, if you won't need to be on your back the entire time?"

"Who is it that always—"

"Yes, yes. I'll call. Love and kisses!" Taube said, and hung up.

Vera stood up and started barking.

Sivving Fjällborg's heavy footsteps were approaching the house. Bella was already scratching away at the front door.

Martinsson let her in. Bella immediately ran to Vera's food bowls in the kitchen. They were empty, but she licked them just to make sure, and growled at Vera, who held back at a respectful distance. When the bowls had been licked clean, they greeted each other and sparred playfully, ruffling the rag rugs in the process.

"What foul weather!" Fjällborg grunted. "The damn snow is coming at you sideways. Look at this!"

He removed snow from the front of his shoulders, where it had formed icy clumps.

"Mmm," Martinsson said. "Soon they'll be singing 'Sweet lovers love the spring' in Stockholm."

"Yes, yes," Fjällborg said impatiently. "Then they'll get beaten up in the streets as they make their way home from the May Day celebrations."

He did not like Martinsson comparing Stockholm and Kiruna to Stockholm's advantage. He was afraid of losing her to the metropolis again.

"Have you got a moment?" he asked.

Martinsson adopted an apologetic expression and was about to explain that she had to go to work.

"I wasn't going to ask you to clear away snow or anything like that," Fjällborg said. "But there's someone you ought to meet. For your own good. Or rather, for the good of Wilma Persson and Simon Kyrö."

Martinsson felt depressed the moment she and Fjällborg walked through the door of the Fjällgården nursing home. They brushed off as much snow as they could in the chicken yolk–colored stairwell, climbed the stairs, and walked across the highly polished gray plastic floor tiles. The plush painted wallpaper and neat, practical pine furniture cried out *institution*.

Two residents in wheelchairs were leaning forward over their breakfast in the kitchen. One of them was propped up with cushions to make sure he did not fall sideways. The other kept repeating, "Yes, yes, yes!" in an increasingly loud voice until an aide placed a calming hand on his shoulder. Fjällborg and Martinsson hurried past, trying not to look.

Please spare me this, Martinsson said to herself. Spare me from ending up in a dayroom with worn-out, incontinent old folk. Spare me from needing to have my ass wiped, from sitting parked in front of a television surrounded by staff with shrill voices and bad backs.

Fjällborg led the way as fast as he could along the corridor with doors on either side leading into individual rooms. He also seemed far from happy with what he was seeing.

"The man we're going to meet is called Karl-Åke Pantzare," he said quietly. "My cousin used to know him. They saw a lot of each other when they were young. I know he was a member of a resistance group during the war, and I know my cousin was a member as well—but he's dead now. It wasn't something he talked about. This is Pantzare's room."

He stopped in front of a door. There was a photo of an elderly man and a nameplate that announced: BULLET LIVES HERE.

"Just a minute," Fjällborg said, holding onto the rail running along the wall for the old folk still able to walk to hang on to. "I need to pull myself together."

He rubbed his hand over his face and took a deep breath.

"It's so damned depressing," he said to Martinsson. "Damn it to hell! And this is one of the better places. All the girls who work here are really friendly and caring—there are homes that are much worse. But even so! Is this what we have to look forward to? Promise to shoot me before I get to this stage. Oh dear, I'm sorry . . ."

"It's okay," Martinsson said.

"I forget, I'm afraid. I know you had no choice but to shoot—I mean, it's like talking about ropes in a house where a man's hanged himself."

"You don't need to censor yourself. I understand."

"I get so damned depressed," Fjällborg said. "Please understand that I think about this even though I try hard not to. Especially with my arm and all that." He nodded toward his dysfunctional side. The one that could not keep up. The side whose hand could not be trusted and kept dropping things.

"As long as I can . . ." Martinsson said.

"I know, I know." Fjällborg waved a hand dismissively.

"And why must places like this always have such cheerful names?" he hissed. "Hillside Garden, Mountain Lodge, Sunshine Hill, Rose Cottage."

Martinsson could not help laughing.

"Woodland Glade," she said.

"It sounds like a tract from the Baptists. Anyway, let's go in. You should be aware that his short-term memory is pretty bad. But don't be misled if he seems a bit confused. His long-term memory is fine."

Fjällborg knocked on the door and they entered.

Karl-Åke Pantzare had neatly combed white hair. His eyebrows and sideburns were bushy, with the stubbly, spiky hair typical of old men. He was wearing a shirt, pullover, and tie. His pants were immaculately clean and smartly pressed. It was obvious that earlier in his life he had been very good-looking. Martinsson checked his hands—the nails were clean and cut short.

Pantzare shook hands with both her and Fjällborg in a pleasant, friendly fashion. But behind his welcoming look was a trace of anxiety: Had he ever met these people before? Should he recognize them?

Fjällborg hurried to allay his uncertainty.

"Sivving Fjällborg," he said. "From Kurravaara. When I was a boy they used to call me Erik. Arvid Fjällborg is my cousin.

Or was. He's been dead for quite a few years now. And this is Rebecka Martinsson, the granddaughter of Albert and Theresia Martinsson. She's from Kurravaara as well. But you haven't met her before."

Pantzare relaxed.

"Erik Fjällborg," he said brightly. "Of course I remember you. But goodness me, you've aged a lot."

He winked to show that he was teasing.

"Ah, screw you," Fjällborg said, pretending to be offended. "I'm still a teenager."

"Of course," Pantzare said with a grin. "Teenager. That was a long time ago."

Fjällborg and Martinsson accepted the offer of a coffee, and Fjällborg reminded Pantzare of a dramatic ice-fishing session with Fjällborg's cousin and Pantzare on Jiekajaure.

"And Arvid used to tell me about how you cycled into town whenever there was a dance on a Saturday night. He said that the thirteen kilometers from Kurra to Kirra was nothing, but if you met a cute girl from Kaalasluspa, that meant you had to cycle back with her first, and it was a long way home from there. And then of course he had to be up at six the next morning to do the milking. He sometimes fell asleep on the milking stool. Uncle Algot would be furious with him."

The usual run-through of relatives they both knew followed. How a sister of Pantzare's had rented an apartment in Lahenperä. Fjällborg thought it was from the Utterströms, but Pantzare was able to inform him that it was in fact from the Holmqvists. How another of Fjällborg's cousins, a brother of Arvid's, and one of Pantzare's brothers had been promising skiers, had even competed in races in Soppero and beaten the outstanding Vittangi boys. They ran through who was ill. Who had died or moved to Kiruna, and, in those cases, who had taken over their childhood homes.

Eventually Fjällborg decided that Pantzare was sufficiently relaxed and that it was time to come to the point. Without beating around the bush, he said that he had heard from his cousin that both he and Pantzare had been members of the resistance organization in Norbotten. He explained that Martinsson was a prosecutor, and that two young people who had been murdered had been diving in search of a German airplane in Lake Vittangijärvi.

"I'll tell you straight, because I know it will go no further than these four walls, that there's reason to assume that Isak Krekula from Piilijärvi and his hauling business were mixed up in it somehow."

Pantzare's face clouded over.

"Why have you come to see me?"

"Because we need help," Fjällborg said. "I don't know anybody else who is familiar with how things were in those days."

"It's best not to talk about that," Pantzare said. "Arvid should never have told you. What could he have been thinking?"

Standing up, he took an old photograph album from a bookshelf.

"Have a look at this," he said.

He produced a newspaper cutting that had been hidden among the pages of the album. It was dated five years earlier. PENSIONERS ROBBED AND MURDERED ran the headline. The article described how a ninety-six-year-old man and his wife, aged eighty-two, had been murdered in their home just outside Boden. Martinsson glanced through it and was disgusted to read that the woman had been found with a pillow tied over her face. She had been beaten up, choked, and strangled, and "violated" after she died.

Violated, Martinsson thought. What do they mean by that?

As if he had read her thoughts, Pantzare said, "They shoved a broken bottle up her pussy."

Martinsson carried on reading. The man had been alive at six that morning when the district nurse had come to give his wife her insulin injection. He had been badly beaten, punched, and kicked, and died later in the hospital. According to the article, the police had conducted a door-to-door, but without success. As far as anybody knew, the couple had not kept significant sums of money or other valuables in their home.

"He was one of us," Pantzare said. "I knew him. And no damn way was this a robbery, I'm absolutely certain of that. They were neo-Nazis or some other gang of right-wing extremists who had discovered that he had been a member of the resistance. Nobody's safe, even though it was so long ago. Youngsters impress old Nazis by doing things like that. They made the old man watch while they beat his wife to death. Why would a robber want to violate her? They wanted to torture him. They're still looking for us. And if they find us . . ."

A shake of the head completed the sentence.

Of course he's scared, Martinsson thought. It's easier to risk your life when you're young, healthy, and immortal than when you're shut up in a place like this and all you can do is wait.

"We simply had to do something," Pantzare said, as if he were talking to himself. "The Germans were sending ship after ship to Luleå—lots of them never recorded in the port registers. Many of them left again with cargoes of iron ore, of course. And provisions and equipment and weapons and soldiers. The official line was that the soldiers were going on leave. The hell they were! I watched SS units marching on and off those ships. They took trains up to Norway, or were transported to the eastern front. We often considered sabotage, but that would have meant declaring war on our own country. After all it was Swedish customs officials and police officers and troops guarding the ports and depots and supervising the transports. If we'd been an occupied country, the whole situation would have been different. The Germans had far more problems in occupied Norway, with the local resistance movements and the inhospitable terrain, than in comparatively flat and so-called neutral Sweden."

"So what can you tell us about Isak Krekula and his hauling company?" Fjällborg said.

"I don't know. I mean, there were so many hauling contractors. But I do know that one of the hauling firm owners up here informed for the Germans. At least one, that is. We didn't know who it was, but we were told that it was a hauler. That got us nervous, because a large part of our work was building up and servicing Kari."

"What was that?" Martinsson said.

"The Norwegian resistance movement, XU, had an intelligence base on Swedish territory, not far from Torneträsk. It was called Kari. The radio station there was called Brunhild. Kari passed information from ten substations in northern Norway to London. It was powered by a wind turbine, but it was located in a hollow so you couldn't see it unless you came within fifteen meters of it."

"Are you saying that there was an intelligence base in Sweden?"

"There were several. Sepal bases on Swedish territory were run with the support of the British secret service and the American OSS, which eventually became the CIA. They specialized in intelligence, sabotage, and recruitment, and training in weapons, minelaying, and explosives."

"It was thanks to those services that the British were able to sink the *Terpitz*," Fjällborg said to Martinsson.

"Both the radio stations and the wind turbines had to be maintained," Pantzare said, "and they needed provisions and equipment. We needed haulers, and it was always a dodgy business initiating a new one, especially as we knew there was a hauler who was a German informer. My God, once a new driver—a man from Råneå—and I were on our way to Pältsa. We had a cargo of submachine guns. We took a shortcut via the Kilpisjärvi road, which the Germans controlled, and they stopped us at a roadblock. The driver suddenly started talking in German to the officer in charge. I thought he was informing on me; I didn't even know he could speak German, and I was about to leap out of the truck and run for my life. But the German officer just laughed and let us through, after we'd given him a few packs of cigarettes. The man had simply told him a joke. I chewed him out for that. He could have told me that he spoke German, after all! Although of course there were quite a few who could in those days. It was the first foreign language in Swedish schools. It had the same sort of status that English has now. Anyway, everything went well on that occasion."

Pantzare fell silent. A hunted look flitted across his face.

"Were there occasions when things didn't go so well?" Martinsson asked.

Pantzare reached for the photograph album and opened it to a particular page.

He pointed at a photograph that looked as if it had been taken in the 1940s. It was a full-length picture of a young man. He was leaning against a pine tree. It was summer. Sunlight was reflected in his curly blond hair. He was casually dressed in a shirt with the sleeves rolled up, and loose-fitting pants with the cuffs turned up untidily. He gripped his upper arm with one hand, while the other held a pipe.

"Axel Viebke," Pantzare said. "He was a member of the resistance group."

Sighing deeply, he continued.

"Three Danish prisoners of war escaped from a German cargo ship moored in Luleå harbor. They ended up with us. Axel's uncle owned a hut used at haymaking time to the east of Sävast. It was standing empty. He put them up there. They all died when the hut burned down. The newspapers called it an accident."

"What do you think really happened?" Fjällborg said.

"I think they were executed. The Germans discovered they were there and killed them. We never found out who had leaked the information."

Pantzare grimaced.

Martinsson took the photograph album and turned a page.

There was a picture of Viebke and Pantzare standing on each side of a pretty woman in a flowered dress. She was very young. A nicely trimmed lock of hair hung down over one eye.

"Here you are again," Martinsson said. "Who's the girl?"

"Oh, just some local he'd picked up," Pantzare said, without looking at the photograph. "He had a weakness for the girls, our Axel did. He was always with a different one."

Martinsson turned back to the photograph of Viebke by the pine tree. That page had been opened often; the edge was well-thumbed and darker than the others. The photographer's shadow was visible.

He's a charmer, she thought. He's really posing. Lolling back against the pine trunk, pipe in hand.

"Were you the photographer?" she said.

"Yes," Pantzare said, his voice sounding hoarse.

She looked around the room. Pantzare had no pictures of children hanging on the walls. There were no wedding photos among the framed ones on the bookshelf.

You did more than just like him, she thought, looking hard at Pantzare.

"He would have approved of you telling us about this," she said. "That you continued to be brave."

Pantzare nodded and his eyes glazed over.

"I don't know all that much," he said. "About the hauler in question, that is. The British said there was someone reporting to the Germans, and that we should watch our step. They were particularly concerned about the intelligence stations, of course. They called him the Fox. And there's no doubt that Isak Krekula was on good terms with the Germans. He made lots of shipments for them, and it has always been the money that counted as far as he was concerned."

"Pull yourself together!" Tore Krekula said.

He was standing in Hjalmar Krekula's bedroom looking at his brother, who was in bed with the covers over his head.

"I know you're awake. You're not ill! That's enough now!"

Tore Krekula opened the blinds with such force that it sounded as if the cords were going to snap. He wanted them to snap. It was snowing.

When Hjalmar Krekula had failed to turn up for work, his brother had taken the spare key and gone to his house. Not that a key was necessary. Nobody in the village locked their doors at night.

Hjalmar Krekula did not respond. Lay under the covers like a corpse. Tore Krekula was tempted to rip them off, but something held him back. He did not dare. The person lying there was unpredictable. It was as if a voice under the covers were saying, Give me an excuse, give me an excuse.

This was not the old Hjalmar Krekula who could be kicked around however you liked.

Tore Krekula felt helpless. This was an emotion he found difficult to handle. He was not used to people not doing as they were told. First that police bitch. Now Hjalmar.

And what could Tore Krekula threaten his brother with? He had always threatened Hjalmar.

He made an impatient tour of the house. Piles of dirty dishes. Empty chip and cookie packages. The kitchen smelled of stale food. Big empty plastic bottles. Clothes on the floor. Underpants, yellow at the front, brown at the back.

He went back to the bedroom. Still no sign of movement.

"For fuck's sake," he said. "For fuck's sake, what a mess this place is. What a pigsty. And you. You disgust me. Like a damn big beached whale, rotting away. Ugh!"

Turning on his heel, he marched out.

Hjalmar Krekula heard the door bang closed behind him.

I can't go on, he thought. There's no way out.

There was an opened package of cheese nibbles next to the bed. He took a few handfuls.

He heard a voice inside his head. His old schoolmaster, Fernström: *"It's up to you to decide what you're going to do next."*

No, Fernström never understood.

He did not want to think about all that. But it made no difference what he wanted. Thoughts came flooding in like water through an open floodgate.

Hjalmar Krekula is thirteen years old. On the radio Kennedy is debating with Nixon in the run-up to the U.S. presidential elections. Kennedy is a playboy; nobody thinks he is going to win. Hjalmar Krekula is not interested in politics. He is sitting in the classroom with his elbows on the varnished lid of his desk. His head is resting on his hands, his palms against his cheekbones. He and Mr. Fernström are the only ones there. Once all the other children have gone home and the smell of wet wool and stables has disappeared along with them, the smell of school takes over. The smell of dusty books, the sour smell of the rag used to clean the blackboard. The smell of soft soap from the floor, and the peculiar smell of the old building.

Hjalmar Krekula can sense Mr. Fernström occasionally looking up as he sits at his desk, correcting exercise books. Hjalmar Krekula avoids meeting his gaze. Instead, his eyes trace the wood grain of his desk lid. It resembles a woman lying down. To the right is an imaginary creature, or perhaps a ptarmigan: The mark where a twig branched off is an eye.

The headmaster, Mr. Bergvall, enters the room. Mr. Fernström closes the exercise book he has been marking and pushes it to one side.

Bergvall greets him.

"Well," he says, "I've spoken to the doctors in Kiruna, and with Elis Sevä's mother. His wound needed six stitches. His nose wasn't broken, but he has a concussion."

He pauses, waiting for Hjalmar Krekula to react. Hjalmar Krekula does what he always does: Says nothing, fixes his eyes on something else, on the wall chart featuring a map of Palestine, on the harmonium, on the pupils' drawings pinned up on the wall. Tore Krekula had taken young Sevä's bicycle. Sevä had told Tore Krekula to give him the damn thing back. Tore Krekula had said, "Come on, I'm only borrowing it." A fight had ensued. One of Tore Krekula's friends had gone to fetch Hjalmar Krekula. Sevä had been furious, hitting out left, right, and center.

Mr. Fernström looks at the headmaster and with a barely noticeable shake of the head indicates that there is no point in waiting for an answer from Hjalmar Krekula.

The headmaster's face becomes somewhat flushed and he starts breathing heavily, provoked by Hjalmar Krekula's silence.

He says that this is bad, very bad. Assault and battery, that is what it is—hitting a schoolmate with a wrench. For God's sake, there are laws against that, and those laws apply in school as well.

"He started it," Hjalmar Krekula says, as usual.

The headmaster's voice goes up a tone, and he says he thinks Krekula is lying to save his own skin. Says his friends might back up Hjalmar's story to save their own skins.

"Mr. Fernström tells me that Krekula is a talented mathematician," the headmaster says.

Hjalmar Krekula says nothing, looks out of the window.

Now the headmaster loses his patience.

"Whatever good that will do him," he says, "when he is failing virtually every other subject. Especially conduct and attitude."

He repeats the last sentence.

"Especially conduct and attitude."

Hjalmar Krekula turns to face the headmaster. Gives him a disdainful look.

The headmaster immediately starts to worry that he might have his windows smashed at home.

"Krekula must try to keep his impulses under control," he says in a conciliatory tone.

And he adds that Krekula will have one-on-one tutoring with the deputy head for two weeks. Get away from the classroom for a while. Have an opportunity to think things over.

Then the headmaster leaves.

Mr. Fernström sighs. Hjalmar Krekula has the impression that the sigh is a reaction to the headmaster rather than to himself.

"Why do you get involved in fighting?" Mr. Fernström says. "You're not a fool. And you're really gifted when it comes to math. You ought to continue your education, Hjalmar. You have a chance to catch up in your other subjects. Then you could go on to high school."

"Whatever," Hjalmar Krekula says.

"What do you mean, 'whatever'?"

"My father would never allow it. We have to work in the hauling business, me and Tore."

"I'll have a word with your father. It's up to you to decide what you're going to do next. Do you see that? If you stop fighting and . . ."

"I couldn't give a crap," Hjalmar Krekula says vehemently. "I have no desire to continue at school anyway. It's better to get a job and earn some money. Can I go now?"

Mr. Fernström sighs again. And this time the sigh is definitely aimed at Hjalmar Krekula.

"Yes, you can go," he says. "Go away."

But Fernström really does have a word with the old man. One day when Hjalmar Krekula comes home, Isak Krekula is bubbling over with rage. Kerttu Krekula continues making pancakes with a grim expression on her face while Isak Krekula lays down the law in the kitchen.

"I want you to be quite clear that I sent that schoolmaster of yours packing," he bellows at Hjalmar Krekula. "I'll be damned if a son of mine is going to become a walking fucking calculator, and I made sure he understood that. Math, eh? Who the fuck do you think you are? Too snooty to work in the trucking business, is that it? Not good enough for your lordship? I'll have you know that it's the hauling business that has put food on your table for your entire life."

He gasps for breath, as if his fury is well on the way to choking him, as if it were a pillow over his mouth.

"If it doesn't suit you to help take responsibility for your family, then you're not welcome to stay here, is that clear? Work away at your math if you like, but in that case you'll have to look somewhere else for a place to live!"

Hjalmar Krekula wants to tell his father that he has no intention of going to high school. This is all something thought up by Mr. Fernström. But he does not say a word. His fear of his father gets in the way of what he wants to say. But there is something else as well. A flash of insight.

He really is good at math. Even talented. Just as the headmaster said. He is a talented mathematician. Fernström told the headmaster, and Fernström drove all the way to Piilijärvi to tell his dad.

And when Isak Krekula yells, "Well, what's it going to be?" Hjalmar Krekula does not reply. Isak Krekula gives him a box on the ear, two in fact, making his head spin and throb. Hjalmar Krekula has the feeling that he can become "a walking fucking calculator." And that is something way beyond the reach of the rest of the family, something that makes Isak Krekula froth at the mouth with rage.

Then Hjalmar Krekula goes to the lake to sit on the shore. Has to turn the ear that has been smacked away from the autumn sun, to prevent it from hurting even more.

He watches two ravens playing tag with a twig. One of them performs wild acrobatics with the twig in its beak, the other chases close behind it. They loop the loop, spin around on their own axes, dive down toward the water, then shoot back up again.

The one with the stick flies straight into the crown of a tree; it seems certain that it will collide with the trunk or a heavy branch and break its neck, but the next second it emerges on the other side—it has found its way through the network of branches like a black throwing knife. It sails out over the lake and gives a reckless *korrrp*, dropping the twig. Both ravens circle above the water before they decide they cannot be bothered and fly off above the tops of the pine trees.

I land on the jetty next to Hjalmar. He's thirteen years old, and his ear is swollen and flaming red. Tears are streaming down his face, although he's trying hard not to cry. And then comes the anger. It hits him with such force that he starts trembling. He hates Isak, who yelled so violently that spit had flown in all directions. He hates Kerttu, who simply turned her back on it all, as usual. He hates Mr. Fernström—why the hell did he have to go and have a word with his father? Hjalmar didn't ask him to. He has never even thought about going to high school. He's had something taken away from him that he didn't have in the first place. So why is he crying?

The fury inside him is like a red-hot poker. He stands up, has to struggle to stay on his feet. He goes looking for Tore, who is messing about with his Zündapp moped, fitting a bigger jet to the carburetor.

"Come on, there's a job we need to do," he says.

Mr. Fernström's black Volkswagen is parked in its usual place, a hundred meters from the school.

Hjalmar has brought a crowbar with him. He starts with the rear and front lights. Soon the glass is lying like heaps of diamonds on the asphalt. But that's not enough: He still has so much anger pulsating inside him that needs to come out, out. He smashes the windshield, the side windows, the back window. There is a loud bang as the panes splinter, the glass shoots out in all directions, and Tore takes a couple of paces backward. Some children walk past.

"If you tell on us, it'll be your skulls next time," Tore *says, and they run off like startled mice.*

Tore *places one foot on the frame of a shattered side window and vaults up onto the roof, bounces up and down several times until it is completely dented and ruined, then jumps down onto the road via the hood.*

It happens very quickly, all done within three minutes, and then it's time to run.

"Come on," Tore *shouts, already on his moped, having driven some way off.*

Hjalmar's arms ache, and he feels sweaty. He's calm now. He'll never cry again.

Opening the car door, he searches through the briefcase on the front passenger seat. Tore *is shouting away, worried in case some adult should turn up at the scene. There is no wallet, just three math textbooks—Tekno's Giant Arithmetic Book, Practical Arithmetic, Geometry Manual—and a paperback titled* Turning Points in Physics—A Series of Lectures Given at Oxford University. *Hjalmar tucks them all inside his jacket—apart from the Giant Arithmetic Book, which is simply too big: He has to carry that under his arm.*

I leave them to it. Soar up with the thermals. Up, up.

I shall start things moving with regard to Prosecutor Rebecka Martinsson and Hjalmar Krekula.

Martinsson is sitting in her office after the morning's proceedings. They comprised cases of reckless driving, assault, and fraud. The documentation needs putting in order, and decisions must be made. She knows that if she knuckles down, it will take half an hour, no more. But she doesn't feel like it; she is finding it hard to concentrate.

The snowy weather has passed over. Quickly. As it tends to do in the mountains. Just when it felt as if it would never cease. When the wind was raging and howling, and the sticky April snow was forcing its way inside people's upturned collars, wet and icy. Suddenly, everything died down. The clouds blew away. The sky became light blue and clear.

Martinsson checks her cell phone. Hopes her man will call or text her. Outside the sun is shining down on the façades and roofs of buildings, onto all the newly fallen snow.

Two crows are sitting in the tree outside her window. They are calling to her, enticing her out. Although she has no awareness of that.

People don't think about birds. Birds inspire them with big, ambitious thoughts, but people never ask themselves why this is the case. Never wonder how it is that twenty little birds in a birch tree at winter's end, chirping and warbling, can open up people's hearts and let happiness come flowing in. The barking of a dog doesn't awaken such feelings.

Then Martinsson looks up into the sky and sees a skein of migrating birds; all those massive emotions take possession of her. Just as when a hundred crows gather to form a croaking choir on a summer's evening. Or an owl cries dolefully, or a great northern diver appears on a summer's night. Or a swallow arrives with a clatter to feed its squeaking fledglings in their nest under the eaves.

Nor do people ask themselves why it is that their interest in birds increases the older they get, the closer they come to death.

Ah well, people don't know very much until they die.

The crows are cawing loudly, and Martinsson feels that she really must go out for a walk and make the most of the lovely weather. It occurs to her that it has been a long time since she visited her grandmother's grave. Good. She stands up.

≈≈≈≈

A flock of ravens lands in the parking area at the front of Hjalmar's house. Their beaks and feathers glisten in the sun.

My God, how big they are, Hjalmar thinks as he watches them through his window.

He has the feeling that they are staring straight at him. When he opens the front door, they shuffle to one side, but none of them flies away. They caw and croak quietly. He is not sure if he should think this is creepy or captivating. They stare at him.

I'll pay a visit to Wilma's grave, he thinks. Nobody could possibly think there was anything odd about that. I live in the village, after all.

Snow covers Kiruna cemetery. High drifts between the cleared graves and paths. It is almost like walking through a maze. Martinsson looks around. It takes her some time to get her bearings. The snow makes everything look different. Hardly anybody has had the time to clear the graves since this morning's storm. They lie hidden beneath the snow. The sun is glistening on all the whiteness. The beech trees form imposing portals with their hanging branches, heavy with wet snow.

Martinsson usually reads the inscriptions on all the gravestones as she passes by them. She loves all the old-fashioned titles: smallholder, certificated forester, parish treasurer. And all the old names: Gideon, Eufeia, Lorentz.

The grave of her grandparents is hidden under the snow. It was buried even before the latest storm. Her conscience pricks as she goes to fetch a spade.

She starts digging. The newly fallen snow is light and easy to shift, but the snow underneath is wet, icy, and as heavy as lead. The sun hurts her eyes but warms her back. It occurs to her that she never gets the feeling that her *farmor* is present when she comes here. No, she meets her *farmor* in other places. Without warning in the forest, or sometimes in her house. When she goes to the grave it's more of an act of will, an attempt to make her thoughts and feelings home in on her *farmor*.

But I know you'd want me to keep things neat and tidy here, she thinks to her grandmother, and vows to become a better gravekeeper.

Now memories of her *farmor* start to surface. Martinsson is fifteen years old and riding her moped the thirteen kilometers from Kiruna to Kurravaara, chugging up to the house on her Puch Dakota with her bookbag over her shoulder. It's almost the end of the term, and in the autumn she'll be starting high school. It's six in the evening. *Farmor* is in the cowshed. Martinsson throws her jacket over the big cast-iron cauldron built into the wall. There is a grate underneath it. *Farmor* uses it to heat up water for the cows in winter. She sometimes uses the warm water to soften up dried birch sprigs so that the cows have birch leaves to eat together with soaked oats; Martinsson often helps her *farmor* tear the sodden leaves from the twigs. *Farmor*'s hands are always rough and covered in wounds. When Martinsson was a little girl she used to bathe in the cowshed cauldron every other Saturday. Short wooden planks were placed at the bottom so that she didn't burn herself on the hot iron.

All those noises, Martinsson thinks as she stands by the grave. All those calming noises that I shall never hear again—cows chewing, milk spurting onto the sides of the pail as *Farmor* does the milking, chains rattling as the cows stretch to reach more hay, the buzzing of flies and the chattering of barn swallows. *Farmor* giving me strict instructions to go and change—you can't mess around in the cowshed wearing your elegant school uniform. Me saying, "Who cares?" and turning my attention to brushing down Daisy.

Farmor never argued. Her strictness was only in her voice. My life with her was one of freedom.

Then she died alone. While I was in Uppsala, studying for my exams. But I'm not ready to think about that yet. There are so many things for which I can never forgive myself. And that is the worst one.

Martinsson is sweating, digging into the heavy snow with the spade, when a shadow falls over her. Someone is standing behind her. She turns around.

It's Hjalmar.

He looks like a man on the run. A man who has been sleeping in his clothes in stairwells, a man who has been searching through Dumpsters and trash cans for bottles and cans he can return for a deposit.

Martinsson is frightened at first. But then her heart becomes heavy and she feels sorry for him. He looks really awful. He's going rapidly downhill.

She says nothing.

Hjalmar looks at Martinsson. He hadn't expected to see the prosecutor here. He passed through the new part of the cemetery on his way to Wilma's grave. All the new graves were free of snow, neat and tidy. The relatives must have been here the moment the sun came out. They had certainly spent their lunch breaks making sure everything looked presentable. MUCH LOVED AND MISSED it said on nearly all the stones. Hjalmar wondered vaguely what it would say on his own stone. Whether Tore's wife, Laura, would look after the grave. She might, simply to stop people talking in the village. He paused for a few moments in front of a child's grave. Calculated quickly on the basis of the inscribed dates how old Samuel had been when he died. Two years, three months, and five days. There was an image of the boy on the top left-hand corner of the stone. Hjalmar had never seen anything like that before. Not that he visited the cemetery all that often. There was a wreath with a teddy bear in it, flowers, and a lantern.

"Poor little boy," he said, feeling a tug at his heartstrings. "Poor little boy."

Then he couldn't bring himself to stop at Wilma's grave. Just walked past the temporary plastic nameplate on an aluminium peg: PERSSON WILMA. Gifts, flowers, a few candles. He walked back through the old part of the cemetery wondering why the hell he had come, and then caught sight of the prosecutor.

He recognized her by her overcoat and long, dark hair. He didn't know why he decided to walk toward her. He stopped a few meters short. She was frightened when she turned around. He could tell.

He wants to tell her she has nothing to be afraid of but can't produce a sound. Just stands there like an idiot. But that is what he's been all his life. An idiot people are afraid of.

She says nothing. The fear disappears from her eyes and is replaced by something else. Something he finds difficult to cope with. He's not used to it. He's not used to people being quiet. He's usually the one who says nothing and lets the others do the talking, lets the others decide what to do.

"They can scatter my ashes to the winds," he says eventually. She nods.

"Have you come to visit the people you killed?" he asks after another pause.

He knows about that, of course. He's read about her in the evening papers. And people talk.

"No," she says. "I've come to visit my grandmother. And my grandfather."

She nods toward the grave she is clearing.

Then it dawns on her what his question sounded like. There was an "also" there that he didn't actually say. But it was there. Have you also come to visit the people you killed?

She turns her head and points. Adds in a calm voice: "The ones I killed are over there. And there. But Thomas Söderberg isn't buried here."

"You were acquitted," he says.

"Yes," she says. "They said it was self-defense."

"How did you feel?"

He stresses the "you." Looks her in the eye. Then looks down at the snow as if he were standing in front of the altar at church, showing due deference.

What does he want? Martinsson wonders.

"I don't know," she says hesitantly. "At first I didn't feel anything much. I didn't remember much either. But then things got worse. I couldn't work. I tried to get a grip, but in the end I made a mistake that cost my firm lots of money and prestige—they had a good insurance policy, but still . . . Then I went on sick leave. I hung around the apartment. Didn't want to go out. Slept badly. Ate badly. The apartment was a terrible mess."

"Yes," he says.

They fall silent as someone else approaches. She nods as she walks past. Martinsson nods back. Hjalmar doesn't seem to have noticed.

It occurs to Martinsson that he might be going to confess. What the hell should she do if that happens? Ask him to accompany her to the police station, of course. But what if he refuses? What if he confesses and then regrets having done so and kills her instead?

She looks him in the eye for a while. And she recalls one of Meijer & Ditzinger's clients, a prostitute who owned a number of apartments. She made no attempt to hide her profession, having commissioned the law firm to sort out a tax problem. On one occasion when they had gone out for an afternoon drink, Måns Wenngren had gotten drunk and quite irresponsibly started asking her if she was ever afraid of her clients. He had been flirtatious, flattering, fascinated. Martinsson had been embarrassed, had looked down at the table. The woman had remained friendly but never wavered in her integrity—it was obvious that she was used to this kind of curiosity. She said no, she wasn't afraid. She always looked new clients in the eye long and hard. "That way you know," she had said, "if you need to be frightened or not. Everything you need to know about a person can be seen in his eyes."

Martinsson looks Hjalmar in the eye long and hard. No, she doesn't need to be afraid of him.

"You ended up in a psychiatric ward," he says.

"Yes, in the end I did. I went out of my mind. It was when Lars-Gunnar Vinsa shot himself and his boy. I couldn't cope with another death. It sort of opened all the doors I was trying to keep closed."

Hjalmar finds it almost impossible to breathe. That's exactly what it's like, he wants to say. First Wilma and Simon. That had been bad enough, although he managed to cope. But then there was Hjörleifur Arnarson . . .

"Did you sink all the way down?" he says. "Did you hit rock bottom?"

"I suppose I did, yes. Although I don't remember much of the worst part. I was in such bad shape."

They gave me electric-shock treatment, she thinks. And they kept me under close supervision. I don't want to talk about this.

They stand there, Rebecka Martinsson and Hjalmar Krekula. For him it is so difficult to ask questions. For her it is so difficult to answer. They battle their way forward through the conversation like two hikers in a blizzard. Heads bowed, struggling with the wind.

"I don't remember," she says. "I sometimes think that if you recall a situation in which you were really depressed, you feel all the sorrow flooding back when you think about it. And if you recall a situation in which you were really happy, the happiness comes back to you. But if your memory of a situation fills you with anxiety, the feelings you had don't come back, no matter what. It's as if your brain simply goes on strike. It's not going to go back there. You can only *remember* what it was like. You can't *experience* how it felt."

Depressed? Hjalmar thinks. Sorrow? Happiness?

Neither of them speaks.

"What about you?" Rebecka says eventually. "Whom have you come to visit?"

"I thought I'd come and say hello to her."

She realizes that it's Wilma he's talking about.

"Did you know her?" she says.

Yes, his mouth says, although no sound is produced. But he nods.

"What was she like?"

"She was okay," he says, and adds with a wry smile, "She wasn't very good at math."

Wilma Persson is sitting at Anni Autio's kitchen table with her math textbook open in front of her, practically tearing her hair in desperation. She has to read up on math and Swedish in order to be able to apply to high school. Autio is at the sink washing up, watching Hjalmar Krekula through the window as he clears away the snow from the parking area in front of the house with his tractor. Autio is his aunt, after all.

Frustrated beyond measure, Persson curses and swears over her math book. It would have made a convict blush to hear her.

"Hell, damnation, shit, fuck, cunt!" she says, snarling.

"Hey, calm down now," Autio says disapprovingly.

"But I don't want to," Persson says. "I'm stupid, I can't understand a thing. Damn algebra shit-talk. 'When we multiply a conjugate pair, the radical vanishes and we are left with a rational number.' I've had enough of this crap. I'm going to call Simon, and we can go out on the snowmobile."

"Do that."

"Aaaargh! But I really have to learn this stuff!"

"Don't call him, then."

Autio sees that Krekula has almost finished. She puts the coffee pot on the stove. Five minutes later he sticks his head in the door and announces that it is all done. Autio will not let him go. She tells him she has only just put the coffee on. She and Persson will not be able to drink it all themselves. And she has thawed out some buns as well.

He allows himself to be persuaded and sits down at the kitchen table. Keeps his jacket on, unzipping it only halfway as a sign that he does not intend to stay long.

He says nothing. He hardly ever does; people are used to it. Autio and Persson take care of the talking, know better than to try to include him by asking lots of questions.

"I'm going to call Simon," Persson says in the end, and goes out into the hall where the telephone stands on a little teak table with a stool beside it and a mirror behind.

Autio gets up to fetch a fifty-krona note from an old cocoa tin standing on the edge of the stove hood. It is part of the ritual: She will try to persuade Krekula to accept the money for clearing the snow. He always refuses, but in the end he usually takes a bag of buns, or some beef stew in a plastic jar. Or something of the sort. While Autio fumbles around in the cocoa tin, Krekula pulls over Persson's math book. He glances quickly through the text, then in about a minute flat he solves nine algebraic equations, one after the other.

"Wow," Autio says. "Look at that, I'd almost forgotten. You were very good at math when you were at school. Maybe you could help Wilma? Her math is driving her up the wall."

But Krekula has to leave. He zips up his jacket, grunts a thank you for the coffee, and grabs the fifty-krona note in order to avoid arguing.

That evening Persson turns up at Hjalmar Krekula's house. She has her math book in her hand.

"You're good at this stuff!" she says without preamble, marches into his kitchen and sits down at the table. "You're a genius, after all."

"Oh, I don't know . . ." Krekula says, but is interrupted.

"You must teach me. I can't understand a damned thing."

"No, I can't," he says, and starts struggling for breath, but Persson has already wriggled out of her jacket.

"Oh yes!" she says. "Yes you can!"

"All right," he says. "But I'm no schoolmistress."

She looks at him entreatingly. She positively pleads with him. So he feels obliged to sit down beside her.

They slog away together for more than two hours. She shouts and moans as she usually does when things are not going well for her. To her surprise, he shouts as well. He slams his fist down on the table and says that for God's sake she must stop gaping out of the window and concentrate on her math book. Is she meditating? What the hell is she doing? And when she starts crying, worn out by second-order polynomials, he taps her awkwardly on the head and asks if she would like a soda. And so they drink Coca-Cola together.

In the end she understands how to solve "those damn quadratic equations."

They are both utterly exhausted. Washed out. Krekula warms up some Russian pastries, which they eat with ice cream.

"My God, you're a clever bastard," she says. "Why are you driving trucks? You ought to be a professor."

He laughs.

"Professor of ninth-grade math!"

How could she possibly understand? Ever since he finished reading the math books he stole from Mr. Fernström's car, he has been doing his sums. He has ordered books from university bookshops and antiquarian booksellers. In algebra he is busy with Lagrange's theorem and groups of permutations. He has been taking correspondence courses for years, and not just in math. Driven down to Stockholm in order to take the exams at Hermod's Correspondence College. Pretended that he was going to Finland to do some shopping. Or to Luleå to collect an engine. When he was twenty-five he took the high school graduation examination at Hermod's. He drove out to his summer cottage the following weekend. He had bought a bottle of wine. Not that he was much of a drinker, and especially not of wine. But he sat there with a glass of red. It tasted foul. Krekula smiles at the memory.

They work for a bit longer, but eventually it is time for Persson to go home. She puts on her jacket.

"Don't tell anybody about this," he says before she leaves. "You know. Not Tore, not anybody. Don't tell them I'm good at math and all that."

"Of course not," she says with a smile.

She is already elsewhere in her thoughts. Presumably with Simon Kyrö. She thanks Krekula for his help and leaves.

Rebecka Martinsson and Hjalmar Krekula are standing in the cemetery. Martinsson has the feeling that she is sitting in a boat and Hjalmar has fallen into the water. He's clinging on to the rail, but she doesn't have the strength to pull him into the boat. He will soon be dangerously close to hypothermia. He will lose his grip on the rail. He will sink. There's nothing she can do.

"How are you?" she says.

She regrets it the moment she's said it. She doesn't want to know how he is. He's not her responsibility.

"I've got heartburn or something," he says, thumping his chest with his fist.

"Really?"

"I have to go," he says. But he shows no sign of moving.

"I see."

She has the dog in her car. She ought to go, too.

"I can't stop wondering what I should do," he says. His face is twitching.

She looks away in the direction of the trees. Avoids looking him in the eye.

"When I felt at rock bottom, I used to go out for a walk in the country. Sometimes that helps."

He trudges off.

Impotence weighs her down.

Martinsson arrived back at the police station at two fifteen in the afternoon. In the entrance she bumped into Anna-Maria Mella. Vera, overcome with joy, jumped up to greet Mella. Left wet paw marks on her jeans.

Mella's eyes were shining and full of life. Her cheeks were red. Her hair seemed to be longing to be free; strands were working their way loose from her braid and looked as if they wanted to fly away.

"Have you heard?" she said. "We've had a report from the lab. There was blood from Hjörleifur Arnarson on Tore Krekula's jacket."

"Wow," Martinsson said, feeling as if she had been jerked violently out of a dream. Her thoughts had been totally immersed in the meeting with Hjalmar Krekula at the cemetery. "What are you—"

"We're going to arrest Tore Krekula, of course. We're about to go to his house right now."

Mella paused. She looked guilty.

"I ought to have called you. But you've been busy with proceedings all morning, haven't you? Do you want to come with us and help nail him?"

Martinsson shook her head.

"Before you go," she said, placing a hand on Mella's arm to hold her back, "I was at the cemetery."

Mella made a heroic effort to hide her impatience.

"And?" she said, pretending to be interested.

"Hjalmar Krekula was there as well. To visit Wilma's grave. I think he was on the brink of . . . well, I don't know what. He's not well. I had the feeling he wanted to tell me something."

Mella became a little more attentive.

"What did he say?"

"I don't know. It was mainly a feeling I had."

"Don't be angry," Mella said, "but don't you think your imagination might be running away with you? All this business might have triggered memories of your own experience. How you felt bad when you . . . you know."

Martinsson could feel her emotions tying themselves in knots.

"That's a possibility, of course," she said stiffly.

"We can talk more about it when I get back," Mella said. "But keep away from Hjalmar Krekula, okay? He's a dangerous swine, remember that."

Martinsson shook her head thoughtfully.

"He would never hurt me," she said.

"Famous last words," Mella said with a wry smile. "I'm serious, Rebecka. Suicide and homicide have a lot in common. We had a guy last year who ran amok in his cottage out at Laxforsen, releasing first his wife and then his children, ages seven and eleven, from the sufferings of this world. Then he succeeded in taking his own life with an overdose of ordinary iron tablets. His kidneys and liver shut down. Mind you, it took more than two months for him to die. He was in the hospital in Umeå with tubes wherever you looked, under arrest for murder."

Neither of them spoke. Mella wanted to bite her tongue off. She thought about when Martinsson had shot those men at Jiekajärvi. The circumstances had been quite different, of course. And how she had gone crazy and wanted to kill herself. But those circumstances had also been quite different. Why was everything always so complicated? The ground around Martinsson was a minefield. Why the hell did she have to bump into her in the doorway?

Rantakyrö and Olsson came charging down the corridor. Greeting Martinsson hurriedly, they looked questioningly at Mella.

"Okay, we're off to pick up Tore Krekula," Mella said. "I expect you'll want to be present at the interrogation?"

Martinsson nodded and the pack raced out of the door, baying and howling, sniffing the ground.

She remained where she was, feeling left out.

Oh dear, she said to herself, how little and insignificant you are.

Vera suddenly started barking. Krister Eriksson had just parked his car and let out Tintin and Roy. His face lit up when he caught sight of Martinsson. He went over to her.

"I was looking for you," he said with a smile so big that his pink skin seemed tightly stretched. "Do you think you could look after Tintin for a while? I'm going to put Roy through his paces, and Tintin is always so miserable when she's left behind in the car."

Vera stood submissively still, wagging her tail in a friendly greeting, as Tintin and Roy sniffed at her, under her stomach and around her rump.

"I'd love to," Martinsson said.

"How are things?" he said. Martinsson had the feeling he could see right through her.

"Fine," she lied.

She told him about Tore Krekula's jacket, about how he was about to be arrested.

Eriksson said nothing, just stood there and waited. Looked sympathetically at her.

Fine, stand there and wait, Martinsson thought. Wait on.

She had no intention of telling him about Hjalmar Krekula and their meeting in the cemetery.

Then he smiled suddenly. Patted her gently on the arm. As if he simply could not keep his hands off her.

"So long, then. I'll pick her up this evening."

He instructed Tintin to stay with Martinsson, went back out to his car, and drove off with Roy.

Laura Krekula took her time before opening the door. She eyed the police officers standing outside. Mella could not resist flashing her ID.

She could see the fear in Laura Krekula's eyes. Rantakyrö and Olsson were wearing their serious faces.

I don't feel sorry for her, Mella thought. How on earth could she marry such an idiot?

"Here you are again," Laura Krekula said in a weak voice.

"We're looking for Tore," Mella said.

"He's at work," his wife said. "You won't find him at home in the middle of the day."

"Is that his car parked over there?" Mella said.

"Yes, but he's making a delivery to Luleå today and won't be back home until late tonight," his wife said.

"Is it okay if we take a look around the house? One of the drivers at the garage said Tore was at home."

Laura Krekula stepped to one side and let them in.

They opened wardrobes. Checked the garage and laundry room. Laura Krekula remained in the hall. After five minutes, the police thanked her and left.

When they had driven off, Laura Krekula went upstairs. She collected the big, long, hexagonal wrench they used to open the hatch to the unheated attic. Turning the wrench, she let the hatch fall open and unfolded the ladder.

Tore Krekula climbed down.

Walking past his wife, he bounded down the stairs to the ground floor.

Laura Krekula followed him. Said nothing. Watched him pull on his boots and jacket. He went into the kitchen wearing his outdoor clothes. Spread some butter on the side of the crispbread with the deepest holes and cut some slices of sausage, which he laid on top.

"Don't say a thing," he said with his mouth full. "Not a word to your mother or your sister. Is that clear?"

Hjalmar is skiing through the forest. The afternoon sun is warming everything. There are big balls of new snow in the trees, but it has started to melt and drip. I'm sitting in the birch trees among all the watery pearls, watching him. Moving from tree to tree. Being weightless, I can perch on the thinnest of twigs. In winter they are black and the frost makes them straggly. Now they've assumed a violet tinge. The color of spring. I run like a lynx up a pine trunk smelling of resin. The bark is golden brown, just like Anni's ginger cookies. The branches are dressed in her green cable-knit cardigan. I hide inside the cardigan. Lying in wait for Hjalmar.

It must be at least twenty years since he last went skiing. His boots and skis are much older than that. Old-fashioned, untarred, unwaxed skis with ancient bindings. He can't make them slide. He has to keep stopping in order to scrape away the snow clinging onto the bottoms. He sinks down into the snow even though he is trying to follow the snowmobile tracks. His ungreased, cracked leather boots are soon soaked through. His pants as well.

His poles sink into the snow. Deep down, and it's hard work pulling them out again. The baskets get stuck. When he manages to pull them up again they look like cylinders with thirty centimeters of snow clinging to the poles above the baskets.

He thinks he's making wretchedly slow progress, but he wouldn't have been able to progress at all without skis. And if skis like these were good enough for his father and his friends, why shouldn't they be good enough for him? Don't forget that in the old days the Lapps used to roam far and wide through the forests with much worse equipment and only one pole.

Occasionally he looks up. Sees drops of water trembling hesitantly on the branches.

Sweat runs down his forehead and makes his eyes smart.

At last he comes to the shelter he and Tore built twenty years ago just south of Ripukkavaara.

Hjalmar sits down in the shelter and takes the thermos of coffee and box of sandwiches from his rucksack. The sun warms his face.

Taking the sandwiches out of the plastic box, he is overcome by exhaustion. He puts them down beside him.

The wind sighs soothingly in the crowns of the trees. Like Anni's wooden spoon in a pot. The branches sway from side to side, offering no resistance. Allow themselves to be rocked to sleep. Not long ago Hjalmar thought the birdsong was hurting his ears. It sounded like knives being sharpened by rubbing against each other. But now it sounds quite different. A chirping and chirruping. A woodpecker is hammering at a tree trunk in the distance.

Hjalmar lies down on his side. Water drips from the roof of the shelter.

A sentence comes into his mind: "Therefore is my spirit overwhelmed within me; my heart within me is desolate." Where does it come from? Is it something he's read in the Bible in his cottage at Saarisuanto?

Why should one have to worry about things that happened in the past? When his father held his head under the icy water. That was fifty years ago. He never thinks about it; why would he start now?

His eyes close. The snow sighs in the forest, made weary by the coming of spring. The sun is roasting hot. Hjalmar dozes off in the warmth of the shelter.

He is woken up by a presence. Opens his eyes and at first sees only a shadow blocking out the sun. Shaggy and black.

Like a shot he is wide awake. A bear.

It stands up on its hind legs in front of him. Hjalmar can make out more than the mere outline. Its snout, its fur. Its paws and claws. For three long seconds it stands still, staring him in the eye.

This is the end, Hjalmar thinks.

Three more seconds. During those three seconds, everything in Hjalmar comes to a standstill.

Well, this is it, he thinks about his own death.

God is looking at Hjalmar through the eyes of the bear.

Then the bear turns around, flops down on all fours, and ambles away.

Hjalmar's heart starts pounding. It is the beating heart of life. It is the fingertips of the shaman on the skin of a drum. It is the rain on the tin roof of his cottage at Saarisuanto, an autumn evening when he's lying in bed and the fire is crackling in the hearth.

His blood flows through his veins. It is the spring water starting to flow beneath the ice, forming rivulets under the snow, finding its way up into the trees, cascading over cliffs.

His breath floats in and out of his lungs. It is the wind that lifts up the rollicking raven, that whips the snow into whirling, sharp-edged spirals on the mountainside, that caresses the lake tenderly in the evening, and then lies down to rest and enables everything to become still and mirrorlike.

My God, says Hjalmar in the absence of anybody else, anything else to turn to while he wallows in the feeling of deliverance that has overwhelmed him. Stay, stay with me.

But he knows this is a sensation that will not last. He sits still until it dies away.

Now he notices that his sandwiches are no longer there. They were what lured the bear to the shelter.

He skis home, feeling exhilarated.

Anything at all can happen now, he thinks. I'm free. The bear could have killed me. It could have been the end.

He will search through the Bible in his cottage and see if he can find that line. "My heart within me is desolate."

Anni looks completely transparent now. She's been asleep on the kitchen bench. I'm sitting next to her, looking at her chest. The muscles inside are so tired, there's no strength left in them. Her breathing is shallow and fast. The spring sunshine pours in through the window and warms her legs. Then suddenly she opens her eyes.

"Shall we put the coffee on?" she says.

I realize that she's talking to me, even though she can't see me. Although she is far from certain that I'm there.

She sits up slowly: Her left hand finds support behind her back while she holds onto the white-painted wooden back of the bench with her right one. Then she needs to use both hands to move her legs closer to the edge of the bench until they overlap it and she can lower them to the floor. Feet into her slippers, hand on the table to get some leverage. A little gasp reflecting effort and pain, and a "there-we-go" slides over her lips as she stands up.

She pours water into the pan, opens the coffee tin, and transfers some spoonfuls into the pan.

"I thought we could fill up the thermos and drink our coffee on the steps outside. Now that the sun's so warm."

Then it takes half a year for her to get out the thermos, fill it with coffee, put on her jacket, and shuffle out of the front door. Not to mention the difficulty she has in sitting down on the steps. Anni laughs.

"I have my cell phone in my pocket. So I can call for help if I can't stand up again. I don't suppose you'll be able to help me."

She pours out the coffee. It's hot. She drinks slowly, enjoying the warmth of the sun on her nose and cheeks. For the first time since I died she is happy to think that she might live long enough to *experience another summer. Tells herself she must take care not to fall, so that she doesn't end up in the hospital.*

Three ravens land in the parking area in front of the house. At first they saunter around as if they owned the place. The sun makes their black feathers sparkle and gleam. They point their curved beaks in all directions, but don't have much to say for themselves. I have the impression they are putting on an act. Pretending to be serious fellows. Dragging their wedge-shaped tails behind them like peacocks. If I were really sitting here with Anni, I would joke about it. We would try to work out where these important gentlemen came from. Anni would say straight away that they were three Laestadian preachers who'd come to convert us. I'd guess that they were the boss of Social Services, a school principal, and a district judge. "I'm done for now," I'd say.

Anni pours herself a refill. She wraps her hands around the mug.

I would also like to wrap my hands around a mug of steaming-hot coffee. I want to be sitting here on the steps with Anni for real. I want Simon to drive up to the door. Oh, his smile when he sees me! As if someone had given him a marvelous present. I'm so full of desire that it's painful. My hands are unable to touch anything.

When a car does in fact drive up, I almost believe it is him. But it's Hjalmar. The ravens fly up into the trees.

Hjalmar switches off the engine and clambers awkwardly out of the car.

Now he's standing in front of Anni, but can't work out for the life of him how he's going to come out with what he wants to say. At first it doesn't matter. Anni does the talking.

"I'm sitting here speaking to the dead," she says. "I must be going crazy. But what else can I do? Soon there won't be any living people left whom I know."

She falls silent. Recalls an old aunt who always used to sit around complaining about how lonely she was. Remembers thinking what a pain it was to have to visit her. Now I sound exactly the same, she thinks. It's enough to drive me up the wall.

"Are you going to the cottage?" she says, mainly to change the subject.

He nods.

"Anni," he manages to say.

Only then does she become aware of the strange expression on his face.

"What's the matter?" she says. "Is it Isak?"

Hjalmar shakes his head.

"But what's the matter with my little boy? Poika, mikä sinulla on?"

He can't help smiling at the way she still calls him her little boy.

She grasps the iron rail with her birdlike claws and manages to stand up.

Then he says it.

"Forgive me."

There isn't much of a voice. You can tell how unaccustomed he is to using it. And how unaccustomed he is to that phrase. His voice is hoarse as it stumbles out of his mouth. As if it were written on a piece of paper that he's had in his mouth for so long that it's become all scrunched up.

The last time he said it must have been very long ago, when he'd been thrashed by Isak. And in those days it meant "Have mercy."

"For what?" Anni says.

But she knows what for.

She looks at him and she knows.

He realizes that she knows.

"No!" she shouts so loudly that the ravens in the tree beat their wings together.

But they don't fly away.

She clenches her bird's claws and shakes them at Hjalmar. No, she will not forgive him.

"Why?" she shouts.

Her body might be skinny, but the air around her on the front steps is vibrant with powerful forces. She is a priestess with damnation in her clenched fist.

Hjalmar reaches out with one hand and leans awkwardly against his car. He holds the other hand against his heart.

"They were planning to go diving, looking for an old airplane," he says. "But Father heard about it. That was when he had his heart attack. You shouldn't poke around in the past."

He hears what that sounds like. As if he were defending himself. That would be wrong. But he doesn't know what else to say.

"You?" Anni shouts. "On your own?"

He shakes his head.

"It's not true," Anni says.

Her voice has lost all of its strength. It's as if she has an animal in her throat. And once the animal has bellowed out its lamentation, it turns on Hjalmar. Her eyes are blazing. The words tumble out in a rush of gurgling fury.

"Get away from here! You swine! Don't ever, ever come here again. Do you hear me?"

Hjalmar gets into the car. He holds both hands in front of him like a bowl and places his face in the bowl. He will go. But first he must pull himself together.

Then he drives away from Anni's house, heading north. As soon as the lump in his throat has subsided, he will call the police station. And ask to speak to that prosecutor, Rebecka Martinsson.

Isak Krekula is lying on his back in the little room off the kitchen. His feet are ice cold. He is freezing. The wall clock is ticking ponderously in the kitchen. Like a death machine. It first hung on the wall in his parents' house. When they died it ended up with him and Kerttu. When he passes on, Laura will take it to her and Tore's house; they will listen to it ticking and wait for their turn.

He shouts for Kerttu Krekula. Where the devil is the woman? "Hey there! Get yourself in here, woman! *Tule tänne!*"

She turns up eventually. He moans and groans as she pulls the covers over his feet.

He has been shouting for her for ages. How come she has not heard him? Stupid deaf bitch!

"I'll put the coffee on," Kerttu Krekula says, and goes back to the kitchen.

He continues fanning the flames of his anger. That woman has to come the moment he shouts for her. Can she not understand that? He is lying here helpless.

"Can you hear me?" he shouts. "Are you listening? Damn whore."

He adds the last comment in a somewhat quieter voice. He has always made such remarks without a second thought. He is the one who has paid for the food served up at mealtimes, and he has always been the boss in his own house. But what can you do when you are confined to bed like this? Dependent on others?

He closes his eyes, but he cannot sleep. He is freezing. He shouts to his wife, telling her to bring him another blanket. But nobody comes.

Inside his head it is August 1943. A hot day in late summer. He and his wife are in Luleå. They are standing outside the German military depot next to the cathedral in the town center, talking to William Schörner, the SS man in charge of security. A fleet of trucks is being loaded with sacks, all marked with an eagle, as well as some exceptionally heavy wooden crates that need to be handled with care.

Schörner is always smartly dressed, clean-shaven, dignified. He does not even seem to sweat in the hot sun. The depot commander, Oberleutnant Walther Zindel, who is stationed in Luleå, sticks two fingers inside his collar and gives every appearance of being on the warm side. The only times Krekula has seen Zindel raise an arm in a Hitler salute have been when Schörner has been in the vicinity.

It is plain that Sicherheitschef Schörner and depot manager Zindel are under pressure.

The tide has turned against the Germans. Everything is changed now. Sweden is accepting more and more Jewish refugees. Public oppos-ition to the German trains passing through Sweden has increased during the spring and summer. The writer Vilhelm Moberg has published articles about these trains, claiming that they contain not only unarmed soldiers going on and coming back from leave but also soldiers armed with bayonets and pistols. At the end of July the Swedish government canceled the transit agreement with Germany, and Swedish Railways will soon stop transporting German soldiers. People have started to hate Hitler. Four Swedes have been sentenced to death in Berlin for espionage. The Swedish submarine *Ulven* was sunk in April, and news is emerging of another Swedish submarine, *Draken*, coming under fire from the German transport vessel *Altkirch*. In July the Germans sank two Swedish fishing boats off the northwest coast of Jutland, and twelve Swedish fishermen died. People are furious when Berlin responds to the Swedish protests by claiming that the fishermen had been sabotaging German light buoys.

Both depot manager Zindel and Sicherheitschef Schörner have noticed that their reception in Luleå has become cooler. The atmosphere in the post office, in restaurants, and everywhere else is different now. People avoid looking them in the eye. They receive fewer dinner invitations from local middle-class families. Zindel's Swedish wife spends most of her time at home, alone.

When Krekula drove down to Luleå, he had in mind that it was time to renegotiate the fee he was being paid for his transport services. Now that Swedish Railways has terminated their arrangements, the Germans will be totally dependent on road-hauling companies to supply their troops in Finnish Lapland and northern Norway. Krekula is also feeling the effects of people's objections to the way he is placing his trucks at the Germans' disposal. He wants compensation.

But the moment he jumps down from his truck outside the depot, he realizes that there will be no renegotiation. Sicherheitschef Schörner is in Luleå. Krekula prefers not to have dealings with him, but when Schörner is in Luleå, which is often, he takes charge of every detail. The last time he was due to pay Krekula, he snatched away the envelope containing the money just as the hauler was about to take it. Krekula was left standing there, holding his hand out and feeling silly.

"Isak," Schörner had said. "A genuine Jewish name, *nicht wahr?* You're not a Jew, are you?"

Krekula had assured Schörner that he was not.

"I can't do business with Jews, you see."

Again Krekula assured Schörner that he was not of Jewish ancestry.

Schörner had sat in silence for what seemed an age.

"Ah well," he had said eventually, and handed over the envelope containing the money.

As if he was not entirely convinced.

Now Schörner is a powder keg on legs. All the setbacks the Germans experience on the battlefield, all the indulgence displayed by Sweden toward the Allies, everything seems to be conspiring to create a minefield around him. Last week, for instance, he heard that three Polish submarines were lurking in Lake Mälaren just off Mariefred, and nobody was doing anything about it—not even the German government. He is calm, and flirts with Kerttu as usual, but there is a field of energy surrounding him, just waiting to go off. He is ready to explode. In fact, he is longing to explode.

Sweden's foreign minister has expressed his worry about terminating the transport arrangements this way: "The final blows of a wounded beast of prey can be devastating." Schörner is that beast.

But Kerttu notices nothing. Krekula watches stoney-faced as she purrs in response to Schörner's flattery. Her chestnut hair sweeps over one eye à la Rita Hayworth. She is wearing a summery blue dress with white dots. The skirt is bell-shaped, and the waist is high. Schörner tells her she must be careful, or one of these days someone will eat her up.

Schörner has a soft spot for Kerttu. She has done him a lot of favors in recent years. Passed on bits of information she has picked up here and there. Just over a year ago a German transport plane with a cargo of machine guns had to make an emergency landing somewhere in the forest several kilometers inland. Kerttu and Krekula were in Luleå, and Kerttu took the opportunity to go to the hairdresser's. When she came out, she was able to tell Schörner exactly where the plane had come down; the wife of the forest owner had mentioned it while having her hair cut. The landowner had not reported his find to the police. Perhaps he had hoped to earn some money on the side. The pilot and all the passengers had died in the crash. On another occasion Kerttu was able to tell Schörner about a journalist who had taken photographs of railway wagons full of German weapons. That kind of thing.

Important and trivial. That is how it is with Kerttu. People want to tell her things. They want her to look at them with her greenish-brown eyes. It lifts your soul when a beautiful young girl looks at you. Schörner usually writes down the information she gives him in a little notebook. It is bound in black leather, and he writes in it with a pencil. Then he puts the notebook away in his briefcase. If the information turns out to be correct and is of use to the Germans, Kerttu usually gets paid. The time she told him about the German transport plane, he gave her a thousand kronor. That is more money than her father earns in a whole year.

So she has acquired a tidy little sum. And she has not wasted it. She lives with her parents and does not have to pay for board and lodging, and she has lent money to Krekula, who has in turn invested it in his hauling business. Krekula is paid well by the German army. He does not ask many questions, and he delivers the goods to their destinations.

Now Schörner takes Krekula and Kerttu to one side and asks if Krekula is prepared to lend Kerttu to him for a little job.

Kerttu pretends to be offended and asks Herr Schörner if he does not think he ought to be asking her instead of Krekula. She is not Krekula's property, after all.

Schörner laughs and says that Kerttu is an adventuress. He knows that she will want to do it.

Krekula says that Kerttu will make up her own mind, but of course he is wondering what it is all about.

"Ah well," Schörner says. "The thing is that three Danish prisoners of war have escaped from a German ship moored in Luleå harbor. I want them recaptured."

He smiles, winks, and offers them a cigarette.

Krekula realizes that, behind his smile, Schörner is furious. The resistance movement in Denmark has become properly organized during the summer, and the Germans have been having enormous problems with sabotage and other anti-German activities.

Schörner knows only too well that ruthlessness must be met with ruthlessness. An eye for an eye. In Norway the Germans have escalated the level of terror imposed on the civilian population, which is essential to keep people under control now that the 25th Panzer Division has withdrawn to France.

"Someone has hidden them," Schörner says. "There is a resistance movement here in Sweden as well. And I have a pretty good idea that a particular young man probably knows where those Danes are. And that young man has a weakness. He's very fond of attractive girls."

And he tells them what he has in mind. Promises them generous payment.

Krekula's head fills with images. He pictures Kerttu coming back from her little outing with bits of straw clinging to her back and her hair tousled. But it is a lot of money. And Kerttu says yes without so much as a glance in his direction. What can Krekula do about it? Nothing.

Krekula is eighty-five years old. Lying on his back in the little room, he says to himself—as he has been saying to himself ever since—I couldn't have stopped her.

He shouts for her again. Says he is thirsty. That he is still freezing.

She appears in the doorway with a glass of water in her hand. When he turns to look at her, she empties the glass in a single swig.

"You've always revolted me," she says. "You know that, don't you?"

Even as she is saying it, the doorbell rings. The police are outside. That little, fair-haired inspector Anna-Maria Mella.

With two men standing at the bottom of the steps. Mella asks if Tore is in.

Kerttu Krekula realizes that this is serious. The police say nothing about a warrant. Nor do they need to. Kerttu Krekula is furious. Absolutely furious.

"Are you mad?" she yells. "Out of your minds? Why are you harassing us? What do you want him for?"

And she stands there screaming as if someone had stuck a stake through her body while the police enter the house and take a look around.

"My boy," she screams. "My poor boy!"

And when the police have left, she slumps down at the kitchen table with her forehead resting on one arm. She puts her other arm over the top of her head.

Isak Krekula is lying in the little room, shouting. "Who the hell was that?" he wants to know. "Who was it?" She does not answer.

I've landed on all fours on Kerttu's drainboard. Standing like a cat on the palms of my hands and the soles of my feet. I want to see this. Damn Kerttu! There's only the two of us in the kitchen. I accompany her to the open-air dance floor at Gültzauudden just outside Luleå. It's August 28, 1943.

There is a dance at Gültzauudden near Luleå. The Swingers are playing. "Sun Shines Brightly on Your Little Cottage," "With You in My Arms," "Ain't Misbehavin'," and other popular songs. The mosquitoes and horseflies join in the "Sjösala Waltz," and the telephone wires sag under the weight of the swallows sitting in a row like season ticket holders.

The young men are wearing suits finished with French seams. The girls are in home-sewn outfits with stiffened bell skirts.

Everyone is slim and willowy in these straitened times of food rationing.

Kerttu is not in a particularly good mood. She has come to the dance without a partner. And Schörner would not let her wear her best dress either.

"You mustn't stand out too much," he said. "You must look like an ordinary young girl. You come from wherever it is you come from."

"Piilijärvi," she said.

"But you don't have a fiancé, of course, and you're staying with your cousin here in Luleå, and you're looking for a job."

She buys a bottle of soda and stands around at the edge of the dance floor. Two young men come up and ask her for a dance, but she says, in a friendly way, "Maybe later," explaining that she is waiting for her cousin. Drinking her soda slowly to make it last, she feels like a cross between a wallflower and an ice queen. Out of the corner of her eye she sees the man Schörner is trying to trap. Schörner had shown Kerttu a photograph of the man. Axel Viebke.

Here comes Schörner. He has borrowed the depot manager's Auto Union Wanderer. Young boys who have been hanging around the dance floor and sitting in the birch trees like a flock of thrushes gather around the smart-looking sports car.

Schörner, who has a quick eye for the leader of any flock, gives one boy a five-krona note to keep an eye on the car. He does not want it scratched. Or to find that some joker has dropped a sugar cube in the gas tank.

Then he saunters over to the dance floor. He is in uniform. Those near him stiffen noticeably.

He buys a soda, but hardly touches it. Then he walks over to Kerttu and asks her for a dance.

"No, thank you," she says in a loud voice. "I don't dance with Germans."

Schörner's face turns white and strained. Then he clicks his heels, marches over to the car, and drives off.

Kerttu turns to look at Viebke. Stares hard at him. Gazes into his eyes. Then looks down. Then gazes back into his eyes.

He leaves his group of friends and walks over to her.

"Do you dance with boys from Vuollerim, then?" he says. She laughs, flashing her white teeth, and says yes, of course she does.

While they are dancing she tells him how she has moved to her cousin's in Luleå while she looks for a job. Her cousin seems to have forgotten that they were going to meet at the dance and has not turned up. But that doesn't matter as Viebke and Kerttu dance together all evening.

When the dance is over, he wants to walk her home. She says he can come part of the way. They go down to the riverbank. The leaves on the weeping birches will soon be turning yellow; it will not be long before summer is over. That is both sad and romantic.

Viebke says he admires the way she snubbed the German soldier who asked her for a dance. Who did he think he was, rolling up like that in his stylish car!

"I hate the Germans," she says.

She falls silent and gazes out over the river.

Viebke offers her a penny for her thoughts. She wonders if he has heard that three Danish prisoners-of-war have escaped from a ship in the harbor.

"I hope they'll be all right" she says. "Where will be safe for them?"

Viebke looks at her. She feels as if she is in a film. Like Ingrid Bergman.

"They'll be all right," he says, stroking her cheek.

"How can you be so sure?" she says with a smile.

And the smile has a trace of condescension in it. As if she thinks he is just a young man at a dance who could not possibly know anything at all. Although in fact she is much younger than he is.

"I know," he says. "Because I'm the one who's hidden them."

She bursts out laughing.

"You'd say anything to get yourself a kiss."

"You can think whatever you like," he says. "But it's a fact."

"Then I'd like to meet them," Kerttu says.

Two days later she is sitting in Zindel's Auto Union Wanderer beside Sicherheitschef Schörner. Two German soldiers are in the backseat. Their rifles are lying on the floor.

It is a lovely late summer's day. Haystacks stand in rows in the fields, and the scent of sun-warmed hay is lovely. In the meadows where the hay has been harvested, cows are grazing on the last of the late summer grass. The car has to keep slowing down because farmers are out on the roads with their horses and carts. The rowan trees are laden with clumps of bright red berries. A father and his three daughters are on the way home from berry picking in the woods. You can see from the way he is walking that the birch-bark rucksack on his back is heavy with fruit. The girls have small enamel buckets full of blueberries.

Kerttu and the Germans walk the last part of the way. The path runs through the forest and alongside some swampy meadows. Eventually they come to Viebke's uncle's hut, used by farmhands as a base at haymaking time. It is small and unpainted, but in the sunshine that day everything is beautiful. The hut gleams like silver in the middle of the clearing.

Schörner orders the others to keep quiet as he draws his pistol and approaches the hut.

It is only when he does this that Kerttu becomes vaguely aware that Viebke will feel that she has betrayed him. That had not occurred to her before. It had all been a sort of adventure.

Schörner and the other soldiers walk cautiously toward the hut. They go inside. After a short while they come out again.

"There's nobody here," Schörner says disapprovingly.

He looks accusingly at Kerttu.

She opens her mouth to defend herself. She was here only yesterday with Viebke and met the Danes. Nice guys, all three of them.

At that very moment they hear voices not far away in the woods. Laughter. It is the Danes. Schörner and the others hurry back into the trees. Dragging Kerttu with him, he whispers that she should lie down and keep quiet.

Here they come, walking through the trees. Viebke and the Danes. He is so handsome with his curly hair and happy laugh. They have been fishing. Viebke is carrying a pike and three perch. He has threaded a switch of willow through their gills. He is holding a pipe in his other hand. The Danes are carrying fishing rods made of birch branches.

Kerttu's spirits rise when she sees Viebke. Then her stomach ties itself in a knot.

Sonja on the switchboard transfers the incoming call to Martinsson's cell phone.

Martinsson has been out for a walk with the dogs. The afternoon sun is exuding warmth. Tintin and Vera are strutting around, exploring the parking area in front of the house. Vera is digging away eagerly at the woodpile, sending wet soil and moss flying in all directions. Some poor field mouse is no doubt sitting petrified underneath all the wood, its heart pounding, convinced that its end is nigh. Tintin waltzes off toward the paddock where the neighbor keeps his horses. They are used to dogs, and do not even condescend to glance at her. She finds a fresh pile of horse manure, guzzles down half of it, then rolls around in what is left. Martinsson decides not to intervene. She can put both dogs in the shower when they eventually come inside. Then they can lie in front of the fire to dry. She considers calling Krister Eriksson and telling him how his pretty girl behaves the moment his back is turned. Joking about having made up her mind that she needs a vacation so that she can act like a dog.

No sooner has she registered the thought than the phone rings. At first she thinks it is Eriksson, sensing that she has been thinking about him, but then she realizes that it is the police switchboard. After Sonja tells her she has a call, Martinsson hears a man clearing his throat.

"Er, hi. It's Hjalmar Krekula. I want to profess," he says.

Then corrects himself.

"Confess."

"I see," she says.

Damn it! she thinks. No tape recorder handy, nothing.

"It was me who killed them. Wilma Persson. And Simon Kyrö."

There's something wrong. Martinsson can feel it in her bones. She can hear that he is in his car. Where is he going?

Thoughts as quick as lightning.

"Okay," she says calmly. "I'd like to record this. Can you come to the police station?"

Holding the receiver away from her face, she swallows. He must not hear that she is worried or afraid.

"No."

"We can come to you. Are you at home?"

"No. This will have to do. I've said it. So now you know."

No, no. He must not hang up. She can see a little boy in front of her, his eyes red with crying.

"No, that won't do," she says. "How do I know that you're telling the truth? People call us to make confessions all the time."

But he has already hung up.

"Shit, shit, shit!" she yells, making the dogs pause and look at her.

But as soon as they realize that she is not angry with them, they continue about their business. Vera has found a pine-cone and laid it at Tintin's feet. Backing off a few paces, she has crouched down. Come on, she is saying. Let's play a game. See if you can grab it before I do. Tintin yawns demonstratively.

Martinsson tries to call Anna-Maria Mella, but there is no answer. "Call me right away," she tells the voicemail.

She looks at the dogs. Vera has soil and clay on her legs and belly. Tintin has applied horse-shit perfume to her neck and behind her ears.

"Filthy swine," she says to them. "Criminals. What the hell do I do now?"

The moment she says that, she knows. She must drive to his house. So that he does not— The dogs. She will have to take them with her. Despite the filthy state they are in.

"You're coming with me," she says to them.

But no. Nobody answers the door when she gets to Hjalmar Krekula's place. And his car is not there. Martinsson trudges all the way around the house through the wet snow, peering in through the windows. She knocks on them as well. But she decides that he is not at home.

Anni Autio. Maybe she will know.

Nobody opens the door at Autio's house either.

A flock of ravens is circling above the house, around and around.

What's the matter with them? Martinsson wonders.

The door is unlocked, so she goes in.

Autio is lying on the kitchen bench. Her eyes are closed.

"Sorry to disturb you," Martinsson says.

Autio opens one eye.

"Yes, well, the door wasn't locked, so . . . I'm looking for Hjalmar Krekula. You're his aunt, aren't you, Anni? Aren't you? Do you know where he is?"

"No."

She closes her eye again.

If I were him, Martinsson thinks, I'd run away to my cottage.

"Does he have a cottage somewhere?"

"If I tell you where it is, and I can draw you a map, will you leave me in peace? I don't want to hear his name ever again. I don't want to speak to anybody. Help me up. You'll find a pen and paper on the countertop, by the scales."

What if I get there too late, Martinsson thinks as she drives like a madwoman along the E10 and then turns off along the Kuosanen road down to the River Kalix. What if he has shot himself? What if he is lying on the floor in a pool of blood? If the back of his head has been shot away? If he does not have any face left? That could be what is in store for me. It could be.

She tries to ring Mella again. Gets the answering machine again.

"I'm on my way to Hjalmar Krekula's cottage," she says. "He's con-fessed to the murder of Wilma and Simon. And I have a nasty feeling . . . Don't panic, there's no danger. But call me. If I can pick up, I will."

Then she calls Krister Eriksson.

"Hi," he says before she has chance to say anything.

It is such a tender-sounding "hi." It sounds happy over the fact that she has called him, and ever so intimate. It sounds like a "hi" the second before a man slides his hand under his lover's hair and around the back of her head. He saw from the display that it was her, and so that is how he sounds.

She is thrown off balance. Feels warm from somewhere between her ribs and her pelvis.

"How's my little girl doing?" he says, and at first she does not realize that he is talking about Tintin.

She tells him that all is well and then mentions that Tintin felt the need to break away from her policing role and just be a dog for a while. So she has been rolling around in horse shit.

"That's my girl," Eriksson says, laughing proudly.

Then Martinsson tells him where she is going, and why.

"We searched his house last Tuesday," she says. "I really don't know how to explain this."

Becoming serious, Eriksson says nothing. Does not tell her that in no circumstances must she go there alone.

"I saw an entirely different person when I looked right at him," she says. "It was as if I should, well, not that I should help him, but that we shared similar problems. There was something in the atmosphere. A compulsion to do something."

She is fumbling for words to explain her feelings, but suddenly feels that she is just making a fool of herself.

"I understand," he says.

"I don't believe in that sort of thing," Martinsson says.

"You don't need to. Just do what you feel is right. And look after Tintin."

"I'd never allow anything to happen to her."

"I know."

A brief silence follows. There is a lot waiting to be expressed, but in the end he simply says, "Bye for now," and hangs up.

Hjalmar Krekula's cottage at Saarisuanto is built of brown-stained logs. The window frames and door are painted blue, and the two sets of steps leading up to the door have been fused together crudely. The roof is corrugated iron, but the chimneys are properly built in. Beautiful pine trees grow on the slope down to the riverbank. An old red-painted boathouse leans provocatively under the snow. It might survive one more summer, but that is far from certain. Not far from the cottage, at the very edge of the water, is the sauna. A circular iron chimney sticks up into the air. A wooden jetty has been beached; the half of it that has thawed peers out from the snow.

The barrier is up and the road has been plowed, but not all the way to the cottage. Krekula's car is parked where the road comes to an end. Martinsson has to walk along the snowmobile tracks for the last bit. Someone has walked there before her. It must be him. Far from easy going—his feet have sunk into the snow after every third or fourth step.

Vera and Tintin are racing around like crazy, noses to the ground. There are spoors made by reindeer that have followed the snowmobile tracks to conserve energy. Ptarmigans have scuttled back and forth among the birches. At one point there are traces of an elk. It takes more than fifteen minutes to get to the cottage.

Martinsson knocks on the door. When she gets no response, she opens it.

The cottage consists of one large room. The kitchen area is just inside the door. On the wall to the left are old kitchen cabinets with sliding doors above a hot plate and countertop.

Turned upside down on the countertop is an orange bowl for washing up, with a brush lying neatly by its side.

In front of the cabinets and countertop are a small dining table and three unmatched Windsor chairs, painted with several layers of thick paint, most recently cornflower blue. A bit further into the room is a padded bench. The knobbly ivory-colored cushions, striped nougat, green, and dark brown down the middle, are on the floor, leaning against the armrests, so that they will not become too damp and moldy underneath.

A fire is burning in the hearth, but it has not yet dispersed the raw smell of damp.

Krekula is on the bench. Instead of using one of the cushions, he is sitting directly on the hard wooden frame. He is still wearing his jacket and his fake-fur peaked cap.

"What are you doing here?" he says.

"I don't know," Martinsson says, and remains standing. "I have two dogs outside who are scratching your front door to bits. Is it okay if I let them in? They're absolutely filthy."

"Yes, let 'em in."

She opens the door. Vera almost overturns the table in her eagerness to greet Hjalmar. Tintin ignores him, tours the room sniffing every nook and cranny, and eventually lies down on her side in front of the open fire.

Krekula cannot resist stroking Vera, who takes this as a sign that she is welcome to jump up onto the bench.

Martinsson says, "Vera!" in a stern voice, but Krekula gestures that it's okay. Vera, feeling that they are now ready to take their relationship a step further, clambers onto his lap. It is not easy to find enough room as his stomach is so big, but she eventually settles down and licks him heartily on the mouth.

"Calm down!" Krekula says, trying to sound stern.

But he immediately starts picking clumps of snow out of her fur. She likes that. She leans on him with all her weight and licks his mouth again.

"She's just eaten a field mouse," Martinsson says. "I thought you might like to know."

"Oh, what the hell," he says, and there is laughter in his voice.

"Not my fault," Martinsson says. "I'm not the one who brought her up."

"Is that so?" Krekula says. "Now then, old girl, that's enough. Who did bring you up, then?"

Martinsson says nothing.

But then she thinks, No lies.

"She's Hjörleifur Arnarson's dog," she says.

Krekula nods thoughtfully and strokes Vera's ears.

"I never noticed that he had a dog," he says. "Would you like some coffee?"

"Yes, please."

"Maybe you could make it? I'm a bit busy here. There's a package in the cupboard."

Martinsson starts to make coffee. Next to the stove is an open Bible. She reads the sentence that has been underlined.

"'Therefore is my spirit overwhelmed within me; my heart within me is desolate.' Are you fond of the Psalms?"

"Not really, but I read them sometimes. The Bible's the only book I have out here."

Martinsson picks it up and thumbs through it. It is small and black, its delicate pages gilded along the edges. The print is so small that it is almost illegible.

"I know," he says, as if he has read her thoughts. "I use a magnifying glass."

The Bible feels pleasant and used in her hand. She admires the quality of the paper. Printed in 1928, and it has not even begun to turn yellow. She sniffs it. It smells good. Church, *Farmor*, another age.

"Do you read it?" he says.

"Sometimes," she says. "I have nothing against the Bible. It's the church that . . .

"What do you read?" she asks.

"Oh, it depends. I like the prophets. They are so sharp. I like the language they use. And they are so human. Jonah, for instance. He's such a whiner. And unreliable. God says, 'Go to Ninevah and preach the word.' And Jonah prances off in the opposite direction. And in the end, when he's been in the whale's belly for three days, he prophesies the destruction of Ninevah. But then, when the people of Nineveh do penance, God changes his mind and decides not to destroy them after all. Of course, then Jonah is miserable as sin because he'd prophesied death and destruction, and thinks he has lost face when his prophesy turns out to be wrong."

"After being in the belly of a whale no less."

"Yes," Krekula says, "it's interesting that he has to face death before he can repent. And even then he's not a good, enlightened man, not a man changed for the rest of time, you could say. It's a journey he's barely set out on. What do you read?"

She opens the Bible to the place marked by the lilac-colored ribbon.

"Job," she says, and checks the underlined extract. "'O that thou wouldest hide me in the grave, that thou wouldest keep me secret, until thy wrath be past.'"

"Yes."

Krekula nods like a Laestadian congregant.

A troubled man reading about a troubled man, Martinsson thinks.

"God seems to be just like my father—as angry as they damn well come," Krekula says, tickling Vera's stomach.

He smiles to indicate that he is joking. Martinsson does not smile back.

Vera sighs with contentment. Tintin responds with a sigh from in front of the fire. This is how a dog's life ought to be.

Martinsson continues reading to herself. "'And surely the mountain falling cometh to nought, and the rock is moved out of his place. The waters wear the stones: thou washest away the things which grow out of the dust of the earth; and thou destroyest the hope of man.'"

She looks around the room. Hanging somewhat haphazardly on the walls, framed in yellowed pine boards, are all kinds of decorations. An unsigned oil painting of a windmill in an inlet at sunset; a Lappish knife and a badly carved wooden spoon; a faded stuffed squirrel on a tree branch; a clock made out of a copper frying pan, with the hands attached to the bottom. A vase on a window ledge contains a bunch of artificial flowers. And there are a few photographs pinned up as well.

"Let me show you my secret," Krekula says without warning, and stands up. Vera jumps reluctantly onto the floor.

Pulling the rag rug to one side, Krekula removes a rectangular piece of linoleum. There is a loose floorboard underneath; lifting it up, he produces a package. Three math books are wrapped in a piece of red-and-white-striped oilcloth. There is also a plastic folder. Opening the package, he places everything on the countertop in front of Martinsson.

She reads the titles out loud: "*Multi-dimensional Analysis, Discrete Mathematics, Mathematics Handbook.*"

"The same books as they read at the university," Krekula says, not without pride.

Then he adds angrily, "I'm not an idiot, if that's what you thought. Look in the folder; the proof's all there."

"I didn't think anything in particular. Why have you hidden all this away under the floorboards?"

She leafs through the books.

"My father and my brother," he says, with sorrow in his voice. "And Mother as well. There'd be a huge fight if they knew."

Martinsson opens the folder. It contains an Advanced Level Certificate of Education from Hermod's Correspondence College.

"I spent all my free time sitting here. At this very table. I struggled and studied. With the other subjects—I've always found math very easy. I don't have a problem with math. The mark I got would have been good enough to get me into college, but . . ."

He remembers the summer of 1972. He was twenty-five years old. He spent the entire summer thinking seriously about telling his father and brother that he was going to stop working for the hauling business. He would apply for a study grant, go to college. He lay awake at night, rehearsing what he was going to say. Sometimes he would tell them that it was just a temporary thing, that he would return to the firm once he had his degree. But sometimes he would tell them they could go to hell, that he would rather run away than go back into the family firm. But in the end he said nothing at all.

"Ah well, it just didn't happen," he says to Martinsson.

She looks at him again. He is in pain. Something is breaking inside him. He has to sit down. The chair by the kitchen table is nearest.

The dogs are there like a shot. Both of them. They lick his hands.

"Damn it to hell," he says. "My life. Damn it to hell. I've grown fat and I've worked. That has been my only . . ."

He nods in the direction of the math books.

He presses his hand over his mouth, but he cannot prevent it—he starts sobbing loudly.

"Have you brought a tape recorder?" he says. "Is that why you're here?"

"No," she says.

And she stares at him. A witness to his sorrow. As it comes cascading out of him. She does not touch him. Vera places a paw on his knee. Tintin lies down at his feet.

Then she looks away. Krekula stands up and puts the books back under the floorboard. Martinsson notices a black-and-white photograph of a man and woman sitting outside a front door, at the top of some steps. Two boys are sitting on the bottom step. It must be Hjalmar and Tore Krekula and their parents. Isak and—what's their mother's name? Kerttu. There is something familiar about her, Martinsson thinks. She tries to remember if she had seen the same photograph when she had visited Anni Autio. Or when she was at Johannes Svarvare's. No.

Then she remembers. It was in the album in Karl-Åke Pantzare's room. She is the girl who was standing between Pantzare and his friend Viebke. Yes, it must be her.

Kerttu, she thinks.

And then it strikes her that Hjalmar and Tore Krekula are white-haired in the way that red-headed people become. Now she thinks about it, it is clear that they must have been red-haired, and they have very light-colored skin.

The Fox, Rebecka thinks. Didn't Pantzare say that the British called the Germans' informer the Fox? The Finnish for "fox" is *kettu*. *Kettu*. Kerttu.

〜〜〜

I hover above Anni's head as she makes her way to her sister's with the aid of her kicksled. There's a delay of at least five minutes before Kerttu opens the door. About two centimeters.

"What do you want?" *she says in annoyance when she sees it's Anni standing there.*

"Was it you?" *Anni says.*

"What do you mean?"

"Come off it," *Anni says, her voice trembling with rage.* "Hjalmar came to see me. He was on his way to his cottage. He told me that he . . . You put them up to it, didn't you?"

"Have you lost your mind? Go home and lie down."

"And Tore! He should have been given a good beating ages ago."

Kerttu tries to close the door, but Anni is furious. "You . . ." *she says, forcing her spindly arms in through the crack and grabbing hold of Kerttu's dress. She pulls her sister out onto the top step.*

"Come on, out with it," *she says, giving Kerttu a good shaking.*

I'm sitting on the rail, laughing. This isn't at all funny, in fact, but my God! It's like watching two scraggy old hens fighting. Kerttu howls, "Let go of me!" *But they don't have enough strength to fight and talk at the same time. They pant and struggle for all they're worth.*

"Go on, Anni!" *I shout.* "Sock it to her!"

But only the ravens can hear me. They are making a racket on the roof of the barn.

Anni holds onto Kerttu's dress as hard as she can, shoving her against the iron rail, over and over again. Kerttu slaps Anni in the face. Anni starts crying. Not because of the pain in her cheek, but because she is hurting deep down inside. She hates Kerttu, and that hurts.

"Traitor," *she snarls.* "You damn—"

That's as far as she gets because Kerttu gives her a head-butt. Anni loses her grip on her sister and falls down the steps.

With considerable difficulty she gets up on all fours. She's sobbing loudly, out of frustration and sorrow.

"Go away," Kerttu says, gasping for breath. "Go away before I set the dog on you."

Anni crawls to her kicksled and struggles to her feet. Pushes the sled ahead of her and hobbles along behind it. Crosses the parking area with difficulty, and comes out onto the road.

When she is out of sight, Kerttu goes back indoors. Tore is standing in the kitchen.

"Did you hear that?" she says.

He nods.

"Hjalmar has gone crazy. And Anni! I think everyone's gone mad. He can ruin us. He doesn't think. He doesn't think about you and your family. About your life."

She pauses and massages her sore back where it has been banged against the iron rail.

"He's never cared about your life. We know that, of course."

"Is he at his cottage?"

Kerttu nods.

"I'll take your snowmobile and go out there," Tore says.

"Your father won't survive this," Kerttu says, sitting down with difficulty at the kitchen table. She rests her head in the crook of her arm.

It's August 1943. In the clearing is a silver-colored haymakers' hut. She's lying on her stomach in the trees. Viebke and the three Danish prisoners-of-war have disappeared into the hut. Sicherheitschef Schörner whispers into her ear.

"Go over to the hut and shout for them," he says.

She shakes her head.

"Just go," he says, "and everything will be okay."

So she does. Stands outside the cottage and shouts for Viebke. She needs to shout his name twice.

He emerges onto the steps. He is surprised, and his face lights up in a smile. The three Danes come out as well.

Then Schörner and the other two soldiers step out of the trees. They are not in uniform, but the pistol in Schörner's hand and the rifles the other two are carrying say all that needs to be said. In broken Swedish Schörner instructs Viebke and the Danes to place their hands behind their heads and kneel.

Kerttu looks down at the moss. She wants Viebke to think that she has somehow been forced to do this. She does not want him to think ill of her. But Schörner catches on to what she is thinking and will not allow that kind of deceit. He walks over to her, his pistol still aimed at Viebke, and caresses her cheek.

Kerttu cannot see the disgust in Viebke's eyes, but she can feel it.

Schörner points his pistol at Viebke's head and demands information about other members of his resistance group.

Viebke says he has no idea what Schörner is talking about, that he . . .

He gets no further before Schörner points the pistol away from Viebke's head and pulls the trigger.

Two seconds pass, then one of the Danes falls over. Blood pours out of Viebke's ear; the gun went off so close to it. The other two Germans exchange glances.

Kerttu has screamed. But now the forest is silent. Her legs are shaking. She looks down at her trembling knees. White parnassia and eyebright are blooming in the grass at her feet. After a short pause she hears the birds twittering in the trees once more, and the woodpigeons cooing.

She stares at the hair moss and stair-step moss and reindeer moss as Schörner kicks Viebke in the stomach and drags him toward the hut.

She stares fixedly at the spent flowers of the wild rosemary and juniper bushes while one of the German soldiers lifts Viebke up so that he is standing with his back to the hut. Schörner takes his captive's sheath knife and stabs it through his hand so that Viebke is nailed to the silvery-white wall.

"Out with it!" Schörner shouts.

But Viebke does not say a word.

Kerttu can see his white face, so very white. She watches as he loses consciousness. Then she sees the lingon sprigs and blueberry sprigs and crowberry sprigs and bog bilberry.

And then Schörner curses in frustration, tries to bring Viebke around by removing the knife and punching him in the face. But Viebke remains unconscious.

Then Kerttu hears three shots, and thinks, This isn't happening, this can't be true. One of the German soldiers walks over to the car and comes back with a gas can. When they drive off, the hut is burning like a parched fir tree.

Schörner hands Kerttu over to Isak Krekula and tells him that his fiancée has done a beautiful job. Then he strokes Kerttu under her chin and says he knows he can trust her, and that she will get a handsome reward. She will have to be patient for a while, but Schörner will personally ensure that she is paid.

Krekula notices the spots of blood on Schörner's face, and he has to tell Kerttu over and over again to get into his truck. In the end one of the Germans lifts her in.

A few days later there is an article about the fire in the local paper, *Norrbottenskuriren*, saying that it had not been possible to identify the three men who died in the accident alongside

Viebke. Kerttu notes that it is the only time she has not seen the newspaper on Krekula's desk in the garage office. But he never says anything. Asks no questions. And she does not say anything either. It is a matter of forgetting, of carrying on.

She never receives payment. They never see Schörner again. In September, depot manager Zindel informs them that there is a parcel for Kerttu in a transport plane from Narvik, which is due to land in Kurravaara.

But Krekula, Johannes Svarvare, and three young men from Kurravaara employed to assist with loading and unloading wait in vain for that airplane, all evening and half the night. And after that, the matter is never mentioned again. Krekula is informed that the transport plane has disappeared, and Kerttu has constant visions of it crashing somewhere in the forest, and someone finding it, and discovering a briefcase. A brief-case similar to Schörner's black pigskin briefcase. And that in it are details of everything that she, Kerttu the Fox, did to help the German army. Every time berry-picking season comes, she is worried to death.

"Are you going to tell me?" Martinsson says to Hjalmar Krekula. "Are you going to tell me what happened?"

She has made some coffee. Krekula has put his mug on the little table in front of the bench. Vera is lying at his feet; Tintin has fallen asleep in front of the fire. Martinsson is finding it dif-ficult to stop looking at the photograph of the Krekula family. She would like to go and fetch Pantzare's photograph of the girl and Viebke in order to compare them. But she is sure it is her. It is Kerttu.

"Where to begin?" Krekula says. "We drove there. To the lake."

"Who did?"

"Me . . ."

He hesitates. Then he takes a deep breath and says, "Me and Tore and Mother."

It is October 9. Hjalmar Krekula is sitting in the backseat of Tore Krekula's car. Tore Krekula is driving. Kerttu Krekula is in the passenger seat. She has been to see Anni Autio. Asked about Wilma Persson. As one does. In passing. Autio said that Simon Kyrö had been by to collect Persson that morning, and they had gone off on some adventure or other. They would be out all day. Autio did not know where they were going. But Kerttu Krekula knew. She went to the garage. Spoke to her boys.

"They'll be at Vittangijärvi, that's for sure. That's where Svarvare thought they should start looking. We need to go there."

That was all Kerttu Krekula said. Tore Krekula loaded the four-wheeler onto the trailer. Now they are driving along the Luonatti road. Gravel clatters against the underside of the chassis. Tore Krekula drives skillfully between the potholes.

Hjalmar Krekula thinks, What the hell are we doing?

Nobody speaks.

Hjalmar Krekula looks at Martinsson. He is searching for words.

"You know," he says, "it didn't happen like you might think it did. Nobody said, 'We'll kill them.' It just happened."

"Try to explain," she says. "And drink your coffee. Before it gets cold."

A tune plays in her pocket. She takes out her cell phone. It is displaying Wenngren's number.

Oh hell! she thinks.

"Answer it," Krekula says. "I'm not bothered."

"No," Martinsson says. "Sorry, I should have switched it off."

She lets the phone ring until Wenngren gives up, then turns it off.

"Sorry," she says again. "Go on."

"There's not much to say. We got there. Mother cut the safety line. I fetched the door."

"And you laid it over the hole in the ice?"

"Yes."

They are driving through the forest in the four-wheeler. It is almost unbearably beautiful down by the lake. When they turn off the engine, it is totally silent. The sun is shining on the bare ice. It is glittering like a silver brooch in the middle of the forest.

And there is the hole in the ice. With a wooden cross over it.

They pause for a while and watch the bubbles of air plopping up through the hole.

"Give me the knife," Kerttu Krekula says to Tore Krekula. He pulls it out of the sheath on his belt and hands it to her.

She says to Hjalmar Krekula: "Go and fetch a door from up there."

She nods toward the farmhouse, which appears to be deserted. Hjalmar Krekula looks over at it. Kerttu Krekula becomes impatient.

"There's bound to be a door to the outhouse or something. Get a move on."

He walks to the farmhouse, lifts the shed door off its hinges, and carries it back to the frozen lake. When he gets to the hole in the ice, he sees that his mother has cut the line and removed the wooden cross.

"Put the door there," she says, pointing at the hole.

He does as he is told. And when she tells him to stand on the door, that is what he does.

The light is dazzling. It is almost impossible to see. Hjalmar Krekula screws up his eyes and looks at the sky. Tore Krekula whistles a tune. A few minutes pass. Then someone appears beneath the ice. Scratches at the door. It is just someone. It could be anybody. Hjalmar Krekula does not think about Persson and Kyrö.

Kerttu Krekula says nothing. Looks the other way. Hjalmar Krekula also looks away. Only Tore Krekula stares at the door with interest. It is as if he has suddenly come alive.

"What did Tore do?" Martinsson says.

"Nothing," Hjalmar Krekula says. "It was me. I was the one who . . ."

The person beneath the ice swims away from the door. Tore Krekula, staring like a raptor at its prey, stops whistling.

"It's her," he says quietly. "She's so little. It's her."

Hjalmar Krekula does not want to hear. It is not her. It is someone.

Now someone starts cutting a hole through the ice, stabbing and jabbing with a diving knife.

Tore Krekula seems amused.

"Damn she-cat!" he says, seeming rather impressed. "She's got spunk, you've got to give her that."

He stands a couple of meters off and watches as the hole grows bigger and bigger. Eventually a hand sticks up through the ice.

Tore Krekula immediately runs over and grabs hold of it.

"Hi there, pleased to meet you!" he says, laughing as he pulls the hand back and forth.

He looks provocatively at Hjalmar Krekula. The same sort of look he used to give his brother when they were growing up. Stop me if you can, it says. Say something if you dare.

Hjalmar Krekula says nothing. He switches off his face, just as he always did. Lets Tore Krekula carry on.

Suddenly Tore Krekula is standing there with nothing but a diving glove in his hand. Someone has managed to shake off his grip.

"Oh, fuck!" he says in annoyance.

Then he sees someone swimming away beneath the ice. He runs behind, waving the diving glove.

"Wait!" he shouts, and starts laughing. "You've forgotten something! Hello!"

All the time he remains above the person swimming beneath the ice.

"Whore!" he shouts.

He sounds angry now. Keeping above her. Panting. He is not used to running. The ice is shiny and slippery, and she is swimming quite fast underneath it.

"Fucking Stockholm whore!"

She is back beneath the door now, scratching and hammering. Then she swims off again. With Tore Krekula after her. Then it is the end. She stops. So does Tore Krekula.

"Now," he says, breathing heavily. "Now."

He kneels down and presses his face against the ice.

"Let's put out an APB on Tore Krekula," Anna-Maria Mella says to Stålnacke, Rantakyrö, and Olsson.

They have assembled at the police station.

"Inform the duty officers in Gällivare, Boden, Luleå, Kalix, and Haparanda for starters. Fax a list of all the vehicles owned by the hauling company and by members of the Krekula family."

Her cell phone pings; there is a voicemail message. She dials the number and listens.

"Oh, shit!" she says.

Her colleagues raise their eyebrows.

"Rebecka has driven off to Piilijärvi to talk to Hjalmar Krekula. Apparently he called her to say he wants to confess."

She dials Martinsson's number. No answer.

"That's fucking inconsiderate," she says.

Her colleagues say nothing. Mella looks at Stålnacke. She can see that he is thinking about Regla. If there is anyone who is inconsiderate, it is Mella.

Suddenly she feels exhausted and miserable. She tries to steel herself for anything Stålnacke might say, but she feels vulnerable and defenseless, does not have the strength to clench her fists, roll up her sleeves, put her guard up.

I'll resign, she thinks. I can't take any more. I'll have another child.

A few seconds pass, but an awful lot can happen in a few seconds. Mella looks at Stålnacke. Stålnacke looks at her. Finally he says, "That's over and done with. Let's go to Piilijärvi."

The burden falls from Mella's shoulders. Like melting snow from a roof in the spring.

Hjalmar Krekula takes a sip of coffee. Holds the mug with both hands. Vera scratches reprovingly at his leg; he is not allowed to stop stroking her.

"I didn't realize that it was her," he says to Martinsson. "I just didn't have the strength to think about it. She died there. I stood there."

"But you've thought about her since?"

"Yes," he says. "A lot."

"How did she get into the river?"

"Mother said we ought to move her. She didn't want Wilma's body to be found there. The airplane, you know. People shouldn't know about that. We pulled her out. We waited for him, but he never came up to the surface."

Krekula closes his eyes. He relives the way they smashed up the door and threw the bits into the hole in the ice.

And we forgot the rucksacks, he thinks. You're convinced you're keeping a cool head, but in fact you're not.

Wiping his face with his hand, he goes on.

"We took the four-wheeler into the forest. I was holding her in my lap. That's when it started to feel unbearable. And that feeling never went away. If only I hadn't held her in my lap. Then, maybe, I don't know, I might have been able to forget. We put her in their car, where they'd left it near the track. I drove the car to Tervaskoski. The river still hadn't frozen there. There was only just enough gas. Tore drove our mother home. Then he drove our car out to where I was. We carried her as far as the rapids, then threw her in. Hid the car keys in the wheel arch."

"Your mother," Martinsson says to Krekula. "I believe she sold information to the Germans during the war."

Krekula nods.

That could well be, he thinks. He recalls a dance he and his brother went to when they were teenagers. He remembers a young man about their own age giving them a scornful Hitler salute. The boy's dad was a Communist. It ended up in one hell of a brawl. They did not stop fighting until someone yelled that the police were on their way.

He remembers his mother shouting from the bedroom when his brother lost his way in the forest, "This is the punishment."

He remembers his father in the sauna. That was not all that long ago. After Johannes Svarvare had told them he had spoken to Wilma about the airplane. After Isak's heart attack. After the killing.

The mood at home was troubled and the atmosphere heavy with everything that could not be said or referred to. Kerttu

Krekula was wracked with pain. Worse than ever. She complained loudly about how difficult it was to look after her husband. Even so, he was better then. Last winter. One morning at the beginning of March, he was unable to get out of bed. The doctors said he probably had had a series of small heart attacks during the night. He had to stay in bed. But it was better last winter.

"He smells," Kerttu Krekula says to Hjalmar Krekula.

She is sitting at the kitchen table wearing her best coat and shoes and with her handbag on her lap, waiting for Tore Krekula's wife, Laura, to collect her and drive her into town. Kerttu Krekula has a doctor's appointment. Such occasions are the only times she ever leaves the village, when she has to go to the "doctors's," as she puts it. With an extra *s*.

It is clear why she has become aware that her husband smells. She herself has just had a shower and sprayed herself with deodorant and is wearing clean underclothes.

Isak Krekula is out in the village. Walking around despite the serious heart attack he had last autumn. This is something the villagers do now and again—make the rounds. You pay a call on a few other residents, sit in their kitchens, drink coffee, and exchange information about the latest goings-on. There are a few other villagers Isak Krekula can still visit. Johannes Svarvare, and one or two more. But he no longer talks to most of them. You can fall out with a lot of people during your life. A lot of people no longer want to see him. Business is business, Isak Krekula has always said, and there are folk who get angry and feel they have been cheated.

"I can tell you, he's not easy to get along with, in case you thought otherwise," Kerttu Krekula says, including the absent Tore Krekula in the conversation.

Her voice sounds hard, flat.

"I can handle him, but you'll have to make sure he cleans himself up. I've had more than enough."

Tore Krekula's wife arrives and sounds the car horn.

Hjalmar Krekula sighs. Is he meant to pick a fight with his father over this? What is he supposed to do? Tie his father up and hold him under the shower? Go over him with a scrub brush?

An hour and a half later, Isak Krekula returns from his rounds. Hjalmar Krekula is sitting at the kitchen table.

"I've started heating up the sauna," he says. "Do you want to join me?"

On the table is a six-pack of strong beer.

Isak Krekula has no desire to go in the sauna. He has been visiting someone who has served up something stronger than coffee, that much is obvious to his son. But Isak Krekula eyes the beer with interest.

Hjalmar Krekula handles his father skillfully. He does not nag him. Does not ask the same question twice. Gives the impression that it is all the same to him—in no circumstances must Isak Krekula catch on to the fact that Hjalmar Krekula has been set the task of making sure his father has a bath. Isak Krekula stands in the doorway and says nothing. Hjalmar Krekula picks up the beer and a towel—only one. Isak Krekula lets him pass. Hjalmar Krekula makes his way down to the sauna.

He puts the beers in a bucket full of snow to keep them cold. He gives himself a good wash, then sits down in the sauna and pours water over the hot stones. There is a hissing and a spluttering, and the hot steam rises to the top bench, where he is sitting. His skin feels burning hot. He tries to ignore the fact that his stomach is resting on his thighs—it is disturbing to realize how fat he has become.

Instead, he thinks about how it has become obvious that the house is now the home of two elderly people. In the old days, whenever you started up the sauna there was always a dry smell of pine wood, Russian soap, and the fire in the stove. Now when he pours water onto the stones, there is a smell of ingrained dirt—it is a long time since the benches were last given a good scrubbing.

He has almost forgotten his father when he hears the outside door slam. Bending over, he fishes a beer out of the bucket.

Isak Krekula comes in and clambers up to the top bench. Hjalmar Krekula hands his father a beer, which he swigs rapidly. Then takes a long swallow.

There is not much of him left, Hjalmar Krekula thinks. A frail old body, thinning hair that is far too long, coarse skin covered in the pock-marks and blotches typical of old age. It does not seem very long since muscles rippled when Isak Krekula rolled up his sleeves, or since he could lift the tailgate on one of his trucks without assistance.

Wrath, Hjalmar Krekula thinks. Isak's anger is just as strong as it ever was. It provides the backbone that keeps him upright. The anger he feels, knowing that the other villagers are whispering behind his back, the bastards, half of whom would've been unemployed if it hadn't been for his hauling business; the anger directed at the tax authorities, those damned bloodsuckers, desk-bound wimps who have no idea what life is all about; the anger directed at local politicians, at insurance companies, at company directors, at the jerks in Stockholm, at the evening tabloids, at celebs (junkies, the lot of 'em), at the unemployed and assholes on welfare—idle swine who malinger and cheat and live off the hard work of others;

at everything he sees on the television—news bulletins, game shows, reality shows, why the hell should he pay for cable to watch shit like that?; at whoever is responsible for the fruit in the supermarket at Skaulo—a pile of rotting crap surrounded by swarms of fucking fruit flies; at immigrants and gypsies; at academics—a gang of pretenious jerks with broomsticks shoved up their assholes.

At Hjalmar. When Hjalmar Krekula passed his thirteenth birthday, his father stopped beating him, reduced it to an occasional box on the ears or smack in the face. When Hjalmar Krekula celebrated his eighteenth birthday, his father stopped all that as well.

But his anger did not subside. All that changed was the way it was expressed. Isak Krekula's body has grown weaker as he has become older. He can no longer lift a kitchen chair and smash it to pieces by bashing it against the wall. His voice is now the bearer of his anger. It has become shriller. His choice of words is cruder. He searches for words at the very bottom of the dunghill. He wallows in sexual references and swearwords like a village dog in the body of a dead cow.

And now it is directed at Kerttu Krekula. It simply has to come out. All that wrath boiling and fermenting inside Isak Krekula.

"That fucking woman. So she's gone off to the doctor's now, has she?" he says.

Steeling himself, Hjalmar Krekula takes a swig of beer.

"I suppose she has to find someone she can flash her tits at," Isak Krekula says, and fortifies himself with another swallow.

He goes on to argue that it is good job there are folk around who get paid for gaping at naked old crones. So that nobody else has to look at their drooping tits, their sagging bellies, their dried-up pussies. No, it's better to feast your eyes on young women, isn't that right, Hjallie? But then, for Christ's sake, Hjallie hasn't a clue about that.

"I don't suppose you've ever had one, have you? Eh?"

Hjalmar Krekula wants to say, "Stop this now." But he knows better.

Nevertheless Isak Krekula notices how distressed his son has become as a result of his ranting. That he has hit the nail on the head. With what he has said about Kerttu Krekula, and what he has said about his son's inexperience. The fact that Hjalmar Krekula has never had a woman. Isak Krekula cannot know for sure, but he keeps on nagging.

"Not even a good screw with some dead-drunk tart?" he says.

That seems to have eased things for Isak Krekula. The pressure inside him is reduced when he tortures his son. Hjalmar Krekula looks down at his fat belly draped over his thighs.

"I don't want to hear any more about Mother," he says, pouring water over the stones so that the steam fizzles and splutters.

Isak Krekula pauses for a moment. His son does not usually have anything to say for himself. But the older man cannot hold back.

"You think," he says, and the influence of the toddies he drank in the village and the strong beer in the sauna is making itself felt. "You seem to think that she's a saint."

Leaning back against the wall, he farts loudly.

"A saint in hell," he says. "You should know. August '43. The resistance hid Danish and Norwegian freedom fighters and Finnish deserters. She was damn brilliant at getting people to talk. Sweet and young and innocent, you know what I'm saying. In those days. Some Danish resistance fighters had escaped from a German iron-ore freighter in Luleå harbor—they'd been working as slave laborers. Three of them. She went to a dance and persuaded a young man to tell her all about it. Everything. Made a damn whore of herself, that's what she did. They were in a hut in the forest. Things didn't turn out well for them at all."

Hjalmar Krekula is filled with horror and disgust. What? What is his father saying?

Isak Krekula turns to look at his son. Something resembling a smile creeps over his face. A grin. Hjalmar Krekula thinks he looks like a snake, a bug, something you find when you turn over a stone. His old-man's teeth protrude provocatively. He does not have false teeth, but what he does have is enough to send shivers up your spine.

"What's happened to Simon and Wilma?" Isak Krekula says.

Hjalmar Krekula shrugs.

Isak Krekula does not know. Nobody has told him. Of course he has his suspicions. The alcohol encourages him to ask. He is raving over having been excluded, shut out. He has been shrugged off, an old man who does not count. Someone who has to be protected. Someone who cannot be trusted. He is not allowed to know. He is not allowed to drive a car. Anger is gnawing away inside him like a parasite.

"She'll burn in hell," he says. "You probably think that's what will happen to me. But she'll be a few levels farther down. So there."

His tone of voice changes. He becomes self-absorbed.

"So there, so there," he says over and over again.

Then he falls silent. Seems to regret having said too much.

"It isn't all that hot in here," he says petulantly. "You didn't make the fire hot enough. There's still too much of a chill in the walls."

He clambers down from the bench and goes out into the cooling room. Hjalmar Krekula can hear him splashing away in the wash basin. Then the outside door closes with a bang.

"What about Hjörleifur Arnarson?" Martinsson says. "What happened to him?"

"That was Tore," Hjalmar Krekula says. "He hit him with a piece of firewood. We couldn't risk him having seen something. We moved him. Knocked the kitchen stool over. Opened the cupboard and put one of the rucksacks inside it. It was supposed to look like an accident." Closing his eyes, he recalls his brother telling him to hold up Arnarson's blood-covered head so that it would not leave a trail on the floor when Tore Krekula dragged him along by his legs.

Thank you, God, Martinsson thinks. That means we can put Tore behind bars. The spots of blood on his jacket plus Hjalmar's testimony. An airtight case.

"What are you intending to do now?" she says. "You're not thinking of shooting yourself, I hope?"

"No."

She starts talking more quickly.

"Because if you did," she says. "I couldn't cope. Not after Lars-Gunnar Vinsa. I was there when he shot himself and Nalle. He'd locked me in the cellar."

"I know. I read about it. But I'm not going to."

Looking down at his mug of coffee, he shakes his head.

"Mind you, I did think about it."

He looks up at her.

"You told me to go out into the forest. And I did. Something happened that I can't explain. A bear looked at me. It came really close."

"And?"

"It was as if there was something bigger than me. And I don't mean the bear. Afterward I just knew that I had to confess. I had to get it all out of me. All the lies."

She looks at him doubtfully.

"So why did you come out here?"

"I thought I'd better come here and wait."

"Wait for what?"

"I don't know. For whatever was going to happen. For everything that had to happen."

Tore Krekula stops the snowmobile beside Hjalmar Krekula's car. There is another car parked there as well. But smoke is only coming from Hjalmar Krekula's chimney. So who is there with Hjalmar? Tore Krekula texts the Swedish Road Administration, asking who owns a car with that registration number. The reply comes immediately. Rebecka Martinsson, Kurravaara. Prosecutor. Her being there is not a problem. He will finish her off. And then his brother.

The death of Hjalmar Krekula will have to look like suicide. Given the state he seems to be in at the moment, he might kill himself anyway. Maybe he just needs a bit of persuasion. Tore Krekula will fix that. Hjalmar killed Wilma and Simon. And as for Arnarson, let's see . . . Hjalmar borrowed Tore's jacket . . . No, that's no good: Hjalmar's so damn fat, he would never fit into his brother's jacket. No, here we go: Tore was standing next to Arnarson, they were only going to talk to him—but suddenly, without warning, Hjalmar lashed out with the lump of firewood. A splash of blood landed on Tore's jacket. Yes, that'll do the trick. Hjalmar murders the prosecutor, then kills himself. Somehow. Tore will have to improvise a bit, but it will be all right. It will all turn out okay. No problem.

That damn Hjalmar! What the hell does he think he's doing? There's not a grain of sense in that fat head of his. He lets himself crumble under pressure. But not Tore. He has a family to think about. Laura. His sons. Even if they are grown up now. And Mother and Father. Tore Krekula has been running the firm more or less on his own ever since he was fifteen. He has never had a week's vacation in the whole of his adult life. He has worked and taken on more responsibility. Worked and taken on more responsibility. And for what? So that his brother can take it all away from him? No.

Tintin is the first to hear the snowmobile. She raises her head and listens. At which point Vera barks. Only then do Martinsson and Hjalmar Krekula hear the sound of an engine coming closer. Krekula gets up and looks out of the window.

"Bad news," he says. "It's my brother."

Martinsson jumps up—but where can she go? Out the door? What would happen then?

"There's no time for that," Krekula says. "He's here."

Martinsson hears the snowmobile's engine being turned off.

Now he's getting off the snowmobile, she thinks. Now he's going to come in.

Krekula turns to Martinsson and speaks. The words come tumbling out of his mouth faster than they have ever done in his life.

"Get into the bathroom," he says. "Lock the door. There's a window. Climb out. Run down to the river and across it. Stick to the snowmobile tracks. They'll have frozen over and with luck will take your weight. It's your only chance. I'll try to slow him down. But I can only talk to him. I can't lay a hand on him. I simply can't lay a hand on Tore."

~~~~~

The bathroom door locks from the inside. Martinsson fumbles with the hasp: She has to lift up the handle in order to thread the hasp through the metal ring. The window is tiny, high up in the wall above the toilet. Martinsson stands on the toilet lid and releases the window catches. Using both hands, she opens the window. There are bottles of shampoo and detergent on the window ledge. She tosses them out into the snow. Then she grabs hold of the window frame and heaves herself up onto her elbows until she is hanging halfway out of the window. She wriggles through it until her hips are resting on the ledge. It is farther up from the ground than she expected. She will have to do her best to avoid breaking her neck when she tumbles out.

This is going to be disastrous, she thinks, as she thrusts herself headfirst through the window.

At that same moment Tore Krekula flings open the door of the cottage.

"Where is she?" Tore Krekula says to his brother.

Hjalmar Krekula says nothing. Vera stands up and starts barking. As does Tintin.

"In there?" Tore Krekula says, nodding in the direction of the bathroom. Marching over to the door, he tugs at it.

"Come out of there!" he shouts, banging on the door so hard that it rattles against the frame.

"What the hell have you told her?" he says to his brother. "Tell me!"

"The truth," Hjalmar Krekula says.

He is still sitting on the bench.

"The truth!" Tore Krekula says, mimicking his brother's voice. "You stupid, bloated asshole!"

He kicks the bathroom door in. It flies open instantly. Thuds against the washbasin.

Tore Krekula peers inside. Empty. But the window is wide open.

Martinsson falls headlong out of the window. Lands on her back like a beetle. The snow is wet and soft, so she is unhurt; but it is nearly impossible to get up. She struggles in vain to stand.

Manages in the end. But with every step, she sinks into the snow up to her waist. The river had seemed very close, but now it seems far, far away. She fights her way through the deep snow. Sinks down after every step. Her muscles tremble with the strain. The sun is broiling. Sweat pours off her. If only she can get as far as the snowmobile tracks. The frost has hardened them. They will support her, and she will be able to run across the river to the other side.

Tore Krekula looks out of the window. Down toward the river. Sees the prosecutor wading through the snow. She manages to crawl up onto the icy snowmobile tracks, and is heading for the river. What is she thinking? That she can get away?

"Is the ice thick enough to take the snowmobile?" he says to his brother.

"No," Hjalmar Krekula says.

The dogs are restless. They are running around in circles and howling.

Tore Krekula does not believe his brother.

"You're lying," he says.

He pulls on his gloves. He will drive after her and mow her down. She is dead. She is already as good as dead.

When he opens the door, Tintin sneaks out.

Martinsson runs along the snowmobile tracks toward the river. It is like a strip of shiny ice on top of the powdery snow. She is a reindeer calf on wobbly legs. The wolf is not far away. Her limbs are exhausted after wading through the deep snow. She finds it hard to stay on the track. Her temples are throbbing. Her strenuous efforts have produced a bitter taste in her mouth.

She hears the sound of an engine behind her, and looks back. It is Tore Krekula on the snowmobile.

He will run her down. She will die in the snow, her insides mashed to a pulp, blood pouring out of her nose and mouth. Run, run.

Tore Krekula drives down the slope toward the riverbank. He is standing up on the snowmobile. The engine is roaring. He is catching up to her. It will not take long. Martinsson stops on the frozen river and turns to face him.

I'm not going to survive this, she thinks.

He is only ten meters away now. She shuts her eyes.

She thinks about her *farmor*. How she always smelled slightly of the cowshed and tobacco smoke. How she used to get up at the crack of dawn and light the fire in the kitchen stove. Martinsson would drink tea with honey and milk, and eat a cheese sandwich. Her *farmor* would drink coffee and smoke her hand-rolled cigarettes. Martinsson thinks about her father. How he and *Farmor* and Martinsson would sit at *Farmor*'s place stemming lingonberries. They each have a tray. Under one edge of the tray is a folded newspaper. Pulling off the stems and leaves, they nudge the trimmed berries so that they roll down the sloping tray. Martinsson finds spiders and other creepy-crawlies that must be rescued and released outdoors.

Then she hears the sound of the snowmobile sinking through the ice. The ice gives way with a crash. The engine bubbles away in the water, but finally falls silent. She hears Tore Krekula screaming.

When she opens her eyes only the rear end of the snowmobile is sticking out of the water. It is sinking rapidly. After a few seconds there is no trace left of it or of Tore Krekula. No sign at all. The ice crackles and sings as if glasses were floating in the water. A thick layer of slush covers the water where he sank. Soon there is no trace left of the hole. The ice seems to be rocking. A wave of terror flows over Martinsson.

She feels the ice beginning to sink beneath her feet. It becomes like a hammock. She sinks farther and farther. Although the ice does not crack and break, she is horrified to see how the hole she is standing in is filling with water. It comes up to her ankles, then her knees.

Tintin comes running toward her across the ice.

"Get away!" Martinsson shouts. "Be careful! Get away!"

But the pregnant dog comes closer and closer.

From his window Hjalmar Krekula sees his brother disappear through the snow-covered ice. Then he sees the dog struggling as far as the frozen snowmobile tracks and scrambling up onto them. Then it races off toward Martinsson.

"Oh God!" he says, and really does mean it as a prayer.

Martinsson is standing in the middle of the ice, as if she herself is frozen. She shouts at the dog, trying to make her turn back. It is as if the prosecutor is standing in a bowl.

Then the ice collapses beneath her feet. Krekula sees her flailing arms. The next second she has disappeared.

I am flying in circles above the river. Me and three ravens. Around and around. I see Hjalmar come out of his cottage. He closes the door behind him carefully, so that Vera cannot sneak out. Then he starts running. But he does not run very fast. He is running along the snowmobile tracks made by his brother, but they have not had

time to freeze yet, and are soft and mushy. When he reaches the
riverbank, he sinks up to his waist in the snow.

He is stuck. He cannot move. He struggles, but it is like being
cast in concrete.

"Rebecka," he shouts. "Rebecka! I'm stuck in the snow!"

I croak with the ravens. We land in the trees. Cut through the air
with our loud, rasping, ominous-sounding cries.

The ice sinks. The water rises. Martinsson is getting wet.

She is up to her knees in water. Then she hears the crust of
ice over the old snowmobile tracks cracking. The next moment
she is immersed.

Snow and ice fall over her. She gropes for the edge of the
hole, searching for something she can hold onto. She hears
Hjalmar Krekula shouting her name. He shouts that he is stuck
in the snow.

The ice is thick, half a meter at least, but loose; it just keeps
breaking. She is lying in a soup of ice and snow. Whenever she
tries to grab onto the edge of the hole, the ice breaks and falls
onto her in big chunks.

Tintin comes running over to the hole.

Krekula cannot see Martinsson; the edge of the hole is too
high. But he can see the dog.

"The dog!" he shouts. "The dog's coming after you!"

And then he sees the dog fall into the hole. The edges are not
strong enough to support her.

He hears Martinsson yelling.

"Oh, shit!" she screeches.

And the dog is howling like a banshee. Screaming with fear.
Then it falls silent. Is fully occupied with trying to stay alive. It
is swimming for all it is worth and scratching at the edge of the
hole, but the ice just crumbles away.

Martinsson gropes for the edge of the hole with one hand and grabs hold of Tintin's fur with the other.

The current is strong; she can feel it trying to drag her legs under the ice. She cannot resist it; it is too strong. The cold is sucking her strength away.

She summons all the strength she can muster and kicks hard with both legs. At the same time she tries to lift Tintin up by her fur.

Tintin scrambles up. She claws her way onto the ice. And it holds.

"Shout to the dog," Martinsson yells to Krekula. "Shout to her!"

Krekula shouts, "Come on, girl! Over here! There's a good girl!"

The dog makes her way over to him. Teetering with exhaustion the last few meters. Staggers up to Krekula. Collapses by his side.

"Have you got her?" Martinsson shouts.

Her legs are sliding under the ice. As if someone were pulling her feet.

"Have you got her?"

Krekula responds, sobbing.

"I've got her. She's here with me."

"Don't let go of her," Martinsson shouts.

"I'm holding on to her collar," he shouts. "I won't let go."

Now she cannot shout to him any more. She has to . . . She has to . . . Try to resist.

Martinsson struggles in vain as her hips are pressed up against the edge of the hole and she finds herself almost lying on her back. She is well on the way to being dragged under the ice. Snow is tumbling over her face. She wipes it away, only now realizing how fiendishly cold she is.

She cannot resist any more. Her shoulders are under the edge of the ice. The current is tugging at her, pressing her body against its underside.

Then she hears Krekula starting to sing.

Krekula has hold of Tintin's collar. He is holding on to her with a grip of iron. She is shivering.

He tries once again to lift himself out of the snow, but it is impossible.

Martinsson shouts and asks if he has the dog. He tells her that he does.

He holds on to the dog and thinks yes, he has her. She is all he has just now. At least the dog is alive. It is going to live. It starts whimpering. It sounds as if it is crying. It lies down in the snow and whines.

And then Krekula also starts crying. He cries for Persson. For Martinsson. He cries for his brother and for Arnarson. For himself. For all the fat stuck in the snow as if in a vise.

And then he starts singing.

It starts of its own accord. At first his voice is hoarse and unpracticed, but then it becomes more forceful, stronger.

"I lay my sins on Jesus, the spotless Lamb of God," he sings. "He bears them all and frees us from the accursed load."

It is many years since he heard that hymn. But the words come without any hesitation.

"I bring my guilt to Jesus, to wash my crimson stains white in His blood most precious, till not a spot remains."

The early spring sunshine scorches the glittering white snow on top of the ice. There are no human beings for many kilometers around apart from Martinsson, in the hole in the ice, and Krekula, in the snow. The shadows lie blue in the snowmobile tracks and in the footprints where dogs and people have sunk down into the snow today.

Martinsson is lying in the water. Most of her body is under the ice. Over the edge around the hole she can see the tops of trees at the perimeter of the forest on the other side of the river. She did not manage to get that far. The firs have black trunks and are laden with cones near their tops.

The birches are spindly. In the south these slender-limbed trees will be blossoming now. Flowering magnolias and cherry trees will be gracing the parks like young girls in their best dresses. Here the birches are thin, but not at all like young girls. Knobbly, straggly, and bent like old crones, they stand at the edge of the forest looking out for spring.

It wasn't really that far, Martinsson thinks apathetically as she gazes at the trees. I ought to have kept on running. I shouldn't have stopped. That was stupid.

Krekula is singing his head off on the other bank. His voice is not half bad. "O guide me, call me, draw me, uphold me to the end; and then in Heaven receive me, my savior and my friend." As he comes to the climax of the hymn, the ravens seem to want to join in. They caw and croak up in the trees.

Then Martinsson panics as the water comes up over her mouth, her nose.

And the next moment she has been sucked under the ice. Its underside is sharp and uneven. She glides helplessly along with the current through the black water. She rolls over, the back of her head hits against the ice, or maybe it is a stone. She does not know. Everything is black. Thump, thump.

Mella, Stålnacke, Olsson, and Rantakyrö clamber out of Mella's Ford Escort next to where Krekula's and Martinsson's cars are parked.

"I have a nasty feeling about this," Stålnacke says, looking toward the forest where a wisp of smoke is coming from one of the chimneys.

"Me too," Mella says.

She has her gun. So do her colleagues.

Then they hear someone screaming. The silence all around them makes the sound even dreadful. It is a scream that does not seem to want to end. It is inhuman.

The police officers look at one another. Nobody can bring themselves to say anything.

Then they hear a man's voice shouting, "Shut up! Stop screeching!"

They do not hear anything else as they race for all they are worth along the old snowmobile tracks. Rantakyrö, who is the youngest, is in the lead.

Martinsson glides along beneath the ice. There is no air. She struggles and scratches in vain.

The cold threatens to split open her skin. Her lungs are bursting.

Then she bumps against something with her knees and her back at the same time. She is stuck. She is stuck, crouching on all fours. The current has pushed her into the riverbank. She is on her hands and knees on ice-cold stones, with the sheet of ice above her back.

The ice is flexible. It has become thin and brittle in the shallows. She pushes through it and is able to stand up. Her lungs suck in fresh air. Then she starts bellowing. Screams and screams.

Krekula stops singing abruptly, and stares in shock at Martinsson, whose head and torso have shot up through the ice like an arrow.

She screams and screams until her voice cracks.

"That's enough!" he shouts in the end. "Shut up! Stop screeching! Come and get the dog."

Tintin is lying motionless by his side.

Then Martinsson starts to cry. She wades through the brittle ice and onto dry land, sobbing loudly. Krekula starts laughing. He laughs until his stomach aches. He has not laughed for many years. He can hardly breathe.

Martinsson walks up to the cottage to fetch a spade. She vomits twice on the way there.

When Mella and her colleagues reach the cottage, they see Martinsson and Krekula down by the riverbank. Krekula has sunk into the snow; they can only see the top half of his body. Martinsson is digging away the snow from around him. Her clothes are soaked through, as is her hair. Her coat has been flung on the ground. Blood is pouring from a wound on her head. Her hands are also bleeding, but Martinsson does not seem to notice. She is digging away frenetically. Krekula has started singing again. "He heals all my diseases, He doth my soul redeem. Hallelujah." Snow is flying in all directions.

The police officers approach cautiously. Rantakyrö and Olsson put away their pistols.

"What's happened?" Mella says.

Neither Krekula nor Martinsson answers.

Krekula is clinging to Tintin and singing away. Tintin is also soaked through. She is lying in the snow. Lifts her head, manages a wag of her tail.

"Rebecka," Mella says. "Rebecka."

When she does not get an answer, she walks over to Martinsson and takes hold of the spade.

"You must go inside, into the cottage," she begins, but does not have the opportunity to say anything more.

Martinsson snatches the spade back and hits Mella over the head with it. Then she drops it and falls backward into the snow.

Rebecka Martinsson is sitting on a kitchen chair in Hjalmar Krekula's cottage. Someone has taken all her clothes off her, and she is wrapped in a blanket. The fire is burning vigorously in the stove. She has a police jacket around her shoulders. The whole of her body is vibrating with cold. In fact she is bouncing up and down on the chair. Her teeth are chattering, rattling. Her hands and feet ache, as do her thighs and her ass. A flour mill is grinding away inside her head.

She has a mug of warm water in front of her.

Sven-Erik Stålnacke is also sitting at the kitchen table. He occasionally presses a towel against her battered, blood-stained hands, and against her head and face.

"Have a drink," he says.

She wants to drink, but does not dare to. She feels that she will simply throw it back up immediately.

"Tintin?" she says.

"Krister came and got her."

"Is she okay?"

"She'll be all right. Come on now, have a drink."

Mella comes in. She has her cell phone in one hand. The other is pressing a snowball against her forehead.

"How is she?" she says pointing to Mella.

"Everything's fine," Stålnacke says. "She has a thick skull."

"I've got Måns on the phone," Mella says to Martinsson. "Do you feel like talking to him? Are you up to it?"

Martinsson nods and reaches for the phone, then drops it on the floor.

Mella has to hold it for her.

"Yes," she croaks.

"Is there no limit to what you'll do to draw attention to yourself?" Wenngren says.

"No," she says with a laugh that comes out as a cough. "I'll do anything at all."

Then he turns serious.

"They tell me you were stuck in a hole in the ice. That you drifted under the ice and then managed to break through it and climb out."

"Yes," she says in her hoarse, rasping voice.

Then she says, "I must look like a huge fucking mess."

Silence at the other end. She thinks she can hear him crying.

"Come up here," she says. "Come up here, darling, and give me a big hug."

"Yes," he says. His voice sounds strained, then he clears his throat. "I'm in a taxi on my way to the airport."

She hangs up.

"Let's go," Mella says to Stålnacke. "We'll get Hjalmar's confession on tape."

"Where is he?" Martinsson says.

"He's sitting on the steps outside the front door. We had to let him rest."

"Hang on a minute."

Martinsson goes down on all fours. Every movement is agonizing. But she manages it eventually. Sliding the rag rug to one side, she lifts up the linoleum and the floorboard, then produces the oilcloth package with the math books and the Advanced Level Certificate of Education.

"What's that?" Mella says.

Martinsson does not answer.

"What is it?" Mella says again, with irritation in her voice. But she falls silent when she notices Stålnacke's expression.

Leave her alone, his eyes say.

Martinsson staggers out through the door. Krekula is sitting at the top of the steps.

Olsson and Rantakyrö are standing beside him. She puts the package on Krekula's knee.

"Thank you," he says.

The moment he says it, he realizes that he has not used that expression for a very long time.

"Thank you," he says again. "That was kind of you, really kind."

He taps the package with his hand.

Martinsson goes back indoors. Rantakyrö supports her discreetly with a hand under her elbow.

Anni has fallen asleep on the sofa in the drawing room. It is a puffed-up leather affair, not especially attractive. Much too big for the room. Hanging over the back of it are small, white embroidered cloths, presumably to protect against the ill effects of someone sitting on the sofa with dirty hair or too much pomade.

I sit in the armchair and look at her. We never used this room. It feels unfamiliar. We always sat and talked in the kitchen. And when I was alive, the television was always on upstairs, which was big enough to use as a room. The drawing room was used only for special occasions, for coffee after funerals or for christenings. Whenever the vicar came to visit, we always served coffee in the best china in the drawing room.

It's evening. The sun is going down. The atmosphere in the room is warm and conducive to an afternoon nap.

When I died, Anni asked Hjalmar to carry the television down to the drawing room. Now she often has rests here. I assume she doesn't have the strength to climb the stairs. She has a woolen blanket over her legs. It's an exquisite blanket whose sole role used to be to hang decoratively over the armrest. It still shouldn't really be used, and so Anni hasn't unfolded it completely; it's lying doubled over her legs. If I could, I would open the blanket out to cover her completely. Silly old Anni! What's the point of not making full use of everything now?

I look around. Everything is so neat and tidy, but it's not really Anni. It's a collection of all the finest things she possesses. The dark-stained bookcase has books—not all that many, mind you—in neat rows. Cheap ornaments, a hollow swan made of glass and containing a red fluid that rises up its neck when the pressure is high, a painted plate from Tenerife on a stand—Anni has never been there. Professionally taken photographs of relatives in dusty frames. There's one of me when I was a child. I look totally weird, with my hair newly washed; properly combed and blown dry, it's sticking to my forehead. I remember the dress I'm wearing: the seams chafed against my skin. The crotch of my tights was halfway down my thighs. How on earth did they get me into that outfit? Did they drug me?

Anni is so thin under her two cardigans. There's nothing more than skin and bones left of her. But she's still breathing. And now her eyelids are flickering. Her hands and legs start jerking like those of a sleeping dog. She has a bruise on her cheek where Kerttu slapped her.

I'm sitting in her best armchair, trying to remember if I ever told her how much she meant to me. I want to thank her for loving me unconditionally. And I want to thank her for never restricting me— I could come and go like a pet cat, but she was always there to heat up a bowl of soup or make me a sandwich or two if I was hungry. Mother used to say that Anni spoiled me. It's true. She did. I want to thank her for that. My mother was so different, with all her hang-ups: drama, *tears, screams, and curses one minute; red-eyed, emotional, and guilt-ridden the next. "Please forgive me, sweatheart; you're the best thing that's ever happened to me. Can you please forgive me?" In the end I became an ice-cold teenager. "Pass the barf bag," I used to say when she became devastated and wet and tearful and hiccupy. Anni said, "Wilma can come and live with me. If she needs a bit of a break. And she can start reviewing her math." Mother thought I'd go mad out here in the sticks. "I did when I lived there," she said. But she was wrong.*

I'm sitting in Anni's best armchair and thinking how much I loved her. I never told her, perhaps because I'm allergic to the word. Mother must have used it thousands of times, but she's about as mature as a baby chick. I ought to have told Anni, though. All those times when she sat on the kitchen bench with her legs up, trying to reach her feet so that she could massage them: I ought to have massaged them for her. I ought to have brushed her hair. I ought to have helped her up the stairs every night. I never realized. I used to lie on my bed, listening to music.

I look at her more closely. The light is dim in the room, and I can't see her chest moving. Is she breathing?

I hear a voice from the kitchen doorway saying, "Is that you, sitting there?" And when I turn around, there she is.

She looks exactly like she always did, but not at all like the Anni lying on the sofa.

"No," she says with a smile when she catches on to my unspoken question. "I'm just asleep. I'm going to live for another sixteen years. But it's time for you to go now. Don't you think?"

Yes, says something inside me. And suddenly there we are, standing on the shore of the lake. It's summer. The far shore doesn't look at all like the other side of Piilijärvi. But the boat is Anni's. It's her old rowboat, the one her cousin made for her ages ago. The water is gurgling beneath the bow, which smells of tar. The sun glitters like diamonds scattered in the ripples. Mosquitoes sing their hymns to summer as Anni unties the painter and holds onto the boat while I jump aboard and lay the oars in the oarlocks.

Anni pushes off, then jumps aboard as well. I do the rowing.

As I'm rowing, I see Hjalmar.

He's standing in the prison chapel, singing away. He's with seven other inmates. The prison chaplain is a thin-haired man in his forties. He's quite good on the guitar, and they're singing "Childhood Faith," the religious song made famous by the north's favorite singer, Lapp-Lisa. The sound echoes back and forth, to and from the melancholy walls. The chaplain is glad that Hjalmar has joined his group. Hjalmar is big and commands respect, and, as some of the other prisoners want to keep on his good side, they turn up for every Wednesday service. The chaplain can demonstrate the results of his prison activities to his own congregation, so everyone is happy. For it is surely marvelous that these criminals are allowed out on parole to attend Sunday service at the Philadelphia Pentecostal Church. They pay homage to Jesus. And are only too pleased to describe the miserable lives they led before they saw the light, so that the whole congregation is inspired.

Happiest of them all is Hjalmar. He has new math books in his cell.

His fat cheeks are rose-pink. He enjoys singing, likes to belt out "Childhood faith, childhood faith, you are a golden bridge to heaven."

He always jokes that he's never going to appeal his sentence.

I carry on rowing. Two ravens come flying over the tops of the pine trees. They circle above us. Around and around. I glance up at their long, black, outstretched pinions, their wedge-shaped tails. I hear the sound of their wings beating above our heads. Then they glide down and perch on the rail of the boat. Just as naturally as if they were taking seats they'd booked in advance. I wouldn't be surprised if they each produced a little black suitcase from under their wings. *Their feathers are shimmering like rainbows in the sun; their beaks are so full of strength, curved and sharp, with little mustaches near the base; and they have thick, feathery collars. One of them lunges at a horsefly that has accompanied them out over the water. They chat to each other with all their r-sounds; they seem to be saying, "Rave-rave-raven." But then one of them suddenly sounds like a clucking cockerel, and the other one seems to burst out laughing. I don't know what to think about these birds.*

I carry on rowing. Dip the oars deep into the water. I enjoy feeling my body again. The sweat running down my back. The wood of the oars made smooth by many years of handling. The feeling in the muscles of my back and arms with each stroke, summoning up the strength, the effort, the tiredness, the recovery.

The sun is hot. The ravens open their beaks. They are silent now. I feel nothing but happiness. It wells up inside me like the sap in a birch tree.

The ravens cry and take off. They fly with powerful beats of their wings in the direction from which I came. Disappear through the sky.

I row. I am strong and as untameable as a river, and I row.

I press hard with my feet, and row with long, powerful strokes.

I'm coming, I think happily. I'm coming now.

sunday, may 3

The weekend is over. The soft light of the evening sun glides into Martinsson's kitchen in Kurravaara.

Måns Wenngren looks at Rebecka Martinsson. She is sitting only half a meter away, and he wants her so badly. Her dark, straight hair. Her eyes with that gray edge around her irises. He has hugged her. Made love to her. Albeit cautiously. She is covered in bruises. Still feels sick, has dizzy spells, and is very tired from the concussion.

He looks at the scar above her lips. He particularly likes that scar. Especially as it is ragged. He is filled with the same kind of tenderness he felt when he held his daughter for the first time.

"How do you feel?" he asks, pouring a glass of wine.

Martinsson reads the label. Much too fine. Wasted on her.

"I'm okay," she says.

She has no feelings about what has happened. No thoughts. What was it like, being in that hole in the ice? Being dragged under the ice? Awful, of course. But it is all over now. She can feel that Wenngren is worried. That he thinks she is going to have a relapse. His voice is gentle, too gentle.

There is some kind of barrier between them. She longed so much for him to come up and give her a hug, but now that he is here she is hiding herself away in her tiredness and her bruises.

And there is something she cannot stop thinking about. When Tore Krekula came toward her on the snowmobile and she thought her number was up. When she almost drowned under the ice. At no time did she think of Wenngren. She thought about her *farmor* and her father. But not about Wenngren. She did not think of him until Mella handed her the phone.

They hear a car pull up outside. Martinsson walks over to the kitchen window. It is Krister Eriksson. He gets out of the car and walks toward her front door, stooping noticeably. She taps on the windowpane, points at him, making a come-on-up gesture with her other hand.

Then he is standing in the kitchen doorway. Wenngren gets up.

"Forgive me," Eriksson says. "I didn't know. I should have called first."

"No, no, it's okay," Martinsson says.

She introduces the two men. Wenngren puts out his hand.

"Just a moment," Eriksson says. "I'll just—"

He unzips his jacket.

Inside it is a puppy. Small and snub-nosed. Having fallen asleep in the warmth of the jacket, it sniffs and starts treading with its paws when Eriksson opens the zipper.

"If you can hold it, Måns and I can shake hands," he says to Martinsson, handing over the puppy.

The delighted look on her face makes him laugh.

The puppy wakes up. It is still blind. So little that she can hold it in one hand.

"Oh God," she says.

It is so soft, warm, and helpless. It smells of puppy.

Vera comes over and fusses at Martinsson's feet.

"You can say hello another time," Marinsson says.

"Is it Tintin's?" she says while the men are shaking hands. Wenngren has pulled himself up to his full height and tucked in his stomach. Gives Eriksson's face an inquisitive look, but is careful not to stare.

"Yes," Eriksson says. "It came a bit early, but everything went well. It's yours if you'd like it."

"You can't be serious," she says. "A puppy of Tintin's, it must be worth—"

"I've heard what you did," Eriksson says, looking right at her.

He ignores the fact that her boyfriend is there. All the men in the world can be there if they want. He looks into her eyes as deeply as he can.

She looks back.

"You certainly can't have a dog," Wenngren says to Martinsson. "You've said yourself that you don't know what you're going to do with Vera. You work so hard. And when you move in with me in Stockholm . . . Dogs shouldn't live in cities."

He takes hold of Martinsson's neck playfully but firmly. The gesture is aimed at Eriksson. She is mine, it means.

Then he asks Eriksson if he would like a glass of wine. Eriksson replies that he is driving, unfortunately. Martinsson looks at the puppy.

"What's happened to Kerttu Krekula?" Eriksson says.

"She hasn't been interrogated yet," Martinsson mumbles, her lips and nose pressed against the puppy. "She says that she and Tore tried to stop Hjalmar. We've let her go. There's no proof apart from Hjalmar's statement, and that's not enough to charge her."

Eriksson closes his eyes briefly. Tries to imagine Kerttu Krekula isolated in her home in the village, with only Isak Krekula for company.

"She had an opportunity," he says. "But she's condemned herself to a tougher punishment than a court would have given her."

"I'll have to go," he says eventually. "I can't keep her away from Tintin for too long. She's at home with the other three."

He wants to feast his eyes on Martinsson for just a little while longer.

"You don't need to make your mind up now," he says. "Think it over. She'll become a lovely dog."

"Do you think I don't realize that?" Martinsson says. "I don't know what to say."

"How about 'thank you'?" he says with a smile.

"Thank you," she says, and smiles back.

She hands over the puppy. Their hands touch as Eriksson takes it from her. Wenngren coughs impatiently.

Krister Eriksson carries the puppy down the stairs inside his jacket. He holds tightly onto the banister rail—he certainly does not want to fall with the little guy.

He gets into the car. The puppy is wrapped up cozily in his jacket on the passenger seat.

He turns the ignition key. Purses his lips. Looks at the puppy, which has fallen asleep again. Thinks about how Wenngren held Martinsson by her neck. Imagines them kissing back there in the house. Hears Wenngren saying, "He's very fond of you, that police officer."

When Eriksson gets home, he hands the puppy back to Tintin, who licks it thoroughly.

He strokes Tintin's head. She has lain down on her side so that the puppy and its siblings can feed. The blinds are drawn. It is dark in the room, although outside the spring evening is light.

What did I expect? Erikkson asks himself. That she would throw her arms around my neck?

He thinks about her lying in the hole in the ice and managing to rescue his dog. Imagines her being dragged under the ice. He tries to convince himself that love is about giving, not taking. It should be okay simply to be a giver. To love without expecting anything in return. But he finds that difficult. He wants her. He wants her for himself.

"I think I love her," he says to Tintin. "How the hell did that happen?"

acknowledgments

Dead people crop up in all of my books. I very much hope that this life is not the only one allotted to us, even if it is big enough in itself.

A lot of what happens in this story is true. For instance, the German army really did have large depots in Luleå. Other things besides soldiers going on and returning from leave were transported by Swedish Railways. Swedish drivers and trucks were rented out to the German army to transport supplies to the eastern front. Walther Zindel actually existed. A lot of German ships were never recorded officially in the harbor ledgers of Luleå.

But most of the plot is made up. I have done what I always do when I write my stories: I borrow incidents, people, and places that I have experienced myself or heard about, and combine them with my own inventions. Once upon a time, for instance, two young boys really did get lost in the forest near Piilijärvi, and one of them did not find his way back home until a week later. But they were not brothers. And they did not fight: The younger boy grew tired, and the elder one went to fetch help. I heard about the incident, and my mind immediately began to turn it into part of a plot.

I have read about the war, of course. I should mention especially *Slaget om Nordkalotten* (*The Battle for Arctic Scandinavia*), by Lars Gyllenhaal and James F. Gebhardt; *Spelaren Christian Günther* (*Christian Günther the Gambler*), by Henrik Arnstad; and *Svenskarna som stred för Hitler* (*The Swedes Who Fought for*

Hitler) and *Där järnkorsen växer* (*Where the Iron Crosses Grow*), both by Bosse Schön.

Many people have given me valuable assistance, and I would like to take this opportunity to express my special thanks to some of them: Dr. Lennart Edström, who helped me to understand what happens when people go over the edge; Dr. Jan Lindberg, who helped me bring the dead to life; Dr. Marie Allen, a senior lecturer who can explain the genetic makeup of watery life so lucidly that I almost understand what she is saying; Cecilia Bergman, a prosecutor; Pelle Hansson, a diver; Jan Viinikainen of the Kiruna municipal archives; and Göran Guné, who knows about airplanes. Many thanks to all of you. If there are mistakes in the book, they are not of your making.

Special thanks also to my editor, Rachel Åkerstedt, and my publisher, Eva Bonnier, who give me encouragement or bring me down to earth in the correct amount at the right time. All the lovely people at my publisher who work on my books in various ways. The intelligent, helpful staff of the Bonnier Group Agency. And Elisabeth Ohlson Wallin and John Eyre for the original dustjacket.

And thanks to my mother for her perpetual "Come on, get on with it, I want to know what happens next—I've been thinking about Hjalmar all week." Thank you for your patience when I have been out of sorts and my head has dropped onto my desk. Thanks to my father and to Mona, who read my texts, check Kiruna facts, help me with Tornedalen Finnish, and a thousand other things. Many thanks to Perra Winberg and Lena Andersson and Thomas Karlsén Andersson.

Life is totally unpredictable, but pretty good even so. Thank you, Per. This book is almost our third child, after all. There are a thousand things I would like to thank you for, but you know about them already. And thank you, Christer, for your love and for putting up with me when all I had time for was the book, the book, the book, and everything else was of no interest whatsoever.

Read an excerpt of Åsa Larsson's

THE SECOND DEADLY SIN

How can a dog possibly scream like that? Samuel Johansson has never heard a dog make such a noise before.

He is in his kitchen, making a sandwich. His Norwegian elkhound is on a running leash in the backyard. The calm before the storm.

Then the dog starts barking. Loud and angry at first.

What is it barking at? Certainly not a squirrel. Johansson recognizes the way his dog barks at a squirrel. Surely not an elk? No, elk barks are less strident, more substantial.

Then something happens. The dog screams. Shrieks as if the gates of hell have just opened up before it. It is a sound that fills Johansson with cold terror.

And then silence.

Johansson races outside. No jacket. No shoes. No clear thoughts.

He stumbles his way through the autumnal darkness, toward the garage and the dog kennel.

And there, in the light from the lamp over the garage door, stands the bear. It is tugging at the dog's body, trying to drag it away, but the dead dog is still attached to the leash. The bear turns its bloodstained jaws toward Johansson and roars at him.

Johansson steps back somewhat unsteadily. Then he summons up superhuman strength and runs faster than he has ever run before, back to the house to get his gun. The bear stands its ground. Nevertheless, Johansson seems to feel the beast's hot breath on the back of his neck.

He loads the rifle with his wet hands before cautiously opening the door. He must keep calm and shoot accurately. Otherwise it could be all over in a flash. A wounded bear would take less than a second to pounce.

He creeps through the darkness. One step at a time. The hairs on the back of his head are sticking out like nails.

The bear is still there. Gobbling down what is left of the dog.

When Johansson cocks the gun, it looks up.

Johansson has never trembled so much. There's no time to lose now. He tries to stand still, but it is impossible.

The bear shakes its head threateningly. Snarls. Huffs and puffs like a pair of bellows. Then it takes a deliberate step forward. That is when Johansson shoots. There is an explosive blast. The bear falls. But quickly it stands up again. And disappears into the darkness.

It has vanished now into the pitch-black forest. The light over the garage door is no help at all.

Johansson walks backward to the house, aiming the gun left and right as he does so. Ears pricked, listening for sounds from the forest. That bloody bear might come bounding toward him at any moment. He can only see for a few feet.

Twenty paces back to the door. His heart is pounding. Five. Three.

He's inside.

He's shuddering now. His whole body is shaking. He has to put his cell phone down on the table and hold onto his right hand with his left in order to push the right numbers. The leader of the local hunters responds after only one ring. They agree to meet at first light. There's nothing they can do in the dark.

As dawn breaks all the men from the village gather outside Johansson's house. It is 28°F. Tree branches white with frost. Leaves have fallen. Rowan berries gleam rust-red among the gray. Something feathery is floating through the air—the kind of snow that never settles.

They stare at the devastation in and around the dog kennel. More or less all that is left, attached to the running leash, is the dog's skull. The rest is blood-soaked slush.

It is a hard-boiled collection of men. They are all wearing checked shirts, pants with lots of pockets, belts carrying knives, and green jackets. The young ones have beards and a peaked cap on their heads. The older ones are clean-shaven and wear fur hats with ear flaps. These are men who make their own motorized carts for dragging back home the elks they have shot. Men who prefer cars with carburetors, so that they can mess around with the engines themselves and are not dependent on service garages where they nowadays just attach computer cables to the cars.

"This is what happened," the hunt leader says, as the more gnarled members of his team stuff new wads of chewing tobacco into their mouths and glance furtively at Johansson, who is having difficulty in controlling the tics in various parts of his face. "Samuel heard the dog howling. He grabbed his gun and went out. We've had bears prowling around here for quite some time now, so he realized that might be the problem."

Johansson nods.

"Anyway. You go out with your rifle. The bear is gobbling away at the dog, and turns to attack you. You shoot it in self-defense. It was coming toward you. You didn't go in and get your gun, you had it with you from the start. No messing around in this case. Nobody's going to be prosecuted for breaking hunting laws, right? I rang the police last night and put them in the picture. They had no hesitation in classifying it as self-defense."

"Who's going to hunt it down?" somebody wonders aloud. "Patrik Mäkitalo."

That piece of information is followed by total silence while all present consider the implications. Mäkitalo comes from Luleå. It would have been good if somebody from their own local hunting team had been commissioned to track down the bear. But none of them has a dog as proficient as Mäkitalo's. And deep down they wonder if they are proficient enough themselves as well.

The bear is wounded. And so highly dangerous. It is essential to have a dog that dares to hold the bear at bay, rather than panicking and running back to its master with the ferocious beast hard on its heels.

And the hunter must not get cold feet either; when Teddy comes crashing through the undergrowth he might have no more than a second in which to react. The lethal target area on a bear is no wider than the base of a saucepan. And the hunter is aiming without a rifle support. It's like shooting a flying tennis ball. If he misses, it is by no means sure that he will get a second chance. Hunting bears is not something for anybody with shaky hands.

"Speak of the devil," the hunt leader says, looking along the road.

Patrik Mäkitalo gets out of his car and greets the assembled group with a nod. He is about thirty-five. He tends to screw up his eyes; his beard is long and narrow, like a goat's. A Norrbotten Mongol warrior.

Mäkitalo doesn't say much, but listens intently to the hunt leader and asks Johansson about the shot. Where exactly was he standing? Where was the bear? What ammunition did he use?

"Oryx."

"Good," Mäkitalo says. "A high residual weight. With a bit of luck it might have gone right through the beast. That would make it bleed more, and make it easier to track."

"What do you use?"

It is one of the older hunters who plucks up the courage to ask. "Vulkan. It usually stops just inside the skin."

Of course, the old-timers think. He doesn't shoot to wound a bear. Killing it outright means he doesn't need to track it down. And he's keen to preserve the bearskin in good condition.

Mäkitalo cocks his rifle and disappears into the trees. He returns after only a minute or so, with blood on his fingers.

He opens the tailgate. His hunting dogs are in a cage, their tongues dangling out of broad doggy smiles. They have eyes for nobody but their master.

Mäkitalo asks to see a map. The hunt leader gets one from his car. They spread it out on the hood.

"This no doubt shows the route it took," Mäkitalo says. "But it's heading into the wind, through newly planted woodland, so there's a risk it might have veered off over here somewhere."

He points to the beck that flows down into the Lainio River. "Especially if it's a mature varmint that's learned how to outwit dogs. You'd better make arrangements for a boat that could come to meet us, if necessary. My dogs aren't afraid of getting their feet wet, but their master isn't as hardy as they are."

Everybody summons up a smile, signaling their empathy for the task ahead.

The hunt leader gets down to practicalities and asks, "Do you want to take somebody with you?"

"No. We'll follow the trail and see where it leads us. If it takes us over here and toward the marshes, it would help if you could go and stand guard here and there." He gestures at the map. "But let's get some idea first of where it's gone."

"He ought to be easy enough to find, if he's bleeding," one of the men says.

Mäkitalo doesn't even condescend to look at him when he replies: "I dunno about that; they often stop bleeding after a while and then they hide away in the thick undergrowth and tend to double back and creep up on whoever is following them. So if I'm unlucky it could be him who finds me."

"Too bloody right," the hunt leader says, giving the colleague who spoke out of turn a withering look.

Mäkitalo sets his dogs loose. They disappear up the hill like two brown streaks, sniffing at the ground. He follows them, GPS device in hand.

Full steam ahead. He looks up at the sky and hopes it will not start snowing in earnest.

He is making rapid progress. He thinks briefly about the hunters he has just met—the type that sit around boozing and snoozing when they're supposed to be on the lookout. They would never be able to move as quickly as he does. Never mind track down the prey.

He crosses the dirt track. On the other side is a sandy slope. The bear seems to have run straight up it, legs wide apart, making heavy weather of it. He puts his hand in the obvious footprints.

The people in Lainio are already on edge. They know the bear has been around now and again. Dung next to an overturned garbage can, steaming in the cold morning air, as red as a mushy porridge of blueberries and lingon. There's been a lot of bear talk. Old stories have been dusted down.

Mäkitalo examines the claw marks in the ground where it has dug its paws deep in order to thrust itself up the hill. It must have a claw the size of a knife in each toe. The villagers have measured the prints, placed matchboxes beside them, and taken pictures with their cell phones.

Women and children have been kept indoors. Nobody has dared to venture out into the wood to gather berries. Parents pick up their children by car from the school bus stop.

It must be a pretty big varmint, Mäkitalo thinks as he examines the tracks. An old carnivore. That's no doubt why it took the dog. Now he comes to a pine forest. It's flat and the going is easy.

The pines are tall, widely spaced, a colonnade, straight trunks, no branches; the wind is sighing in the crowns high above. The moss that usually crackles underfoot in the summer is damp, soft, and silent.

Good, he thinks. Nice and quiet.

He crosses an old boggy meadow. In the middle is an ancient barn that has collapsed. The rotten remains of the roof are scattered around the skeleton. It has not been cold enough for the ground to freeze. His feet sink deep into the swampy turf; he is becoming very sweaty. There is a smell of mud and iron-rich water.

Soon the trail veers away toward the coppices and brushwood in the direction of the Vaikkojoki River.

A few ravens croak and caw in the distance through the gray morning air. The vegetation is growing more dense. The trees are shrinking, fighting for space. Spindly pines. Messy gray spruce twigs. Stunted birches: most leaves have blown off; those remaining range from yellow to dull green and gray. He can see no further than fifteen feet in any direction. Barely that.

He is down by the beck now. He has to keep brushing away twigs with his arm. He can only see a couple of feet ahead.

Then he hears the dogs. Three loud barks. Then silence.

He knows what that means. They have tracked down the bear. Disturbed it, forced it to move away from where it was lying wounded. When they detect the pungent smell coming from such a hideaway, they usually bark.

After another twenty minutes he hears the dogs barking again, more persistently this time. They have caught up with the bear. He checks his GPS. A bit over half a mile away. They are barking while on the move. Barking and chasing the bear. Best to keep plodding on. No point in getting too excited yet. He hopes the young bitch doesn't get too close. She is rather excitable. The other bitch works more calmly. Good at standing still a safe distance away, holding the hunted animal at bay, barking. She seldom goes any closer than ten feet. A wounded bear is not a patient bear.

After half an hour they start barking from a stationary position. Now both the bear and the dogs are standing still.

Typical! Just where the vegetation is at its thickest. Nothing but undergrowth and no view at all. He keeps going, and is now only six hundred and fifty feet away.

The wind is coming from the side. Not a problem. The bear should not be able to smell him. He cocks his rifle. Presses on. His heart is pounding.

It's okay, he thinks. He wipes his hand on his pants leg. A bit of adrenaline goes with the territory.

One hundred and sixty-five feet to go. He peers into the undergrowth where the barking is coming from. Both dogs are wearing jackets that are luminescent green on one side and orange on the other. To distinguish them from the bear in circumstances where that is necessary. And also to see what direction the dog is facing.

Now he sees a glimpse of something orange up ahead. Which of the dogs is it? Impossible to tell. The bear usually stands between the dogs. Mäkitalo screws up his eyes, peers into the undergrowth again, moves as quietly as he can to one side. Ready to shoot, reload, shoot again.

The wind veers again. At the same time he catches sight of the other dog. There are about thirty feet between the two of them. The bear must be in there somewhere, but he can't see it. He must get closer. But now the wind is coming from diagonally behind him. That is not good. He raises his rifle.

Then he sees the bear. Thirty feet away. No clear view for taking a shot. Too many tree trunks and too much under-growth in the way. It suddenly stands up. It must have gotten wind of him.

It charges at him. It all happens so quickly. He hardly has time to draw a breath before it is almost upon him. There is a creaking and crashing and snapping of branches.

He shoots. The first shot makes the bear swerve to one side, but it keeps on coming. The second shot is perfect. The bear col-lapses ten feet short of him.

The dogs pounce on it immediately. Bite at its ears. Chew its fur.

He lets them do whatever they want. That is their reward.

His heart is slamming like an open door in a storm. He tries to get his breath back in between praising his dogs. Well done! There's a good girl!

He takes out his cell phone. Calls the local huntsmen.

That was a close shave. A bit too close for comfort. He thinks briefly about his little boy and his partner. Then he banishes any such thoughts from his mind. Looks at the bear. It is big. Really big. And almost black.

The local huntsmen arrive. The air is heavy with autumn chill, pungent bear, and admiring respect. They tie up the body of the bear with ropes and attach straps running over their shoulders and under their arms so that they can drag it to a clearing not far from a track that can be accessed by their four-wheel drive pickup truck. They work like slaves, and agree that it is a hell of a big beast.

The inspector from the county council arrives. He inspects the place where the bear was shot to make sure that no laws have been broken. Then he takes no end of samples while the hunters are recovering from their efforts. He clips off a clump of fur, cuts out a skin sample, cuts off the testicles, and pries out a tooth with his sheath knife so that the age of the bear can be established.

Then he cuts open its stomach.

"Shall we check what Teddy's been eating?" he says.

Mäkitalo has tied his dogs to a tree trunk. They whimper and strain at their leashes. It's their bear, after all.

Steam rises from the contents of the bear's stomach. And the stench is awful.

Some of the men take an involuntary step back. They know what's inside there. The remains of Johansson's Norwegian elkhound. The inspector knows that as well.

"Ah well," he says. "Berries and meat. Fur and skin."

He pokes around in the slushy mess. His face suddenly assumes a suspicious expression.

"But for Christ's sake, this isn't . . ."

He falls silent. Picks up a few pieces of bone with his right hand, which is protected by a plastic glove.

"What the hell is this it's been eating?" he mumbles as he pokes around in the slush.

The huntsmen come closer. Scratch at the back of their heads so that the peaks of their caps slide down over their foreheads. One of them takes out a pair of glasses.

The inspector straightens up. Quickly. Takes a step backward.

He's holding a piece of bone with his fingers. "Do you know what this is?" he asks.

His face has turned gray. The look in his eyes sends shivers down the spines of all the others. The forest has fallen silent. There is no wind. No birdsong. It seems that it is refusing to reveal a secret.

"It's not a dog in any case. I can assure you of that."